BLOODLINE ORIGINS

Book I

IULIANA FOOS

*To Christina and Steve
Thank you for your support. Enjoy!*

Iuliana Foos

SOUL MATE PUBLISHING
New York

BLOODLINE ORIGINS

Copyright©2018

IULIANA FOOS

Cover Design by Wren Taylor

This book is a work of fiction. The names, characters, places, and incidents are the products of the author's imagination or are used fictitiously. Any resemblance to actual events, business establishments, locales, or persons, living or dead, is entirely coincidental.

All rights reserved. No part of this publication may be reproduced, stored in a retrieval system, or transmitted in any form or by any means (electronic, mechanical, photocopying, recording, or otherwise) without the prior written permission of both the copyright owner and the publisher. The only exception is brief quotations in printed reviews.

The scanning, uploading, and distribution of this book via the Internet or via any other means without the permission of the publisher is illegal and punishable by law. Please purchase only authorized electronic editions, and do not participate in or encourage electronic piracy of copyrighted materials.

Your support of the author's rights is appreciated.

Published in the United States of America by
Soul Mate Publishing
P.O. Box 24
Macedon, New York, 14502

ISBN: 978-1-68291-671-1

ebook ISBN: 978-1-68291-651-3

www.SoulMatePublishing.com

The publisher does not have any control over and does not assume any responsibility for author or third-party websites or their content.

To my love,

my rock,

my husband Marcus.

Chapter 1

Ana dared a quick glance behind. The group of three approached with unnatural speed. An accelerated pulse throbbed in the back of her throat.

She lived in a city where people got murdered or disappeared too often. Ana didn't want to become the latest statistic. With a hand tightened on the edge of the white canvas tote on her shoulder, she ran for her life. Flip-flops jumped inside, mixing with her towel and keys. The phone and tablet only added to the turmoil in the bag.

I knew those guys were trouble the moment I saw them. Should've started to run sooner.

Their footsteps echoed heavy in Ana's ears, mixing with the calming swoosh of the waves. With the sun setting behind the steel and glass buildings, dusk quickly swallowed the remote beach.

Shiny windows revealed lights popping one after another into a mesmerizing play. Streetlamps turned on like watchers over the cars parked in their designated spots.

She enjoyed the salty smell of the ocean. The mix of algae, salt, and water had a euphoric effect on her brain. But not at that very moment. *What if I'm not going to make it? I swear my building moved further.*

Ana peeked over her shoulder.

The group was getting closer. Black boots kicked the sand with every step, creating the illusion of a cloud surrounding their feet. Strong, chiseled jaws jutted out and eyes as cold as ice chilled her skin. Their determined and murderous attitude made Ana think of a horror version of *The Three*

Musketeers with long, black coats billowing behind them, frayed and dirty.

Her lungs screamed for air, and her heart rushed to supply the extra blood. Every day she relaxed on the beach, reading and daydreaming about her deepest, most secret fantasy: vampires. Now, for the first time, she wished she wasn't there.

Sheer terror crept into her mind and spread through her body like wildfire. Her bones shook and she picked up the pace.

Ana never liked rules, and always tried to bend or go around them. She knew to keep her eyes ahead, especially when running. With the group of three behind her, she couldn't help but look back.

Almost close enough to catch her, they skidded to a halt, and she hit something hard, like a brick wall. The impact knocked her backward and she lost her balance.

"Celina, get her to safety," a commanding voice said with a strong French accent.

One of the two women grabbed Ana, breaking her fall, and pulled her to the side with one quick and fluid movement before the two groups met. *Where did they come from? And what's with all those long coats? Aren't they hot? It must be about ninety degrees.*

Ana tried to catch her breath and wiped the thin sheen of sweat off her hairline.

She was still close enough to see their eyes. One of the men who chased her stared at her with hunger, like a wolf that just missed out on catching a lonely little lamb. Another tremor coursed through her body.

Ana freed herself from Celina's hold and half-hid behind her. She squeezed the arm of the woman now protecting her, trying to get her attention. Soft leather delighted her fingertips.

"What's going on? Who are you?"

Celina ignored the questions. Her emerald eyes focused on the two confronting groups. Long, auburn hair partially covered her face.

For the first time, Ana had a moment to observe the newcomers in detail. All four of them wore identical leather coats, perfectly tailored. Their clothing resembled a uniform.

One of the men who had given chase glared at Celina. "You again." He took a step forward, pointing to Ana. "That's my dinner."

His eyes bored through her, and she took a half-step to the side, hiding a little more behind Celina. The other two in his group laughed at her reaction—sinister laughs, like a bunch of hyenas on the prowl.

The man's scar, traveling from the corner of his right eye to just under the jaw, made him look tough and terrifying. His bloodshot, dark-colored eyes had something evil in them as if inner demons peeked through. They sent chills up Ana's back.

A frigid sensation, as if someone had replaced her blood with an icy-cold matter froze her brain, made thinking impossible. She couldn't move or even blink. Yet her heart thumped in her chest, ready to make the leap into the fine sand.

"This is your second warning, Ivan. You cannot hunt humans in our territory. Next time I see you, you will die." The woman with the French accent and light-blond hair cascading down her back stood her ground.

He glared at her with disgust, his lips turned into a frown. His chin shot upward.

"You think so highly of yourself. I'm sick of your superiority complex. Fight me, *Your Majesty*." He enforced his mockery with a courtly bow. His arms moved on the sides in a poor impersonation of a graceful ballerina.

Ivan and his two cohorts drew swords and daggers. The group who protected Ana reacted instantly, and their blades and knives came out from under the buttery-soft leather coats.

Celina held a gun in her right hand. Ana peeked at it with curiosity and fear. She'd never seen one up close before. All their weapons glimmered in the faint glow of the dusk.

Caught in the middle of the ongoing conflict between the two groups, all air squeezed out of Ana's lungs. Tiny, rushed and shallow breaths followed.

Threatening hisses filled the air. Ana's heart stopped. Eyes wide, she covered her mouth with her hands. Goosebumps erupted. Every single one of the people in the confrontation had fangs.

Are these people vampires? It can't be. They must be fake. But earlier, she had said something about not hunting humans. What the hell is going on? How can all this be? Ana was intrigued and scared at the same time. She wanted to take advantage of the situation and run, but she also wanted to stay.

One of the attackers toyed with the tip of a pointed dagger, hissed, and sprang forward, swinging the blade in an arched half-circle.

"Your Majesty!" One of the men dressed in leather jumped in front of the blond woman. The sharp edge of the knife sliced through the sleeve of his overcoat, revealing pale, white flesh unblemished by the sun.

With fearsome rage and blinding speed, the two groups engaged, fighting one another. Her Majesty, beautiful and deadly in equal parts, resembled an elite supermodel dancing with daggers. Her feet barely touched the ground, moved with mesmerizing speed and grace.

A rare cocktail of fear and excitement paralyzed Ana. Vampires existed only in the books she read, in the movies, not on the same beach she came to every day.

The weapons seemed old, but the bright shine of the sharp edges convinced Ana they were more than capable of doing their job. Swords with long, flat blades had handles encrusted with what appeared as precious gems or highly polished motifs. They clashed against each other in a rapid dance of death.

She couldn't see the daggers well, but Ana guessed they were just as sharp. Their higher pitch whistled in the air, a choir of fatality.

Two screams pierced the night, one after the other, like twins, covering the hypnotic splash of the waves.

From where she stood, through the fast-approaching darkness, Ana saw Ivan's companions blazing in a bright amber color for a couple of seconds, only to extinguish just as fast and turn into black ashes. *What the hell?*

Ana had to blink a few times at the sight of their remains flying in the breeze before slowly settling in the same fine sand she loved.

"Stop." Ivan took a step back.

Celina kept her gun pointed at him, following his movement.

"Are you giving up that easy?" The woman with the French accent kept her daggers inches from his skin, ready to plunge them into his chest.

"I hate and despise you, but this isn't a fair fight, not anymore. There are four of you against me. I'm not stupid."

"And yet, you are here." Her Majesty raised a perfectly groomed eyebrow.

Ana smiled inside. *Ha. I like this lady.*

The blonde stashed her daggers away and signaled the others to lower their weapons. The fight seemed to be over, and Ana let out a breath, not sure how long she had held it.

"You and your friends are not welcome in our territory. Leave and never come back, unless you have a death wish," her Majesty snarled.

Growls from her escorts saturated the warm air and fangs glimmered.

Without another sound, Ivan turned around and ran so fast, Ana swore he vanished into thin air. The remaining group closed in, and she found herself in the middle of them.

They measured her from head to toe with interest and sniffed the air.

I hope I don't stink. Or worse yet, smell like dinner. More goosebumps rose and covered her skin under a thin layer of cold sweat.

"Who are you? What just happened?" Ana's blood flowed once again and her pulse accelerated.

"Considering we saved your life, you could call us your guardian angels." Her Majesty readjusted her clothes. "A few seconds later and you would have been dead." She tilted her head, first to the right then left. A small crease appeared on her smooth forehead. "There is something about you, a presence." She inhaled loudly. "Something I have never sensed before. And it is strong."

"I saw you fight, your fangs. Are you . . .?" Ana couldn't bring herself to finish the question, avoiding the fantasy word, the one she didn't have the courage to say out loud.

"Yes. We are, and the word you are looking for is *vampires*." The blonde squared her shoulders with pride. "Now go home and do not tempt your fate by staying out this late, alone, in isolated places like this. Oh, and you should keep our meeting tonight to yourself."

The stunning leader spoke with a superiority characteristic of someone with a high rank. At her discreet nod, the whole group walked away from Ana, following the woman in charge.

As if anyone would believe me? "Wait!" Ana ran after them, kicking up some sand in her tracks. "Thank you for saving my life." She saw the beginning of a tiny smile in the azure eyes. "Please." Loose grains of sand slowed her pace. "I want to be like you."

They all froze and stared at her. Ana saw the raised brows, and the unspoken questions. She heard her own words and wondered what in the world was she thinking. It sounded way better in her mind than out loud.

As unreal as it seemed, Ana's obsession with vampires surfaced. If they were real, then this was a once in a lifetime chance. She didn't want to miss it. Not this one.

"You want to be like us?" Her Majesty tilted her head again with renewed interest. "Do you even know what you are asking?" Her eyes narrowed. "Humans hate us. They have hunted us for centuries, thinking it is in their right and power to kill us. And you want to be one of us?"

"Yes," Ana answered without any hesitation.

"Why?"

"It's hard to explain."

"May I?" The leader motioned to Ana's hand, extending her own between the two of them.

For a few moments, the striking vampire kept Ana's hand in hers, the tension palpable around them. Her touch was gentle, her hands warm and the skin soft. *I thought they were supposed to be coldblooded.*

The light-blue eyes lost their silver glow and seemed lifeless and empty. Her Majesty released Ana's hand, then took a step back.

Ana didn't know if she should be scared or intrigued.

"I am not sure what it is, but you are different." She pursed her lips. "You can probably have anything you want, and you want to become one of us, a vampire?"

"Yes, I do. Like I said, it's hard to explain why. I don't feel like I belong anywhere. No matter where I go, or what I do, I feel like I shouldn't be there. Until now . . ."

Ana noticed the leader listening to her words, carefully, without blinking.

Even in the fast-growing darkness, Ana saw the leather suit the tall, beautiful woman wore under the long coat:

Acknowledgements

Thank you, Michelle, for teaching me things I had no idea I should know, for opening my eyes to what I didn't know was there. Your friendship, guidance, and patience are and will always be close and dear to my heart. Without you holding my hand on this new path I was lost on, I would have never made it.

To all my family and friends who believed in me when I didn't, thank you for your support.

Tanya, I would have never had the courage to embark on this journey without you and your encouragement. You gave me hope and I thank you for every kind word.

Brenda, I will always be grateful to you. Your honesty, knowledge, and friendship are precious and make me one of the luckiest people in the world to have you on my side. Thank you for pushing me forward.

I would also like to thank my critique group, a mix of talented and good-natured people I was fortunate enough to know. Too many to mention, I will still try: Karen, Miranda, Kevin, Daron, Sheila, Roy, Cynthia (both of you), Kim, Dee, Fernando and everyone else, I love you guys. Your opinions, views, and advice helped me along the way.

We all know it takes a village to raise a child, well, it takes just as many, if not more, to write a book.

black with red accents. A sophisticated medallion rested in the middle of her chest. It resembled a coin with a design Ana couldn't make out.

"Are you serious? Are you willing to give up being a human to become one of us?" Her voice went up with doubt. "There is no way back, you know. Turning into a vampire is painful, you would be sick for days." Her Majesty waved her right hand discreetly between them. "And lose anything that is remotely human in you. None of us are vampires because we wanted to be."

"But I do." Ana stared straight into the woman's hypnotic eyes. For a short second, they glimmered like the sun reflecting off ice crystals.

Her Majesty surveyed their surroundings as if she heard sounds. Her nose twitched a couple of times. It seemed she sensed something, and her escorts scoured the area. Ana heard their loud sniffing and saw their eyes searching all around. The two men took a few steps in different directions, only to come back full circle and empty-handed.

"Take some time and think about it. Keep in mind everything you would lose. And if, a week from today, you still want to become one of us, meet me here." She gestured to the sand with a delicate hand. "Right now, you might be under the influence of what you saw. Search inside your soul, look into your heart, and make sure that it is what you want." Her perfectly manicured index finger pointed to the left side of Ana's chest. "Tomorrow, I will send you a book. It will give you some insight into who we are." She glanced at the woman entrusted with Ana's protection that night. "Celina, take her home and make sure the human is safe."

The green-eyed woman nodded. "Understood."

"Celina will visit you every other day to help you understand more. Fair enough?"

"Yes, thank you." Ana bobbed her head a couple of times with excitement. "I don't even know your name."

"Emelia De Croix, Queen of the Third Coven."
"I'm Ana, Ana Duma."
"You should go now. *Bonne nuit.*"
"Goodnight."

Ana walked away with Celina by her side. She couldn't even indulge in the feeling of the fine, warm sand caressing the bottom of her feet and squishing in between her toes like she usually did.

Later, in the safety of her apartment, Ana allowed herself to think about what happened. It was still hard to believe she had just seen vampires. And moreover, that she had asked them to make her one of them.

Her obsession with everything to do with vampires started in her teenage years. Yes, she gagged at the thought of drinking blood, but if it made her fast, strong, and immortal, it would be worth it. She'd drink blood the same way she ate fish during childhood: eyes closed, nose pinched, and not thinking about it.

Growing up poor, the food consisted mostly of fish, chicken wings, chicken gizzards, and chicken feet, for over five long years, in her teens. It was that, or go hungry. Unable to give chicken bits a second chance, she hadn't touched one in over a decade.

When she first crinkled her nose at the stink of garlic, her father joked, *What, now you're a vampire? It's healthy, and you're going to eat it.* She could still hear his voice, even now, six years after both her parents had died in an accident. *Damn drunk drivers.*

At the time, she didn't know about vampires. After researching and learning about them, her fascination and obsession started over twelve years ago and never stopped.

Ana shook her head. With shaking hands and rubbery legs, she walked to the kitchen for a drink.

A good part of the water she tried to drink trickled down her chin and all the way to her chest. The cold fluid dribbled onto the white beach dress she still wore from her prior outing.

At least I know this is real. She tried to wipe off the cold water. *Can it be right? Do they really exist? Am I going to be one of them? I so want this to be true. In the next few days, I'll get either my proof that it's real or the wake-up call that I'm losing it.*

Late at night, Ana went to sleep only to have the familiar vampire dreams. Most of the time, these events were composed of disconnected short fragments. As one of them, a creature of the lonely night, sometimes she would play pranks on people. Other times, she would scare and punish the ones who had wronged her, or reward those who had helped her.

In her dream world, she even visited her ex-husband and scared him out of his old and ugly handknitted socks. She'd endured his abuse for years. He'd managed to shatter her confidence and break her spirit.

When she divorced him, Ana experienced liberation. *You are nothing without me.* His last words addressed to her still echoed in her mind even all these years later. They still made her doubt herself, and that night, they woke her up: heart hammering, skin clammy, and body trembling. *I thought I was doing better at getting over it.*

The morning found her anxious. With her first cup of coffee in hand, Ana sat and waited to see if anyone would show up. She glanced absentmindedly over the almost finished painting. It was one of her commissioned works. Her freelance job was satisfying and paid the bills, a win-win situation. Another landscape with her signature detail: real sand mixed in her paints, and some more sprinkled over the essence of free rolling waves, surreal sunsets, and the comfort of a warm, inviting sandy beach.

Her eyes examined the surroundings. She loved the tiny apartment and leased it even if it cost an arm and a leg. At

BLOODLINE ORIGINS | 11

least she had a 'peek-a-boo' view of the ocean. She couldn't afford a full view. She would've had to add a kidney to the price.

A knock broke the silence. Ana opened the door to find Celina holding an old-looking book.

"You're here. You really came." Ana forgot all manners for a few seconds. She stood in the doorway, her eyes opened wide and blinking fast.

"You didn't think I would?" Celina brushed past her, a slightly amused expression on her face.

"No. I didn't even think you existed. Hey, don't I have to invite you in first?"

"That's in the movies and those fantasy books you most likely read. So, do you still want to become one of us?"

"Yes. I'm just finding it hard to believe." Ana locked the door then motioned to the couch. "Have a seat."

"Here's the book." Celina sat, extending her hand and offering the timeworn hardcover to her host.

Ana grabbed it and joined her. "*How to Become a Vampire for Dummies*?"

Celina couldn't hide her amusement. Her full lips stretched over small, even teeth.

"You're funny. The book's called *Run with Us*, and it's a collection of what some of us have experienced. It will make more sense when you read it."

"Would you like some coffee?"

"No, thanks. I'm a pureblood, not a hybrid."

Celina's answer raised more questions in Ana's mind. She wanted to know what the difference was.

"How come you didn't fry in the sun? It's a beautiful day out there." Ana waved toward the window overlooking the parking lot.

"I took a daylight serum, and I have another one with me for later." Celina pulled a vial, with a glowing green liquid inside, out of her pocket. "You should start reading. Pretty much everything you think you knew about us is a myth. The reality, my kind's reality, is quite different." Celina made herself comfortable.

Ana's eyebrows rose, and she tried to smooth away a couple of horizontal lines marking her forehead with doubt. The book seemed ancient, with discolored red hardcovers and ripped fabric around the edges.

She slowly opened it. A pale shade of yellow paper retained a musty, old smell. The words on the first page captured her attention: *Some call us undead, cursed souls, bloodsucking monsters. We just laugh . . .*

From the first few sentences, Ana committed herself to learning about her future, a vampire's life.

Chapter 2

"I'm going to kill her. When I'm done with them, the Third Coven will be a memory." Ivan's words mixed with anger, echoing against the worn walls.

Heavy boots crushed the glass shards littering the floor. A few low, portable lights fought the darkness. Tiny particles of dust floated in the air mixing with the smell of mold and salty water.

Dirt and sand covered the fractured cement floor. Pebbles dislodged from the long, deep cracks. Layer upon layer of rust accumulated on pieces of discarded industrial equipment.

A few broken windows, high up, near the thirty-foot-tall ceiling, let the sound of cresting waves washing against the shore partially blend in with the noisy traffic in the distance. Thick, heavy beams supported the metal roof with holes in it.

Ivan picked up a broken bottle and threw it across the empty space. It shattered against one of the bare walls. Hundreds of chips fell on the ground, landing at the base of the dark green moldy spots in the abandoned warehouse.

One of many massive buildings forgotten in the industrial area right by the port, it served as a meeting place he had for the group of independents who shared his hatred against humans.

Earlier, after his friends died, he had to flee from the Queen. But he turned around and hid nearby. Special abilities in his kind were not unusual. He could focus his energy and render himself undetectable by any other vampire.

He could easily pass as a human, as if his immortal presence ceased to exist. He heard the whole conversation with the human he chased.

Ivan sensed something different about her, too, but he didn't pay any attention or care. She looked good enough to have some fun with before drinking her blood to the last drop. The Queen's interest in the human made Ivan want the weak creature more than before.

"I need a plan. A damn good one," he muttered and sat on the old couch shoved in one of the corners. *I wish my brother was here. The man was brilliant. I miss his strategy, but he wouldn't have helped me. His love for humans ran deeper than our blood.* A deep sigh left his chest.

His hand traced over the long scar marking his face. The darker, and smoother skin healed over the silver burn. It was a *gift* from his brother, given to him the last time they saw each other. That fight stayed fresh in his memory throughout the two centuries. They almost killed each other that night. Every time he touched it, Ivan remembered the pain from the silver-coated blade slashing his flesh mixed with the bitter taste of betrayal.

A noise outside—breaking glass—attracted his attention, like someone or something crashed to the ground on top of a bottle. His nose twitched and he sniffed the air. "Human blood." He rushed out the back door. Blending into the surrounding night, Ivan rounded the corner with silent steps. Grass, littered with weeds, absorbed the sound of his boots. A drunk human stumbled against his own feet in an attempt to walk. On impact with the hard ground, the man scrapped his arm on a glass fragment. A few drops of blood escaping through the abraded skin beckoned Ivan. His sense of smell wasn't just superior to those of humans. In general, with one sniff, he and his kind could tell if it was animal blood, human, or another vampire's.

Ivan saw the opportunity for a snack falling right into his lap. His fangs descended, and he licked his lips with anticipation.

Every single muscle in his body tensed with need and thirst. A low growl and he launched forward pinning his victim to the ground. The drunken man, wasted beyond any rationality, didn't fight back. His breath reeked of alcohol. Ripped, dirty clothes covered the smelly body, like he hadn't taken a shower in months.

Good, no one will miss him. Stupid human. Ivan's fangs tore into the soft flesh. Warm blood filled his mouth. His eyes rolled back and closed with ecstasy. Alcohol and drugs didn't affect his kind. They would alter the taste of the life-giving fluid, but without any other side effect.

Ivan needed the nourishment. His energy had seriously depleted after using his unique ability earlier that night. Just like all the vampires' special powers, his came at a great cost. Every use took a good chunk of energy.

The animals he had fed on that week provided a weak imitation of what he craved: human blood. Quenching his thirst, he drank every ounce of life from his victim, and, a few minutes later, he stood and glared at the form at his feet.

He had to dispose of the body. *Good thing we are right by the water.* Ivan pulled his sword. The sharp blade cut with ease through flesh. A slight resistance of the bones sent a pleasant tingle through his veins. After one more glance at the head in his left hand, he flung it into the water.

Blade to flesh, he carved out a handful of tissue from his victim's neck, close to the shoulder. Since he'd sucked it dry, he didn't have to worry about a bloody mess. The mixture of muscle and bruised skin, bearing the marks of his bite, jiggled, soft between his fingers, before he tossed it to the fish to devour.

With only a partial body left, Ivan laid his sword flat on the ground. *I'll clean this in the warehouse. I know there are some rags somewhere.* He lifted the remains with ease and dropped them into the water.

After another glance, to make sure it sank, he picked up his sword.

Ivan wiped the blood off his lips and returned to the warehouse. He had to talk to his friends, they needed a solid plan. After feasting, his mind worked quicker, his energy restored, and ideas started to pour.

Before morning, he assigned two of his people to follow the human. He needed more time to figure out what his next move would be.

~ ~ ~

"Having second thoughts?"

Startled, Ana quickly turned her head in the direction of the familiar voice. Celina stood, flanked by two guards she recognized from the previous week's encounter.

"No, I was waiting."

"You still want to go through with this?"

"I do."

"Let's go, then. Her Majesty is waiting for us at the castle." The green-eyed beauty motioned toward the street.

Ana followed Celina to the black SUV. Her heart raced a bit faster with each step. At the vehicle, Ana glanced back. She took in her refuge, the beach, she had come to almost every day for the past year. *I'll miss you.*

The powerful engine purred, and the hypnotic movement of the car caused her to relax. Ana napped for most of the way, tired after the recent sleepless nights.

With the Queen's approval and Ana's willingness, Celina had picked her up a day early.

About four hours later, the car pulled in front of a mansion. Gravel crunched under the tires and dislocated tiny pebbles hit the undercarriage.

Her eyes feasted over the landscape reminding her of paintings she'd seen in museums. Well-manicured, with perfectly trimmed round bushes and straight hedges, it looked tranquil and classy. Even the trees were impeccable, not one leaf out of place.

Ana couldn't ignore the guards everywhere, standing tall in their leather uniforms, like statues decorating the breathtaking grounds. A few of them sniffed the air when she walked by, which made her feel like prey on the evening menu.

Celina led the way, and two guards flanked Ana, offering her an additional layer of protection. At the moment, she wasn't sure who or what she needed the extra show of force for.

An elegant entrance with straight, white columns on either side of the massive wood double-doors welcomed Ana. Skimming a hand over the smooth edge of the door, she took in all its beauty and craftsmanship.

The moment she stepped into the round, grand foyer, Ana stopped. A light breeze danced around, lingering in her proximity, only to infuse deep into her bones. She shivered and wrapped her arms around her body.

White, immaculate floors made her think of ice and her toes curled inside her shoes, with a cold sensation. In the middle, a crest made of black marble was embellished with gold inlays. The double sweeping staircases followed the round shape to the second and third floor. Balconies wrapped around the circumference of each. Guards stood by some of the closed double-doors, their faces emotionless.

On the other side of the foyer, a spacious, open room, had an exterior wall made completely of glass. Black velvet draperies trimmed with gold tassels partially obstructed the view of a garden built around a white stone fountain.

Servants and guards went about their business or stood in militant assigned positions. *Why all the security? Is this the way it always is, or is something about to go down?* Under one of the staircases, Ana noticed another door. It appeared heavy and old. Made of dark-colored wood with exposed grain running along the full height, the structure was held in place by oversized black metal hinges.

Two guards stood on either side. With their immobile faces, and weapons in plain view, they wore the same black, uniform-like leather suits. *Whatever's behind that door, it's safe. Who in their right mind would get near those two? They're terrifying.* Ana's short hairs at the base of her skull stood straight out.

Celina glanced at her then headed straight for the guards, unfazed by Ana's discomfort.

"Miss Celina, Her Majesty is expecting you in the ceremony room." The guard on the right side spoke with a deep, gravelly voice then pulled open the door.

A massive slab of brushed steel with the same crest in the middle came into view. The shield, with two daggers crossed in the middle, was painted in black and gold. Four symbols shone in the quadrants created: a tree on the left side, a sun on the top, a heart on the right side and a moon in the bottom. She paused wondering what they meant. Air swished passed her. The double doors split open, granting access to the next point of entry.

"This way." Celina stepped in and invited Ana to follow.

She shrugged and advanced with shaky, small steps, barely touching the floor with her heels. Ana tried her best to keep as much distance as she could from the guards, who kept sniffing the air. *What the heck are they smelling?* She drew in a deep breath, filling her nose with floral scents.

The doors slid shut, surrounding Ana in steel. "An elevator? This thing is huge."

"It can transport about twenty to thirty people at once." Celina pressed a button, the bottom one out of only two.

After a smooth and short descent, Ana wanted to ask another question. She opened her mouth, but a melodious ring resonated in her ears, silencing her where she stood.

From the first step outside the elevator, Ana entered a new, different world. Now it was clear why everyone called it 'The Castle.'

Throughout the vast area, four-story-high, arched ceilings dropped into strong, straight columns rooted in black marble floors. Chandeliers hung from the peaks of the intricate ceilings, like frozen upside-down fountains of crystals. *How in the world did they lift them so high? Those things must weigh a ton. And how do they clean them?*

Ana's gaze travelled all across the room in awe and excitement.

The first impression left her breathless. She couldn't believe how airy and luminous the space appeared in spite of the fact that it had no windows. Twenty-foot-tall mirrors with ornate gold frames hung on the walls. Oil paintings, towering double-doors and heavy banners with the same crest, completed the simple yet elegant décor.

Celina stopped for a second and opened her arms gesturing around.

"This is the ballroom. It's where we have our celebrations, and sometimes our Queen greets guests here." She pointed toward the back of the room. A throne-like chair dominated the back wall. "The house on top is only a cover-up for everything down here."

The sound of footsteps echoed once again. Ana trailed the other woman between the columns on the right side, and down one of the many hallways. Unlike in the ballroom, black with gold trim runners covered the cold, tiled floors.

On raw, uneven walls carved into stone, crystal sconces matched the opulent chandeliers. The smell of burning fire reached Ana's nose, and she focused her attention ahead. She did her best to ignore her rushed, erratic heartbeat, caused by excitement and nervousness. An arched doorway marked the end of the corridor a few steps ahead.

"Do you remember how to greet our Queen?" Celina stopped right before the next room.

"Yes, of course I do."

Ana bowed with all the grace she could muster, proving to Celina she'd practiced.

"Good, you'll have to do it now and every time you see her." Celina's words marked the end of the walk through the corridor.

Ana entered into an amphitheater, carved into limestone, or some other type of light, off-white stone. She had a moment to examine the benches, each row higher than the one in front, following the perfect semicircle shape of the room. They resembled a deep, oversized staircase.

The air, heavy and solemn, surrounded her like a thick cloak. *I wonder what they do in here. It seems important.*

The Queen stood in the middle of the room, giving instructions to some of the servants, and glancing over what seemed to be renovation blueprints. "I want this section here in a darker color stone." She pointed to a spot on the paper, then glanced toward the middle of the section she faced. The man beside her made a note and nodded.

"Your Majesty." Celina bowed before the Queen.

"Your Majesty." Ana tried to make a good impression, afraid she would slip and fall not so graciously in the middle of the immaculate floors.

"So you came. You decided to go through with it after all."

"Of course. Why is everyone surprised by my decision? I'm the one who asked to join you."

"Because you are the first one to do so in hundreds of years."

"Your Majesty, I have news on the matter I was telling you about two days ago." Ana heard Celina's whisper.

"Give me a minute, *cherie,*" Queen Emelia stepped away from her and stared at Celina.

Taking advantage of the few seconds, Ana examined her surroundings. Multiple high-domed entrances opened in the amphitheater. On the walls, more of the heavy flags hung, each bearing different coat of arms embroidered with shimmering thread.

Between them, burning torches filled the space. Two of the large banners with the same crest she'd seen throughout the castle flanked the only straight wall. In the middle portion of it, an area resembling a honeycomb nested hundreds of rolls of paper.

"What do you think?"

Ana stared at the Queen, lost for words, overwhelmed, and not sure yet it wasn't a dream.

"I apologize, Your Majesty," Ana whispered. "Everything is just incredible. I can't believe all this is real."

Queen Emelia gently placed her hands on Ana's shoulders causing her to jump. *Nope. Not a dream.*

"First things first, when we are not in public, please call me Emelia. In case you have not noticed yet, I am taking a special interest in you."

"Thank you, I promise to try and do my best, but you're a Queen. Celina told me you were once a real royal blood princess. I'm just an ordinary, average, plain Jane."

"I was born a princess, it is true. You, *chérie*, are anything but ordinary. There is something about you, a presence, something that makes you different from all the humans I have ever encountered. And trust me, I have met a lot throughout my six centuries of life."

"You're six hundred years old?" Ana felt her eyes widen.

"*Oui.*" Queen Emelia's answer came with a bittersweet smile. "But let us first go upstairs and make you comfortable." She walked toward one of the arched exits. "In the next couple of days, we will spend a lot of time together. You are under my personal protection, and you will be staying with me, in my suite, just to be on the safe side. I would never forgive myself if anything happened to you."

The last words stuck in her head. It was hard to imagine anything happening in a place like this without the Queen's approval. "I have a question, if I may," Ana hesitated.

"Of course. Ask what you will."

At Queen Emelia's nod, Ana continued. "Celina already explained to me the three covens and their territories. It's my understanding that your coven is the smallest, under four hundred people, and in permanent conflict with the others. Why exactly is that? And why don't you turn more humans and get your numbers up?"

"It is not that simple. We are a few thousand vampires spread throughout the world. Most are independents. Only a small portion, about ten percent are sworn into a coven."

"Why is that?"

The Queen tilted her head in the direction of a couple of bowing servants. "A matter of personal preference, really. Most prefer to remain independents. There are enough of us. Turning more would only attract unwanted attention to us and would throw the balance off."

"What balance?"

"Most vampires refuse to admit it, but we depend on humans, the main species populating this world. Your kind," she quickly corrected herself. "They are the ones who do all the work. We just enjoy the fruits of their hard labor."

Oh, so we're nothing more than workforce? The thought bothered Ana.

"Humans might outnumber us, but we are more powerful. We can control pretty much everything we want, from politics to economy."

Ana tried to understand. In spite of the Queen's elaborate explanations, she still fought confusion.

"We made the transition to only feed on animal blood. Sadly, most vampires do not understand that our survival depends on the humans' existence." Queen Emelia glanced toward Ana. "They can procreate, and they do, but continuing to kill them will eventually lead to their extinction." A sad undertone hit the marble columns like in a game of pinball. "Many of us are stuck in different times. Even if we are immortals, we still need to evolve, to keep up with the progress around us. We need to think about the future, not only about the next meal."

The Queen's words left Ana wondering. She already knew from Celina, she had to marry a vampire or be adopted by one in order to be accepted and turned. What if nobody wants her? What if all men reject her and no family wants her under their roof? Would she have to go back to her previous life? Knowing what she knew now, nothing could ever be the same.

"Then why turn me?" Ana voiced her concern.

"Because you asked, and because you are different. It is not forbidden to turn humans. Unlike the old times, when a vampire would turn a human and run, leaving them to figure out things on their own, now we have to take responsibility." Her lips stretched over tiny white teeth. "New vampires would attract the unwanted attention I was telling you about. When first turned, the unexperienced, young ones have little control over their urges and without the proper training would feed, unrestrained, upon the humans. They would not only expose themselves but also endanger all of us. It is the one aspect all vampires agreed on."

"So, a vampire will act as my mentor?" Ana pinched the bridge of her nose and pursed her lips. Her mind churned, trying to process all the information. *Damn, I am so confused right now.*

Chapter 3

"Is everyone clear on what you have to do tomorrow?" Ivan's question resonated in the large, empty space the warehouse offered.

"I have to go in, shove her into the suitcase, preferably without breaking her, and get her into the car. It's not complicated." Tamara, a petite woman with long, brown hair and light-blue eyes answered first.

"I'll wait at the door with the car running and then drive to the exchange location." A husky-looking man, Fred, gloated with pride, more than likely because he remembered what his job was. He definitely wasn't the sharpest tool in the bunch.

"Tamara, you are going to use your magnetism on her, and you should be the one waking her. Don't forget, scare her a little as soon as you are on the move," Ivan glanced, with a sadistic glint in his eyes, to the last one the group. He believed the guy's name was Peter.

"You said not to touch her," a tall, skinny man objected.

"That's right, Peter. Just make her understand whom she's dealing with." Ivan growled, and his angry hiss caused the tall man to lower his beady eyes to the ground.

"Do you want me to go with them?" Collin brushed dust off his oxfords then took in his reflection.

Ivan turned to his right, to his best friend, literally his partner-in-crime, Collin. He knew he could trust him.

"No. I need you with me at the exchange location. We'll have to cross into the Second Coven's territory."

"Do you think they would go to such lengths to follow us?" Collin asked. "For a human?"

"She's different. The Queen wants her, and she went out of her way to protect her. I hope they won't risk venturing into rival territory even if they figure out what's going on," Ivan explained, and Collin nodded in agreement.

A loud noise made all of them turn their attention to the door. A blonde entered and rushed to the group gathered in the corner.

"We have a problem." Panic and hesitation mingled in her voice.

"What is it, Karina? Aren't you supposed to be on watch right now?" Ivan furrowed his brows and rose to his feet with a bad feeling in his gut.

"Celina took her to The Castle today. I saw them leaving with a suitcase and headed that way."

With a loud growl and fangs extended, Ivan flipped the low, wooden table placed in front of the couch, reducing it to kindling. "What? Why?"

"I think Celina made us a few days ago, when she assigned guards to patrol the area. They figured she is not safe and took her a day early."

Ivan paced. Heavy boots punctuated every step, and his fists tightened. His own people feared him and scurried out of reach. Dust and tiny pebbles crunched under their feet, and the sound grated in Ivan's ears.

"We should have grabbed her days ago." He threw his hands in the air. "Why did I think it was a good idea to wait until the last moment?" Ivan lowered his hands and held his head between them.

"Because you wanted to make it look like she changed her mind and didn't show up. The plan had potential and would have been perfect." Collin tried to calm him.

"Damn it! Not good enough." Ivan's anger sent everyone

except Collin cowering in fear toward the exit. "Now I have to go get her from The Castle. I need a new plan."

The determined words hit the bare concrete walls and echoed in the silent space. From experience, Ivan knew that sooner or later the two of them would come up with something. They always did.

~ ~ ~

The next morning, Ana entered the spacious, private living room where Queen Emelia waited for her. Heavy, black draperies sunlight-proofed the north-facing windows.

All the furniture spread throughout the vast room belonged to a different era. Every single piece rested on elegant, curved legs. The detail in every sculpted inch of wood shimmered in a gold patina matching the fabric covering the sofas and the uncomfortable-looking chairs. Everything seemed old and expensive.

As an artist, she appreciated the craftsmanship. Growing up poor in Romania, an isolated country at the time, Ana liked everything modern and comfortable. The smell of new furniture always made her smile. Antiques, to her, meant old junk people didn't want to give up, and considered *charm* and *character* to be just fancy words for *old* and *crappy*.

"*Bonjour.*" Queen Emelia greeted and moved toward Ana. It seemed she glided over the shiny floors.

She wore an elegant, fashion-forward dress, contrasting with her surroundings, with the same ease as the leather suit a week ago. The black fabric, with red trim, trailed behind her in a short train.

"Good morning, Your Majesty." Ana rushed to bow.

"Emelia, please."

"I'm sorry. I'm working on that."

They both sat, and Ana poured some coffee for herself. One side of the space had the clear designation of a dining room. The long table and chairs had the same museum quality as the rest of the furniture in the Queen's suite. The total opposite of Ana's contemporary taste, it made her uncomfortable.

An assortment of toast, pancakes, waffles, muffins and croissants were joined by about six various jams. Scrambled eggs and different types of omelets were paired with crispy bacon strips and sausages. Fresh fruits and pastries alone, occupied three double-tier trays.

"I had no idea what you would like, so I ordered you a little of everything." Queen Emelia hurried to explain, no doubt noticing Ana's shocked stare.

"Oh. For a moment I thought this was an open buffet for the whole state." She waved at the abundant spread occupying more than half the table.

"Sometime today I will ask you to make a list for our cook with what you like and what you don't." The Queen waved to the food. "That way, this won't repeat," she added.

"I will do that." Ana nodded and picked up some toast.

"As I promised, while you have your breakfast I will reveal how I became the person I am today. After that, we need to do some shopping. You will need a dress for tomorrow night's ceremony and a wardrobe to get you started. I will not negotiate this," the Queen added right away. "You need things either way, no matter what you decide tomorrow night. My family is one of the wealthiest in the world, and I insist that you will have a good start. Are we clear so far?"

"Yes," Ana muttered after the first sip of coffee, her opposition defeated before she had a chance to decline the offer. She took a bite of toast. The delicious apricot jam perfectly balanced sour and sweet, her favorite.

"Good," the Queen continued. "I was born in the year 1405. My father was Louis De Orleans, younger brother of Charles VI, the King of France. So yes, I was born into the royal family. I entered the world as a Princess, even if my mother hid me and my twin brother from everyone.

My parents feared we would be killed. Due to politics and powerplay, enemies assassinated my father about two years later." A sigh left the Queen's lips. "My mother took us to one of her family's estates, outside France. Soon after, a fever ravaged her body, and she died. My grandmother raised us. We lived in hiding for a few years. I returned to France a couple of months after I turned sixteen, to attend the ball season as my debut in the Parisian high society."

The Queen stopped for a few seconds, with a dreamy glimmer in her eyes. Sadness resurfaced.

"I will never forget my first ball, the divine music, and all the elegant women in their evening gowns. Rich, opulent, crystal chandeliers illuminated the ballroom. I wore a light baby-blue dress, with matching ribbons in my hair, and satin shoes." She stroked a lock of her hair. "That night I met my future husband, Count Edward De Croix. From the second I saw him, I knew he was the one. He was dashing with his dark-brown hair tied in a ponytail and his big, baby-blue eyes."

A sweet smile stretched the Queen's lips and Ana smiled with her.

"We fell in love with each other that night, and in a few short months, we got engaged and then married. We were so happy, so in love. I lived the perfect life, convinced that nothing could ever change it. I was wrong. One night . . ."

The Queen stopped for a few seconds, out of breath, and unable to finish her sentence. The demons from her past haunted her eyes. Her fixed gaze held inside the terror and pain.

Ana realized how much those memories affected her.

"Still in love almost two decades later, and after another ball on a mid-February frigid night, it started to snow. We heard the coachman's scream. The horses snorted, and their hooves hit the cobblestone. The attackers forcefully dragged us out of the carriage. With coats ripped and muddy, they smelled as if they had not bathed in months. We offered them money and jewelry, but they only seemed amused by our attempts."

The Queen stopped again and took a few steps away from the table.

Guilt surrounded Ana. She was the one bringing back all the haunting memories.

"I did not understand why until I saw one of them sinking his teeth into my husband's neck." A tremor shook her body. "We all knew about the rumors, beasts that drank human blood. They wanted our life essence, not our money, or other possessions. I stood, so terrified that I could not even scream." Her voice failed her, and the Queen paused a few seconds. "I watched my husband, who I loved so much, die in front of me, the life slipping out of his body, out of his eyes. Our son, Phillip, died next. He was only seventeen."

The Queen paled, as if she relived those moments of terror and pain. Her breathing became shallow.

"I'm so sorry."

Ana completely forgot about her breakfast, captivated by the story. She took a forkful of scrambled eggs and a bite from a bacon strip. *I feel bad, but I'm hungry.*

Queen Emelia stared at Ana as if she just saw her for the first time. A sad, painful smile crossed over her perfect red lips.

"I have never forgotten the details of that horrendous night. After I saw my family slaughtered right in front of me, I knew it was my turn. This man, this monster, who seemed to be their leader, held my face up, staring into my eyes. He reeked." The queen covered her heart with the palm of her right hand. "I could smell the blood on his hands, knowing it was my husband's and my son's." She slid her fingertips over her face. "It felt warm and sticky on my skin, in spite of the cold night. White snowflakes covered everything. I could hear my own breathing and the snow falling in tiny, soft sounds." She slowly returned to her seat. "I saw the demonic glow in his eyes and heard him whisper: *"You should thank your child for your life."* His teeth tore my skin. His fangs sank into my flesh, the blood started to leave my body . . ."

Ana covered her mouth with her hands in an attempt to cover her tiny cry. She failed.

Queen Emelia glanced at her, and let out a deep, loud sigh.

"Later, I found out that my transition lasted six days, and I was pregnant, which was the reason why he had spared my life. He couldn't bring himself to kill a pregnant human. I became one of the monsters everyone feared." Queen Emelia sat and leaned against the back rest. "Around that time, I met my dear friend Mara, the Duchess of Stael, already one thousand years old. She and her husband taught me everything I needed to learn about being a vampire." With a graceful, fluid movement, the Queen tucked a strand of hair behind her ear. Poised, she looked like a photo in a magazine. Only something was different, anger flickered in her eyes. "When I became strong and fast enough," the warm undertone in her voice changed to hate and vengeance, "I took my revenge and killed all the ones involved in my family's death." An almost sadistic glint sparked in her gaze. "Their empty hearts throbbed for the last time against my dagger's blade. That day I accepted who and what I had become. I went for the last time and visited my family's graves, said my farewells, and never looked back."

Ana wanted to say something, but nothing came to mind. The Queen's pain suffocated her, and she couldn't find the right comforting words.

"It is all in the past. You will find that most of us became what we are in similar situations, always some tragedy, always a life to regret being stolen from us. There are exceptions, but very few."

Finally, something came to Ana's mind. "What happened to the baby?"

"He grew into a powerful man." She smoothed an imaginary crease on her dress. "For many years he was the only reason that kept me going. So many times, I wanted to end my days." Another wave of shadows darkened the Queen's eyes. "You will eventually meet him. For now, if you are finished with breakfast, we should start our shopping."

Later that evening, after dinner, she still had many questions. Ana refused to go to sleep and stayed up, talking to Queen Emelia until late into the night.

She couldn't remember going to bed, but she woke to a new morning: the day she had to decide her future.

"Good morning." Ana entered the living room with a big smile, a lot of energy, and a bounce in her step.

"*Bonjour*. I hope you slept well."

"I did, thank you. Since you mentioned it, I don't remember going to bed."

"I put you to sleep. Today will be a long and full day, so you needed rest."

"Wait a minute. Did you use that magnetism thing on me?" Ana knew from Celina that all vampires had a power over humans. It allowed them to place the individuals in a hypnotic-like trance, or simply to put them to sleep.

"*Oui.*"

The hand-carved double doors opened, and a servant entered the room with breakfast. This time only one plate with French toast and assorted fresh fruits. *I'm not even mad at her for getting me to sleep that way. Should be, but I'm not. Heck. It was the most restful night I had in months.*

"Now, we can talk about tonight's ceremony." The Queen sat, inviting Ana through a simple gesture to do the same. "*Bon appétit*," she added with a smile.

"I have a few questions for tonight. What am I supposed to do, to say? How everything is going to—?"

"I got it," Queen Emelia interrupted her. "Before we get into those answers, you should know that today, you will have to stay here all day. I am sorry for the inconvenience, and I do not want you to feel like a prisoner. It is for your safety. There are extra guards at the door, and nobody will enter this room without my permission. You will not accept any food or drink unless it is from me or in my presence."

Ana eyed her food suspiciously. "Do you think someone wants to poison me?"

"I do not know, but I want to be cautious. You would be surprised to what lengths some vampires go for a human. I am not thinking about poison as much as drugs. The members of our coven, I can vouch for, but there will also be others who I do not know, and I cannot guarantee their intentions." The Queen pointed to Ana's food with a smile.

After one more hesitant second, she sipped some of the coffee. As always, Ana enjoyed the taste, and curled her toes with pleasure.

"About tonight, the first and most important thing I want you to keep in mind is that it will ultimately be your decision. You are my protégée, which puts you in a good position, where you can pick and choose. The ceremony itself has two parts, or if you decide to marry one of the men interested in you, just one part. Do you have any questions so far?"

"How do I choose? What if I'm making the wrong choice?" Nervousness got the best of her. Ana's excitement was shadowed by the fear of making yet another mistake.

"No matter what you choose, or when, always listen to your instincts and follow your heart. If you do anything else, you will spend the rest of your life wondering *What if?* And that would be a very long time."

For a quick second, Ana remembered her mother's advice—to always do the right thing. She did, and nothing good came out of it from her experience. For as long as she could remember, she had placed other's needs before hers.

Ana spent years more preoccupied with doing the right thing for the rest of the world, even if it wasn't what she wanted. Following her heart was new territory.

"Now, we are different from humans, and the perception of age might be tricky. A vampire's appearance is the same as it was when he or she transitioned. The older we grow, the more experienced, more powerful we turn. Unlike humans, who the older they get, the weaker they become. In the invitations I sent out, I have expressed the preference for nobles."

"So, if I understand this right, I should choose an old noble?"

Her confusion brought a smile to Queen Emelia's lips.

"Choose the one your heart tells you to. Do not forget that you are going to spend the rest of your life with this man, look at him every single day for hundreds, maybe thousands of years. You do not want to be disgusted every time he touches you." The Queen patted Ana's hand over the table. "I am asking you to keep an open mind, ask questions when it is your turn to do so, and constantly search inside yourself. There might even be some combat if the ones wanting you are willing to fight. But, by that time, you will already have a favorite, if any at all."

"What questions do I voice? Do I ask them in front of everyone?"

"You may ask anything you want to know about them. The only time you can spend a couple of minutes in privacy, in a small room attached to the amphitheater, will be with the one you choose, or the winner of the fights, if you still do not have your heart set. Once you come out, your decision will be made public, and becomes official." Queen Emelia took a sip from her golden goblet. Ana already knew it was blood. "The wedding ceremony will be three days later, followed right away by your turning ritual. You can change your mind until the last moment and walk away from the marriage. Do not forget, once you marry, there is no way back. You will be husband and wife for the rest of your lives. Vampires do not divorce."

"And if I don't like any of them?"

"If you do not want to marry any of them, we will move on to the second part, and families willing to adopt you will step forward. Once you are adopted, we will plan the turning ritual for a date that I imagine you would want to be soon."

The Queen stopped for a second and Ana nodded in agreement.

"After you are turned, the hard part will start. You will be in training for a year, after which you would have to demonstrate what you have learned, how you have adapted to your new life." Queen Emelia paused, then continued. "Only after you pass your final tests will you truly be one of us, join us in fights, allowed to hunt on your own, and have the same rights and duties as everyone else. Until then, you will be considered a young vampire, always supervised and pretty much never alone."

"It's the same if I get married?"

"No. Your husband will be responsible for you, and your actions. He will train you and make sure you are ready for your tests, which you can take anytime you want, when you both think you are ready."

"So, it can be less than a year if I'm learning fast, or longer if I'm slow?"

"*Oui*, being married allows you to do that."

"I see. If I am adopted, is marriage still an option later or not?"

"Of course, and you would be doing it on your own terms, not pressed by time or circumstances."

After lunch, Celina came into the Queen's suite, reminding Her Majesty she needed to attend to her duties. Queen Emelia hesitated for a couple of seconds. As gracious as always, she slid out a booklet from the nearby bookcase and handed it to her protégée.

"Here, while I am gone you might want to read this. I should not be long."

"I'll be fine." Ana assured her and took the booklet.

She sat down in a chair, under the light of one of the elegant table lamps. They matched the impressive chandeliers, and their shimmering crystals attracted her.

Queen Emelia and Celina left the room leaving Ana alone, well-guarded, and safe.

Still holding the booklet, Ana skimmed her fingertips over the crystals. Their clinking sound made her smile. Tiny reflected lights chased on the walls. Ana tried to read, but the words danced before her eyes. She read the same sentence three times. Her mind could not focus on anything.

Marrying for love is overrated. It would not be the first time I'd do it. But my marriage failed, so maybe it is not the right approach. Adoption's tempting and looking better by the minute. Perhaps I should go with that. But what if there is a man I like? Can I even like vampires? Ana continued to try reading. The words on the page mixed with images of vampires. Her mind transformed into a battlefield between adoption and marriage.

About three hours later, the Queen returned. Ana lifted her eyes from the booklet to meet Queen Emelia's gaze. "Any decision yet?"

Ana shook her head and failed to smile.

"It will come to you. Trust your instincts."

Ana heard the encouragement in the Queen's words, and tried to hold on to it, feed her mind and soul on it.

"I will get ready for tonight, so everyone can focus on you when the time comes. I hope you don't mind an early dinner." Queen Emelia stopped for a brief moment in the doorway to her dressing room.

"Not at all." Ana returned to her thoughts as soon as the door closed.

Trust my instincts? Do they even work? I have been ignoring them all my life. I made mistakes too often to admit. All this thinking is not helping. Or does it? Does acknowledging my failures count as progress? Ana massaged her temples and closed her eyes. More thoughts flooded her already busy mind.

They were so many of them, so intertwined, she found it impossible to follow them. Something bothered her, but she had no idea what. *Why do I feel like I am missing something?*

Chapter 4

"What do you think? Brown or hunter-green?"

Ivan stared at Collin in disbelief. His friend still tried to chose between the two leather suits with an arched brow.

"Are you kidding me? I came here as fast as I could. You said it was important." The irritation in Ivan's voice made Collin smile and he turned around to face him.

"It is important. I have to make sure I look good tomorrow night for the Acceptance Ceremony. Don't you think so?"

"What are you talking about?" Ivan asked with a deep crease on his forehead and narrowed eyes.

"You didn't check your emails, did you?"

"No. I haven't made it home in three days. I should get my phone back soon, too. This damn new technology is driving me crazy. Everything was so much simpler in our time." Ivan shook his head frustrated. "I hate all the tiny buttons the new phones have and the need to swipe a finger over the screen in order to make them work. Sucks when the screen is cracked."

Collin tried but failed to hide a smirk, took a few steps, and sat on the black leather sofa, inviting his friend to join him.

"Tomorrow night the Queen's coven is holding a ceremony at The Castle, and I'm going. Your human's name is Ana, by the way."

"Wait. What? They're having a ceremony for her?" Ivan let the soft cushions of the couch mold around his body.

"Precisely. I'll get your human."

Collin's explanation caused a new question to rise in Ivan's mind.

"Why? You said you're not interested in her."

"I'm not. You are, so I'll get her out of their place. Where should I bring her?" Collin asked with a humorous curtly bow.

Finally, Ivan understood his friend's plan. A demonic light glinted in his eyes.

"Do you think it'll work? What if she doesn't accept you?"

"How many women have rejected me?"

Collin's question had a strong offended undertone, and Ivan weighed their chances.

"None that I know, but she's different. She might—"

"If I have to, I'll get into her mind a little. She will accept me."

"And then what?" Ivan insisted, seeing potential in his friend's plan.

"I bring her to you, and you do whatever you want with her. We have to make it look like I was attacked and lost her, though. I want to keep my relationship with the Third Coven. It's quite useful. At least until they figure out our friendship."

A few seconds of silence fell between them as Ivan mulled the plan over in his mind.

"It might work. But if it doesn't, we need a Plan B."

"Hey, I came up with Plan A. The backup is all yours. Just keep in mind that security will probably be increased."

Collin rose to his feet and returned to his leather suits. He stared at them with an undecisive stare.

Ivan's gaze followed his friend. If played right, Collin's plan could drop the human straight in his lap. He could use her to his advantage, against the Third Coven and their leaders. His jaws clenched with anger, hate overtaking his judgement. For the first time in what seemed a long while, he hoped for a break. He could almost taste her blood on his lips.

"The green one," Ivan suggested. "It brings out your eyes."

They spent the next few hours discussing the ceremony, and planning everything in detail. Collin had to play his cards right, make a good impression on Ana. She had to accept him. By the time he left, Ivan believed that one way or another, Ana's blood would quench his thirst.

~ ~ ~

After a while, Ana pushed all the fears and insecurities aside. She finally managed to read a few pages, even if she couldn't remember what from one paragraph to the next. At least her mind was not preoccupied with the impossible choice she had to make soon.

The heavy double-doors opened and hit the wall. Ana jumped out of her seat and stared toward the direction of the commotion. Her heart beat in her throat, forcing her to swallow hard in the hope to send it back into her chest.

A man entered the room. His dominating presence made everything around him shrink.

"You can't be here. This is Queen Emelia's suite." Her voice sounded screechy, and she hardly recognized it.

Ana didn't know if she should be scared or show confidence. *Whoa. I could look at him for the next few centuries.*

The man stopped, and his intense gaze cut through her. Bright silver lights in his dark-blue eyes made her think of a storm in the deep ocean. His expensive-looking suit and perfect haircut contrasted with the angry and ready-to-fight attitude. He showed off his long, straight, and incredibly white fangs with a low hiss. Ana took a step back.

"Do I look lost to you?" His question sent a weird mix of chills and tingles up her spine.

"How did you get past the guards?" Ana asked when she saw one of them closing the doors behind him.

"With my irresistible charm."

His sarcasm didn't go unnoticed. *Who the hell is he?* Ana wondered, and thought quickly of a smart answer, but nothing came to mind. She figured that as always, all the good comebacks would pop in her mind afterwards, too late to consider.

"Of course, how silly of me to ask." Ana managed to sound sarcastic, if nothing else.

She folded her arms around her waist but tried to act brave under his fixed gaze, narrowing on the side of her neck.

In the few seconds since he had entered the room, Ana took in all the details, from his spotless black shoes to the azure silk tie.

She didn't need enhanced senses to detect the sudden charge in the air. Tension sparked, like a coil ready to snap. *Damn, this is one big, angry vampire. Do they all look like this? He's easily double my size. Maybe I shouldn't goad him even more. He's not happy I'm here.*

"You should go. Queen Emelia will be here any second."

Instead of leaving, he moved closer.

"The door is that way," Ana insisted and pointed behind him.

"You must be the human that everyone is buzzing about."

He started walking in an agonizingly slow circle around her.

"I'm human, but I wasn't aware of any buzz."

"You smell good."

His hiss, dangerously close to her back, made Ana uncomfortable with him standing behind her.

"I take showers."

"And you wear perfume, I know. I can smell your blood running through your veins, hear your heart beating out of control."

He replaced his initial sarcasm with a whispered, low, rumbling voice. All her insides tied up in an impossible knot, furious he saw right through her. *Damn it, how do I keep cool when I want to jump in his arms? I should pretend he doesn't impress me. But he does. Okay, fake courage and confidence, it always works.*

The mysterious man displayed a superior, satisfied smile, and took his time to walk in front of her. He leisurely bent down to her height and stared into her eyes, only inches away from her face.

Ana smelled a mixture of cologne and natural musk. It made her bones go soft. His lips, close to hers, arrested her every breath.

"You are not afraid." Surprise and admiration surfaced in his voice.

"I'm not."

"You should be. You should be very afraid. You should start running as fast and as far as you can."

He continued to stare deeply into her eyes, as if he tried to see straight into her soul.

Ana blinked a few times. *I hope he's not going to use that magnetism thingy on me.*

"No. I'm here because I want to become one of you. You don't scare me."

Her answer made his head tilt to one side.

"Do you realize where you are, what you have gotten yourself into? Do you know what the difference is between being turned or killed?"

"About five seconds and a few ounces of venom."

"I see you have done your homework."

"And I wasn't even aware that there would be a test."

It's working. All I have to do is not let him see beyond my mask. Ugh. Easy to say.

Slowly he straightened up, holding her chin in his hand, forcing her to look in his eyes, dwarfing her with his stature. His touch made Ana's blood boil. Heat dispersed through her body.

"Hmm . . . There is something about you . . ."

"Everyone keeps telling me that. What's wrong with me?"

"Why do you think there is something wrong?" The beginning of a smile tugged at the corners of his lips.

"I don't know. Nobody has said there's *something about me* and then started jumping for joy."

"You are so naive. Do you realize how easily I could kill you?"

His stare cut deeper into her soul, with his unusual cobalt blue eyes.

"You could, but you won't." Ana braved. "If you wanted to kill me, I'd be dead already. Unless you are one of those people that like to play with their food." She decided to provoke him, show him she would not back away from a challenge.

Busy confronting him, Ana didn't hear the door when Queen Emelia entered the room. "Andree."

Ana startled, and tried to turn her head toward the Queen. He held her face in place, eyes locked.

"Mother."

Ana took in a sharp breath. "Mother?"

She stepped back quickly and freed herself from his gentle hold. Ana glanced at the Queen, then at him, and finally back to the Queen.

"Yes. I am sorry, *chérie*, but with everything else going on I have not had a chance to tell you more about my son, Prince Andree." The Queen turned her attention to him. "I was not expecting you back until next week. This is a nice surprise."

"I cut my trip short when I saw your official invitation. I need a drink, anyone else?"

Ana realized he waited for her answer, and she hesitated.

"Oh, *chérie*, you can trust Andree with your life. He would not hurt you."

"Thank you, water is fine." She eyed him suspiciously while he poured her the water and accepted the glass with trembling hands. *Trust him? With my life? He's not the trustworthy kind of guy with kind eyes and a sweet smile. I am going to pass on the trust part.*

Andree sipped from his drink and before he had a chance to say something, the Queen turned to him again.

"We will have an early dinner in a few minutes. Do you care to join us?"

No. Please say no and leave.

"Sure."

Ana had the uneasy feeling that he accepted the dinner invitation just for fun. He didn't appear hungry. Not for food, anyways.

From the corner of her eye, Ana saw Andree take off his jacket and the blue silk tie, throwing them carelessly on the back of a chair. Next, he rolled up the sleeves of his white shirt, revealing strong forearms webbed with thick veins. He sat and continued to study Ana's every move.

She caught herself breathing fast to keep up with her racing heart. The first couple of buttons of his shirt were undone and her eyes glued to his chest peeking through.

When she realized the source of her rushed and shallow breaths, she shook her head, turning her attention to the Queen. The sip of cold water didn't help.

Another satisfied smile tugged at the corner of his lips.

"He's the one who saved your life the night you were turned?"

Ana focused on the Queen and did her best to ignore him. He was extremely dangerous and sinfully good-looking. Something about him made her feel completely transparent and inexplicably attracted to him.

"Yes. I owe my life to Andree. He is the last gift I had from my husband."

Ana directed her attention on the glass she held. Tiny beads of condensation ran along, racing to the bottom. At least her hands stopped trembling before spilling the water all over the place.

Andree broke the uncomfortable silence. "Mother, I did not know you got so bored, or that our coven is so desperate for members that you started recruiting humans to be turned."

"Neither. The first night after you left on your business trip, Ivan showed up again."

"What? That bastard never learns. I hope you took care of him."

In the next few minutes, the Queen told Andree how the events of that night took place.

Ana did her best to disregard him and his glances. If he'd stop undressing her with those deep blue eyes, she might have succeeded, too.

"Why do you want to be turned, to become one of us?"

Ana gave up her detailed study of the floor. She knew she had to answer. Her eyes left the intricate design of the rug to look at him.

"I've always felt out of place, like I was living in the wrong time or world. It's hard to explain. When I met Queen Emelia for the first time, I felt I belonged somewhere." Ana turned her gaze toward the Queen. "I knew right away that my place is with you."

"I know, *chérie*. It is why I did not decline your request."

"And it was why you decided to take her as your protégée?"

Queen Emelia's smile faded away when she turned to her son, silently confronting him.

They both have those sparkles in their eyes. I wonder if all of them do. Will I get them, too? They look kind of cool.

"Yes. I did not know I was supposed to ask for your permission."

Right on, Queen!

Andree didn't answer. He turned away and nursed his drink.

A couple of servants entered the room with dinner. Ana already knew now, the golden goblet filled with blood was for the Queen. To her surprise, they brought regular food for Andree. That night, grilled chicken breast and vegetables were on the menu.

"I am a hybrid. I eat regular food." His explanation made Ana glance in his direction.

That is why he had a drink. I'm not even hungry. So he's the Queen's son, a Prince. Damn it. I talked so inappropriate to him. But I had no idea. He should've told me, or not provoked me the way he did. He deserved it. And why this impossible attraction? He's trouble and way out of my league. I know his type too well and—

"You are not hungry." The Queen pointed at the way Ana pushed her vegetables around.

"Not really, I'm sorry." She stopped playing with the broccoli and sipped some more water. The carrots were arranged into a straight line, as if they were parading soldiers.

"Give her a break, Mother. She is anxious to get herself a husband."

His remark won him a deadly glare from Ana, sharper than any dagger. It took all her will to speak respectfully instead of jumping at him to slap that smug grin right off his face.

"I'm not. I might opt for adoption."

"Speaking of that . . ." The Queen intervened again in an attempt to dissipate the thick tension. "If you decide that none of the men tonight are right for you, I would like to adopt you myself."

Ana's eyes opened wide, and her jaw almost hit the table. "You can do that?" Her knife and fork clinked against the plate when she dropped them. Luckily, she didn't have any food in her mouth at the time. She would've choked.

"You have got to be kidding me." Andree's indignation filled the room. He pushed back the chair and threw his black napkin on the table, revolted.

"I do not need your approval."

The Queen kept an impossibly calm expression.

"She . . ." His index finger pointed to Ana. "She cannot be my sister." Andree raised his voice.

Ana wished she could hide under the table. His accusatory tone lashed her ears and caused Ana to make herself small in the chair. She didn't ask for all this, she was most surprised by the Queen's decision.

"Why not? I think you would be a great big brother. You could teach her a lot."

"No. She. Cannot. Be. My. Sister."

He spoke in a low, restrained tone accentuating every word with purpose.

Andree picked up his jacket and exited the room the same way he came in, storming through the double doors.

"Your Majesty . . ." Ana couldn't finish her sentence. Her lower lip trembled and tears filled her eyes.

"This is not your fault, *chérie*. Finish eating. I will have a word with my son. This is not like him."

Queen Emelia exited the room the same way Andree did, hurrying through the doors.

Can't they just walk like normal people?

~ ~ ~

The Queen followed her son to his suite and marched into his living room.

"Andree, what—"

He rushed to his mother and eased her hands into his in an invitation for her to use her power on him and read his emotions. The lights in her son's eyes became stronger and brighter.

The Queen calmed down and whispered, "Andree. I did not know."

Her initial concern and anger at his display of disrespect melted away. Deep inside his heart, she found the real reason, the shock causing him to act out of character. It was just as unexpected for her, and she decided to respect his wish, not saying the burning words out loud.

Pride and tenderness enveloped her heart. She had been waiting for that moment for centuries, worried that would never happen.

Andree withdrew his hands out of his mother's and walked away from her, starting to pace. He resembled a caged wild beast, ready to tear apart anything or anyone in his way.

"Now you know why she cannot be my sister."

"I had no idea. Jumping to conclusions was clearly a mistake."

"Did you leave her alone?" He stopped pacing for a moment.

"She is safe. The guards are at the door, and Celina is with her."

"Please, Mother, just go back. It is not safe enough for her." He ran his fingers through his hair. "I have to come up with some damage control."

"Yes, you do. I am not convinced this was the best approach. You left her crying, and—"

"I know," Andree interrupted. "And she just decided to

choose a husband tonight. She dismissed the adoption a few seconds ago."

The Queen hid her surprise, but suspicion surfaced.

"Are you in her mind right now?"

"Yes," he added under his mother's stare. "I have been in her mind, and I have created a link to her."

The Queen walked toward the door. She stopped in the doorway and glanced one more time at her son.

"You should tell her that, too. Nobody likes to have their mind read at all times, especially without their knowledge."

~ ~ ~

"Your Majesty." Ana rushed toward the Queen the moment she re-entered her suite.

"Everything is all right, *chérie*. We have to get you ready for the ceremony. Andree will apologize, of that I promise."

An hour and a half later, Ana stared at her reflection in the tall mirror. She examined the beautiful crimson silk dress she wore and twisted sideways to peek again at the laced-up back. She had loved it when she first tried it on, and now she absolutely adored it. The image of the bluest eyes she'd ever seen flashed in her mind, distracting her from the outfit. *I wonder how he's going to apologize? Send me flowers, or simply let me live? He sure looks like he's killed before. But man, he's nice to look at.* With a smile she pushed away the troubling thoughts.

The simple, red stilettos officially became her new favorites. She'd never looked so perfect before. Ana took a deep breath and walked into the living room where the Queen and Celina waited for her.

"Ready?"

"Yes." Ana didn't recognize her own voice.

"You look beautiful. You will probably break some hearts tonight." The Queen's voice sounded far away, as if it traveled a great distance to land on her almost deaf ears.

Overwhelmed by the moment, Ana didn't notice they were going a different way to the ceremony room. If an abyss would've opened before her, she would've walked straight into it. Servants and guards bowed, whispering behind her, but she couldn't make out the words. Her hands clasped and unclasped a few times. Her whole body shivered, as if it didn't belong to her.

When they arrived in the ceremony room, Ana realized they stood somewhere behind the straight wall, in an alcove, off to the side.

"I'll stay here with you," Celina whispered. "When you hear your name, you must go and stand beside our Queen."

Ana nodded. A sudden lump in her throat stopped her from speaking. A heavy drapery and a few minutes stood between her and her future.

Chapter 5

Ana's mind scattered. She couldn't understand what Queen Emelia was saying to the members in the audience. Words refused to register.

"When you step out of there, remember to hold your head up and look straight forward."

A voice echoed in her mind, and Ana massaged her temples. *Am I losing it? Do I hear voices now? Damn, this is not the right time for me to go crazy. I have to focus.*

Celina touched her arm. "Are you all right?"

"I might be losing it here." Ana shook her head. "I hear voices."

"Must be His Majesty, Prince Andree. He's the only one powerful enough to communicate with you that way."

Celina's answer did nothing to help Ana. *Oh, goody!* She turned around, and rolled her eyes, taking her position, ready to walk into the amphitheater when she heard her name. Not even a second later, his voice invaded her thoughts, again.

"Celina is right. It is me. I will help you get through this as an apology for my behaviour earlier. When we locked eyes before dinner, I established a link between us. It is how I am communicating with you now."

Again, Ana shook her head.

"Get out of my mind. I need to concentrate here. Might be fun for you, but this is distracting as hell," she whispered, and even if she couldn't see Celina's smile, she sensed it, causing her to turn her head. "It's true." A cool sheen covered the back of her neck, and she tried to ignore it.

"Your cue. Go." Celina gently gave her a small push toward the room.

Whispers and hisses filled the amphitheater the instant she entered. With every bone in her body chilled and muscles about to disintegrate, she managed to make her way to the Queen.

Ana peeked around the room. At least a couple hundred people had gathered there that night. She found some comfort and confidence in Queen Emelia's smile.

When she finally stood by her, Ana found the courage to glimpse at the guests sitting on the stone benches. Blood red, plush pillows covered the hard, cold seats for extra comfort. She saw their faces, their eyes, and quivered.

"You did great. Now try smiling. You want people to like you, right?"

For the first time, Ana grasped she stood in a closed room, underground, with over two hundred vampires. A thin layer of sweat covered her body. Her discomfort with the situation was only topped by his voice resonating in her mind. When she finally saw him, she did a double-take.

Prince Andree sat on the first bench, relaxed, with one ankle resting on the opposite knee. His arms spread on the next bench up that he used as a backrest. Good thing nobody tried to sit near him. He occupied at least three seats. Andree gazed at her with a familiar arrogance.

The all-black leather outfit he wore made him appear broader and more powerful. His boots came up over his knees. Pockets on the sides nested a few daggers, their handles sticking out.

Her eyes traveled higher to the pants hugging long and strong legs in a way that set her cheeks on fire. The vest didn't leave much to imagination: tanned skin, taut over hard muscles. His chest moved slowly up and down and her breath followed the hypnotic rhythm.

Ana discreetly wiped her palms, suddenly clammy, against her dress. She wanted to ignore him. *Wishful thinking.* She tried and failed to tear her eyes away.

Around his thick arms, two thin leather strips fastened with silvery buckles, had the ends trailing down a couple of inches.

The perfect hair Ana saw earlier must've been part of his work or office attire. Now it was a controlled, messy mix of different shades of blond and light brown strands. Ana couldn't stop thinking about running her fingers through it.

His eyes, the same electric blue shade that intrigued her all evening, had something different in them. If she didn't know any better, she would've believed he liked her, especially judging from the smile causing a few slight wrinkles near his temples.

The grin persisting on his lips when he glanced at his mother made her realize the Queen talked to her. Her lips moved, and Ana wanted to understand the words, her mind still busy processing Andree's new appearance.

"My mother just asked you if you are ready to start."

Ana smiled and nodded to the Queen.

"I'm a little out of it." Ana glanced at Andree, just to see him smile again and barely nod to her.

"I know exactly what you think at all times. I have to admit, I am flattered."

Warmth spread up her neck then came to a stop on her checks. She was sure, visible blush covered her face for everyone in the room to see. And from his broad grin, she doubted anyone had overlooked her reaction.

The next few minutes seemed an eternity. Some of the men came close, walked around, studying her every gesture and expression, sniffing the air that no doubt carried her scent.

"Relax, you are safe. My mother and Celina are right beside you. No one will touch you."

His reassurance didn't help. Ana found herself shifting her weight from one leg to the other. She wished she could be invisible.

A few men remained in the center, willing to marry and turn her. Ana peeked at them and, for the first time, she managed to see their faces. Some looked decent, but a couple of them made her skin crawl. A tremor coursed through her body. Goosebumps covered her skin.

"We already have six solid contenders here, if there is anyone else interested please step forward, or we are moving on." The Queen's voice rose over the murmurs.

Thank God. I was ready to run out of here. Ana finally tried to relax.

Her tiny second of relief ended when Andree rose from his seat. *What in the world is he doing? This must be a joke. It can't be.*

He walked slowly, with a controlled laziness. Murmurs filled the vast amphitheater.

The turn of events didn't surprise Ana alone. One of the six men already lined up ran his hand through his hair and glared at the Prince.

She saw Andree's eyes measuring her from the top of her black hair to the sexy ruby shoes she wore.

"I am as entitled to this as anyone else. I am an eligible bachelor."

Ana perceived his message. It seemed like a bad dream from which she couldn't wake up. She glanced at the Queen. Unsuccessful in attracting her attention, Ana stood still, afraid to even move a muscle.

Andree took his sweet time to walk around her. The scent of his cologne made the entire world spin around her. His breath burned the back of her neck and sent tingles through her body. After what she believed to be another eternity, he walked just as slowly to the end of the line and stood, with the other men, now as an official candidate.

"This is going to be fun. Do not forget to ask questions."

Ana wanted to ignore his words so badly, but she couldn't.

"What the hell are you doing, Your Majesty?" She waited for a response, convinced he heard her loud and clear, but none came.

One at a time, the men bowed in front of her and introduced themselves with their name, occupation, and age. The first two, Ana heard almost nothing they said. She needed to get a grip on her wild emotions before it was too late. Gradually she found her calm, and the next man bowing before her was a Count.

"Ask him about his wife." Again, Andree's interference made her mad. It took all her will to keep smiling.

"Have you been married before?" Ana asked.

"Yes, I lost my wife about a hundred years ago. You remind me of her."

From the Count's confident stance, he had no idea his answer took him right out of the competition. *You are out, buddy.* Ana forced another smile and the Count went back into the line with the others, chest puffed out, convinced he had a shot.

She glanced at the first two men she didn't pay any attention to earlier. *I can't see myself with either of them.*

Ana's considerations got interrupted by the next contender, and she listened to him. He constantly avoided eye contact, preferring to focus his beady eyes to anything but her. His slender, close to willowy built and pointy nose reminded her of a weasel. *So not my type. I don't trust him as far as I can throw him.*

The fifth candidate, Ana had to admit, she would have considered. Duke Verre belonged to the coven, almost seven hundred years old with honey-colored eyes, and a kind smile. She could see herself living a long, eventless life with him. Perhaps boredom would become a factor at some point in the future, but he appeared to be the type of man she could trust. A convenience marriage with him didn't look as terrifying as she thought it might.

The sixth man, Collin, presented himself as an independent. His leather suit, a deep shade of hunter-green, molded to every curve of his athletic body. Ana lost herself, mesmerized by his emerald eyes. An unusual calmness wrapped around her.

A fuzziness overtook her, as if she floated in a thick mist. She fought to keep her heavy eyelids open, even if every pore of her body craved the promised relaxation.

"Look away. He is trying to control your mind. Since he is not good at it, you are not in any danger."

Ana followed the advice breaking eye contact and immediately regained her sharpness.

She knew Andree followed in line.

"Do not forget that we are in public, and I am the Prince of this coven. You have to be respectful even if you want to scratch my eyes out."

Ana giggled involuntarily, realizing the man in front of her thought she smiled at him.

He thanked her for being open-minded and returned to his spot with confidence, reminding Ana of a peacock. His plumage would have matched his clothes.

The moment she feared arrived, and Andree tilted his head before her.

"I am Andree De Croix, Prince of the Third Coven, and I am five hundred and seventy-six years old. I can offer you the one thing you desire most." He paused, and Ana stared at him, convinced he did it on purpose.

"And what would that be?"

"I can make you happy."

His condescending air, the full of confidence appearance, made Ana want to slap him more than ever. The palm of her hand itched and she wiped it against her hip. She remembered they were in public and it wouldn't look good for her to whack the Prince of the coven she wanted to enter. Instead, she bowed.

"You honor me, Your Majesty." Sarcasm poured from her words, and she hoped it wouldn't be lost on him.

After another one of his arrogant smiles, Andree went back to his place and stood poised and content.

"You did well. Better than I expected."

"Go to hell."

Andree couldn't help letting out a chuckle that he masked into a cough. He partially covered his face with his right hand.

The Queen smirked and returned to business. "Do you have a favorite?"

Luckily, this time Ana paid attention and hurried to answer. "No. Not yet."

"Is there anyone you know for sure would not be a match for you? If so, please send those men back to their seats."

Without a word, Ana eliminated three of them in a record time of less than ten seconds. All she had to do was walk in front of them and tilt her head in a way she would express how grateful she was for their offer, and how sorry she was to decline. She kept the Count, Collin, Duke Verre, and Prince Andree in competition.

"All right, so we have four gentlemen left. Now, who is willing to fight?"

The Queen's question provoked cheers from the crowd, and Ana looked around amazed at the reaction. They expected a fight.

Andree stepped forward.

"I will." He spoke loud enough to be heard over the noise of the excited crowd.

Silence fell over the amphitheater, and the other three contenders measured each other up. Andree's confidence radiated from him like heat from the sun.

Ana saw him draw two daggers. He stood tall, and holding the weapons in a resting position, he waited, calm and conceited, for anyone to accept his challenge.

"With all due respect, I have to decline. Your Majesties." The Count bowed and went back to his seat.

"I'll fight." Collin accepted the challenge and stepped forward.

"When you are ready."

The two opponents faced each other, and their hisses rose covering the Queen's words. The Duke stood aside, near Ana.

Ana swallowed hard a couple of times. Her mouth dried and her throat tightened. The crowd started to cheer again, encouraging the two fighters.

When Andree motioned to fight, Collin lunged into an unexpected, early attack. The daggers clashed cutting and stabbing the air. Both men surprised Ana with incredible acrobatic jumps in spite of their size. *I can hardly see anything. They move so fast. I can't wait to be just like them. It would be so cool to be able to fight like the Queen did that night on the beach.*

Andree was taller and broader, but Collin seemed to be faster, lighter on his feet, and attacking non-stop.

All the cheers from the spectators melted in the background. A cold claw tightened around Ana's heart. Her lips trembled and she pressed her hands against her chest. In her effort to see the fight, she forced her eyes open, delaying blinking as much as she could. Curiosity blended with fear in a concoction that had no problem overtaking her already shaken nerves.

Andree's daggers cut right through the leather jacket Collin wore. Two red lines marked his chest. She had to blink.

When she reopened her eyes, Andree's arm started to

bleed. *I knew it.* It only took a fraction of a second for Andree to get injured. Anna's knees turned soft.

Both stopped momentarily to assess the damage.

"Merely scratches," the Queen whispered in her ear and Ana closed her eyes, letting out a long, silent breath.

~ ~ ~

Collin retreated from a quick flurry of attacks. No match for Andree, his chances diminished rapidly. His reputation and his ego took a hit. He wanted to help his friend, but fighting Prince Andree wasn't exactly a walk in the park. As the fight progressed, he became more enraged.

It was bad enough the Prince surprised everyone with an untimely return. His interest in the human made Collin doubt his plan would work. He remembered how Ana broke free earlier from his attempt to control her mind and he suspected Prince Andree was responsible for it. Aversion against him escalated to anger and then pure hate.

He had to call Ivan and let him know what was happening as soon as he could catch a good moment.

~ ~ ~

Ana covered her mouth with her hands, trying to stop the yelp that escaped. Andree glanced at her for a fraction of a second. The distraction worked in Collin's favor and he rushed toward the Prince.

Ana's heart stopped when Andree flew backward. Her pulse roared in her ears. The empty seats he landed on crumbled under the hard impact.

Collin followed and, in a moment of desperation, Ana advanced one step, like she wanted to jump between them. She saw Andree's stare, and knew from the glimmer in his eyes he expected it, he enjoyed her reaction.

The instant Collin landed on his knee beside him, Andree jumped and twisted in the air before the other man could react. He landed behind his opponent, and Andree's blade stopped less than an inch away from his throat.

"You are defeated." Andree's declaration made the crowd explode into cheers.

Forced into submission, Collin surrendered and lifted both his arms over head.

"You won this time. Good fight." Collin gathered his slashed jacket and faked a jovial air. They both stood and bowed.

Visibly displeased with the result, Collin returned to his seat. The proud feathery tail of the personality he displayed earlier, now dragged behind him on the tiled floor, a little ruffled and perhaps a few plumes missing.

Ana didn't realize she had tears in her eyes until they blurred her vision. She wiped them away discreetly, hoping no one saw. It wasn't her lucky night.

"Were you worried about me?" Andree's question echoed in her mind.

She ignored him, trying to get her heart under control.

Queen Emelia waited until Andree retook his position and turned to the last contender.

"Duke Verre."

"There is no way I can defeat Prince Andree. Your Majesties." Just like the Count before him, the Duke bowed respectfully and went back to his seat.

Andree's triumph caused more cheers from the excited crowd. He put his daggers away and approached the Queen and Ana. With an elegant and distinguished tilt of his head, Andree stood in front of his mother.

Dust from the stone seats he had crushed minutes before clung to him. The cut on his arm had already stopped bleeding.

"As per our tradition, the victor, Prince Andree, and Ana will now have a few minutes of privacy. We will be awaiting your decision once you return. Unless you would prefer someone else."

The Queen glanced at Ana and saw her shake her head.

All of her earlier emotions washed away, and she seemed once again in control. Aware that every eye in the room studied her, she kept the calm appearance. A storm of emotions ravaged her soul. She couldn't decide which prevailed, if she was furious, frightened, numbed or curious. Each emotion took turns, leaving her with an empty stare.

The whole crowd stood in silence. Andree extended his arm, with a satisfied smirk on his face.

"Put your hand over mine and walk with me."

Ana hesitated, suddenly interrupted from her inner turmoil. An unusually strong charge floated between them.

"I will not bite you, at least not yet. Not literally."

The moment she placed her hand over his, an electric shock coursed through her body. In spite of her decision not to look at him again, she did. *I wonder what he feels right now? Did he notice the tremor? I hope not.*

After they entered the small room, Andree closed the door behind them. He dusted off some of the small rubble still attached to his clothes and straightened his frame.

"Your Majesty," Ana started, but as soon as their eyes met, she totally lost it. His superior smirk threw her in a new direction from the one she wanted to follow. She had every intention to remain calm and respectful. After all, he was the Queen's son and she adored her. "What the hell do you think you're doing?"

Chapter 6

"We do not have much time. Please, just listen, and—" Andree took a step toward Ana.

"Stay away from me." Fear mixed with anger glimmered in her eyes. "If you come any closer, I'll scream."

Andree stopped and measured her with the same snobbish air that drove her crazy. His eyes roamed up and down her body. He watched her backing into the wall behind.

She continued to retreat until the cold stone stopped her. Discomfort caused by his insistent stare made her even more nervous and seeing his lips curling into a smile only added to her agitation.

"You do realize I could get near you before you had a chance to open your mouth, right? I am only walking out of respect."

"Respect? Is that what you call it?" Ana didn't care to listen to whatever he had to say.

His body blurred for the instant it took him to cross the space between them. Tipping her chin up, he forced her to look at him.

She had never seen anyone move as fast and had to blink a couple of times.

All her efforts to keep distance between them failed. The wall behind halted her escape, and his body right in front of her, only inches away, stopped her from moving altogether. She didn't even have time to turn her head and assess the distance. The firm, cold stone assured her there was no way for her to move into that direction.

"I know you hate me and don't want me in your family. I got it. I—" Her eyes stung, and tears threatened, but she fought them back.

"Why would you think that?" Andree interrupted her. A crease appeared between his brows.

"You said so, earlier. It's why I had decided to marry whoever wanted me and get out of your way."

"I never said I do not want you in my family."

"Yes, you did." Ana insisted trying to avoid his inquisitive eyes. Seeing her cry was out of the question, and she steeled her will. Weakness was not an option.

"No. I said you could not be my sister."

"Same difference." Ana threw her words with poorly controlled fury.

"You cannot be my sister because I want you to be my wife," he muttered as if it was the biggest secret in the world.

His whisper reduced her to silence. All her attempts to free herself ceased. She stared at him in disbelief. "What?"

Since she finally stopped fighting him, he continued. "Do you remember when I came into my mother's suite?"

"It only happened a few hours ago. My memory is not that bad." His image entering through the wide opened doors flashed in her mind, hastening her blood.

"Funny girl. I am talking about the second I entered the room and laid eyes on you for the first time."

"You mean when you scared the life out of me?"

"Yes, that second." Another one of his arrogant smirks stretched his lips. "Look back, do you remember it?"

His insistence won, and, annoyed, Ana rolled her eyes. How could she forget it? Tingles spread in her body at the memory of him. She felt the flames rising to the tips of her ears.

"It is the precise second I fell in love with you," Andree murmured in a soft, soothing voice she didn't recognize.

"Yeah. Right. Love at first sight." It made her think of caramel, silk, and sunsets. *Is this a joke? It can't be true.*

"It is true. I never joke around when it comes to my life."

"It can't be. The way you talked to me, and—"

"It was one of the hardest things I ever had to do. I have waited for the right woman to come into my life for over five hundred years. I had to make sure you were the one."

The distance between them gradually diminished. His breath brushed hot over her skin. It interfered with her judgment. An avalanche of images blended with feelings, making Ana dizzy. She didn't want to believe him, it would've contradicted the promise she made to herself. It had been years since she decided not to allow love back into her life.

"I don't believe you. I don't know why you are doing this."

Ana shook her head and attempted to push him away. It felt like she tried to move a wall with her bare hands. Men like him don't fall for women like her. She knew that much.

"We are running out of time. I will answer all the questions you have later. For now, accept me. Be my wife, and I can promise you will never regret it."

Andree touched her lips with his thumb so gently, Ana thought she just imagined it.

More images popped into her mind. Her ex, his drunken stupors, and their fights. She had suffered enough. All of it had happened because she allowed it to, she let a man hurt her, and she wasn't going to make that mistake again.

But Andree was not her ex, and it wasn't fair to compare. *My life wasn't fair either.* She pushed everything to the back of her mind trying to mute the irresistible attraction toward the man in front of her.

"But I don't—"

"Do not ever try to lie to me." His interruption came

before she could finish her sentence. "I already know how you feel, how attracted you are to me."

Ana froze. That second, she found out how a thief feels when caught stealing. *How does he know?*

"I know every single thought you had tonight and earlier today. Everything. When I told you I was flattered, I spoke the truth," he reminded her.

"Please stop. Is this some sort of a game for you? I came here to become a vampire, not to be toyed with. I don't care who you are." Ana tried again to push him away. His superior smile infuriated her. "And stop smirking."

"This is only one of your qualities among many." He licked his lips, drawing her attention to his mouth. "You are not afraid of me, nor intimidated, and you speak your mind. You even sent me to hell." Andree reminded her with an arched brow. "I love that about you." He paused for a short second. "Just think about it, marrying me will make you a Princess." Complicity sparked in a bright shade of blue inside his mesmerizing irises and made her pulse reach for never heard of high speeds. "You will have a special status in our coven. In time, you could become more powerful than my mother."

His offer tempted her. So much so, Ana almost said yes. But she couldn't afford to let attraction and hot blood make the decision for her. She'd made mistakes before, too many of them.

Ana's mind fought the battle of all fights. She could marry him to ensure her place. Yes, she tried to convince herself she'd accept his proposal strictly to become a vampire—nothing else.

She dared a quick glance at the man in front of her. *Who am I kidding? He's hot, a Prince, and loves me, if it's true. What more could I ask for? What if I'm wrong? What if he's going to hurt me like everyone else? Can I take that chance?*

It would've been much easier if she hated him, or at least disliked him, instead of being attracted to him. She could've considered everything a compromise, a sacrifice she'd have to make in order to become a vampire.

"Will you turn and train me?"

Ana stared into his eyes, two pieces of a blue heaven she was tempted to enter. The fear of getting hurt again held her back. If she was going to allow another man in her life, at least she needed some assurance.

"You have my word."

"That means squat to me."

"I know you have trust issues, and I cannot blame you. If you knew me a little better, you would know that my word is more valuable than any written contract."

"But I don't." Ana's eyes narrowed to dark, suspicious slits. She hoped to catch him in a lie, anything she could use against him.

"You will. Soon. Just trust me."

"Why should I?" Ana noted his hesitation when he took a few steps away from her. For a moment she thought he acted against his wishes.

"We are running out of time. We have to go back in there, and you must make your decision public."

Ana nodded and walked toward the exit with her head down. The fight inside her grew more intense. A roller coaster of *yes* and *no* caused her emotions to spike. Fear confronted courage, adventure faced comfort, and unknown stared down monotony.

Before opening the door, Andree wrapped one arm around her waist, squeezing her against his body.

"Follow your heart and listen to your instincts. I am nothing like the men who took advantage of you. If you accept me, I will spend every day, for the rest of my life, doing anything and everything in my power to make you happy. That is my promise to you."

Ana stared at him again. She wanted to believe him. Her body did. But her mind struggled. *Why does he have to be so damn perfect? If it's true, and he really loves me, I could miss the chance of a lifetime. He could give me everything I ever wanted or dreamed of.* She closed her eyes in a desperate effort to regain her sharpness. His proximity dulled most coherent thoughts and messed with her senses.

He gently let her go, which allowed her a few seconds to regain her needed calm.

"Not following your heart would be the biggest mistake you could make," he whispered and opened the door. Andree placed her hand over his, and they returned together to the ceremonial room.

Silence fell heavy and deafening. The clicking of her high heels on the stone floor echoed in her ears. She swore her heart thumped somewhere between her throat and her ears. For the few seconds it took them to walk back to the center of the room, Ana saw herself as a pendulum, swinging non-stop from accepting him to not.

She didn't have enough time to compare all the pros and cons, she could hardly find enough strength to stand.

They stopped on either side of Queen Emelia, and she turned toward Ana with a gracious smile.

"It is time to tell us your decision. Will you choose a husband tonight, or do you prefer adoption?"

"I've chosen to get married." The words rolled off her tongue surprising her.

The spoken answer provoked cheers from the crowd, and everyone's eyes turned to their Prince. He strode in front of Ana and seized her hands. Silence covered the amphitheater again like a suffocating blanket.

Ana trembled.

"Relax, and do not think of anyone else. This is between you and me."

Ana perceived his words and gazed at him. For the first time, he dropped the arrogant air she'd grown accustomed to, no more smirks either. Instead, she discovered in his deep ocean-blue eyes everything he'd just told her. She stopped shaking.

"Ana, would you be my wife?"

His question resonated in the silent space, hit the rough stone walls only to bounce back into her thoughts. Her heart and mind fought like Titans at war over her life, her future. The internal battle threatened to overwhelm her senses. The constant pounding in her brain became unbearable until she took a stand.

Ana swallowed, trying to find her voice, but when she opened her mouth to answer, no sound came out. Her mind still fought and didn't let her speak.

Her hesitation floated around the room, like a silent, wounded bird. Not one blink of an eye disturbed the thick air. Anticipation and curiosity stopped everyone from moving. The amphitheater seemed filled with live statues.

"Yes." Her whisper brought the crowd to their feet in an explosion of cheers.

Gently, Andree lifted her right hand to his lips. The soft kiss sent her blood into a raging inferno.

"Thank you. You will never regret it," he murmured in a low voice, only for her ears.

"The wedding will be in three days." The Queen made her last announcement of the evening, lifting her right hand. "While I am sure our couple has a lot to talk about, the rest of us will celebrate their engagement in the ballroom. Starting now, Ana is under Prince Andree's protection."

Andree scooped Ana in his arms, and after gracing the audience with another classy tilt of his head, he exited the chamber. She closed her arms around his neck. When he started to run, flashes of her surroundings—walls, chairs, people, ornate sculptures—all zipped before her eyes.

The dizzying speed of his fluid movements nauseated her, causing what little food she picked at earlier to swirl in her stomach. *I should've passed on the peas, too. They would've looked good lined up with the carrots.*

~ ~ ~

Ivan received the message and read it with glowing eyes. *Ana just accepted a proposal to marry Prince Andree. Call off Plan B. It is too dangerous.*

His fangs extended, a hiss pushed through, and his left fist hit the desk hard enough to crack the solid wood.

Definitely not the kind of news he had expected. Unfortunately, he couldn't call his people back.

The Prince was supposed to be out of the country. *Are you sure?* he messaged back to Collin and waited for his response.

Yes. His friend's message flashed across the LED screen. *I fought him and lost. I swear I am going to take him down one day.*

Ivan couldn't hold back a demonic grin.

I can't call off Plan B. They went silent already. He hoped his people would make a choice for themselves and abandon their mission if it looked too dangerous.

~ ~ ~

After what Ana thought to have been mere seconds, Andree stopped in front of the double-doors opened by the two guards and entered into the spacious room.

"I could've walked." She swallowed hard, forcing the contents of her stomach back where they belonged along with the butterflies now circling in a flurry.

Andree lowered her in the middle of the thick, luxurious white rug that hugged her red, high-heeled shoes.

"Not fast enough."

"Where are we exactly?" She glanced around to take in the new surroundings.

"Our suite."

Ana noticed the modern and comfortable style she loved, a lot different from the Queen's suite. She wanted to be cautious and keep her distance, but with only one glance in his direction her blood heated.

Her eyes stopped on the low table, where a champagne bottle and two glasses waited beside a small arrangement of scented white flowers. She whirled around, facing him.

"You were sure I was going to accept?" Suspicion poured through her words and radiated from her being.

"No."

"Then what is this?" Ana's perfectly manicured, red-tipped, index finger pointed to the table.

"I hoped you would say yes. I know everything you like, or dislike for that matter, all of your fears, dreams, and hopes."

His answer left her speechless. It bothered her, and she threw a disapproving glance at him. Her eyebrows lowered without another word. Transparent, was the first word that came into her mind. Being vulnerable made her hide behind a wall of suspicion and curiosity.

"Just as my mother can read anyone's feelings by holding their hands, I can get into anyone's mind by looking in their eyes. I can find out everything about anyone. It is one of my special abilities."

"One of them? What else can you do?"

"You have experienced how I communicate with others, through a link I create with that person. I can also influence anyone's decisions, and make others think what I want them to."

"You can control people's minds? How is this possible? How did you get all this?" Genuinely curious, Ana joined him near the sofa.

On second thought, if she had his power she would use it, too. A multitude of images flashed in front of her eyes. Past moments when she could've used his ability. Her life would've been so different. *Wait a minute, he didn't manipulate my mind, did he?*

"I would never do that. I love your mind as is." Andree poured champagne into the glasses and gave her one. "Would you like a drink?"

Ana accepted the tapered glass with bubbles racing to the top. "Thanks."

"To us. To a long and happy life together." Andree clinked his glass against hers.

The crystal touching against crystal sang the unmistakable song of promise. *Maybe. There is potential but it's a long road ahead.*

She sipped from her drink and sat. Ana doubted his toast and preferred to remain silent. She still didn't forgive him for invading the privacy of her mind.

"Unlike most vampires, who were at some point turned, I was born one." Andree sat beside her. "I always had these skills, and I have trained long and hard to utilize them to their fullest." A smile worked its way up to his eyes. "Has anyone explained the differences between purebloods and hybrids?"

"As far as I understand, hybrids eat and drink regular food, and can stand in sunlight. Purebloods, who live strictly on blood, are vulnerable to the sunlight, unless they use daylight serums." With a sense of pride in her tone, Ana showed she had learned something.

"That is correct. But hybrids still need blood to survive. Every few days, but we need it. Since I will turn you, you will become a hybrid. Any human becomes the same type as the vampire turning them."

"I knew that." Champagne bubbles tickled her nose. "Oh, and the born vampires are all hybrids, too.

He nodded. "There is another big difference between the two." He volunteered more information. "Hybrids use their energy a lot faster and they regenerate it at a slower rate compared to purebloods. Also, the latter tend to be faster, but with training, all disadvantages can be overcome."

Andree stopped and jumped to his feet. His nose twitched a couple of times. Quickly, he grabbed Ana and hugged her close to him.

"What is it?" Hard, lean muscles contracted under the palms of her hands, and tension exuded from his body.

"Stay close to me."

"Why? What's going on?"

"We are about to have some unwanted company. No matter what, you stay close, do you understand? This is not a joke."

Ana nodded. Three men entered the room through the wide-open glass doors and her head turned in their direction. The intruders showed their fangs and hissed. Their clothes reminded her of the incident on the beach, mismatched, and in different states of filthy.

The attackers' faces were mostly covered by overgrown, ungroomed beards. Only their eyes held a wild, demonic stare.

She had just seen Andree fight earlier, but against one adversary, not three.

Andree turned to face them and drew his daggers, different from the ones he used in the fight with Collin. Shinier. Ana remembered Celina telling her they all had, at all times, silver coated weapons for emergency situations. She couldn't tear her eyes from the sharp blades.

With one step, Andree put himself between Ana and the three intruders, blocking her view. He opened his arms, protecting her with his body.

Hidden behind him, Ana held on to his waist. The tension in every one of his muscles made her hands tighten, ache with stiffness. Andree's hiss sent chills down her back, it sounded different from before—primal.

"For your sake, I hope you are lost." Andree's voice rumbled from deep within his chest.

"Give us the human and nobody gets hurt," one of the intruders demanded. Ana couldn't see them from behind Andree, but the gruff tone of his voice sent tremors through her body.

"You know that is not going to happen. I will only tell you once. Leave, and you will walk out of here. I would hate to have to kill all three of you in front of my fiancée."

"There are three of us against one of you. Do you really think you stand a chance?"

An odd static energy crackled in Ana's ears, and the air changed. Andree's muscles relaxed in her hands. He straightened his frame.

What the hell is he doing? He's not going to turn me over to those guys, is he?

"Do you have any idea who I am?"

"The smug Prince Andree." The same raspy voice that seemed to belong to the one doing the talking sent more chills up Ana's back. She closed her eyes and leaned her head on his back.

His muscles tensed and relaxed, in a quick dance, then stopped. The intruder's screams filled the room, echoing against walls and hurting Ana's ears.

She held her breath and wished she was anywhere but there. The sound of weapons hitting the wood floor covered the hisses that stopped abruptly.

"Who is next?"

Ana reopened her eyes and peeked around Andree's body. To her shock, the two remaining men put away their weapons and knelt.

"Your Majesty, please," said a bald man with tattoos covering his head.

"Please forgive us, Prince Andree." The second guy, with blue-black hair bowed his head further.

Their murmurs left Ana in disbelief.

Still shaken, she glanced around them. Ana figured he must've killed one, since ashes covered the floor, surrounding the abandoned weapons.

She noticed the deep cut on Andree's arm, the blood, and she covered it with her hands.

"Andree," her voice cracked.

Her panic must have distracted him because he turned around. Her fingers, covered in his blood, pulsed to the beat of his heart, and tears pooled in her eyes.

"Are you hurt?" he asked, quickly checking her hands.

Ana shook her head. "You are."

"It is superficial."

The doors opened, and four guards rushed into the room. With his attention split three ways between the guards, Ana, and the two remained attackers, Andree lost control of the intruder's minds. The two kneeling men glanced at each other and quickly ran the same way they came in, jumping off the large balcony. Without waiting for orders, the guards followed them.

"Son-of-a—" A deep, throaty hiss escaped Andree's clenched teeth. He refocused his attention on Ana and rushed her into the bathroom, washing her hands.

"I have to make sure he didn't hurt you, that his daggers didn't nip your skin. If your blood mixes with mine I can't detect it."

Ana barely registered his explanation. Her fixed stare focused on the blood diluting under the stream of warm water. A pink swirl formed around the drain, and she followed the hypnotic movement.

"I am sorry." He drew her close to him, pressing her against his muscular chest. "Are you sure you are all right?"

Ana didn't blink, and her lips trembled. She hadn't realized how intimately he held her in his arms. They returned to the living room, and she avoided looking in the direction where ashes feathered the floor. Knowing they were the remains of someone who had been alive until only minutes ago knotted her insides. A gag reflex caused her to completely turn her back to the spot.

"Ana." With one bent finger under her chin, he lifted her face to him. "Talk to me."

"I've never seen anything like that," she murmured.

The captain of the guards rushed into the room, his swords drawn and glimmering in his hands. With no enemies left in sight, he placed the weapons on his back and bowed. For the next few minutes, Andree explained what had happened.

"You and your sentries need to figure out how the attackers managed to get so close." Andree touched with the tip of his boot one of the weapons on the floor. "I expect a full report before morning."

Ana tried to recover control of her emotions. The surge of adrenaline from earlier left her trembling. Her arms crossed over her abdomen. Who wanted her badly enough to risk death? Why? Fear and curiosity took turns, but neither brought answers.

Fragments of the conversation stuck in her mind. Andree had blamed himself for losing control over the two attackers. He had never once mentioned she had caused his distraction by calling out to him. *Next time I'll keep my mouth shut.*

Still trying to figure out who was after her, deep in her thoughts, she had no idea when the captain of the guards left. *Why do they always have to move as quiet as the wind?*

Andree closed the glass doors and whirled around to face her.

"When you turn me, I'm going to get some of your powers, right?"

"That is correct," Andree answered with a slight amusement dancing over his face.

"Will I get that one?" She rubbed her temples. "Am I going to be able to control other's minds?"

"That is not how it works. It depends on what your body accepts, what will assimilate in the turning process."

Ana thought about it a few more seconds in silence. "If I do, please train me well."

Andree smiled and took her in his arms, holding her close to him. Gently, he lifted her face to his again. His touch, soft and gentle, gave her an inner sense of calm and offered sanctuary and warmth.

"I will train you well no matter what. I need to know that you will stay alive."

His lips brushed hers lightly, like a feather at first. She lifted her eyes to his and completely lost herself in their blue vortexes. Fear dissipated, passion enveloped her like a fuzzy cloud, and she surrendered to him.

From the instant Andree kissed her for the first time, Ana felt she was safe with him. Could she trust him? Was she ready for such a huge step?

Chapter 7

Ana sat on the sofa, still a little dizzy from his kiss, and took another sip from her drink, trying to calm and organize the chaotic thoughts. She had questions, and the man who'd entered her life so abruptly held the answers, just as he held her until a few seconds ago. It made her wonder what other deep, dark secrets he held locked away.

Focused on her thoughts, she relived the moment when her blood rushed, her bones melted, and her limbs trembled. What was it about this man that made her senses reel? Sure, he was attractive—more than a little, but looks were often deceptive. Or so her past had shown her, especially when it came to her ex-husband.

Warm arms encased her waist, warming her to the core. His touch, unexpected, rekindled the flaming inferno ravaging her heart.

She struggled to accept the attraction between them, the undeniable chemistry.

"In a few seconds, servants will come in to bring your things from my mother's suite. Do you need to get anything you might have left behind at your old place?"

"I have everything I need with me." Ana quickly shook her head. "I rented a locker in a storage facility for my painting stuff."

The door to the suite opened. "Your Majesties." The servants, wearing the same drab grey uniforms, bowed humbly then carried her clothes and belongings into her new dressing room.

All the questions from earlier resurfaced in her mind. One after another, they peeked their heads like a bunch of curious creatures, torturing her with the lack of answers. One stood out in her mind: *Did I make the right choice?*

As soon as they were alone again, Andree continued. "I see you have a lot of questions for me. Before I answer, I have to tell you a few things. Do you think you can hold on for just a little longer?"

Ana nodded and glanced at him. Her eyes went to the already healing cut from minutes ago. One of the things she had learned from the books Queen Emelia had given her, was that vampires healed a lot faster than humans.

"Since I already admitted I have been in your mind, I know you do not like needles. Our doctor, Daniel—my best friend for the past four hundred years, is on his way here to take a sample of your blood." His hand covered hers and squeezed it lightly.

"Samples? Why? What are they used for?"

"Do not worry. We all have blood stored in the vault, preserved, just in case we need it at some point in the future. We must renew them once in a while, but it is good to have it for emergencies. Daniel is also using it to make daylight serums, and for research. He will make sure you do not feel a thing."

Andree stopped for a second.

"I will need your official documents, everything with your name on it, so I can start working on your new paperwork." He released his hold. "The contents of the storage unit you mentioned will be transferred to a more appropriate place. In the meantime, please think about what last name you would like. I noticed now more and more women prefer to keep their names even after marriage."

"Okay." Thoughts of her finished paintings and partial ones came to mind. She'd been so rushed to pack, many of them lacked proper packaging to preserve the medium used. "My work, it needs a climate-controlled environment."

Ana rose, collected her purse, gathered what he had asked for and a few seconds later, she handed him a white plastic folder containing the information of who she was in the upside-down world she left behind.

"As far as the name goes, I'll take yours, if that's all right."

"I am honored." His right hand covered the left side of his chest, on top of his heart. "Every twenty to twenty-five years we change identities, and move, so we do not attract attention."

"What? Why?" Ana hurried to ask, suddenly afraid to live on the run.

"We do not age, so we cannot look the same for too long." He paused and set the folder beside him. "It is not inconvenient at all. And I promise to make sure our homes will surpass your expectations," he tucked a rebel strand of her hair behind her ear. "However, all of our original documents shall remain secured in a safe. Any questions so far?"

"I have one. How are you going to start on my paperwork if we're not married yet?"

"We have people working for us everywhere. Right after the ceremony, you will have to sign a pile of documents, in the presence of witnesses, and only after that, will you receive your new credentials." A slight smile played with the corners of his lips. "I want it all done and over with before we leave for the honeymoon. You will need a new passport as well."

"When you say that you have people everywhere, what exactly do you mean?"

"Our kind, mostly. In the last four hundred years or so, more and more hybrids have come along. We blend in with humans more so than purebloods since we are not bothered by daylight." He sipped from his drink. "There are vampires employed in every single place you can think of: the government, fashion, finances, restaurants, the military, the list goes on and on. They also rotate every few years for obvious reasons. Most of them are independents. When it comes to hiding from humans, we set aside any conflicts or differences." His glass clinked against the smooth surface of the table.

Ana tried to wrap her mind around all the information. Their unity as a species impressed her. She couldn't wait to be one of them.

"There are quite a few humans working for us as well."

"There are humans that know about your people?" Ana heard her voice grow shrill.

"Yes. They all signed silence agreements, or non-disclosures, as you may know them as. They would pay with their lives for betraying us or breaking the provisions of the contractual agreement. It is not worth it."

Ana blinked fast a few times. She wished she would've known about them a long time ago. Perhaps she wouldn't have had to go through hell and back, lose her ability to fully trust anyone. Doubt crept into her mind, once again.

"Why would any vampire work in an office, doing a boring job, when you guys can do anything you want?" Her question caused the wrinkles around his eyes to appear again. Those fine lines looked good on him.

"Not all of us are the best fighters. Some chose to support from behind the lines, sort of speaking. What they do it is important. Keeping our kind hidden from humanity goes beyond any internal conflicts, or beliefs."

"So even if it is an enemy of yours, you will still provide them with fake documents?"

"Not only me, everyone else. Most of them are

independents, and they stay neutral. Our safety as a species is their job—everyone's job."

Ana pursed her lips into a thin line. His explanation made sense to a certain degree but some gaps still remained.

"I already mentioned Daniel to you." He waved his hand between them. "My other best friend, Mike, is my general manager. He takes care of all our business. You probably know from my mother that we are wealthy." Andree paused and continued, but only after Ana nodded her agreement. "We have been accumulating our fortune for centuries, and I am pretty sure that, unofficially, we have shares in almost every single big-name business out there. I am saying *unofficially* because there are different identities we have been using throughout time, but it is all recorded carefully in our archives."

The servants leaving the suite stopped and bowed.

"Your Majesties." The taller of the two women spoke with a British accent and stiffness. "All items are in place." She bowed again, with the grace of a dancer.

They both headed for the exit, but the door opened before they reached it. A tall man entered, holding the door ajar for the two women slipping into the hallway and out of view. His athletic build made Ana wonder if vampires worked out.

"Come on in, Karl. Ana, this is Karl, my assistant."

Ana nodded in his direction and Andree handed him the white folder.

"Karl, I need you to do a few things. First, here are Ana's official documents. Make sure her new paperwork is done in time, and safe." He stopped and waited for his assistant's nod. "Next, I will need you to place an ad in our network, for a personal assistant for Ana. I would like to have the position filled before the wedding. You can make appointments for the interviews as soon as possible."

"Yes, Your Majesty, I'll do those right away. And if I may, congratulations, to both of you."

After another bow, Karl left the room.

"What do I need an assistant for?" Ana asked.

"She will do everything for you, from hunting, to using her contacts to get whatever it is you want. An assistant will help you train, will protect you with her life when I am not around, and at least until you learn our way of life, she will guide you every step of the way."

"Die for me? Who would want to kill me? Is this because of the earlier incident?"

"I do not know who or why and this has nothing to do with the incident. At least until you can hold your own, you will be vulnerable. Your assistant will be your shadow, always there for you. You will also need a maid, but for the time being, I will have Veronica with you. My mother told me that she's been helping with your needs since you got here, and you are satisfied with her work." Andree paused and waited for Ana to nod her agreement. "She has been with us for over a century."

Without a word, Ana lowered her gaze. Her fingertips detected the small crease between her eyebrows. She started to understand the magnitude of the changes in her life. Whether she was ready for them was a different story.

Andree lifted her chin up. A smile stretched his lips, exposing perfect teeth. *How will it feel when he turns me, when his fangs bite into my neck?*

"See, this is another thing you will have to learn. Never look down in front of anyone. You will be a Princess. Others will bow before you, but you always hold your head high, be proud of who you are."

"I have a lot to learn," Ana admitted and tried to look away from him. With a firm but gentle grip, he held her in place, staring into her eyes. She felt vulnerable, naked under his gaze.

"And you will, in time. Until then, you should trust me.

Since we are on the subject, I have to talk to you about our societal rules of engagement and . . ." His nose twitched in a sniff. "It will have to wait. Daniel has arrived."

Great, more rules to look forward to. Just what I always wanted. Not.

The doors opened, once more. She drew in a deep breath, collecting her thinned and frayed nerves, unsure of what to expect next.

A well-dressed man, in his early thirties entered. He had an air about him, grave and serious, a coldness which made Ana unsure of how to receive him.

Arm to waist, the man bowed with a masculine, yet elegant flare. "Your Majesties." His deep, crisp voice hummed in the room.

"Daniel, you know you do not have to do that."

"It wasn't for you, but for Her Majesty, Princess Ana." His answer embarrassed her. Out of habit, Ana cast her eyes down.

"Head up, look straight ahead." Andree cupped her chin, guiding her head back. "When someone bows in front of you, you may respond with the tilt of your head, but you will keep looking forward, never down." He quickly demonstrated for her.

Ana repeated the gesture, eager to learn everything.

"Very gracious. You were born for this." Daniel stopped in his tracks and examined her with increased attention. "There is something . . ."

"You sense it, too?" Andree flashed a quick glance at Daniel.

"I do, but . . . What is it?" Daniel sat across from Ana and placed his black leather doctor's bag on the floor.

"Here we go again." Ana rolled her eyes.

"We have no idea. My mother sensed it first, but she cannot tell what it is, either. Head up, my love."

"You people have way too many rules, ceremonies, all this *royalty* stuff," Ana couldn't keep her irritation to herself any longer.

"It is what has kept us alive for many centuries. Traditions and rules helped us evolve and make it throughout time." Thus far, Andree had kept his promise to answer all her questions, and then some.

"But in the real world—" Ana tried to make her opinion known. She didn't believe in all the rules and their customs. Evolution was the reason they didn't exist anymore, at least in human civilization.

"The real world? Whose? This is our reality, what you see here." Andree gestured around him. "Whatever is out there"—his index finger pointed to the closed glass doors—"the human domain, it is unwelcoming to us. This is where we are ourselves, where we do not hide, where we do not have to use fake names." Andree's eyes concealed a longing she couldn't understand. "This is where we can be who we are and not be judged for it or hunted because we are different. The human world, where you lived until now, will become just as hostile for you as it is for us."

Ana considered his words. She'd never thought about it from his perspective. For the first time the secret society she wanted so badly to enter revealed itself in front of her in a completely new light. Vampires envied humans for their mortality. Ana finally understood the longing in Andree's eyes. His kind was denied access to humankind.

"Do not forget that most of us were born centuries ago. We grew up, formed our personalities, our characters, in a different era." He continued with a softer tone. "In those times, bowing before a noble was a show of respect. Today it is mockery. The human world has changed and not necessarily for good. We have preserved our traditions, our beliefs, and yes, we do have rules—rules that kept us safe from humans."

As much as she opposed strict rules, Ana understood the need to adjust, to conform and fit into their society. Becoming a vampire meant more than a bite and drinking blood. It was a lifestyle, a mentality, and she doubted she had what it took to be one of them.

~ ~ ~

A faint, floral breeze infiltrated Andree's nose. The familiar and intrusive scent distracted his attention from Daniel and the current conversation with his head-strong fiancée.

"Hello, Mother." Releasing a heavy sigh, he propped his feet on the edge of the coffee table.

Queen Emelia entered the wide opened doors. "I am sorry for the interruption, but I have a question that cannot wait until tomorrow."

"Your Majesty." Daniel bowed with respect.

"What is it, Mother?" Andree didn't hide the slight irritation in his voice.

"It is about the wedding ceremony." The Queen shot him a stern glance then approached. "You will have a traditional ceremony, but would you also like a human one?" She turned to Ana. "I mean, considering that you are human, would you like your white dress and walk down the aisle?"

Andree checked Ana's mind. He had to know what she thought, not what she would answer. Her thoughts swirled in a tight ball of emotions.

Fragments of her words entered his mind forming sentences. *Last time it didn't end well. Do I want to walk down the aisle again toward a man who might end up hurting me? Would Andree? He seems different from my ex. This could be a chance to make it right, to move on from a failed past.*

Her decision to at least try and cover a bad memory with a good one caused a muscle to twitch in Andree's jaw. But she'd compared him to her ex. His hands balled into fists. From his previous incursions into her mind, he knew her ex was a lousy excuse for a man. He didn't deserve to be compared to him. Anger sparked and went away just as fast. It wasn't Ana's fault, she only tried to protect herself against more hurt, more suffering, and moreover, against the whole world. *That is going to be my job.*

"If that would be all right," Ana cast her eyes downward. Her head lowered for a couple of seconds then, shoulders back, she tipped her head up, holding the Queen's gaze.

Pride made his chest swell. "We should have both ceremonies." His bride to be was as bright as she was beautiful, the perfect combination, worthy of a Princess. "I do not want Ana to have to give up her wedding day." He nodded his approve. "We will need an official regardless to make it legal for the outside world."

"*Magnifique*. We will have them both then, back to back, first the human ceremony and then our traditional one. Daniel, since you are here, I request a batch of serum." Queen Emelia smiled toward her son's friend. "The wedding ceremony will be held outside, on the north lawn, right before sunset. We will need about two, maybe three hundred daylight applications. Will that be a problem?"

"It shouldn't be. I have a couple of days and nights to make them, but I'll need full access to the lab here. Using my own would take more time to go back and forth." Daniel planned out loud.

"*Bien sûr*, you are the only one using those facilities. Do you need help?" the Queen asked with her well-known attention for detail.

"I'll summon my assistant. Between the two of us, we should be done with time to spare."

"You are going to need it." Andree's words caused his friend to redirect his attention.

"I will? Why?" Daniel's eyebrows shot upward in confusion.

"I was hoping you would be my best man." Andree couldn't imagine getting married without his best friend by his side.

A wide smile covered Daniel's face. "I'd be honored."

"It is set then. We will discuss the details tomorrow, and Andree, do not forget that Ana needs to sleep," Queen Emelia added on her way to the door.

"I know, Mother."

With a slight tilt of her head, the Queen left the room, and Daniel took the bag he had set aside earlier.

"We should extract your blood now and get this done and over with, especially since you're not looking forward to it. Andree told me that you're afraid of needles."

About ten minutes later, Daniel left with the blood sample. He had work to do.

Andree turned to Ana and smiled. "I said you wouldn't feel a thing."

~ ~ ~

Andree's kiss had the same effect on her as it had the first time. As much as she tried to deny the attraction, Ana felt helpless in his arms. The world reappeared inch by inch around her after his warm, inviting lips left hers. Tiny bubbling volcanos spread through her body refusing to simmer down.

"Are you sure you're as old as you're saying?" She inched away, placing a small distance between them—space she needed to help her think.

"Yes, why are you asking?" His brow arched.

"I'm surprised. I've never liked antiques," Ana muttered avoiding his gaze.

Andree laughed and held her tighter, closer, lifting her face to him.

"Ana, we are going to marry, and we will be together for hundreds, possibly thousands of years. You have to learn not to hold back anymore." He leaned against the sofa's backrest.

His deep and raspy voice soothed her. Ana wondered how he could both calm and excite her at the same time.

"But—"

"You are." Andree touched her lips gently. His fingertips brushed over her skin.

She trembled under his touch. Each living cell in her body craved for more contact.

"I want to make you happy, but you have to let me. If you continue holding back, trying to hide and control the way you feel, you will never be completely happy." His thumb caressed her cheek. "Let go of your fears. I will never hurt you. I need you to trust me. Do not be afraid."

Ana anticipated his kiss from the way he stared at her lips. Fighting against him was harder than she thought. Surrender tasted sweet, at least for the time being. All of her passion and desire surfaced taking her soul by storm.

"I love you." Andree's whisper caused an avalanche in her mind.

She panicked. "I . . ." Her body tensed. All words left her mind. It was too soon. She didn't share his feelings. Yes, she was attracted to him, but not in love. No way. Even if impaired under his seductive presence, she knew that much.

"Shhh," Andree's index finger pressed lightly on her lips again. "Do not feel obligated to say it back. I know exactly how confused you are right now. Take your time. I have never accepted anything less than I am offering, one hundred percent, and that is not going to change. When you are ready, you will know it."

Ana watched the tiny silver sparks growing brighter in his eyes. *Hmm. Does he know something I don't?* She wanted to believe he was the last person in the world to hurt her. Memories of her past shadowed the present. Her guard needed to stay up.

~ ~ ~

Andree sat on the edge of the bed until well after she fell asleep. He listened to the slow, regular rhythm of her breathing. A rebel string of hair fell on her face, and he brushed it away carefully, not to wake her. Ana rolled to her side revealing a partially bare leg that made his heart beat faster. She sighed in her sleep. Andree allowed himself to look at her deeper memories. He wanted to know as much as he could about her.

For the next couple of hours, he dove into her past. Memories of her childhood saddened and made him smile at the same time. The harsh times, only matched by tough parents determined to raise her to be a winner, warmed his heart. In their way, they wanted to prepare her for the worst, without realizing they had robbed her of precious memories.

Encouraged and taught to always do the right thing, Ana grew up ignoring her dreams. She had accepted one wrong decision after another because of failed logic. Following her heart or a dream was still a foreign concept.

The worst was yet to come, and he knew it from what little information he had extracted prior from her married life. He hoped to never come face to face with the man who broke her spirit. His fists tightened. *For his sake.*

Andree only moved when he heard the door. Quietly, he exited the bedroom and went into the living room where Daniel waited.

"You wanted to see me." His friend sat on one of the couches.

"Yes, I need to ask you a favor. I have been in Ana's mind, into her memories, and there is one thing that bothers me." He pinched the bridge of his nose. "She always wanted to have children but never did. She had a surgery, her tubes used to be blocked, but shortly after, she divorced. Would you mind taking a look at her?"

"Of course, I can do that. When do you want me to?"

"Now. She is asleep. I need to know sooner rather than later."

The urgency in his voice put Daniel in motion. He left the comfy sofa and followed Andree back in the bedroom.

"Well." Andree felt as impatient as a kid waiting to open his gifts.

"Give me time to examine her." The opacity covering Daniel's eyes signaled the use of his special ability. Andree remembered the distant times when he helped him train. Without even touching Ana's body, Daniel's gift provided him with the means to see through anything, and he inspected her carefully.

Andree trailed his friend to the living room once he was done, eager to hear what he had to say. Before Daniel had a chance to say anything, a single rap at the door broke the tension in the room.

"Enter." Andree faced the entrance.

In the door frame, the captain of the guards stopped. "Your Majesty." The man bowed.

"Did you catch them?"

"No. I am sorry. I figured out how they got in here." He squared his shoulders. "I found their fake invitations." The man handed Andree the three passes the intruders used to gain entry.

"We also discovered a body, a human guard and evidence that one of our own had been killed."

"Who?" Andree asked, anger starting to build inside him.

"David Dawson. He used to—"

"I know exactly who you are talking about," Andree interrupted.

"Whoever they were, this was premeditated. They had an original invitation from which they made the fakes." The captain hesitated a moment, then continued. "It appears they were made by an amateur, at home. Not superior work but good enough to pass at a glance. Whoever let them in did a poor job of scanning papers. I will make sure it doesn't happen again."

Andree nodded, and the captain bowed then left.

"Sounds like you need to up security." Daniel broke the silence first.

"Yes. I will. What about Ana?" Anger simmered just below the surface of his skin.

"She's perfectly fine. The surgery took care of a minor issue. One of her tubes was blocked and the doctor performing the procedure did a nice job clearing it. I can't tell you why she didn't have children, but she should have no problem." Daniel zipped his bag. "Wait a minute. You are not thinking of . . ." Daniel's shock stopped him from finishing his sentences. "No. You can't be serious."

"Why not? I love her. I want her to have everything she desires, including a child. I want her to be happy."

"You know very well why not." Daniel's index finger pointed at Andree and trembled. "It could kill her."

~ ~ ~

Minutes before sunrise, Collin entered Ivan's living room. Heavy draperies sun-proofed the space. He had to hurry, as a pureblood, he didn't want to be caught in the sunrise with the serum expired.

"Who did we lose?"

"Johnny. Bert and Eric made it out in time."

"Damn it." Collin let himself sink in the cushions of the comfortable but worn couch.

Ivan joined him in silence. Another of their plans had gone south.

"I am going to kill Prince Andree one day. He humiliated me in front of everyone. The smug ass of a Prince forced me into submission!" Collin's rage escalated.

"Take a number and sit in line. He's mine." Ivan claimed the Prince's life.

Collin stared at his friend. It took the previous night for him to finally understand and share his friend's hatred toward the Third Coven's Prince.

"What are our chances of doing something during the ceremony, on their wedding day, and getting away with it?" Ivan's question resonated in the room.

"Slim to none. That place is like a fortress. The security will be tighter, especially after tonight."

"Those bastards. Why was he back so soon? Why—"

"I don't know." Collin glanced at his friend. "All I do know is that one day, he will pay."

Collin's usual calm, nonexistent at the moment, was replaced by hurt pride and a bruised ego. His fury against the Prince continued to build. He clenched his teeth and held back the large assortment of swear words popping into his mind. Words were not going to cut it for him.

"Why is he interested in my human?" Ivan's whispered question made Collin turn his head in his friend's direction.

"In all honesty, she is beautiful. Any man would be lucky to have her."

Ivan's hand cut the air in front of him and a disgusted grimace covered his face.

"I don't care about that. I only want to use her against them. As far as I'm concerned, she is just another human. Did you sense anything in her proximity?"

Collin nodded. He rose to his feet and started to pace. The discolored rug muffled his steps.

"She is different. There is some sort of presence about her. I think she could be valuable. Unfortunately, she's now under his protection. There's no way to get her out."

Ivan ran his hand through his hair. "That smug bastard is tough." His hatred surfaced again. "He must have a weakness."

Suddenly, Collin whirled around and faced his friend.

"He does. It's her." Realization hit Collin like a truck. Everything started to brighten in his mind. Ideas lit up like stars in a clear sky.

"That's not exactly good news." Ivan's confusion amused his friend.

"It is. He's too absorbed in this human. When we fought, his focus was on her instead of me. A handful of times during our scrimmage, her movement and well-being distracted him, leaving him vulnerable. He will make mistakes, and we are going to take advantage of them."

"You lost me," Ivan admitted, taking a few steps away from the sofa.

"We need someone inside."

Ivan didn't seem to share Collin's excitement, but it didn't matter. A spy inside the Third Coven seemed an impossible task—one he intended to see come to light.

"Everyone working for them is loyal. Who would turn on them?"

A half-demonic, half all-knowing smirk covered Collin's face.

"Loyalty, my friend, has a price." The tug of his lips into a grin further brightened his mood. "It is only a matter of paying the correct amount to the right person. I am sure not everyone in there is happy."

"In that case, we should get to work." A malefic light flared behind Ivan's eyes.

Chapter 8

"You are out of your mind. Have you ever been with a human? Do you know how easy you can kill her?" Daniel's lamentation hit the wall of calm Andree struggled to keep. "You said you loved her."

"I do."

Love at first sight was real. It had happened to him earlier that day. Andree knew Ana was the one destined to him the instant he saw her. He searched in her mind and found she was kind, selfless, and protective of the people close to her. After that, all of her other qualities were an added bonus.

"Then why risk her life?"

Daniel had a point, and Andree knew it. He reviewed his past five centuries, remembering the women who accidentally died in his arms. His love for Ana, and his determination to give her everything she ever wanted, seemed to win the battle waged inside him.

"Daniel, there are things that even you do not know about me. I am not proud of it, but I have been with a lot of humans before."

"You have? How many? What percentage survived?" Daniel stared at his friend. "Do you hear yourself?"

"In the first approximately three hundred years, I killed a few."

"How many?"

"More than a handful. I did not keep count."

"We both know you did. Andree, we've been friends for almost four hundred years, I know you never forget anything." Daniel's gray eyes narrowed with suspicion. "I know the level of attention you pay to every detail, and I know how much you have always tried to protect humans. If you killed any, I'm sure you have an exact—"

"Thirty-eight." Andree's answer reduced Daniel to silence.

Andree didn't even try to hide the guilt he still fought to control after all the years.

"That's not bad but let me ask you something. Did any of those women mean anything to you? Did you have feelings for any of them?"

"No. At the time I didn't know why I had to do it. I couldn't stop." Ghosts of the women who died haunted Andree's eyes.

"I'm sorry, my friend, but your feelings for Ana might work against you in this case. You love her. It will be impossible to control yourself when passion and desire takes over your mind and body. It'll only make it harder."

"I will be careful. I have to."

The thick, soft rug absorbed the sound of Daniel's steps. Andree knew his friend worried about Ana's safety, and for good reason. The man's concern, his tension, charged the currents of air in the room.

"Let's assume you can do this. We'll pretend you won't break Ana's bones when you grab her or hug her too hard and crush her. Let's say you manage to keep her alive. You know as well as I do, that no human has ever delivered a vampire baby and survived. Ana is not strong enough to carry the pregnancy to term. She won't make it, Andree."

"That is where you come into the picture. I am going to turn her after she gets pregnant if she does." Andree had to correct himself. "It will be her decision." He refocused his attention to his friend. "You will let me know the right time to do it."

"You are crazy. Does she even know the risks? Do you have any idea how sick and fatigued she's going to be? She's way too fragile for this." Daniel threw his hands in the air. "She's half your size, for crying out loud. I really have a bad feeling about what you want. Just turn her right after you get married. It's the right thing to do, and you know it."

"No. Besides, I need more time to figure out a way to turn her."

"What do you mean?" His friend's brows almost touched in the center of his forehead. "There's only one way to turn a human—a controlled bite."

"That we know of." He paused. "I have to find out if there is any way to turn her without losing all that is human in her." Andree pointed toward the door behind which Ana slept. "You met her, you saw how she is. Ana has this unique, innocent, almost naive way of seeing the world around her. She is a good person, giving without expecting anything in return, easy-going, until you piss her off, of course. Then she becomes more courageous than most people I know."

One of the memories he had discovered earlier flashed in his mind and caused a wave of tenderness to wash over him. During her elementary school years, she stood up for a complete stranger bullied by older kids. She went straight to the leader of the bullies and punched him in his nose. None of the other kids saw it coming, and they stared at her shocked. She broke the guy's nose, and it cost her three days suspension. But the skinny blond-haired girl she stood up for, became her best friend.

Andree glanced at Daniel. His friend didn't seem impressed with his explanations, so he would have to convince him beyond a shadow of a doubt.

"She comes from the world we want to fit into, but we cannot. Yet she feels like an outsider. I have never met someone willing to give up everything to be one of us. She is not afraid. And then there is the presence we all sense in her." Andree hesitated for a short second. "If I had to guess,

I'd be inclined to believe she had a vampire in her family lineage, a powerful one. It would explain a lot."

"Ana is going to become one of us, strong and fast, an immortal. Most changes are physical. She will keep her character."

"And her humanity? There has to be a way to make her strong while keeping those little human traits. Her need for protection empowers me. Her views are refreshing. Her desire to be immortal is stronger than anything else. It will be so much easier for her to adapt."

Daniel ambled toward the door with a defeated air. Stopping, he held onto the frame.

"You should sit down and think this through, my friend." Daniel glanced back. "You are not making any sense. Of all the people I know, you're one of the most rational. Everyone looks up to you." Admiration and sadness mixed together in Daniel's tone. "Against any common sense, you fell in love with a human. You should've known better. Turning her as soon as you can will excuse it. This entire situation will only make more waves. You have to get yourself together, for her sake, and everyone else's." He walked into the hallway and closed the door.

Andree stared at absolutely nothing for several seconds after Daniel left. He sat and leaned forward with his elbows on his knees. Every time he tried to be rational, Ana's image showed up in his mind. He remembered her blushing and smiled. Then he recalled her telling him to go to hell and grinned again. He loved her fire, her existence.

An uncontrollable need to be close to her overwhelmed him, causing him to rush in the bedroom. He didn't see her at first under the soft covers, in the middle of the oversized bed. Heart pounding, he watched her chest rise and fall.

Andree kissed her forehead and her breath fanned over his skin. His blood rushed, surging through his veins. Her alluring scent brought his fangs out. Slow and steady, her pulse throbbed on her neck, beckoning him. Instinctively, he licked his lips and swallowed hard, trying his best to stay in control. Daniel was right. It would not be as easy as he had thought. The vampire in him wanted her just as much as his human side needed her.

Andree let out a hiss and left the room in a hurry. Through a mental link with his mother, he asked her to meet him in his quarters. He wasn't about to leave Ana alone.

Minutes later, a knock at the door announced her arrival.

"Enter." He spoke the single word while lost in thought—thoughts of the passion that drove Ana at the core, thoughts about the children she wanted, thoughts regarding the possibility of creating an offspring together.

His mother entered the room. "What is it?" She smoothed the silk dress covering her frame.

Her question made him hesitate before speaking. *Where should I start?* "Mother, have you ever heard about a different way of turning humans?"

"A different way? There is only one way. I do not understand."

"Ana will lose everything that is human in her after turning. I want to avoid that."

"You love her that much?" His mother's soft and warm voice wrapped around him like a comfortable blanket.

Andree glanced at his mother with sadness. His shoulders dropped, and his head hung low, an act he wasn't accustomed to even in childhood.

"Yes. I do not want to lose her. I do not want her to become like us: cold, indifferent to pretty much everything. It would be a struggle to blend in the outside world, and I do not want that for her."

"I know what you mean. Unfortunately, I only know of one way to turn humans, the way it has been done for centuries. If there is another, I am pretty sure someone would have figured it out by now."

Silence fell over them. After a while, the plans for the wedding took priority.

"I will talk to Ana in the morning. It will be her decision, but I would like to postpone her turning."

"That is not going to sit well with everyone."

"If anyone has a problem with it, they are more than welcome to challenge my decision."

He knew his mother, of all people, understood he had made up his mind, and how stubborn he could be.

After Queen Emelia had left, Andree decided to join Ana before the first signs of a new day emerged along with hope for a renewed future. Still clothed, he slipped between the covers, ever so careful to not disturb her. In her sleep, she cuddled closer to him. He let out a sigh and hugged her, relishing how her soft flesh molded against him.

Images of the women he had killed hundreds of years ago came back to haunt him: broken necks, snapped spines, crushed ribs, and punctured lungs. Their lifeless eyes still followed him in nightmares. Guilt suffocated him.

Their deaths had all been accidents. He never wanted to kill any of them. A force beyond his control pushed him further every time, didn't allow him to stop. He had to learn how to bed a human and not kill her. At the time Andree didn't know why. The question tortured him for centuries. Now he knew why. The one destined to him was a human. Andree struggled to supply his lungs with much-needed air.

Every single one of them made him stronger. He had mastered how to barely touch them, please them, how to keep his hands off when he was about to lose control.

He glanced at Ana, still asleep, with her head resting on his shoulder. She was the answer. It was because of her, he endured the guilt of those deaths. They died so he could be with her.

Andree gave in to temptation and ran his fingers through

her soft and silky hair. He buried his face in it, closed his eyes and inhaled her scent: Lily of the valley.

An old memory flashed in Andree's mind. When he was about ten years old, he got caught in a torrential rainstorm. He had wandered for hours through a small grove near the edge of a city. Still young, he had forgotten what city they had lived in at the time. A few older trees had formed a canopy that offered him shelter. A carpet of lush, green leaves and delicate, white, heavenly-scented flowers covered the ground. Andree had picked a few for his mother, hoping he wouldn't get in trouble for running home soaked. It worked. She had loved them, smiled, and told him their name: *Lily of the valley*. It had been over a half millennium ago.

His attention shifted to Ana's left hand resting in the middle of his chest. Gently, he covered it with his own. *How can someone so small and fragile have this much power over me?*

Andree smiled again. He knew that sooner or later, one way or another, he would have to turn her. Life without her was unimaginable.

Ana's long, black eyelashes fluttered open like a butterfly's wings.

"Good morning, My Princess." Andree kissed her forehead, warm and smooth against his lips. He closed his eyes for a brief second, keeping his desires at bay.

"Morning. Did you sleep, too?" She sighed a sleepy yawn.

"No, I sat here with you. You know we only need a few hours of sleep every few days, right?"

He saw her nod and wanted to smile, but he couldn't.

"We need to talk about something important, and I need you to be as honest as possible, not only with me but with yourself, too." Andree hoped for the best.

"What is it?" She sat in the middle of the bed, waiting for him to speak.

Andree took her hands into his, gazing into her eyes. Decadent, dark, melted chocolate came to his mind. Her image in his bed, the white silk nighty she wore, distracted him, causing him to pause. He tried to find his words. For a moment, they had all fled his mind.

"I have been inside your head some more and learned something—"

"Again? I let you get away with it last time, but you are taking advantage." Her brows scrunched, forming an angry line that only made her more attractive in his eyes. "Stay out of my mind, would you?"

Andree knew not to provoke her any further. Her volatile temper surfaced again, and deep inside, he loved it.

"I promise it is the last time I will search into your past. I needed to know."

"Then do what everyone else does: Ask."

The start didn't seem good and Andree worried he upset her at the wrong time. *Like there is a good time for it.* He needed to repair the damage.

"Would you have told me everything?"

Ana pursed her lips. *"Damn it. He is right, but that doesn't excuse him. Maybe it would be better to drop it."* Andree smiled inside at her thoughts.

"What did you want to ask me?"

"You always wanted something, but never got it . . ."

"You'll have to be more specific. There are so many things I've wanted and never got." A slight smile tugged at the corner of her lips. "Power, money, fame, should I continue? Perhaps a pony?"

"I am talking about having children."

Her smile vanished. The joy in her eyes drained and sadness replaced it. Memories started to pour into her mind through a gate she had sealed for years. Andree witnessed every single one of them unfold before his mind's eye.

"I've tried to have children in the past, but I've been told I can't. I got used to the idea."

"Daniel believes there's nothing wrong, and you should be able to have children if you want. That surgery you had right before separating was successful."

"How does Daniel even know about it?" The flames burning in her eyes told him she was preparing for another confrontation. There was little doubt in his mind that she could deliver him to a delightful life in heaven or a sweltering eternity in hell.

I love her fire. I guess it makes things more interesting. Andree noted her wrinkled brows.

"I asked him to take a look at you last night after you fell asleep."

"You did what?" Her brows sprung up in a mixture of surprise and horror. "Oh, God. Did you make me forget what he did?"

"No, relax. He did not touch you." Andree rushed to add, "Daniel's special ability is seeing through things like clothes, flesh, bones, walls, pretty much everything." He reached for her, but she retreated. "He's like a walking X-ray machine."

"Are you serious? Wait a minute, does that mean that he can see anyone naked?"

Andree laughed at her panic.

"He could, but he is a true gentleman, and never abuses his power. He sees like us, but when he needs to view beyond the surface, he concentrates and does it. He is convinced you should have no problem having children if you still want to." Andree paused again and examined her carefully. "It is up to you if you want to try."

Her mind struggled to process his words. She didn't allow herself to hope again, he could feel it. She'd been down that road, only pain and disappointment had met her at the end. Andree hurt at her thoughts, as much as she did.

It took her close to two years to accept that she would never have children.

"I had no idea. You know, when I was a teenager, I used to dream that one day I'd have twins," she said softly, almost afraid of her words.

"I know. Theodor and Theodora, great names, by the way. My question is: Do you still want them? Do you want to have a child? Mine?"

Ana searched his eyes, and he saw the cobalt pieces of his irises reflected in hers. That moment, he understood the weight of his question. In one of her memories, she had read in one of the books Queen Emelia gave her that vampire women couldn't have children since they didn't ovulate. The thought resurfaced now, and he sighed.

"Women of your kind can't conceive." She pinched the bridge of her nose and frowned.

Andree rushed to clarify her confusion.

"There is a way." He held her hands in his. "If you are willing to try, I will wait to turn you until after you get pregnant, if it happens. You would not survive otherwise. I need to know from you if you want to have a child with me. If you do not want to try because of the risks, I understand."

The sadness in his eyes reflected in hers, and the resigned tone of his voice amplified in her mind. Under his careful observation of her mind, Ana realized she would have taken something away from him if she were to say no. Andree's heart beat faster at her swirling, unspoken words.

"Can I think about it?"

"Of course, I understand this is a tough decision." Andree continued to monitor her thoughts.

"Yes, it is. I don't want you to get your hopes too high in case it doesn't happen. I've done that before, and it's a steep way down to disappointment." She fidgeted with her gown. "In case I decide to try, you won't turn me for a while, right?" Ana avoided his gaze.

Andree lifted her face, his eyes settled into hers. "I promised I will turn you and I keep my promises, all of them, always. I cannot imagine living my life without you. We can wait a few months, years if you—"

"No, not years. We can wait a few months, but no longer. Please." Tears started to gather in tiny pools. "I will let you know."

"As you wish, my Princess."

Andree drew her on his lap and closed his arms around her. His hungry lips tasted hers, clouds of lust threatened self-control. The kiss turned passionate fast. Desire took over his body.

With a throaty growl, Andree gently pushed her away and jumped off the bed. He needed to keep his distance in order to regain control. Her wide-open eyes conveyed the innocence he had fallen in love with, but they also housed a sliver of fear—fear of the unknown.

Ana ran into the bathroom without a word.

Over a half an hour later, they met for breakfast. Their recent kiss replayed in his mind and made him long to hold her, touch her, but he had to take things slow. He needed to control his vampire side. The aroma of coffee flooded the terrace. Before he let her sit, Andree hugged her to him.

"I promise I will try to keep my distance better in the future. It is almost impossible to resist you. I cannot touch you before we get married. It is the way I was raised."

"But it isn't like that anymore. These days, making love before getting married is common, it's human—"

"I know," he interrupted. "But I am not human." Andree kissed her again and held the chair for her.

Chapter 9

Ana's thoughts ran scattered, like fine dust in the wind. She had about an hour before a whole day of shopping started.

For security reasons, Andree and his mother agreed it would be safer to do it at The Castle, instead of dragging Ana through stores. The calls made the night before assured there would be enough to choose from to create a wardrobe suited for a Princess. Andree shared the plan with Ana, and she nodded absently, still lost in her busy mind.

"I need to make a call." Andree let her know before disappearing inside the living room.

A couple minutes later, he returned to the terrace laughing and shaking his head.

"What's so funny?"

"My friends, Mike and Ella, are on their way here to meet you. I have already mentioned Mike to you. His wife, Ella, possesses a very rare ability. She sees the future of the person she touches. I figured that sooner or later you would need friends, and I thought the two of you would get along well."

"So, she could possibly see my future?" At first the idea appealed to her, but then again, did she really want to know what the future held for her? What if she didn't like it? What then? Could she change it?

Andree sat beside Ana and wrapped an arm around her shoulders, bringing her out from the fascination of her own mind.

"Before they get here, there is something else I need to talk to you about."

"Sounds important."

"It is. If you decide to give us a try, things are going to be different for us."

"Different? What things?"

"Like all humans, you are extremely fragile. I could break your bones or crush you to death. I need you to promise that if I ever hold you too tight, you will tell me. I could not live with myself knowing I hurt you in any way."

"I know you won't."

"No, you do not understand. This is serious. If I lose control for even a split second, you could die."

"I'm not made of glass."

"Glass is stronger. You do not realize the differences between us yet. See this?"

Ana looked down and his touch, gentle and warm sent tingles through her body.

"If I squeeze your hand a little more I could break every bone in it. Every single time I touch you, there is a potential danger. I need you to make sure that when I am about to lose control, in the bedroom, my hands are not on you."

Her cheeks burned, and she avoided his expectant gaze.

"I am serious, Ana. I do not care if I destroy a million pillows, they can be easily replaced, but my hands cannot, under any circumstance, be on you. Do you understand me?"

"Yes, but—"

"No *but*. There is only one way we can make this work, and I need your help. Please, promise me that you will do what I ask you."

Andree held his breath in anticipation of her answer.

She couldn't miss the tension in his body, or when he squeezed her hand a tiny bit harder. "Okay, I promise. Now easy on that hand."

Andree let go and jumped away, as if her hand had burned him.

"See? This is what I tried to explain to you. I am so sorry."

"It's all right. It wasn't as bad as you think, just a little too tight for comfort."

"Ana," he whispered and hugged her close to him, pressing her head gently on his chest.

"Your Majesties." A woman and a man's voices mingled together in the warm air.

Andree and Ana turned at the same time.

"Ella, Mike, this is Ana." Andree introduced the newcomers without any formality.

Mike came closer first. Ella hesitated. She studied Ana with curiosity. They both bowed, and Ana tried to remember how to greet them properly.

Mike broke the silence: "I can see why Andree has fallen for you."

Ella tilted her head to the right, continuing to stare.

"This is incredible. Can you guys feel it? There is something about you—"

"You have got to be kidding me. Is this ever going to stop?" Ana couldn't hold back the frustration.

"What is it?" Confusion and concern mixed in Ella's voice.

"Everyone who has met her has said the same thing, even me. Yes, we can all sense it, but we do not know what this is."

"I'm sorry. I didn't mean to upset you in any way," Ella apologized quickly.

"No, it's not your fault. Everyone senses something, but nobody seems to know what it is. I wish I knew what was wrong with me."

Ana tried to excuse her reaction. Her broken confidence surfaced again. For years, her ex blamed her for everything.

Years of abuse were hard to extinguish, but she had promised herself she'd try to overcome her insecurities. For the most part she did. Every now and then, they would show their ugly heads, leaving her broken inside. *Not today, damn it. I am going to marry in two days, and I will enjoy every minute of it.*

"Nothing is wrong," Andree insisted, tightening his hold on her waist.

"He's right. It's not wrong. I don't know how to explain it. It's like this great power that's in you is ready to erupt and blow us all away. It's surprising in a human."

After Ella's explanation, they all sat, and the conversation started to flow easy and light. Ana noticed the inside jokes, even the common gestures and reactions the three of them shared.

"Would you like to have Ella look into your future?" Ana glanced at Andree, his words still echoing in her mind. She nodded with a glimmer of excitement in her eyes.

"Ella, would you peer into Ana's future?"

"It would be my pleasure. Should I look for something in particular?" Ella asked and took Ana's hands into hers.

Andree shook his head and Ella focused on Ana.

"Are you blocking me in some way?" A crease appeared between Ella's eyebrows. She stared straight into Ana's eyes.

"No. How would I do that?"

"Hm. There's only one person in this world so far who's future I can't see, and that's me."

"You can't see anything?" Mike's tone revealed surprise.

"Nothing. Nada. Zero. Zilch." Ella shook her head and glanced at her husband.

"That is impossible. She is right here. You have to see something." Andree's insistence didn't change the facts.

"I don't. Which is why I asked you if you are blocking me," Ella explained, turning to Ana again.

"Maybe I don't have a future," Ana whispered and retrieved her hands from Ella's. The thought was unsettling.

"No, you do. It's like a wall between me and that future, like someone or something stops me. I can't see through it. I honestly believe it has something to do with what we all sense in you. Once you become one of us, I wouldn't be surprised if you were extremely powerful."

Andree's phone rang, and he excused himself to answer. Mike followed him, leaving Ana in Ella's company.

"Do you think I'm that special?"

Ana wanted to believe what Ella just told them. She didn't dare dream it was true.

"I do. And it's not just your power. It's everything else about you. You are human, yet you don't fear us, or hate us. You've done what no other woman has ever done, and believe me, many have tried."

Ella stopped for a brief second as if to make sure she had Ana's attention.

"What?"

"You conquered Andree's heart. He's never been in love before. Both Mike and I know him well, and I've never seen him this happy. Whatever you do to him, keep doing it." She winked and squeezed Ana's hand. "He has always focused on work, training, and this coven. No matter how many times we've tried to introduce him to women, he always said that the one for him wasn't born yet. He's been waiting for you to come along for centuries."

Ella's refreshing company brought Ana some comfort.

"Thank you. I feel better now."

"If you ever need to talk to someone, a friend, an adviser, although I'm terrible at giving advice, please don't hesitate. I would be more than happy to help you with anything I can."

"I don't know anyone here. Thank you for your offer. I might take you up on it."

"Any time."

They both smiled at each other. Ana felt comfortable with her, a kinship she couldn't explain. She knew deep inside, their friendship only started that day, but she hoped it would last for years to come if not centuries. The longevity of vampires' lives was surreal and hard to wrap her head around.

"Ana, we should go." Andree returned to the terrace. "My mother has already asked twice about you." He coiled his arm around Ana's waist.

"I can take her. I'm going there," Ella offered.

"Fine."

"I'll bring Ana back in a couple of hours. If I'm not mistaken, that's when the shopping will move from the Queen's suite to this one, right?" Ella waited for Andree to confirm, and he nodded.

"Wait, more shopping?" Ana turned with surprise toward Andree.

"You need a lot of things." He tightened his arm around her, causing her pulse to escalate to new heights. "Please do not fight me on this one," he murmured in her ear. She couldn't resist him even if she wanted to.

~ ~ ~

As soon as they entered Queen Emelia's suite, Ana noticed racks of bridal gowns lined up. Helped by her new friend, Ella, and the Queen herself, Ana narrowed it down to three, and Veronica carried them to the dressing room.

The reality of trying on wedding dresses hit her. She remembered Andree asking Daniel to be his best man. She couldn't ask any of her friends outside the compound, in truth, she didn't have anyone. For the last few years, after she had lost her best friend to cancer, she kept mostly to herself. When she left Romania, she lost touch with everyone she knew. Her ex's controlling nature stopped her from attempting to make new friends. After the divorce, her trust issues interfered. Now was the time to start building her new life.

Ana turned her attention to Ella, who was comparing two long and narrow boxes containing what appeared to be lace strips.

"Ella, would you be my maid of honor?" The question left Ana's lips, and she held her breath nervously. She wasn't sure what the rules were for that if she had to be friends with someone for longer before asking. Even Veronica had stopped smoothing invisible creases.

"It would be my pleasure." Ella dropped the boxes and hurried to hug her new friend.

Phew, at least she's not stuffy like most of the vampires.

The first dress was a disaster, but the moment she tried on the second outfit, Ana knew she found the perfect one. She always dreamed of a simple, strapless, soft white silk dress. The ruched bodice hugged her body, closing at the back with plain lacing. The bottom, not too puffy, had some volume, and the soft silk had a discreet shine. With the matching shoes on, she stared at her reflection in the mirror.

"This is it," Ana whispered with teary eyes.

"You look incredible, a true Princess." Ella bowed and made Ana laugh.

"C'mon, please, stop that."

Ana, dressed in her gown, along with Ella returned to the living room. The three servants and two designers with their assistants all stopped and turned to face her. She counted three seconds of complete frozen faces, then they all bowed at once.

Queen Emelia rose from the couch and approached her. "Amazing. This is exactly how a Princess should look. All you need is some jewelry, and maybe a veil. Oh, and this," she added.

A servant waited with an open box from which the Queen took out a circlet, placing it on Ana's head.

"What would a Princess be without a tiara?" Queen Emelia arranged it, so the stones sparkled at the right angle.

Ana touched the glimmering gems and approached the nearest mirror. "It's so beautiful . . ."

"It is my first Princess tiara." A tiny smile bloomed on the Queen's lips. "One night I snuck into my old house years after I was turned. I took only two things: this and a brooch I had from my husband."

"I can't take this. The sentimental value . . ." Ana tried to return it.

"Please. I am not a princess anymore. You are. Please, *chérie*, you do need something old." Her eyes smiled with happiness that warmed Ana's heart.

"Thank you." Ana finally accepted, and two big, heavy tears rolled down her cheeks.

For the second dress, which she was going to wear for the vampiric ceremony, Ana trusted the Queen and Ella to make the choice for her. She had no idea what would be appropriate. Since she was alone in the dressing room with only Veronica, Ana turned to her.

"Is this how I'm supposed to look?"

Veronica's head jerked up. The sudden movement caused her long brown hair to slip over her shoulders. She rose to her feet and quickly checked the gown with an expert, detailed scan. Her eyes, deep-set, matched the color of her hair. They made Ana think of dark-roasted coffee.

"That's exactly how you should look, Your Majesty. The traditional ceremony for us is about giving our body, our heart, and our soul for eternity, to the one we choose. We can't change how our hearts or souls are, but we can make sure our bodies are desired." Veronica tilted her head with respect. Her eyes lowered, shadowed by long, thick lashes.

Ana considered the off-white dress again. If desire was the theme of the event then this was the right dress for the occasion. The stretch fabric hugged her every curve. The lace overlay gave it an old glamour and elegance, which brought a classic style to the garment. Strapless, with a small train, the dress fit her tight, flowing loosely at the bottom. She loved the numerous tiny buttons at the back, all the way down, adding a little playfulness. *There must be a hundred of them.* Ana giggled and twirled one more time.

"Thank you." She smiled at Veronica and returned to the living room ready to display her final pick for the celebration.

"Absolutely perfect." Ella skimmed a hand down the length of the delicate buttons. "I kind of feel sorry for Andree." Her joke brought smiles all around, and Ana knew she had the perfect dress.

Both outfits stayed in the Queen's dressing room, so Andree wouldn't see them until the ceremonies. Mike and Ella had to go, leaving Ana to shop the rest of the day alone with Andree, in their suite.

~ ~ ~

"They know me. Are you sure about this?" Her doubt caused Collin to roll his eyes.

He wanted to throw the damn phone at the nearest wall. Instead, he took a deep breath and ran a hand through his already messy hair.

"Yes, I am sure. It might work to your advantage. Just don't think of me when you are there. He can hear your thoughts, remember? Let me know how it goes."

"Fine, but you owe me." The sultry voice resonated in his ear.

"Big time. I will make sure to pay with interest."

His answer provoked chuckles at the other end, and the woman he had been talking to ended the call.

"Did she go for it?" Ivan asked. He paced like a caged beast.

Collin displayed an offended air.

"You underestimate me, my friend. I can make any woman do what I want. I was told my charm is irresistible." He wiggled his eyebrows with a playful twinkle in his emerald eyes.

"Except one."

Ivan's reminder infuriated Collin, and his fangs showed. His loud hiss filled the room.

"He must've told the human how to break free from my control. I know it. He is going to pay for it one day. I swear." Collin's hands balled into tight fists.

He knew they shared a single aligned truth, they both hated Prince Andree, and for a few minutes, silence fell between them. In his mind's eye, he and Ivan each killed the smug prince a few times, and in a several few different ways. The thought of the man's death brought a smile to his lips.

Ivan's voice broke the daydream and sent them both crashing back to reality. "Was that one the last of your contacts?"

"Yes, but I am expecting a few calls back. I had to leave messages."

Ivan nodded and glanced toward the window.

The wistful look in his eyes was one Collin knew all too well. The night attracted his kind, vampires, and a sudden thirst took over his senses. It had been a while since they had both feed, and the need to replenish tugged at him.

"All this talk about humans has made me hungry." Ivan licked an exposed fang. "You?"

"Me too. Let's go get some dinner."

Chapter 10

Andree stared at Ana for a while. She had been sleeping in his arms for a couple of hours. He loved her with every fiber in his body, every thought in his mind. Everything revolved around her, for now, and, hopefully, for centuries to come. Only one thing stood in the way of their eternal bond, her inability to fully trust him. Earning her trust was his top priority.

The feeling of belonging together, so much stronger than anything else he had ever experienced, overwhelmed him.

He closed his eyes and relaxed, for the first time complete, content. Two hours later, after a short nap, Andree left the bedroom to do more planning. Settling for anything less than perfect was unacceptable.

A courier brought him a small package around three in the morning. His jeweler promised he would have Ana's ring before sunrise, and so he did.

After the deliveryman left, Andree's sensed a familiar presence he couldn't place. He sniffed a couple of times. *Must be somebody I have not seen in a long time.* It bothered him, but he didn't sense any danger.

His attention shifted to the black, velvety box, and he took out the ring. The brilliant diamond, flawless in the platinum setting, met his expectations.

After another round of calls, messages, and emails, Andree decided to surprise Ana by wearing her favorite color that day, white. She believed that no other color could exist without white. Not even black.

Her mind was loud from the second she opened her eyes. Andree heard her first thought and smiled: after recognizing the room she woke up in, his name filled her mind.

He needed to keep his distance, resist the temptation to join her, and hurried outside, on the sunny terrace. Thanks to his exceptional hearing, he clearly distinguished her footsteps resonating on the hardwood floors.

Ana stopped inside the spacious living room a few minutes later. She had spotted him waiting for her with breakfast, and her thoughts screamed in Andree's mind. *Is this for real? Am I really marrying this man tomorrow? Am I going to have a child with him? I am definitely attracted to him, but is it enough?*

Andree witnessed her accelerated pulse. He heard the rustling of the fabric when she wiped her hands on the light blue dress. Different images played in her mind. One of them involved the two of them holding their baby.

He could swear there was a shortage of air, suddenly he couldn't keep his lungs going. Andree had never felt so proud before, his own body seemed to be too small to accommodate all his emotions.

"Delicious thoughts, but I am growing old waiting here. Are you going to join me, or should I come inside?"

Ana hurried onto the terrace smiling, embarrassed.

"Today we have three interviews for the assistant position," he tried to sound casual, but sensed her anxiety.

"What am I supposed to do, or say?" Ana sipped coffee from her mug.

"Do you want me to ask the questions?" Andree offered as soon as the soft cushions of the outdoors sofa flattened under the weight of his body.

"If you wouldn't mind. Everything's new to me, I have no idea what I'm doing." Her admittance brought a spark in his eyes. With only a few words she empowered him.

"I need one thing from you. You have to pay attention and let me know if you feel a connection to any of them."

"What do you mean?"

"We form connections to our assistants. You need to be comfortable with her. She will always be a thought away from you. All you have to do is think of what you need, or want, and she should already be on her way, no words necessary."

"But I can't do that. I'm not one of you yet."

"You do not have to be. This connection will be there regardless. You cannot force it. If it is not there, we must move on to the next candidate."

"And if I still don't feel anything?"

Andree couldn't miss the slight panic in her voice. For one moment he fantasised he could snap his fingers and make it happen for her. Unfortunately, the reality was different.

"We will keep looking until you do."

Ana's confusion brought a slight crease on Andree's forehead. She was trying her hardest to adapt, he knew she was, but for the time being, she seemed to feel like a square peg trying to fit through the round hole, and Andree wished he could do more to ease her discomfort.

The first two candidates fell short and were not a good fit. Andree knew both. One of them worked for his mother a while back, as the captain of the guards. Even though her fighting skills excelled, she lacked the finesse necessary for the position.

The second applicant had a solid background in diplomacy. She would have had the contacts needed. Both he and the Queen had used her connections in the past. Like most vampires who chose safe work, her fighting abilities left much to be desired.

Andree cut the interviews short in favor of spending the extra time with Ana. He decided it would be a waste of time to continue through polite discussions leading nowhere, especially when Ana felt no connection or bond to any of them.

He noticed her absent stare, and the slight frown. "Are you all right?" His hand covered hers on her lap.

"I'm not sure all this is going to work." Ana leaned her head against his shoulder with a sigh.

Andree knew he was her support in a world she didn't understand, that in his proximity she found calm, safety, and heat.

He was more than happy to provide all three of them and encircled her body, holding her close to him.

"Do you know how many individuals I interviewed before I hired Karl?"

Ana shook her head. Her hair tickled Andree's arm.

"Twenty-two."

"Are you serious? I hope I don't have to go through twenty-some interviews."

Andree nodded amused at her reaction.

"I do not want you to get upset over this."

"I am not upset, just a little disappointed," Ana admitted and glanced at him.

"You only have that connection with one person, with the right one," Andree explained, then kissed her.

~ ~ ~

Ana broke the kiss and walked away from him. She leaned against the stone banister, squinting her eyes to avoid the sun. The fiery, scorching ball hung over their heads.

She missed the beach, the sound of the waves, and the smell of the ocean. Being near water always helped her think. She had a lot of thinking to do, so many questions inside her head with no answers.

As if listening to her wish, a light breeze danced around her. Ana sniffed loudly.

"Are we near the ocean?" She turned to face Andree.

"Depends on what *near* means to you, but we are not far. Why?"

"I can smell it on the breeze. Do you think we could go see it later?" Ana lowered her eyes on the smooth, white stone tiles. The sun beamed in full force. She wasn't sure if it was safe, or if they had time.

"That is one good nose," Andree joked. "I will see if I can arrange something."

"Thank you."

She rushed back to him, cuddling to his side.

~ ~ ~

"Next one will be . . . Mara." Andree changed the subject after a deep breath. With her close to him, the world seemed perfect again.

"I've heard that name before."

"Probably from my mother. Her best friend's name was Mara, Duchess of Stael. It cannot be the same. She was a pureblood, while this one coming here is a . . ."

"What is it?" Ana's breath quickened.

Andree's attention directed toward the door before finishing his sentence. "There is this presence I sensed last night, and now it is near again." Andree jumped to his feet. His eyes glued to the person walking on the terrace, wrapped in a long, hooded cape.

She advanced toward them with her head down and bowed. "Your Majesties."

"Mara," Andree whispered and rushed to her.

The woman stood tall taking off the cape.

Her long, dark-brown hair glistened in the sun. Same color, almond-shaped eyes quickly surveyed her surroundings. The handles of her weapons stuck out of the pockets of her charcoal leather suit.

Two swords crossed on her back, and the black metal protective gear on her legs and wrists made her seem ready to fight any second.

"Andree," Mara answered smiling, and they hugged.

"Mara, get inside. You cannot—"

"Relax, I am a hybrid now. I will be fine in the sun," she assured him.

"How is that possible? What are you doing here? I thought I sensed a familiar presence last night, around three in the morning."

"Yes, it was me. I came early and spent some time with Emelia. I missed her. But, I am here for the assistant position."

Mara approached Ana, staring straight into her eyes.

"Is this a joke? You cannot be her assistant. You are a duchess."

Andree's objection made her lips curl upwards in a slight smile. "Not anymore. I gave up the title four hundred years ago. I know it is not official yet, but Princess Ana, I am honored to meet you." She bowed again.

Andree noted Ana's desire to make a good impression. She greeted her as he'd taught her, then tilted her head under the woman's scrutinizing gaze. His chest puffed out, with overwhelming pride.

"That was pretty good. Still have a lot to learn, but you are so precious." Mara turned to face Andree and studied him meticulously for the first time.

"You have grown powerful. I heard all kinds of stories about you and . . ."

Mara left her sentence unfinished and turned her head toward Ana. Andree watched both women carefully. An invisible, strong current linked the two of them. He sensed Ana's excitement flooding the terrace.

"You sensed it, too." Mara's whisper caused him to purse his lips.

Speechless, Ana nodded, and her eyes sparkled.

Andree went back to his seat.

"I see you two already have a strong connection. Mara, this is not right. It is a step back for you."

"Not at all. It is a big step forward."

Arm outstretched in a welcoming gesture, Andree invited Mara to join him and Ana.

Sitting across from him, she fluffed a pillow, using it as an armrest. "You know I can be the best assistant anyone could wish for. It is the only way I would return to the coven. I already spoke with Emelia, and she is fine with it—that is if Ana will have me."

Andree considered her words.

"I can hunt better than anyone, fight, and even if I do not have any special powers like . . ." She stopped again scrutinizing Ana. "There is something about you." Her eyes racked the length of Ana's frame.

"Seriously? You too? Please tell me that at least you know what it is." Hope glimmered in Ana's eyes.

"I am sorry, I do not. It is like a great power is concealed inside you. I have never sensed anything like this before, at least not from a human."

"Mara," Andree spoke next. "I know what you can do. You taught me a lot, and without you, I would not be who I am today. But I do not think it is even remotely appropriate for you to be an assistant."

Andree had to admit that Mara would have been an asset if she returned to their coven. Ana liked her, and the two women had a connection.

"Do I need to renew my membership with the coven?" Mara's joke brought a tiny smile on Andree's lips, but didn't change his mind.

"You know what I am talking about." He continued to oppose her idea.

"When my husband was murdered, I stopped being a duchess. He gave me the title and it died with him, along with my heart. It took me three hundred years to get over his death, to be able to feel anything again." A sigh left her lips. "I want to return to the coven and be useful, make a difference. I kept up with the news. I will not come back and sit pretty, get a title, and pretend nothing ever happened."

"How did you become a hybrid?" Andree knew deep inside she would be perfect for Ana. "Would you like a coffee?"

"I would love one." She turned to face Ana with a smile that brightened her face. "I had never had coffee until after I turned hybrid. It is pure bliss."

"Mara, you have the knowledge, the experience, contacts, and everything else, but it does not feel right." Andree tried again to sway Mara his way.

Within seconds, a servant brought one single cup of steaming hot coffee.

"Without Anthony, life became empty, nothing mattered anymore." Mara continued her story. "When I left the coven, I wanted to die." Coffee mug cradled between her fingers, she sniffed the fragrant aroma. "A few years later, I heard rumors about a doctor, a crazy scientist that worked on a *cure* for vampires."

Mara stopped and took a slow, steady sip. A smile caressed her aristocratic features and danced in her eyes.

"As if vampires were sick." She turned again toward Ana. "Humans have the tendency to believe that if someone is different it means sickness lurks." She puffed and waved her hand like she dismissed all humans. "It took me months to locate him in London. I hid in his laboratory, an old warehouse, and saw him place the two vials in a fridge before leaving." Her eyes lowered to her hands, nervously twisting on her lap. "I did not care anymore and injected them both.

I wanted to die. Back in the attic, I waited for a reaction. It seemed it didn't work, and I lost consciousness . . ."

Andree didn't need to examine her mind for the truth, her pain visible in her eyes, said more than mere words ever could convey.

"I woke up dizzy, in the middle of screams and broken glass. Three vampires had attacked the doctor. They wanted the serum. I jumped in the fight and hoped to die an honorable death." She lifted her eyes and gazed at Andree. "Instead, I killed the three attackers. The doctor was almost gone, too."

Andree glanced toward the door. A familiar presence approached them, the shadow of a silhouette swept the floor.

"His injuries were too great, he would not have made it. I did the only thing I knew to save his life. I turned him. All I could think of doing was to apologize. I said—"

"—forgive me. "Daniel, the source of the shadow peered around the doorway. "It is the best I can do." His gaze fixed on Mara.

She waved him onto the terrace with opened arms.

"It was you." Daniel advanced closer. "You turned me and saved my life." He gave Mara a hug.

"I am sorry, but it was that or let you die. It was my fault since I had taken your serum."

"I see it didn't work, which I am now grateful for." Daniel released her.

"Not in the way you thought." Mara winked with a grin. "It turned me from pureblood to hybrid."

"What? Are you serious?" Daniel's lower jaw gapped. "How much did you use?" Daniel's eyes went back and forth from Mara to Andree. "Both vials? Only one?"

"All of it," she whispered. "I wanted to die. Instead, you gave me a whole new life."

Andree noted the mutual gratitude between the two of them. They each had given the other a new life.

"I never had the chance to thank you properly for saving me." Daniel tilted his head in front of Mara. "Thank you."

"If you remember what you used in that serum, you should try and replicate it." Mara placed her hand on his arm. "Perhaps more would like to become hybrids."

Daniel's eyes lit up with excitement, and Andree saw the tiny wheels starting to turn in his friend's mind.

"I do, and I have all my notes. It would of course take me a while to replicate it, reformulate and test, but it could revolutionize our world. Any pureblood could turn hybrid if they wished to do so." Daniel's eyes sparked. "Can you imagine? Our kind wouldn't have to hide from daylight anymore, we could all mix in with the humans. I bet most purebloods barely remember the taste of food."

Songs of distant birds echoed. Andree nodded toward Mara in an invitation for her to continue.

"Since that day, I wandered all over the world. As a hybrid, I did not have to hide anymore from the sun. Slowly, I moved on. I accepted Anthony's death, even if I am stuck being alive and—"

The vibration of a cell on silent rung in Andree's ears. Never one to leave a ringing phone to its own demise, he turned to Mara.

"Do you want to answer that?" His eyes focused on her pocket now lit with a flashing light.

"No, nothing can be this important." She tapped the device silencing it.

"Are you sure? I don't mind," Andree insisted.

"It is probably my former roommate. She must have figured out I left." A grin washed across her face. "I already have everything I need with me, so I can start right away."

Andree nodded, and Mara continued where she left off.

"In my travels, I met many people, and learned a lot. I was thinking of a way to come back and put all my accumulated knowledge to good use when I saw the announcement of your engagement. You are looking for an assistant, so here I am."

Andree still hesitated and glanced at Ana again. She liked Mara, and he didn't need to invade her mind to figure it out. The link between the two women was strengthening with each passing minute. He had no problem saying *no* to anyone, but her. Ana wasn't just anyone, she was his eternal love.

"Mara, are you sure this is what you want?"

"I am sure," she answered with absolutely no doubt.

"In that case, the job is yours." Andree caved in to the guilt for not giving Ana what she wanted.

"Thank you. You will never regret it."

"I know." Andree glanced at Ana again. Her joy filled his heart.

Chapter 11

Ana watched Mara and Daniel leave, both still talking to each other, and couldn't help but smile.

As soon as they turned around the corner, inside of the suite, Andree's arms closed around her. She lifted her gaze to him.

Andree dipped his head, and his eyes lingered on her lips. Her pulse picked up the pace, and her hands rested on his chest, unsure if she wanted to push him away or not.

A gentle, feathery kiss caused her to close her eyes. Her mind ran into a never-ending circle. Desire intensified, and when his lips claimed hers, Ana still tried to figure out if she should reject the advance or surrender to him.

She didn't try to escape him, but she didn't answer his kiss either. Her passivity, she hoped to clue him in. If it wasn't for all those shadows from the past constantly looming over her head, she might've trusted him more.

As if he understood her signals, Andree freed her. He first stood, then knelt in front of her.

"Ana, you know as well as I do how unexpected this is for both of us. A couple of days ago, when I came here, I didn't know it would be the day I would fall in love and ask you to marry me." He reached into his pocket, taking out the ring to place it on her finger.

"I must do it the right way. Ana, will you accept . . . will you be my wife?"

The shining diamond reflected the sunlight in a kaleidoscope of colors.

Seven years ago, when her ex-husband had asked her to marry him, he gave her a bunch of carnations and a box of chocolates. She hated carnations. In his defense, all those years ago, in that part of the world, engagement rings were unheard of. Men would just simply ask.

At the time, she wanted to break free from her parents' control, and her ex was her ticket out. Agreeing to marry him was only one of her many mistakes.

She glanced at the man in front of her. He would be her way into the vampires' world, a new life she desired. Was she making another mistake? Andree's eyes, the gates to her personal blue haven, bored through her with the force of a laser and the heat of the sun.

Her heart whispered clues to the many questions hitting the walls of her mind. Like a traffic jam, all of her insecurities, added to the crowded space. Was marriage, the ultimate price to pay for her dream, too much? Could she do it? What about her promise—that she'd never, ever let another man close to her heart? Andree was inching his way in, and Ana was torn between giving him his chance, or shutting him out, together with the rest of the world. The word *love* scared her, and she dismissed it. She had only met him the day before, she couldn't have any feelings for him. At least not yet. And she had better keep it that way. If someone like her ex, an ordinary man, hurt her that much, the Prince kneeling before her could tear her heart apart. She had to be cautious.

One thing she knew for sure: Andree was more than an access card into a world she had been fantasizing about for years. How much more, she wasn't sure.

Tears pooled in her eyes. She fought them back blinking fast a few times. Unable to speak yet, she pulled him to her in a mind-melting, toe-curling kiss. Her own reaction surprised her. The hand he slipped behind her head, under her hair, pressed her lips firmly against his.

When she needed air, Ana broke the kiss and withdrew from him. "Yes," she whispered, afraid of what kind of future she committed to. How much had she altered it today with a single spoken word? Only time would tell.

Andree pushed the ring on her finger, and she held her breath. It could've been shackles meant to destroy her, or wings to fly her to the happiness she had only heard existed. Ana stared in his eyes, trying to figure out which.

~ ~ ~

The tiny word caused him to close his eyes and smile with his face buried in her hair. *She smells like life.*

"It's the most beautiful ring I've ever seen. I'll never take it off."

Her promise had given Andree hope. Maybe she would trust him, perhaps he was making slow progress after all. *I wonder how long it is going to take her to figure out her own feelings, to accept them.*

After lunch, he dropped Ana off at his mother's suite. On his way back, Andree called Mara.

"Could you come see me please? We need to talk."

"Of course. I will be there in a few seconds, I just finished settling in."

They both entered his living room at the same time.

"I need your help." Andree motioned for her to sit on the couch.

Unsure of where to start the conversation, the muscles in his square jaw twitched, and his hands closed into fists only to unfurl a couple of times.

"I want to congratulate you again. Princess Ana is the perfect match for you." Mara spoke tilting her head to the side.

"Thank you. She is the reason I need your help."

"I do not understand."

"I love her . . . I know she will change with the turning. I do not want to lose the way she is now. I want to make it easy for her to adapt, to blend in with humans while living in our world."

"What is it you are trying to say?"

Andree glanced at her and saw confusion set in her eyes, in the lines that appeared on her forehead.

"Have you ever heard about a different way of turning humans?" Andree voiced his suspicions. He had heard, many years ago rumors about mysteries that some vampires carry and refuse to share. "Or do you know someone who might? You know many people."

He was willing to try anything, even listen to superstitions, whispered conspiracies.

"Andree, you know there is only one way to turn humans. It is true, she will become strong, and fast, and—"

"You do not understand," Andree interrupted. "I do not want her to lose all her humanity. Mara, you know how much time we had to spend on being able to blend in. I do not want her to have to train twenty years just so she can walk on the street. It would be so much easier, to still be part of their world, if she retained what makes her human at the core. I do not want her to have to give up everything."

The skin on his knuckles whitened, and a few veins rose on his forearms.

"I have not heard of a different way to turn humans. But I might know someone."

Andree watched her index finger playing in her long hair, twisting a strand around it. It looked like a chocolate swirl, the same shade as Ana's eyes.

"Who is it? Can I talk to him or her?"

Mara sensed his anxiety and stood. "The man I am talking about is the oldest vampire alive."

"Mihai Veres?"

"No, Jonas Klaas." She took a few steps. "He is almost two thousand years old, an outcast."

"What do you mean? What did he do?"

"When I met him, he had been exiled and banned from both Mihai's and Gabriel's covens. They did not like his ideas."

"What kind of ideas? You are killing me."

Dammit, he wanted answers. For a fraction of a second Andree's mind played terrible scenarios. He feared he would turn Ana into a cold, bloodthirsty monster. Nightmares played with his sanity.

"Jonas' theory about us, vampires, made the others think he was crazy. According to him, long ago, an alien species came to Earth and turned humans into vampires. He swears one of them turned him."

Andree sat with his elbows resting on his knees. He'd heard the theory before. Somewhere deep inside, he believed it to be true. He hoped it was, so he could find a way to turn Ana into the best possible specimen who would combine only the greatest qualities of both species.

"Jonas is a monument of knowledge. If anyone has ever heard of a different way, he would be the only one I can think of."

"Will he talk to me?"

"I could call him and ask. Do you want to go to him, or would you prefer for him to come here? He lives in your territory, only about three hours away. He likes his solitude, and I happen to be one of the few he accepts."

"If he could come here, it would be great. After all, he has never been banished from our coven, and to be honest, if he is not in good terms with the Veres brothers, I already like him." Andree managed a weak smile. "I do not want to let Ana out of my sight, so here would be best."

"Let me see what I can do."

Mara took another few steps away to make the call.

Andree remained seated on the sofa. He slowly massaged his temples in an effort to stop his mind from exploding. *There has to be a way. I hope this man has the answer. I am running out of options, and I am not ready to let go of Ana. I would do anything if I could just keep her the way she is.*

A few minutes later, Mara came back. A victorious light glimmered in her eyes.

"He will be here tonight at eleven, if that is all right with you."

"Perfect. Thank you."

Mara smiled, and after a short bow, she left.

Andree stood in front of the window. The sun started to descend, the same way it always did since he could remember. Heat dissipated under a refreshing breeze. An idea came to his mind.

~ ~ ~

In the Queen's suite, Ana answered questions, little details Her Majesty needed to make the next day perfect. Both ceremonies were already planned in detail.

"*Chérie*, did Andree explain anything to you about our traditional ceremony?"

"No, but he mentioned he would this afternoon."

"All right, I trust he will." The Queen took Ana's hands into hers. "There is something else I should talk to you about since he mentioned he might not turn you right away."

Ana noticed Queen Emelia's hesitation. She wondered what in the world could make the most confident woman she had ever met be so cautious. The night they met popped into her mind for a short second.

Ana wished she could fight with the same grace and ferocity as the Queen. Her speed, the way she avoided hits and her feet barely touching the ground, made Ana want to become like her.

"I guess you know how much stronger vampires are compared to humans, and probably Andree already warned you about the risks . . . in the bedroom."

The tips of Ana's ears burned, and she knew they'd turn bright red any minute now. From the way she felt, she imagined there would be flames coming out of them, too.

"Do not ever hesitate to tell him if he is hurting you. Daniel will come and talk to you for a few minutes, while I am needed downstairs."

"Daniel? Why? What is he going to—"

Ana stopped when the doors opened, and Andree's friend entered the room. He bowed respectfully with his usual grave appearance.

"Your Majesties."

"The guards are outside and so is Celina."

The Queen seemed in a hurry to leave the room. Ana's eyes focused on the Queen, tracked the woman's rushed steps.

"Your Majesty, I have to ask your permission to speak freely." Daniel downcast his gaze.

"Please do, and you can call me Ana."

"It wouldn't be appropriate."

"You're calling Andree by his name." She insisted, hoping she would feel more comfortable if everyone would be less stuffy around her.

Her objection made Daniel smile. The only time Ana saw him relax was in Andree's proximity.

"We have been friends for about four hundred years. It's different. We met days after I finished my transition."

"So, I have to wait four centuries for you to call me by my name?" Her voice went up turning shrill.

Daniel shook his head and ran his hand through his short hair.

"It might take me a while. I'll work on it. You have to understand I belong to different times, most of us do."

Ana didn't miss his hesitant steps, or the way he searched for his words as if he was not sure how or where to start. The steeliness in his gray eyes melted away.

"Andree told me there was a possibility you two might try to have a baby. Nobody else knows about it, but I have to make sure you'll be all right in case it is what you truly want."

Ana sat with her hands clenched in her lap. The subject, as uncomfortable as the couch, caused her to shift. One image kept coming back, flashing before her eyes: Andree and her holding a baby, happy, smiling at each other. As much as she tried to push it away, it kept popping into her mind.

Ana focused on Daniel. His lips moved, a sure sign he talked, and with purpose, but nothing registered.

"As a human, making love to a vampire . . ."

She caught a few words before her mind wandered again. *Andree . . . Dangers . . . Conflict . . .*

More fragments from Daniel's speech echoed in her ears competing with the rumbling of her own blood. She kept staring at Daniel, nodding every so often. Every time she heard Andree's name, or thought of him, her pulse went off the charts. *This is crazy. I have to cool down. I already admitted I am attracted to him. I can't let hormones dictate my life.* She blinked fast a couple of times. It didn't help with the erratic heartbeats.

Daniel held a vial in front of her. A bright, light-blue liquid glowed inside, and Ana lifted her gaze.

"What is this?" She wished she had paid attention and wondered what she had missed.

"Your elixir, the one Andree asked me to make. It will help you." He searched for his words and she sensed the temperature rising on her cheeks. "It's a combination of tonics, stimulants, energizers, all made to react to you and you alone, to strengthen you. I've tested it on your blood. Once the effect wears off, it lasts about three hours, you are going to be tired and fall asleep. No other side effects, and you won't be sore after."

"Thank you. Do I need it?"

Ana couldn't imagine using it, even if it looked pretty. She didn't like taking over-the-counter medications, much less something otherworldly. Out of habit, she opened the container and sniffed a couple of times. She loved wild berries.

"Oh, yes. Without it you'd be in constant pain, all of your muscles would be sore. Vampires and humans don't mix well when it comes to, well, intimacy."

She closed the vial and let her hands play with it. Her fingers twirled it a few times, then she continued to rotate it, each time on contact with a different digit. The shine of the ring caught her eyes, and she smiled absently, her first diamond ever. That image, of a baby, popped into her head again. Having a child was worth any sacrifice she might have to make.

"I'll need you to be honest . . ."

Blah, blah, blah. Damn it, why can't I concentrate? What if he is telling me something important? Envisioning herself as a mother occupied every corner of her mind. She knew she shouldn't hope, but she couldn't stop herself. Did she want to have a child with a complete stranger? Was Andree just a stranger to her? Was the short time spent together so far decisive? Or should she consider the intensity between them?

"Andree asked me to do everything I can to make sure you are well and remain that way." Daniel leaned forward and clasped his hands together. "He's concerned about you. If the drink doesn't work as well as I think it will, let me know. I will make adjustments."

Once again, Ana fought through her thoughts and heard him.

"I will. Thank you."

Andree's concern touched her. If he had been there, she would've jumped into his arms.

The sensations he sent through her body every time he touched her, and especially when he didn't, played hell with her mind and body. Her own desire, the way her soul ached for him, overwhelmed her senses. If somehow, the universe was giving her a second chance, and she could have a baby, Ana didn't want to miss it.

Panic covered her face, her eyes glimmered bright. *I'll do it. I'm going to have a child with him.* She stood the same instant the thought popped into her head, hands covering her mouth.

"You both are going against nature. Don't forget, you belong to different species, natural enemies. Imagine a lion and a gazelle trying to have a baby."

Under different circumstances, Ana would have laughed at his joke. She straightened and grabbed the small vial.

"I must talk to Andree." She ran out of the room, as fast as her heart raced. "Thanks."

"You're welcome." Daniel's words caught up with her before the door closed.

"Celina, which way is Andree's suite?" Ana looked both ways, disoriented. They were on the second floor, that much she knew.

"That way." Celina pointed to her right, shaking her head.

"Thank you." Ana rushed down the hallway, wondering what the future had in store for her. She knew she was provoking it.

~ ~ ~

In his suite, Andree read the short message from Karl. *Everything is set.* He planned a surprise for Ana, and his lips curled slightly upward.

Tension and excitement filled the air, as if the tiny

both seated, and the song of waves filled her ears. His chest moved in the rhythm of his breath against her back.

"Now you can open them." His lips touched her temple.

The never-ending blue ocean glimmered in the sun before her eyes. Waves crashed on the shore with white crowns, and Ana inhaled, saturating her lungs.

Ana turned her head to smile at Andree. He leaned against one of the massive boulders spread on the isolated beach.

"It is breathtaking."

"You wanted to see it."

His deep voice rumbled out of his chest and resonated in her body. Tingles went up and down, inside and around every bone. His hard body sheltered her, and she let her head rest against him. His heartbeats reverberated as always: steady, strong and comforting.

"I want us to try and have a baby," she whispered, knowing he would hear her over the sound of the waves.

Ana lifted her face toward him and gazed into his eyes. Her whole body bathed in comfortable warmth. Andree's lips captured hers and sent her mind in numbness, everything around them disappeared. His right hand arched gently around the side of her neck, holding her face up. Desire enveloped her like a blazing fire, and she clasped his arms. He tasted like coffee and power mixed into the most alluring flavor.

"Are you sure?" Andree broke the kiss, staring into her eyes.

"I am." Ana nodded. She had never been more certain about anything in her life until that day.

He stole her next breath with another kiss. His passion pushed her limits. She was still afraid, had doubts and maintained her reserve. Andree caressed her jaw with his thumb, and his hand slipped under her hair. Her fingernails buried into his forearms, leaving tiny halfmoon prints on his skin.

Ana enjoyed the calmness of the afternoon, and listened to his soothing, hypnotic voice for a while. Thoughts of a prior discussion on the vampire ceremony entered her mind, and she felt a need to understand the process better.

"What exactly do you mean by *taste* your blood?" She suddenly straightened and turned her head to stare at him.

For almost an hour Andree explained the details of the traditional vampire wedding ceremony.

"There will be two ceremonial daggers, sharp, with our names engraved on them. You will use the one—"

"Use? Are you telling me that I have to cut you in a room—an underground room—in the presence of hundreds of vampires? Are you for real? Are you—?"

Andree laughed and held her closer to him.

She could appreciate his gesture, but it didn't help her feel better. It was bad enough she stood in that room the other night, under the scrutinizing glares. Adding blood to the equation wasn't something to look forward to.

"You will cut your initial in the palm of my hand, here," he explained, indicating a spot on his palm, right under his thumb. "I will do the same, and you will not feel a thing. Daniel will be right there with his spray. It will be quick and painless."

"But what about the blood? I mean—"

"Nobody will attack you or me, guaranteed. It is part of the ceremony."

"I'm not sure about it. You guys in general go crazy when you see or smell blood."

"Ana, tasting my blood is a symbol. I am giving you my life, just as you will give me yours. It is what will bind us for eternity." He lifted her hand to his lips and kissed her palm, sending tingles, as if a million tiny ants marched through her veins. "As I already told you, the ceremony is short, but every word we say, every gesture, symbolizes something."

"Can't we do all that without the blood part?" With the tingles melted away, and a nervous energy replacing them, she dared to gaze at him.

"We are vampires, Ana. Blood is life."

Chapter 12

The wedding is tomorrow, and I've got nothing. Ivan had paced his living room for the last couple of hours.

He opened the heavy draperies and welcomed the dark evening. Not one star dared to shine through the thick clouds. The smell of rain lingered in the air, mixed with acrid ozone and fresh-cut grass, which further soured his mood.

In the distance, lightning broke the darkness and thunder followed, booming over the sound of the city preparing to go to sleep.

The flashing light reflected from the window into his eyes with sudden hope and understanding.

"I have to look at the bigger picture," Ivan muttered and straightened his frame.

A huge weight pressed on his shoulders. Drawing breath became almost impossible. His chest filled with anger and hate. They mixed and bubbled together taking over his whole being.

From the corner of his eye, Ivan detected Collin strolling the length of the hallway. Returning his focus to the dark sky outside, Ivan tightened his fists. The lightning display from earlier, long gone, was now replaced by a low rumble of thunder. He turned to face his friend.

"I see that deliciously maleficent light behind your eyes." Collin plopped his body on the soft but worn cushions of the couch. "That's always a good sign."

Ivan was too busy with his struggle against spontaneous combustion to bother playing host.

"Sometimes it is scary how well you know me." Ivan stroked his jaw.

Collin smirked, and Ivan could swear he saw the flames of a green hell burning in his eyes.

"It is why we are friends." Collin crossed his legs and leaned back, further into the cushions.

Ivan's fists unfurled, and he took a deep breath.

"I was thinking. Even if we get the human, it is not enough. I want the Third Coven crushed, wiped from the face of the Earth."

"You really hate them, don't you?" Collin arched a brow and focused his attention on his friend. "Let's not forget, even if they are the smallest, they have the most powerful members." He nervously scratched his scalp, with impeccable, manicured nails, which didn't surprise Ivan. Hell, his friend took his appearance to a whole new level of walking art these days.

"It is inconvenient, yes. With the human in my hands, the smug Prince would be weakened, and hopefully, so shall his mother. We need to make up for their power with numbers, big numbers. We need to overwhelm them."

Ivan's fist closed in front of him, as if he strangled all of them, at the same time, until their lives were forfeit.

"Sounds like you already have a plan, and, judging by the way you look, a good one."

"Don't I always?" The worn wooden floorboards squeaked under Ivan's slow steps. "Who has numbers, power, and hates the Third Coven? *—even more than we do?*"

Collin stared at his friend, expectant. He shrugged.

"The Veres brothers." Ivan's answer caused Collin to lean forward and uncross his legs.

Silence followed, giving the room an eerie stillness. The Veres name demanded respect among all vampires. As the sons of the most powerful vampire of all times, they both were true forces of nature. No sane vampire dared to cross them.

"Are you seriously thinking of asking them to declare war on the Third Coven?"

A few more shuffled steps placed Ivan back in front of the window, gazing at the dark sky again.

"I'm still working on it." Ivan turned to face his friend for the second time in only a few minutes. "I need a way to get an audience with both of them. The brothers are the answer, I know it. I need them so I can crush that bunch of arrogant little pricks calling themselves the Third Coven."

"If memory serves me right, Gabriel Veres wanted an alliance with them. I heard rumors he proposed to the Queen."

Ivan's eyes twitched at the corners. It was the first time he'd heard that. It could create some problems.

"Either it was just a rumor, or she was too proud and stupid to accept. I have to start recruiting, too."

"I'm leaving you with your plans." Collin stood and straightened his clothes. "I have to go meet one of my contacts just outside The Castle."

"Let me know how it goes. I might go out, too. It's a good night for a hunt, I can feel it."

Alone once more, Ivan turned to the window, clasping the frame. The structure squeaked against the glass, and a few chips of paint fell on the floor. Moist, saturated dirt invaded his senses. *A good night for some play and maybe a bite.*

~ ~ ~

As soon as Mara entered the living room, Andree hugged Ana closer to him. "I will be back as soon as I can." His whisper consumed the little air between their lips. His breath caressed her cheek.

"No rush." She sensed his hesitation to leave, but he needed to feed. Ana couldn't stop thinking that one day she would join him, she would also need to drink a creature's blood.

He had only been gone for a few seconds, and she missed the warmth of his body already. Ana remembered Mara, still waiting, and turned to face her.

"I thought Anthony and I had the strongest connection, but when you two are together, I can sense the tension. It makes the air dense around you. It is strange and yet good at the same time."

"Strange?"

"I have known Andree since the second he came into this world." A serene gaze softened her eyes. "I held Emelia's hand when she gave birth to him. Now, seeing him all grown up, powerful, and in love is different. He used to be the sweetest kid ever." A smile bloomed on Mara's lips. "You should have seen him when he learned about emotions, how he tried to make his mother smile. At the time, Emelia suffered, still heartbroken after the loss of her beloved husband and eldest son."

Ana curled on the couch, her legs bent under her, curious to find out more about Andree. "Come. Tell me more." She patted the cushion next to her.

At Ana's invitation, Mara sat across from her, in a proper, straight manner.

"He eventually grew up, and we all knew he would soon learn what he was. Born vampires grow like humans, but around sixteen years old, they have their first thirst. It is when they need to learn the truth." She picked a thin thread off her leather pants. "Andree's manifested a couple of months early, and Emelia explained everything to him."

Mara stopped for a few seconds, toying with the thread. Ana hardly blinked, she didn't want to miss a word.

"That day, the sweet little boy ceased to exist. He resented her." Sadness echoed in the space between Mara's words. "Andree closed up, refusing to talk to anyone until Anthony and I stepped in three years later. Usually around the age of twenty-one, the powers start surfacing." She rolled the thread into a tiny ball and set it on the coffee table. "His showed up before nineteen. In need of training and guidance, he would not even look at his mother. Anthony and I taught him everything we knew, but Andree wanted more. He wanted to become the strongest and the best. Eventually, he did."

"He didn't talk to his mother for years?" Ana couldn't imagine the Queen and her son not speaking to each other. They seemed close and on the best of terms.

Mara shook her head.

"Shortly after he turned thirty-five, he asked Emelia to stop his aging. She gave him the special bite that stops born vampires from aging any further. We all thought he would finally make things right with her."

Ana wanted to say something. *What if history repeats itself? I can't imagine being resented by my own child.* She preferred to keep her thoughts to herself.

"Instead, he isolated himself from all of us even more. Andree threw himself into intensive training. For years, we hardly even saw him. He would only show up for some special events, every time more powerful. It took him close to a hundred years to come to terms with who he was, and to talk to his mother."

Ana's fingertips slid along the crease marking her forehead, and she pursed her lips into a fine line.

"It was his turning point, when Andree took over his responsibilities, and became who he is today. Shortly after that, my husband was murdered. I left and had not seen him until today."

Ana's mind busied with the one insistent, terrifying

thought of being resented. Her eyes followed Mara's silent steps.

"I kept up to date with everything going on in the coven." Mara stopped and whirled, facing Ana. "His overprotectiveness is sometimes criticized. The way he always tries to help others is appreciated, and many owe him their lives. In spite of the ongoing conflicts, Andree has a reputation. He is respected and feared. Many consider him the most powerful vampire alive."

Ana devoured every word. For the first time, she learned about Andree's past. To her disappointment, it wasn't all good. She thought he was perfect. Learning he wasn't, gave her more reason to keep her guard up.

"You are marrying a Prince tomorrow, a vampire. We will have to start working on your training as well." Mara straightened her frame.

"But he won't turn me for a while."

"I know. I wasn't talking about combat. You will be this coven's Princess. You need to learn how to perform those duties."

Ana knew she was nothing like a Princess, and realized she resembled one even less that moment. She noticed the disapproving look in Mara's eyes. Slowly she put her legs down to sit properly. *All this stuffy business is going to be the end of me. Who cares if I curl on the couch or don't keep my back straight? It's not like the posture police will arrest me. Heck, the world won't fall apart because of the way I sit.*

"I'm not used to all this. I'm trying, but not always getting it right."

"It will take some practice. The most important thing for you to understand is who you are. It goes far beyond good posture and being gracious. You have to believe in yourself."

"Everything happening in the past few days, it's so surreal. At times I wonder if I'm not dreaming."

Ana massaged her temples. It could've at least been a better dream, one where she would not have to fight her fears and doubts every step of the way.

"I am back," Andree announced his return before entering from the balcony.

"Do you always get this messy?" Bloodstains on his clothes made Ana ask herself if she would look just as messy after feeding.

The Queen's preference for preserved blood, sipped from her golden goblet, made more and more sense. She might prefer that method of feeding, too.

"Most times." He scratched his scalp, adding to the mess. "I will take a quick shower and be right back." Andree left the room in a hurry.

Ana returned her attention to Mara. "You can go if you want," she said. "I will be fine for a few minutes by myself."

Mara shook her head. "That is not how this works. I will stay with you until Andree is back." Her tone didn't leave any room for negotiations.

Ana faced the balcony and stared into the night. She shoved her hands into the pockets of her jeans and kept quiet. *I can't believe I am getting married tomorrow. I wish mom and dad were here. Maybe it's better they never knew I divorced. It wouldn't have sat right with them.* Preoccupied with her own mind, Ana startled when Andree's hand touched her back.

"I apologize, I didn't mean to alarm you." Ana looked around for Mara. She was gone. "You should go to sleep early. Tomorrow will be a long day." Andree sounded concerned she wouldn't get enough rest.

His care touched her. "I will." She turned to him, curious and worried at the same time. "If we're going to have a child, do you think he's going to resent me the way you did your mother?" Ana finally let out the one scary thought.

Fear surrounded her, like a rough mantle, scratchy and uncomfortable.

"I see Mara told you a few things about my past. Good." He wrapped his arms around her. "It is a possibility. Also, he or she, might take after you and have the desire to be a vampire."

Ana rested her head on his chest appreciating his effort to make her feel better, even if it failed. She never thought she would like her child to resemble her, but anything was better than resentment.

The scent of his cologne tickled her senses. She let out a deep sigh, and her muscles relaxed. An owl called in the darkness, and the sound travelled through the silent night inside their living room. The opened doors allowed warm and fresh air to swirl around. If she tried really hard, she could probably smell the ocean.

"You said most times you would get messy feeding. Why is that?" Ana decided to change the subject, after all, it was possible she wouldn't have a child.

Andree's laugh made her glance at him. The bluest eyes stared at her, surrounded by fine wrinkles. Strong, white teeth sparkled under the bright overhead lights. *God, he's gorgeous.* A smile tugged at the corner of her lips. Ana's hands tightened on his waist at the thought of her fingers running through the dark blond hair. She loved seeing him laugh.

"I am glad you think so," he whispered then winked. "As for the feeding part, it is a messy job. Taking down your prey, killing it, then drinking the blood can get tricky."

"When you say prey, do you mean like a wild animal, or are humans on the menu?" Ana shivered at the thought of taking the life of a human. She would rather die of thirst.

"Mostly animals. Our coven switched to animal blood many years ago. Once in a while, some still struggle with it, which is understandable. The change is deeper, we are trying to alter our essence. I wouldn't kill a human for blood, but depending on the circumstances, I might not completely reject the idea if the need arose."

She saw the lights in his eyes intensifying, a sign of emotional disturbance. *So, what drives a man to kill? This man?*

~ ~ ~

Later, in their bedroom, after Ana fell asleep in his arms, Andree released his hold and barely whispered, "As much as I enjoy holding you, I must go." He kissed Ana's forehead lightly, making sure he would not wake her.

At his request, Queen Emelia joined him in his living room. He and his mother spent a few minutes together, revising one more time the preparations for the next day.

"Sounds like you took care of everything." Andree concluded glancing at the clock. "With two minutes left to spare."

"You know how much I love throwing parties. Besides, you seem to have your hands full." Her arched brow told Andree she wasn't a complete stranger to the challenges he now faced.

His mind wondered to his bride to be. Ana's hesitant behaviour slowed him down. He wished he could douse the flames of her doubt with a snap of a finger. Patience. He knew it would require a lot of him to make their relationship work, but he was up for the task. Nothing was going to stand between him and the woman he loved, not even death itself.

Exactly at eleven o'clock, on the last beat of the second hand, the doors opened.

"Your Majesties, this is Jonas Klaas." Mara bowed quickly and introduced the guest.

Jonas appeared the same age as Andree, only his gaze revealed his age and old soul contained therein. He had dark-brown hair and even darker eyes that Andree was sure hid many secrets, truths, and lies. His pale skin made him a pureblood. The lower half of his face was covered by a short, well-groomed beard.

Andree sensed the man's power, his presence, in spite of his tired appearance, reflecting something more, but what? Jonas wasn't an ordinary vampire. He'd stake his life on that assumption.

"Your Majesties." He bowed with the grace of a dancer.

"Please, come and sit with us. You too, Mara," Andree added, detecting Mara's intention to leave.

His mother's thoughts entered Andree's mind. He had a hard time containing his laughter. In spite of her apparent calm, she had ripped off Jonas' clothes a few times over in her mind. She thought him to be dashing, mysterious, and uncharacteristic to her usage of words, hot.

For the first time in several centuries, the Queen showed an interest in a man. A fact that didn't go unnoticed, and something he could use later to prod her with for a laugh or two.

"By all means," the Queen purred. "Come. Sit." She stoked the fabric of the couch.

Andree peeked at her, sitting right beside him. Her face, calm and beautiful as always, reminded him of one of the porcelain dolls she collected.

"I see at least some of the rumors are true. You're incredibly powerful," Jonas said, approaching. His deep voice rose from the depths of the darkness surrounding him.

His long black coat wafted behind him. Right before sitting, he stopped and took in the room. He sniffed the air around. And if Andree was reading the ancient vampire's body language correctly, the man's senses had shifted to heightened alert.

"Is there something wrong?" Queen Emelia's tone sounded curious and amused at the same time.

"I sense something." Jonas' deep-brown eyes, mysterious, and with a trace of danger, searched for the source of the disturbance. "It's coming from . . . there," he added a few seconds later pointing toward the closed bedroom door.

Prince Andree and his mother glanced at each other, at Mara, and then finally back at Jonas. Andree's eyebrow arched with interest and admiration. The man had just arrived, and already, in a matter of seconds, he had sniffed out the future Princess.

"You can sense her from here, through the closed door?" Mara's hand slid to the dagger hidden under her coat. That night she wasn't wearing her usual swords crossed on her back.

Andree found his reaction to Ana odd and of keen interest. Someone with his longevity must know more about their kind. Perhaps this night he would find out more about the woman he loved.

"I'm not the only one, am I?" Jonas watched, carefully waiting for an answer from any of his three hosts.

"We can sense it, too, but only when we are close to her. Do you know what it is?" The Queen tried and failed to hide her fascination with their guest. Her gaze set deeply into his eyes, and the smile on her lips brightened the room.

"I have to make sure. It seems impossible." Jonas turned his gaze from the Queen to her son. "May I see her?"

"Do you know what it is we all sense in her?"

For a moment, Andree doubted the man in front of him, probing Jonas' mind, he made sure the newcomer wasn't a danger to Ana.

"I might." Jonas took a step in the direction of the room where Ana slept. "I have to see her."

Andree jumped in front of him, blocking Jonas' path.

The Queen asked, "Why?"

A low, throaty hiss escaped Mara's lips. She stood, shoulders back and spine erect, guarding the door.

"She is asleep." Andree kept calm, but alert. He wasn't about to let anyone touch what was his, and Ana was his, there was no mistaking the connection between them.

"I know that." Jonas raised his hands. "You have my word, I would not hurt her." He offered an opened, nonthreatening stance to show his willingness to communicate. "I need to make sure—to confirm what I suspect. After that, I'll tell you everything." He placed a hand on Andree's shoulder. "Please, Your Majesty, I mean no harm. You need to trust me."

Andree's investigation of Jonas' mind revealed nothing. The man didn't have any hidden thoughts, nor did he harbor animosity. For several seconds the two men stared at each other.

"All right." Andree opened the door, taking a couple of steps into the bedroom. He waited for Jonas to follow him.

Mara and the Queen stood on either side of the door, tense, ready to step in at a moment's notice if needed.

Jonas walked slowly, his eyes opened wide, as if he had entered a trance. He fell to his knee in the middle of the room. His head bowed, and his right hand pressed over his heart.

"Forgive me," he whispered.

Andree glanced at Mara and his mother. The two women appeared as confused at Jonas' reaction as he was.

A few more seconds passed in complete silence, then Jonas stood. He bowed respectfully one more time. Retreating, he walked backward and slipped through the opened double doors, his eyes never leaving Ana.

"How do I become a member of your coven?" His head hung low, his face framed by dark locks.

"How about you start by telling us what is going on?" Andree's patience had vanished. He wanted answers, not more questions. Hell, he had more than enough of his own unanswered at the moment.

"I lost her about three hundred years ago. I never thought I'd get a second chance," Jonas answered, still lost in his thoughts.

Jonas' gaze locked onto an imaginary point, and demons stirred in the reflective surface of his pupils.

Andree expected to see his own heart beating on the floor, on the thick white rug. *It cannot be. This is not happening. Ana is mine. This man cannot be . . . No.*

"Ana is twenty-eight years old. How could you have lost her three hundred years ago?" The Queen intervened.

Andree tried to control his fury. His hands ached to kill the man in front of him, and his fists closed tight. The knuckles turned white. Blood roared in his ears. He might need the man in front of him. So he had to hold back his instincts. He had to let him speak.

"I made a promise to a dying man I'd watch over her." He turned his attention to Andree. "I'm her guardian."

Andree's heart returned to his chest. Nothing the man in front of him had said thus far made any sense. He was waiting for an explanation. He needed clarification, and he intended to get it, one way or another.

"To whom did you make that promise?" The Queen's question caused Jonas to lift his eyes to her.

"Vlad Veres."

"What does Ana have to do with Vlad Veres?" Andree waved in the general direction of the bedroom.

"The girl sleeping in that room is of his blood. Vlad Veres is her direct ancestor." Jonas' index finger pointed to the door, his gaze turned to Andree. "She is of his bloodline."

"What?"

Ana's question made everyone turn around. She stood in the doorway, trembling, whiter than her robe. "Who are you?"

Chapter 13

Andree rushed to her side. "Ana."

She barely registered the whisper, grateful for his strong arms supporting her shaking body.

"My Princess." Jonas kneeled in front of her.

Ana checked him up and down, trying to decide for herself if the man before her was crazy or sane.

"What the hell was all that about?" Her hands clasped on Andree's forearm.

From the safety of his embrace, Ana demanded an answer. She had to know why or how she was associated with the name of the most famous vampire of all times.

"My name is Jonas Klaas, and I'm your guardian." With an opened hand, he covered his chest.

"Guardian? What are you talking about?" As far as she knew, guardians were supposed to protect people, usually someone important.

"It's a rather long story." Jonas hesitated to say more and glanced toward the rest of his hosts.

"So, start sooner than later. I'm not getting any younger." The first shock washed over her, leaving room for questions. Every time she thought she had her answers, new questions arose, a never-ending circle.

"Jonas thinks you are Vlad Veres's blood descendent. It would make sense, explain the air about you, what everyone senses in you." Andree gently caressed her back. One by one her muscles relaxed under his touch.

She gazed in his direction. *How can I be related to a vampire? I'm human. No?*

"Are you serious? *The* Vlad Veres?" Her voice gradually lost volume, surprise tightening around her throat.

The books she read contained details about the most powerful vampire in history. Obviously, there were gaps in the information. Being somehow related to him was something she could've never imagined.

"There is only one Vlad Veres, my Princess. And it's true. You are of his blood." Jonas rose to his feet. Her eyes tracked the slow, controlled movements.

Ana massaged her temples. More questions started to pop into her mind like a game of whack-a-mole. Was she already a vampire? If she was somehow related to Vlad did she still need to be turned? Perhaps the marriage wasn't even necessary anymore.

"If he's my ancestor then I'm already a vampire?" Confusion scrambled her thoughts, but that one question, the loudest in her mind, continued to repeat on auto play.

"No, you're human. Nevertheless, you carry his power. It shouldn't be too complicated to prove you are related to his sons, Mihai and Gabriel, your great, great-uncles a few times over, since all the generations in between." Jonas's glanced toward the Queen and her son. "A simple DNA test could prove it, if you can get their blood to compare, that is."

Ana felt her knees giving way, unable to support her, and she reached for Andree. He coiled the other arm around her waist, helping her to the couch. She had relatives? Vampires? *I must be dreaming. This can't be real.* "I need to know how all this is even a possibility." Her eyes turned to the one man, Jonas, who seemed to hold all the secrets—ones only he knew. And as long as they involved her, she had to know.

"It all started about two thousand years ago . . ." Jonas' words resonated in the room.

Ana snuggled closer to Andree, curious to hear about the connection between her and Vlad Veres. In her mind it was still impossible. *A joke or misunderstanding.*

"I never thought I'd have to talk about this again. For hundreds of years, I've been trying to forget." He let out a deep sigh. "This truth, what I'm about to tell you, is what got me banished from the First and Second Coven. The Veres brothers and their followers didn't believe me." Jonas glanced again toward the leaders of the Third Coven, as if he wanted to make sure he wasn't going to be banished from yet another coven.

"Are you sure Ana is who you think she is?" Ana shivered against him, and Andree tightened his hold, cradling her to his chest.

"Yes, I am." He paced away from the group. "The presence is strong in her, even stronger than I remember. I sense all the power he transferred to that girl. None of you ever met Vlad." His eyes moved from one occupant in the room to the next. "If you had, you'd understand what I'm talking about."

"Sit." Queen Emelia gestured to the chair he had walked away from. "Tell us everything from the beginning." She glanced toward Mara, on her left. "We all want to know, and if Ana is who you say she is, she has a right too know, as well." Her gaze moved to Andree, and he nodded.

Ana assumed she had asked her son to investigate in Jonas' mind. She would have.

Jonas nodded, returning to his seat.

"The Roman Empire's expansion, conquering everything in its way, came to a halt just south of where I lived. The mountains formed a natural barrier between their legions and us." His hand cut the air, as if to divide it. "One day, a small group of about twenty Roman soldiers entered our village. As simple people, we farmed crops, raised animals, and had families. We thought they were going to invade, to destroy our way of life. To everyone's surprise, they didn't."

The Roman Empire? Ana's mind wandered away for one quick second to her school years. She never paid enough attention to the lessons taught in history. There were too many dates to remember, too many wars.

"The group appeared impressive. Their leather armors were adorned with shiny buckles, and the helmets decorated with bright-red crests." Jonas' right hand rose over his head as if he tried to show the red plumes. "The soldiers had enough of the fighting, of death, of their marches to conquer new territories." Jonas leaned forward and clasped his hands together. "Their leader, Vladius Veresio, which was the Roman version of his name, offered to defend our village, teach us how to fight, in exchange for a peaceful life. As deserters, they couldn't return to their homes or go anywhere inside the Roman Empire." His head lowered, then rose again. "They stayed and became part of our village. Vlad Veres adopted the version of his name common in Dacia, stripping from it his Roman origin. We became friends and neighbors, started new lives"

Jonas stopped for a few seconds and glanced around.

Andree kept stroking Ana's back lightly, reminding her to relax. So far, she was disappointed with the information. The history lesson was interesting but failed to bring her any real answers.

"On that terrible day, so long ago, I woke early in the morning and fed the animals. Screams rose from the village. Smoke filled the air. We were under attack." Sadness overtook him, and Ana could hear it in his voice, see it in his eyes. "I rushed my wife and two sons to Vlad's house, only a few steps away from mine. He had an underground room the two of us dug ourselves. Before hiding our families, we became overrun by attackers, about a dozen. Vlad and I fought them, but outnumbered, they overpowered us."

Jonas paused, and Ana noticed anger mixed in his words.

"I was badly injured, couldn't move, and soon, Vlad fell to the ground as well. The nomads killed our beautiful wives, my sons, and Vlad's twin girls in front of us. The barbarians laughed, stabbing both of us once more, and left us to die with the mutilated bodies of what had been our families before us."

Jonas gasped, he could hardly breathe. It was as if a claw had tightened around his neck. His pale skin whitened, and his dark irises blackened, glazed by painful memories.

Ana shivered, imagining the two families brutally murdered.

"When I opened my eyes, Vlad lay beside me. We were both badly injured, but alive. The remaining villagers planned an attack, to avenge the lost ones. A few days later, we joined them, still wounded and recovering."

Ana saw his hands clasp together in his lap, shaking.

"Our attack surprised the nomads. Their tents burned and screams of dying men cut through the thick smoke. Death surrounded us, reeking and shrieking. It quenched the revenge we craved." Jonas leaned against the backrest, and the chair squeaked under him. "Out of nowhere, a thick fog appeared above our heads. The air started moving around us in a way I never knew possible. We all floated up, lifted by the small but remarkably strong whirlwinds. The cloud became denser. The stench of death dissipated. Lightning struck, and I lost consciousness."

"What was it?" Ana surprised herself with the question, quickly covering her mouth with her hands. She couldn't stop her curiosity from conjuring images in her head.

"Impatient, like all humans." A bitter-sweet smile tugged at the corners of Jonas' lips.

Ana lowered her eyes embarrassed. *Well, I don't have your time.* A yawn forced her to cover her mouth again. A quick glance to the nearest clock indicated it was already one thirty.

"I have no idea how much time passed before I came back to my senses in a cave." He clasped his forearms, staring at them. "The chains around my wrists and ankles, made of bright blue light, were cold to the touch." He gazed at Ana, and her hands closed on Andree's forearm in front of her. "Every inch of the cave glowed in the bluish hue. I tested the resistance of those strange restrains. Each pull emitted a buzzing sound. I wasn't going anywhere. They were solid."

Ana didn't want him to stop. In her opinion, he had just gotten to the good part. "So what happened next?" Again, curiosity got the best of her.

"Hundreds of us sat chained, some still unconscious. There were people from all over the world, different races, men and women, rich and poor, judging by what we wore. Vlad was there, too, though motionless." His eyes took on a far off, distant stare. "I noticed the others' clothes, stained." Ana was entranced by his hand rising to the side of his neck, and stared, unblinking. "There were bite marks on their necks. The sight of blood, the smell of it, agitated us. A sudden thirst overwhelmed me." He paused. "I assumed I looked the same as them. Others started to wake up, and hisses rose all around me, echoing against the stone walls."

The memory brought his fangs out. Long and sharp, they glimmered for a second under the strong lights.

Out of instinct, Ana cuddled closer to Andree. His nearness made her feel safe.

"I checked to see if I had fangs, too. I did, and they hurt my gums." His tongue skimmed over his upper teeth. "We would've probably attacked each other if we weren't tied up." Jonas leaned forward again and placed his forearms on his knees. "Vlad woke up and hissed at me. All the noise and commotion attracted the ones who seemed to have put us there. They looked human but different."

"Different how?" Ana asked again, taking advantage of Jonas's short break.

"Some had pale skin with dark tattoos. Others had darker skin with luminescent body markings. White eyes beamed toward us, empty, emotionless. Most of them had slightly pointed ears. They were taller and bigger than most people I knew. Some glided, others walked, and all wore long black robes."

That's kind of cool. Ana tried to visualize those chained, and the tall silhouettes gliding inside the cave. It made her shiver.

"They inspected everyone in the room and separated us into groups. We were the lucky ones, they said, chosen to rule the Earth." Jonas ran his hand over the lower half of his face. "They spoke our language with ease." He leaned against the backrest of his chair again, as if he wasn't used to sitting, or he was uncomfortable. "It seemed the ones with darker skin and luminescent tattoos were higher ranked. One of them signaled, and more came in." He glanced at Ana. "On some floating carts, motionless human bodies were piled up, and we each got one dropped at our feet—"

"Where they dead?" Ana interrupted.

Jonas shook his head. "No. They showed us how to feed. That was the first time I drank human blood."

He stopped again. Ghosts seemed to be haunting his eyes, as if trying to escape.

Ana gathered her legs, curling them under her frame. She had dismissed the earlier lesson from Mara in regard to the posture.

"Who were they?" Ana slightly leaned forward, devouring every word.

Jonas stared at her like her words woke him from a trance.

"They told us they were from *Vamphora*. Called themselves *Vamphorians* and named us vampires."

"Wait. Are you saying they were aliens?" Ana couldn't believe her own words.

"Yes." Jonas nodded in agreement. "They were searching for a new home. Theirs was on the brink of extinction."

"I can't believe it. This can't be." Ana opposed every thought in her mind. *Aliens are not real. Are they?*

"It's the truth. Prince Andree, please feel free to examine my mind. I have nothing to hide."

Andree glanced in Jonas' direction. Ana was convinced he already had. She wished she had his power. A trip in Jonas' mind would've been an adventure.

"I lost track of time. We trained every day. They taught us how to hunt at night for our food, which consisted of human blood." He glanced around the room with discomfort. "None of us could stand daylight. We weren't human any longer. The changes were extensive."

Jonas stood and paced slowly.

"They told us we couldn't be killed by humans, only by our kind, and taught us how to use the new powers they'd given us. To my surprise, we stopped aging. Our skin and muscles toned. We were so much stronger than before, faster. Every so often, they took us somewhere deeper underground. When we came back, we had no recollection of it or what they'd done."

His voice started to fail him, lost volume, turned into whispers. Memories, emotions, all swirled together and Ana wondered how it would be to live through something like that.

"In time, I started to have flashbacks. I was always locked in a glass cylinder. Defying the laws of nature, I floated above the ground with sensors connected to me. It was how they stored information." His hand touched his scalp at the base of his skull. "I guess my brain ran out of room after a while. I had a few implants put in. Shortly after that, I started to understand their language."

Jonas shook his head and ran his hand through shoulder-length, dark hair. Ana followed his eyes, glancing toward Queen Emelia and Mara, both seated on the same sofa.

"I saw incredible signs, symbols, I had never seen before and somehow, I understood what they represented. Their advanced technology amazed me. Even today I can't explain some of the things they used, what they did."

As slowly as he walked away from his seat before, Jonas returned to it.

"A few times, while in my cylinder, they brought Vlad there, too. He had his own glass room. They hurt him and taught him how to heal himself. It was unbelievable." A sigh escaped from deep within his chest. "After a while, the initial group started to thin out. Some did not return to the cave in the mornings or were taken away and never brought back. Vlad and I stayed close and watched each other's backs through all of it."

"So, these aliens turned and trained you?" Ana continued to ask questions. She had a difficult time believing him.

"Yes, they did. I know this must sound crazy, but I am speaking the truth."

"Vampires are aliens." Ana's voice sounded screechy. *This guy is crazy. He needs a special vest and one of those tiny padded rooms. Or the entire world is way different from what I thought.*

"Half." Jonas' correction went in one ear and out the other.

"Might as well. It is more believable to me than all the other theories: cursed souls, undead, all the superstitions. This actually explains a lot." Andree spoke for the first time since Jonas had started his story.

"After almost one hundred years, they left." Jonas stroked his beard. "One morning we came back to the cave, and they were gone with their ship."

"They had a ship?" Ana's eyes opened even wider to the point where she felt the discomfort.

"Yes, they did," Jonas rushed to explain. "They lived on it, buried in the cave until their departure from this world."

Ana massaged her temples again and blinked a few times. A new glance toward the clock revealed an hour had passed since last she checked.

"Vlad and I were on our own. We fought together, killed together, fed together. We were inseparable. About a hundred years later, bits and pieces of memories started to come back to us." A slight smile bloomed on his lips. "His desire to have children caused escapades, sometimes lasting for weeks." The smile melted away in more sadness. "He killed hundreds of young women, trying to get them to carry his children. After a while, he finally fathered Mihai. Only a couple of years later, Gabriel followed. We both watched over them."

Ana tried to convince herself she wasn't dreaming. Her fingers tightened on Andree's forearm to make sure. She needed something to ground her.

"He told them what they were, trained them, and made them into what they have become. Our memories improved." Jonas tapped his temple. "We both discovered we had powers we didn't even know about and started training again. Vlad turned into what we all know him as, the greatest vampire of all time."

The greatest vampire of all time, and I am related to him? Is this for real? Ana hid a yawn behind her hand and leaned her head against Andree.

"Some challenged him, some turned into followers. Living in the wilderness got tiresome, and we started to accumulate fortunes. Luxury became a habit we indulged in." Jonas stood, stretching his legs, as if the chair was uncomfortable. "For the next few hundred years, Vlad's reputation grew among vampires, and soon even outside. We started to make up stories to give the humans something to believe, and we alone are responsible for most myths still circulating out there today."

A tiny giggle slipped from her lips and made Ana arch an eyebrow in Jonas' direction. He seemed pleased with himself.

"When Prince Vlad the Impaler, of Walachia, came into the picture, Vlad saw the opportunity to divert attention from us even more. He made a deal with the human, and we helped him fight against the Ottoman Empire. In exchange, he agreed to be portrayed in the stories we all know today." An almost impish smile tugged at the corners of his lips, making Jonas suddenly look younger. "Nobody seems to remember he never lived in Transylvania, the name coincidence sufficed. The myths about him passed the test of time."

"So, Vlad the Impaler never did what I learned about in school?" Ana's candid question brought a smile to Jonas' face, and he shook his head.

"No, it was all us. The impaling idea belonged to him. He used the cruel punishment sparingly. We took it to the proportions that made it into the history books."

His explanation left Ana wondering how much she'd learn was true after all. How much, exactly, had the vampires altered the true line of history?

"Around that time, Vlad told me his end neared."

"He knew he was dying?" Ana rubbed her tired eyes.

"Yes. With only a few years left, he wanted to make sure his legacy would live on. He decided to have a child and bequeath all his power to this offspring." Jonas paused briefly and glanced toward Ana. "Vlad believed that one day, the whole world would be ruled by his blood descendants, his family. His body started deteriorating with each passing day. By the time his daughter entered the world, I had to help him walk."

Again, what do I have to do with any of this? That happened centuries ago, not years. Ana didn't miss Andree's arms squeezing her closer to him.

"That night, we snuck into the house of his newborn baby girl. He touched her forehead. She opened her eyes, identical to Vlad's, and stared at him with a bright glow. I sensed the power he gave her. She became stronger and more powerful than Vlad himself."

"What happened to her, the baby?" Ana could've sworn she saw Vlad's image flash before her eyes. She wasn't sure if she was influenced by Jonas' story, or if it was written in her genes. The image, traveled through centuries, and ignited her blood.

"Vlad asked me to watch over her and her future daughters who would carry his power throughout time. He forbade me from turning her or interfering with the lives of her female offspring. He said I would know when to intervene. I tried to ask him more, but he could barely breathe."

Jonas took a few steps again, trying to regain his composure. He looked like he had lost his friend all over again.

"Why did he die?" Ana asked.

"I don't know. None of us could ever figure out the cause. In his last moments, he told me that at the right time, one girl from his bloodline would rise above all and become the most powerful vampire ever." His eyes fixated on Ana. "I was supposed to recognize her as the one who will carry his spirit within. He asked me to be her guardian. I promised him I would, and he died in my arms." Jonas nodded toward Ana. "You are that girl."

Ana stared at him in silence. She had been thrown in a changed world, foreign, and a little scary. Words failed her.

"You still have doubts that your fiancée is the one?" Jonas asked, turning his attention to Andree.

"I met the Veres brothers. She is nothing like them." Andree's objection brought another tiny smile on Jonas' lips.

"Of course, she isn't. Vlad gave that little girl all he had in him, everything. Transmitted from mother to daughter for generations, throughout centuries, her powers are pure, untamed, untrained." Jonas glanced to Ana and back to Andree. "The brothers have lived, trained, fought, and killed. But in her," he pointed to Ana, "Vlad's presence is strong. There is no mistake."

His words sent shivers through Ana's body. An invisible weight on her shoulders made it hard to breathe. Her blood hummed with recognition. She rubbed her arms with her hands, up and down, on the sides. A chilling air swirled around her.

"After Vlad died, I kept my promise and watched over the little girl. She grew up and had children of her own, and so on for a few generations. Vlad's presence in these girls became weaker and weaker, harder to sense. As I said, hundreds of years ago I lost track of the one carrying his power. I couldn't sense his presence anymore."

Jonas worked his way back and stood in front of Andree.

"I lived all this time with guilt. I had failed to do the one thing my friend asked of me. I'm taking back my guardian role. I see how much you love her, and I know she'll be safe with you, but nothing will stop me from protecting her."

Ana noticed Jonas' determination. He didn't seem to be intimidated. *Everyone wants to protect me now. Where were all of you years ago when I could've used you?* Again, Ana's mind wondered in the past for a brief moment. *How would Jonas have reacted to my ex?*

"I assume you are the one who will turn her." Jonas stared at Andree.

"It is the reason I asked to see you. I will turn Ana, not right away, but I will."

"Not right away?" Jonas' eyebrows shot upward.

"Precisely. I am searching for a different way to turn her." Ana stared at Andree, not sure she understood his words, and if she did, how many ways were there.

"I'm either getting too old to keep up, or I misunderstood you." Jonas shook his head. "You said you are looking for a different way to turn her?"

"Yes. I do not want her to change after turning—to lose her humanity. I know it is how all this works, but I want her to stay as much as possible the way she is." Andree's explanation resonated in Ana's ears rising one question. Why?

"I see." Jonas's fingers slid along his beard in a few slow strokes.

"Have you ever heard of anything like that?" Ana heard hope rising in Andree's voice.

"You do realize there will be some changes. Even if minimal, they are unavoidable. She will become a vampire, after all." Jonas' answer caused Andree to jump to his feet.

"Yes, I do." Andree approached Jonas. "And I see you know something."

Without Andree holding her, Ana felt cold and lost. Why did she? Ana didn't need a man to hold her hand every step. True, she was walking in an unknown world, and Andree wasn't just any man. She could find her way.

"You want to turn her into one of us while keeping as much of her human side as possible. There might be a way, but I can't promise anything." Jonas murmured, as if a terrible secret was about to be revealed.

"I will do anything for her." Andree towered over Jonas.

Ana's heart melted at his words. She knew he would fight for her, protect her. She knew he loved her, and those words made her understand how much.

But why?

Chapter 14

Seconds after Andree jumped to his feet, excited, Ana hugged one of the decorative pillows to her. With her arms wrapped around the fluffy bundle covered in white velvet, she shivered and glanced around the room: The Queen and Mara sitting beside each other, to Jonas, and kept Andree last.

Andree followed Ana's thoughts as she moved from one surprise to another. He needed to know her reactions and struggles. It was the only way he could do anything about them. She would've never admitted, or asked for help, it simply wasn't who she was.

"Why? I mean, I understand what you're trying to do, but why is it so important to you?" Ana finally asked.

Andree whirled around. The sight of her, there on the couch, softened his heart. She resembled a child, all gathered in the white robe, holding on to the small pillow. The fear mixed with confusion in her eyes, touched him deep inside, and he rushed back to her.

"I do not want you to lose everything human in you." He smiled, trying to make her relax, feel better. "We don't cry, or blush, we don't even blink, unless we train to, and that is only to not raise any suspicions among humans. You would eventually adapt like we did—" Andree cupped the side of her face in the palm of his hand.

"So, you like me as a human, but you think you won't if I change into one of you?" Ana jerked back, as if his touch burned her. Andree smelled her fear.

"Nothing in this world could ever change how much I love you, Ana. It would make it easier for you to adapt, and not spend years in training. I don't want you to miss the world you lived in until now."

Andree drew her into his arms. He closed his eyes for a second, kissed the hair on top of her head, and inhaled her fresh and sweet scent.

One quick glance around the room brought him encouragement from his mother, admiration from Mara, and an understanding nod from the man he just met.

After a few seconds, Jonas cleared his throat.

"Please, you were about to say something I am interested in hearing," Andree said.

"They had a huge, heavy tome. They called it the 'Book of Knowledge', or that's the best translation I can make." Jonas gazed at Andree. "It was made of some black metal, with a glowing glyph in the center of the cover and intricate designs in the corners. The pages, made from the same dark alloy, in paper-thin sheets, had symbols imprinted by one of them." Jonas flexed his right hand in front of him, imitating a motion the way Andree imagined the alien had moved. "He would glide his palm over the pages, and a glove-like device strapped to his hand beamed with a blue laser. There were also moving holograms, recordings of their experiments. If there is another way to turn humans, it must be in that book."

"Did they leave it behind when they left?" Andree's curiosity mixed with suspicion. If he could put his hands on that book, maybe he would find a way.

"Yes," Jonas said, "A gift for *the one* to find and understand it. They said whoever that person would be, deserves the knowledge." Another loud sigh pushed through his lips. "I scoured the whole area, without any success. This book would prove our origin. Vampires around the world would finally understand what we are, where we had come from."

"What area?" Andree asked. "Where did all this happen?"

Jonas glanced at everyone in the room before turning his attention back to Andree.

"Near the Black Castle."

"Did you search the castle?" Andree asked the first thing that came to mind.

Jonas shook his head. "It wasn't built back then."

"I have to find it." Andree's resolution echoed in the room.

"Then you believe me. You don't think I'm crazy." Jonas' dark eyes glimmered with hope.

"I know you are not crazy." Andree divided his attention between Jonas and Ana. "I can see everything you told us is the truth."

"Thank you, Your Majesty," Jonas whispered. "I was serious about joining your coven as well." He turned to face the Queen and walked in front of her. With a slow, calculated movement, he lifted her hand to his lips.

Andree noticed the intense glimmer in Jonas' eyes and his mother's light tremor. *Those two are going to be fun to watch. But now I have more important things to do.* He still couldn't look away from them.

"You can do that tonight if you like, or if you want a ceremony, I can schedule one." Queen Emelia kept her apparent calm with grace.

"I don't need any fuss. Where do I sign?"

"We will take care of that before morning." His mother graciously tilted her head.

Andree smiled amused by the new tension between them. His attention switched quickly to Ana. She was his priority.

"Perhaps you should get some sleep?" He lifted her in his arms, and she nodded. He knew he was better than the pillow.

Andree returned the same time Ella and Mike joined the group in the modern suite. They were both scheduled to meet Andree for last moment instructions.

"Maybe I can help find this book," Ella offered after Queen Emelia brought her up to speed with the latest events.

"How?" Andree's attention shifted to Ella.

"I can look into your future and see if you find it, maybe even how," she suggested.

He accepted her offer without a second thought.

Ella searched into Andree's future for a few minutes, and by scanning her mind, he could see what she did. When she came across one specific romantic night of him and Ana, Andree asked her telepathically to keep it their secret. He couldn't wait for that night, turn the vision into reality, make love to his wife.

The vision of the book faded in her mind. "I'm sorry." Ella lost focus.

"Keep looking, please. We have to figure out where it is," Andree insisted.

She tried for another few minutes, but she couldn't see anything else related to the book. Ella stopped and shook her head.

"What did you see?" the Queen asked with curiosity.

"Prince Andree and Jonas will find it. I saw them carrying it, through some underground tunnels, like catacombs." Ella pinched the bridge of her nose. As always, looking into someone's future took a great deal of her energy. "Then I saw them outside, in the rain, the Black Castle somewhere behind."

"I wonder what I've missed, why I haven't found it myself." Silence was the only answer Jonas received.

Andree started planning, formulating a strategy. He needed to move fast. Time worked against him.

"I need you to travel to Transylvania in ten days." Andree glanced at Jonas long enough to see him nod in agreement.

"I require your services too, Ella. Tomorrow, after the wedding, Ana and I will leave on our honeymoon. Karl and you, Mara," he continued turning to face her direction, "will both join us. You will have to make arrangements for the week after that as we go. We will have to search every night for the book. I will send the jet for the rest of you."

"I'll come, too, at least I can help you carry the book," Mike offered.

Andree turned his gaze to his friend. He knew the real reason and nodded in agreement. Mike didn't want to be away from his wife.

"I can use any extra help. Daniel will join us as well." Andree planned out loud, so everyone would know their roles. "Mother, we will keep you up to date."

"Please do. I hope you will not have much trouble finding it."

"Good, we have a plan," Andree concluded in a firm tone.

The Queen left first with Jonas on her heels. They had to take care of his admission in the coven.

Mara rushed out next. Mike and Ella were the last to leave.

Andree called Karl to give him instructions.

I am going to be busy for a while.

~ ~ ~

The alluring scent of lust lingered, filling Collin's nose. His sexual passion now satisfied, allowed him time to embrace the fascinating woman in his arms. Her dark, chocolate eyes peered at him. Lips pressed to the soft, pulsing skin of her neck, he worked his way to her sweet lips, once again. "Are you certain you can do this without raising any suspicions?" He had to make sure. With all the passion and attraction involved, he couldn't forget it was still business. A few more feather-light kisses took his lips near her ear.

The woman smiled, revealing sharp fangs. Her eyes held the same darkness, mystery, and silent promise as usual.

"I already told you. I am as close to her as anyone could possibly get."

"Any chance we can snatch her tomorrow?" Collin tried his luck even if he already knew the answer.

Her long, dark hair danced around her face when she shook her head.

"No. Security is going to be crazy tight. It would be a lot easier for me to kill her than for you to take her away." She arranged her gown and smoothed the fabric. "All the isle seats will be occupied by guards, and friends. Do me a favor and don't try anything stupid."

"I told you, we want her alive." Collin kissed the palm of her hand.

"Suit yourself." She couldn't hold the tiny moan provoked by his hungry lips. "We are leaving for the honeymoon a couple of hours after the ceremony."

Collin stared at her in disbelief. With their clothes back on, she pressed her lips against his in another kiss, then withdrew from him.

"What do you mean?" His hand closed on her arm, holding her in place. "Won't she be in transition? He is crazy to put her on a plane." Collin's voice rose, over the whispered volume they cautiously kept. "But she would be unconscious for at least a day if not longer. Interesting . . ." Collin scrunched his brows under her smiling eyes.

"It is all I know for now. You should go before sunrise. I'll keep in touch."

Another embrace and a passionate kiss sealed their agreement. Then Collin disappeared into the nearby forest.

~ ~ ~

From his window, Andree watched two silhouettes embrace in the early morning fog. The woman rushed across the well-maintained lawn shortly after. She wore a long, hooded cape. He couldn't see her face. The man ran in the opposite direction. *Lovers*, Andree smiled and walked away. For the next couple of hours, he kept himself busy planning the new details for the honeymoon.

The sun started to rise. A bright-red globe, like a lost Christmas decoration hung just above the treetops in the distance. The sky around it lit on fire dissolving the haze of the mist. A few dark-purple clouds lingered around for a short while, then dissipated. The crimson sun gradually turned orange, then bright yellow, with every inch ascending on the luminous sky. His wedding day, the day he had waited five centuries for, had finally dawned.

~ ~ ~

"Do you think I can see Jonas? I have a few questions for him." Ana sipped from her coffee.

"Sure. Let's go find him." Andree lifted her hand to his lips.

She felt the tingles coursing through her body before his lips even touched her skin. He made it hard to remain in control, level-headed.

They found Jonas in the massive underground library. Books lined three of the four walls from floor to ceiling.

"Good morning, your Majesties." Jonas bowed then shelved a book.

Ana remembered what Andree had taught her regarding greetings. As graciously as she could, she tilted her head.

"That was perfect. I am impressed."

Ana received Andree's message, but the array of books surrounding her, along with a few sculptures and weapons on display, distracted her. A few tables spread in the vast area supported more books piled up on them. The musty, saturated smell of old paper tickled her senses. She loved the scent of knowledge. Unlike the old-style furniture, Ana always believed the old books were richer than newer ones.

She smiled, remembering how as a child, in school, she always offered to take the old, recycled manuals. The first day of school she would spend hours covering the books in indigo paper. The new plastic covers were impersonal, and she hated them. All teachers could pick her books or notebooks from a pile, the only ones wrapped in the old fashioned purple paper.

Why the hell do I remember my schoolbooks now? I'm learning about vampires, aliens, and all those incredible stories, and all I can think about are my school days. Ahhh. But look at all these books.

Andree's and Jonas' voices distracted her from memories to their conversation. She remembered why she asked to see Jonas.

"I might not be getting this right, and if I'm mistaken I apologize." She walked closer to them. "You said you had to watch over Vlad's daughter. Wouldn't she have been a vampire if he was the father?"

Jonas smiled with understanding eyes, and Ana quickly searched in her memory to see if she read something in those books the Queen had given her. Perhaps she just forgot?

"No. Born vampires are all hybrids, their human mothers were turned while pregnant. They are very rare because the turning has to be done between eight to twelve weeks gestation. Any sooner or later could kill the unborn baby." Jonas ventured in a detailed explanation. "The children will grow and behave like humans until the age of sixteen when they get the first thirst, and after twenty-one they start developing their powers, if they have any, of course. They will continue to age until they get a special kind of bite, called the *Parents' Touch,* which will stop their aging."

"Like Andree." Ana turned to her fiancé, and her lips stretched into a shy smile. She understood that part.

"Correct. The other hybrids were turned by one. You know, a human turned would become the same type of vampire as the one who bit them." Jonas stopped for a second, and Ana nodded in agreement.

"Now, when the mother remains human, things are different," Jonas continued. "The baby will grow a lot bigger, stronger, and faster. It is why human mothers don't survive the pregnancy unless they are strong enough." A shadow passed over his face. "The birth will definitely kill any human, and it did in this case, too. Vlad was way too weakened even to attempt saving the mother."

Jonas stopped for a second. An apologetic look settled in his eyes.

Ana had absorbed a lot of information from the books the Queen had given her in a relatively short time, but the explanations Jonas just offered, she had heard for the first time. They weren't written down anywhere, she was sure of it, at least not in any of the books she came across. Ana felt bad for the woman that died in birth, and suddenly she realized it was her ancestor. *Should I feel worse? I know there have been centuries since, but still, that woman was family.*

"From the moment the baby is born it's human: aging, getting sick, living a mortal's life. His or her father's genes are present, but dormant, and only another vampire can sense them." Ana's attention focused back to Jonas. "That human will have to be turned to unleash the powers inside, as any human would be. Just like Vlad turned his sons."

"Why is this so complicated?" Ana rolled her eyes and saw Andree smiling. She remembered him telling her he thought she was cute when she acted on her little quirks.

She tried her best to wrap her head around all the information.

"When you are trying to combine different species it's not easy, especially when they are natural enemies." Jonas' justification reminded Ana of Daniel and his explanations from the previous day. *What did he say? A lion and a gazelle? What would that be? A lionzelle?*

"And you are sure I'm one of those who carries the genes?" Ana came back to reality, not that it was any more believable than her fantasies.

"One of the most powerful ones. Vlad Veres is your ancestor, and I have absolutely no doubt about it."

"We have all sensed it in you, Ana. What Jonas is saying makes sense. He is speaking the truth." Andree enforced the other man's clarifications.

Ana took a few steps hugging her waist. Her lips pursed and her mind churned. She knew Andree had been in Jonas' mind, and he knew the truth.

She wasn't scared by the idea of aliens. On the contrary, she thought they were pretty cool. Vampires, aliens, pretty much everything fantasy, had intrigued her for years. Finding out now she had always been different from everyone wasn't exactly breaking news.

"Does this have anything to do with the fact I always felt out of place, like I didn't belong anywhere?" She held her breath waiting for the answer. It would have explained so much about her life.

Jonas nodded. He stroked his beard a couple of times.

"Definitely. All of these people carrying vampire genes, knew they were different at some point in their lives." His words entered her mind, slowly sinking in.

Ana had no problem accepting the reality. Understanding the same reality was still a work in progress and a whole other story. She had a long road ahead and knew there would be more questions along the way. *At least I know where to find answers.*

"Now, Jonas, if you will excuse us, I would like to take Ana back to our suite." Andree ended the meeting. "We only have about two more hours before we have to start preparing for the wedding."

He tossed the body effortlessly and listened. The predictable reptiles went straight for it, splashing in the shallow water.

Ivan's eyes stopped on one of his victim's shoes, left behind. He grabbed the hot-pink stiletto and threw it in the same general direction. *Damn, this hooker only whetted my appetite. I should have known better. Sex with humans is never satisfying. They are way too fragile.*

He remembered hearing four distinctive bones breaking under his hands. Or were there five? Who cared? *At least the alligators are thanking me. I made their job easier.*

Ivan started to whistle a song on the way to his car, parked nearby. His mind channeled on some real fun: he knew Karina would be more than happy to see him. She had proven herself over and over again in the last couple of centuries. Her loyalty and their chemistry made him go back to her every time.

A quick stop at home allowed Ivan to clean himself up and change into fresh clothes before visiting Karina.

An hour later, her eyes lit up with excitement. Standing in the doorway, she beckoned him inside.

With all the events from the past couple of weeks, he hadn't had time to sleep for even a minute. Karina knew all his problems and desires. She helped him every time as much as she could. They had fought together, celebrated, even fed together when the occasion rose. That morning, it seemed, he needed rest.

With their passion consumed, Ivan finally fell asleep in her arms.

~ ~ ~

Ana fought through her swirling emotions, and she barely registered her surroundings on the way to the last halt before walking outside. She stopped in front of the improvised, white curtains.

With the black draperies pulled on the sides and the glass wall opened, the vast room appeared more spacious. The austere décor she'd seen before was softened with a multitude of floral arrangements, decorative crystals, and countless yards of draped white silk and tulle.

A servant wearing white gloves and a pretentious black uniform with gold trims had finished arranging champagne glasses in a pyramid. The last of the afternoon rays were fleeting. Sunbeams glimmered through the crystal, and a multitude of lights chased on the walls. The enchanting dance mesmerized her.

Mara handed her a tiny round bouquet and Ana buried her nose in it. The delicate lily of the valley flowers filled her lungs with a divine scent. *Is this real, or am I dreaming?*

Ana touched the silver brooch Queen Emelia insisted she wear. The one of a kind jewelry represented their house crest. It was her *something borrowed,* and Ana smiled remembering her *something blue.*

Ella gave her a delicate lace garter with thin blue silk ribbon, now resting high on her thigh. One more quick, nervous touch assured her the tiara, her *something old*, was in place.

Whispers and laughter floated in the air. Ana couldn't make out the hushed words, just the background noise. Her mind took a trip into the past.

Her childhood, her teenage years, the day of her first wedding, the years of abuse and pain, all paraded in front of her eyes. She had cried an ocean of tears before finally deciding to walk away from a torturous marriage. Ana always thought she failed. Her spirit remained broken. *Will I ever be whole again? Can I let go of my fears and let Andree mend my soul? Can he do it?*

"Your Majesty, are you all right?"

Startled, Ana jumped and whirled around. Mara stood behind her.

"Yes," Ana said. "Some old memories came out of nowhere."

Mara used a crisp white, embroidered handkerchief to wipe a rebel tear on Ana's cheek with an understanding smile. Her touch was soft, careful not to ruin her makeup.

"Must have not been the best ones. Are you ready? In a few seconds, you will walk out there."

Nodding, Ana turned and faced the white draperies again.

~ ~ ~

Andree waited impatiently in front of everyone for Ana to walk down the aisle and become his wife by the human laws. Through his link with her, he saw every single thought she had. He hurt at her memories. Maybe she had to see everything one more time before it could all be left where it belonged: in the past.

The present and the future were his. He promised himself he would do everything in his power to give her good and happy memories. She would never have to look back and have regrets. At the thought of her ex-husband, and all she had endured at his hand, Andree clenched his fists. He wished he could *have a talk* with that man. *Perhaps I will.*

Daniel touched Andree's shoulder. "Is everything all right?"

"Yes. Ana is fighting some really bad memories."

Andree relaxed and swore she would never have to go through that pain again. *I can, and I will make her whole again. And mine.*

Servants pulled the white draperies on either side of the doorway. Soft music filled the air and Ana took her first step outside. All the guests stood, faced the door and admired her delicate beauty. She walked slowly, taking her time.

Andree knew those memories would stay with her—

them, for hundreds, maybe thousands of years. He vowed to make new ones with her and to savor every second.

~ ~ ~

From the audience, Collin searched for a specific woman. The moment his eyes met hers, he smiled. She moved her head slightly, from right to left, in an almost imperceptible movement. Collin nodded and blinked in acknowledgment.

He didn't expect anything less than tight security, especially after the attack from a few nights ago. He hoped he would catch a break; someone would make a mistake, or at least a few moments of privacy and maybe steal a kiss or two from his brown-eyed beauty.

~ ~ ~

Fully bloomed white trees decorated the whole area. The light breeze made them shed tiny flowers over the lush, green grass. It looked like snow in eighty-degree weather. Their scent competed in the air with the rest of the flowers spread everywhere and the ocean's unmistakable salty signature.

A light tremor coursed through her body. The bouquet shook in her hands. Ana tried to focus on the guests' faces, but her effort failed. She knew if she looked at Andree, his love and strength would make her forget about everyone else. More than anything, she wanted new memories, to erase the old ones.

She approached the halfway mark of the decorative path when more doubt set in. *Am I doing the right thing?*

"You are so beautiful." His words resonated in her mind and marked the end of her avoidance.

Their eyes locked and she became entranced in his deep blue, piercing gaze. Everything and everyone disappeared, swallowed in a blue vortex.

Something about him took her breath away. It could've been the superior, snobby attitude she had seen in the past, the elegant tuxedo he wore, or his confidence. Ana smiled and blushed, wishing her veil wasn't so translucent and covered her better.

Doubt gnawed at her. For a short second, she thought to run away. Ana was about to tie herself to yet another man—this time for an eternity—when she had promised herself she'd never do it again. Was it worth it? Did she want to become a vampire that much? Her steps took her further, as if independent from her will.

As soon as she walked close enough, she handed her bouquet to Ella and nodded to the officiant waiting in front of the white marble fountain. Ana had admired the same fountain days ago from afar. The detailed sculpture representing an ancient Greek god resembled Andree. White, fragrant roses floated in the water.

Four posts decorated in white tulle supported a canopy of light-blue wisteria flowers. Under them, Andree's eyes seemed deeper and more intense.

He held her hands in his when they faced each other. His touch calmed her nerves and sent a wave of hot desire through her body. She didn't want to run anymore.

The officiant asked for the rings. Three times.

"Sorry. I was a little distracted." Andree's voice had a tremor she wasn't used to hearing.

All of the audience giggled, and Ana peered in his direction. She didn't expect him to be nervous. The older man officiating the ceremony lost his serious air and smiled with kind understanding, and an all-knowing smirk.

"I bet you were." Bible in one hand, rings in the other, the man asked, "Do you, Andree De Croix take Ana Duma to be your lawful wife?"

"I do." He gazed straight into her soul.

"Do you," the officiant turned to her, "Ana Duma take Andree De Croix to be your lawful husband?"

She panicked for a second. *Why do I want to run? Maybe I should? But he is different. Andree is not going to hurt me. No. I won't let him.*

"I do." Ana's answer changed both of their worlds forever. They were married.

Her focus started to dissipate, then she heard the officiant say, "You may now kiss your bride."

Slowly, Andree lifted her veil and folded it back. He wrapped his right arm around Ana's waist, and with his left hand, he lifted her face to him.

She had reservations, not sure yet that Andree was the last man in her life, the one to hold her heart forever.

He murmured for her ears only, "I love you."

His same, warm and inviting lips touched hers lightly at first. Her heart slammed against her ribcage, out of control. The doubts might have started to dull, and her body responded to his touch, but somewhere in the back of her mind, Ana swore to be careful.

Still dizzy from his kiss, Ana smiled gratefully when he held her close to him. The guests' cheers and congratulations melted together in a hazy memory.

After they signed the marriage certificate in the office and a whole pile of paperwork, Ana received her new documents. She took the time to read her name: Ana De Croix. She loved it.

Only a few minutes later, behind the closed doors of their suite, Andree continued to hold her close, staring into her eyes.

"Now you are my wife according to the human's laws. By our laws, not yet. I still cannot touch you."

His kiss made her wonder if she dreamed, or not. It seemed too good to be real. She had even wrapped her arms around his neck. Ana feared she would forget about her painful experience and trust again. But she didn't want to. It was only in her power to keep herself from getting hurt.

As soon as she regained her sharpness, Ana started to laugh.

"I thought you just said you couldn't touch me."

"That does not count."

"It doesn't?" Her left brow raised in amusement.

"No." Andree shook his head. "I will show you the difference later."

The promise in his eyes, the playful wink, made Ana's cheeks burn. She hated herself for blushing all the time and hoped she would lose it with her turning.

"We do not have much time left. I am expecting my mother to storm in here at any second and take you away from me one more time."

"Don't let me go." She couldn't believe she had just said the words. Ana fought the impulse of covering her mouth with one hand. Her earlier smile melted away.

"Trust me, it is the last time. After the ceremony, nobody will ever take you away from me again."

"One of your best promises."

What the hell is going on with me? Since when am I this daring? With slow steps, she walked to the sofa.

"Getting tired already?" Andree joked, joining her.

"No, but I think I got something in one of my shoes."

Ana took off the white heel bothering her. One tiny, squished flower fell on the rug. She realized Andree was close to her, his hand on her waist.

"Stop. Don't touch me." Ana jumped to her feet forgetting she only had one shoe on.

"What is it?" A blank stare settled in his eyes. An icy undertone caused the temperature in the room to drop a few degrees. Ana couldn't help but think that it could be one way for their union to function: cold, loveless, rational. Was it what she wanted? Hell no.

"I'm wearing your mother's silver brooch." He followed the direction of her index finger to the mentioned piece of jewelry on her right hip. "I don't want you to get hurt or burned because of it." Ana hurried to unclip it and set it aside in the velvety pouch made specially for it.

Andree drew her on his lap, and his arms closed around her, like a cocoon.

Ana rested her head on his chest. One deep, relieved breath left his lips. The steady sound of his heart resonated in her ears, the movement of his chest hypnotic, and she closed her eyes.

I still can't believe that we are married. He is turning all my fantasies to reality. Vampires, aliens, they are now true. What is next? Dragons flying around? I love dragons. Elves, warlocks, werewolves, unicorns?

"I will make more of your fantasies come true." Andree's whisper ignited tiny fires on her skin.

Ana lifted her head in his direction. The glimmer in his eyes mixed with tiny silver lights. He had a little bit of devil in him, just the perfect amount to send her emotions into an untamed whirlwind. His lips curled into an impish grin causing the tips of her ears to burn in flames. Yet, there was no smoke.

"That was not—" Ana tried to remain in her guarded mode. He made it so easy to lose control, to let herself get carried away.

Andree's laugh interrupted her.

"I know. I was only messing around, hoping to make you blush. I absolutely love when you do." His smile melted away her embarrassment. "I never saw dragons or any of the others. I am afraid that vampires and aliens are all I can offer."

~ ~ ~

An hour later, Ana starred at her reflection in the tall mirror. Mara and Veronica transformed her from a sweet, blushing bride to a sexy, provocative woman. She remembered how different the two were in spite of the fact they both had almost the same color hair and eyes.

Veronica's soft, gentle kindness made Ana smile. Mara's warrior heart contrasted with her gracious, aristocratic flare and intimidated Ana. Her defined muscles trained to wield swords, while Veronica handled the makeup brush easily.

The lace gown, as gorgeous as when she first tried it on, hugged her body. Long, black hair cascaded down her back, except for a couple of locks supporting the tiara. Darker makeup accented her smoky eyes and lush lips.

Ana returned to Queen Emelia's living room almost at the same time Daniel walked in.

He stopped, staring at her in awe.

"Daniel?" The Queen hardly controlled her laugh.

"Huh? Your Majesties." He bowed suddenly woken to reality.

"Did you need something?" Ella asked, and he handed Ana a folded piece of paper.

"What's this?" Ana lifted her gaze to him.

"It's from Andree."

Ana opened the note and read it. *My love, these are the last minutes before you will become my wife for eternity. I want you to know how much I love you, how much you mean to me. Earlier, when all those old memories of yours brought tears to your eyes, I wanted to go out there and kill the bastard responsible for them. But I know you would not like it. I will allow him to live. I want you to have only good memories from today until the end of time. I want you to be happy. I want you, period. See you soon, my love.*

Her heart beat so fast and loud, Ana thought everyone could hear it. Excitement bubbled in her chest, and she had to control herself not to squeal and start jumping around. This was the way she preferred her marriage to be. The coldness she provoked from Andree earlier sent a shiver through her body. Maybe in time, after she was positive he wouldn't hurt her, she could allow him into her heart.

"Could I get a pen and paper, please?" Ana decided to make a bold move and quickly composed in her mind a response.

"Of course, here." The Queen pointed to the small desk in the corner of the room.

Seconds later, she had written her reply.

Andree, there is nothing in this world I want more than to share eternity with you. The memories you saw today are in the past. Maybe not the happiest, but it is what made me into who I am today. I can't make any promises, but I will try my best. Ana

She knew she should have probably been more reserved. But she stayed true to herself. Living forever was still a concept she was going to have to get used to. If she had to share that with someone, Andree was the one.

~ ~ ~

The big smile on Andree's face reminded Daniel how Ana looked, and he thought it was his duty to warn his friend.

"You should know something. Your wife looks . . . amazing."

"I know." Andree couldn't hold back his laugh. He straightened his shirt and glanced into the mirror.

"No, you don't. I just saw her. You're not ready for her." Daniel handed his friend the cape and helped adjust it on his shoulders.

"What are you talking about?" Mike intervened, smoothing an unexisting crease on the black silk. "Don't worry, there are little tricks women pull with makeup and all that sort of things," Mike continued with the experience of a man who'd been married for three centuries.

"I'm telling you, Andree, my friend, I feel sorry for you because you'll have to stand through the whole ceremony," Daniel insisted.

Andree glanced at his friend. "Then I can't wait to see her."

~ ~ ~

The amphitheater filled, and the guests waited for the ceremony to start. Blood red pillows contrasted with the off-white stone. Whispers, murmurs, and laughter danced in the air. This time Ana and Andree were in two separate alcoves on either side of the center of the room. From where she stood, she saw him through an opened fold in the curtain.

As the officiant of the ceremony, Queen Emelia couldn't hide her pride. Weddings were not a common occurrence in their world.

Ana brushed her clammy, shaking hands against her hips, over the delicate lace.

"This is it. I hope you are not getting cold feet now." Andree's voice echoed in her mind.

"I'm not. I'm only worried that I'll forget what to say and what to do."

"I will guide you through if needed. Just follow my lead."

"Are you sure that's good advice?" As soon as her thought left her mind, a smile spread over her lips.

Chapter 16

The Queen stood in the middle of the stage, still as a chiseled statue. "Join me." She waved to both Andree and Ana.

Ana listened to her heels echoing on the stone floor. *Can I be any louder?*

Andre reached the center a couple of seconds before her. She felt his stare all but undress her from head to toe, causing waves of heat to wash over her. For the next few seconds, a void left no air in the room, as if everyone inhaled at the same time.

Ana avoided Andree's gaze again. She wanted to see him first when they faced each other, in front of Queen Emelia.

Unlike her, Andree continued to stare at her from the second she entered the room. She could feel his eyes roaming over her. Tingles ran over her body, and an uncontrollable giddiness overtook her.

"You are killing me. You look absolutely stunning. Now all I can think about is getting you out of that dress. I might be the one in need of guidance for the ceremony."

Ana covered her giggle with a light cough. When they finally stopped in front of the Queen and faced each other, she gazed at the man before her.

All the Princes from her childhood stories flashed in Ana's mind. Prince Charming, Eric, Albert, the Beast, they all but faded and dwarfed compared to him. The half-alien, vampire Prince Andree was not the product of imagination. He was real.

Ana grasped the reality: she was living her own grown-up fairy tale, where fantasy met reality. She lost herself in his eyes, deeper than the ocean and brighter than any stars, struggling to remain guarded. A feat harder than she imagined.

~ ~ ~

Eyes glued to Ana, and the dress hugging every curve he desired, the sounds of the crowd faded into the distance.

The Queen proceeded with the ceremony, gracious and proud, official and warm. "Andree." She paused and waited, then she touched his shoulder. "Andree."

For a few seconds, just as Ana was mesmerized by him, Andree allowed himself to dive into her eyes. The never-ending pools of sweet and decadent chocolate brought him the certainty of happiness. *So it is true, and this is how it feels.* Destiny is real.

Andree had heard in the past stories from older vampires about destiny. He never believed them to be true, not until three days ago when he entered his mother's suite and saw Ana for the first time.

It was the unique moment when time and space ceased to exist, when fate itself laid before his eyes. From that second nothing had been the same. He had crossed into a different dimension.

Ana was his destiny, and everything leading to that moment made sense now: her, being on that beach and chased by Ivan, his mother, saving her life, the presence intriguing everyone, his decision to return early when he read the open invitation for bachelors.

None of the separate events made sense at the time they happened, but all led to the two of them being in the same place, at the same time.

She came into his life for a reason, and they were meant to be together. Every living cell in his body was linked to hers. It was their destiny. Her continuous reservation, the shield she kept between them, bothered him, but Andree knew it was part of the process. Yes, he would've preferred if she would figure out her feelings sooner rather than later, but he didn't want to rush her. Time was on their side.

His emotions swirled, and grew in a whirlwind, filling the vast room. The audience fell quiet, hypnotized under the spell of fate, their senses dulled away. No one even dared to move.

Andree placed his hands in front of Ana's face, and slowly opened them to the sides.

"Ana, look into my heart and see me for who I am. Here, today, in front of everyone I am giving myself to you for eternity."

His words echoed in the amphitheater, and he knelt. The long, black cape he wore pooled behind him, dark and smooth. Only the sound of the burning torches broke the silence. Andree bowed his head and placed his left hand on top of the right one, with palms facing up, in an offering gesture.

"Cut your initial in my palm, on my words."

Ana nodded and took the sharp dagger from the Queen's hands.

Daniel sprayed anesthetic over the small area in Andree's palm, cold against his heated flesh.

"I am giving you my body, my heart, and soul. Everything I am now belongs to you." Andree lifted his head and stared into her eyes. "Will you accept me as your husband from today until the end of time?"

The tip of the blade touched his skin. Ana's hand trembled, but she managed to follow through with the instructions. Beads of blood pooled on the surface of the open cut.

"Now taste my blood."

Ana gave back the dagger, and she touched Andree's bleeding cut with her lips.

~ ~ ~

His blood tasted metallic, coppery, but she didn't scrunch her nose.

"I accept you as my husband."

Andree rose to his feet and let a drop of his blood drip on the marriage contract the Queen held. The whole crowd started cheering. Daniel cleaned his cut quickly and put a bandage over it.

Ana's heart beat faster. A thin layer of sweat glimmered on her hairline. She knew the importance of this ceremony. It was her turn. Uncertainty hit her like a brick wall, she wasn't sure she could say the words. Doubt rose again. *I can do this.*

"Andree, look into my heart and see me for who I am. Here, today, in front of everyone I am giving myself to you for eternity."

She knelt in front of Andree and offered him her hand. The cold spray cooled her palm. For one fraction of a second, in an out-of-body experience, Ana saw herself, offering everything she was to him. *This is so surreal, it's crazy.*

"I am giving you my body, my heart, and soul. Everything I am now belongs to you." She lifted her gaze to him. "Will you accept me as your wife from today until the end of time?"

From the corner of her eye, Ana noticed a few of the guests rising to their feet, hissing and displaying their fangs. *Damn!* Her heart ponded in her chest. *I knew this was a bad idea.* Mara, Karl, Ella, Mike, and Jonas quickly stood and faced the audience with a unified hiss. One second later, everyone returned to their seats. Everything seemed to be back to normal.

"It is only instinct. You are safe." She heard Andree's voice in her mind. *"This is the last chance to change your*

mind. If I accept you, there is no way back. Are you sure you want me?"

Ana was lost for words. A nod would have to suffice, and she swallowed trying to recover her voice. No such luck. *Why do I react this way? All this is just a ritual and the words are just that. Isn't it?* Andree returned the small dagger to his mother. Blood stained the tip of the blade. She had no idea when he had cut his initial into her palm. Their eyes locked. Excitement and fear mixed together and washed over her.

~ ~ ~

Andree experienced pure empowerment coursing through him. Fangs descended as a reaction to her blood, and his clothes tightened, suffocating him. His body struggled to host the power within. He focused and controlled the reaction.

Andree's lips touched the palm of her hand, his receding fangs abraded her skin. Her blood tasted sweet, a bit salty, and belonged to him. Forever.

"I accept you as my wife."

Ana took her turn and let a drop of her blood drip on the marriage contract.

For the second time, the crowd applauded excited, and Daniel cleaned and covered her cut as quickly as he could.

Andree took Ana's left hand into his, with the cuts lined on top of each other, upright, between them. He leaned his forehead on the back of her hand and Ana followed his lead.

"Andree, do you promise to love Ana, support her, and protect her at any cost?" Queen Emelia's voice broke the deafening silence.

"I do." Andree kissed her hand, after which he stood tall.

"Ana, do you promise to love Andree, support him, and protect him at any cost?"

One memory flashed in Ana's mind, her grandmother. She had been dead for almost a decade, but her words echoed in Ana's mind. *"A woman's body, from the neck down, belongs to the man she chooses. From the neck up, only belongs to herself. Always remember, it is up to you to give anyone the power to hurt you."* Ana had to blink a few times, her breath accelerated, and she felt Andree squeezing her hand.

"I do." She touched the back of his hand with her lips, their eyes locked again.

The Queen took the glass box holding the crossed daggers, with their blood on the blades, and showed it to everyone.

"You have promised to love, support, and protect each other, you have given your blood, and you have placed your lives in each other's hands. It is my pleasure and honor to acknowledge in front of our coven, that from this day on, you are husband and wife."

Andree's and Ana's first kiss as a married couple, in front of the coven, marked the beginning of their eternity together. She understood that second, it was only up to her what kind of life she would live. How much power would she give Andree—how much she would retain?

Every single person in the amphitheater rose to their feet, cheering and applauding, waiting for the next ceremony to start.

~ ~ ~

Andree turned to face the guests and lifted his right hand. Silence filled the room again, at his request.

"Most of you are expecting the turning ceremony next. We have decided to wait for a few months."

His words produced confusion among the guests. An avalanche of murmurs replaced the silence. A few of them demanded an explanation.

Collin yelled out, rising to his feet. "Blasphemy!" His

index finger pointed to Andree, and green flames burned bright in his eyes.

Andree's arm tightened around Ana's waist.

Every murmur stopped.

"What did you say?" Andree confronted Collin.

"This is unheard of. She came here asking to be turned." Collin pointed to the immaculate floor with purpose.

"And I will. She is not ready yet."

"You are breaking the rules." His index finger moved toward Andree for a moment. "Any of us that offered to marry and turn her would have." Collin's hand waved to the audience this time, himself included. "You claimed her. Turn her, now."

"Are you challenging my decision?" Andree's growled question resonated between hisses. Every muscle in his body tensed.

All attention turned to Collin. With obvious regret for his outburst, he let himself fall back on the crimson pillow crossing his arms over his chest and shaking his head.

A few moments of silence floated like a mist, cooling all the heated spirits.

"I will turn her at a later date. You will be notified when. Until then, Princess Ana is my wife, and I expect you to show her the respect she deserves." Andree concluded the ceremony, with his usual confidence, and kissed her hand with a respectful bow.

Slowly, everyone came near and congratulated them, on the way to the ballroom, where the glamorous party would continue for hours. No one dared to argue the decision any further.

~ ~ ~

A black limousine with dark-tinted windows drove Ana and Andree straight to the local airport. Ana eyed the private jet, ready to take off. Fear swirled around her and Andree sensed it.

"Where exactly are we going?" She stepped off the platform, through the opening, and entered the luxurious interior.

"Our honeymoon. I know you do not like flying, so I thought you could sleep until we get there." Andree squeezed her hand into his.

He waited for her to approve or decline his idea.

"That might be best. Are you going to use that magnetism thingy again?"

"Yes, if you are okay with it. I do not want you to feel forced into anything." Andree showed her to her seat.

Ana peeked over the seats and saw Mara, Karl, and Veronica already in theirs. She buckled her seat belt with shaking hands.

The engines rumbled, and the aircraft picked up speed. Eyes closed, she didn't have time to notice any details besides the soft leather seats and the black carpet covering the floor.

~ ~ ~

"Are you ready?" Andree buckled his seat belt.

"Yes." Ana's word came out as a soft squeak.

Andree used his magnetism, and she fell asleep, leaning against him. He wrapped his arm around her shoulders and hurried to place a tiny pillow under her head for extra comfort.

About three and a half hours later, Andree's lips brushed on hers, waking her up.

"Welcome to the Azores, Princess De Croix," he whispered and couldn't resist stealing another kiss.

~ ~ ~

Ana opened her eyes and smiled at the sound of his voice. The humming of the engines quieted down. One minute they were getting ready to take off, and now, they had already landed.

"I'm starting to get used to that. Wait." She turned quickly to look out the window blinking fast. Lights flashed and airport service vehicles roamed around in the darkness. "Did you say Azores?"

"Yes, I did." A grin stretched across his lips.

"I can't see anything. What time is it?" Ana asked squinting her eyes.

"It is almost morning. We are in a different time zone."

"How long did I sleep?" Ana ran her hands over her face trying to completely remove any lingering sleepiness. She still had on the make up from the wedding.

"A little over three hours, which is perfect, since our first day together is just starting."

Ana could taste the promise in his words. The tension between them thickened the air. Every atom charged with anticipation.

She giggled and wrapped her arms around his neck. Andree lifted her in his arms and started toward the exit. They were the last ones to leave.

"This dress of yours is coming off as soon as we make it into our room." His whisper sent wave after wave of heat through her body.

"Good luck with those buttons," Ana braved.

"You don't know me very well, do you? You really think some buttons will slow me down?"

Her quivering body molded against his, and Andree smiled. Anticipation tasted sweet.

Twenty minutes later, they sipped champagne and admired the view from their terrace.

In the early morning hours, the ocean glistened under the moonlight. Waves brushed against the coarse sand.

Algae, salt, and fish joined their scents and tickled her nose. The sounds, the smells, everything swirled around her. Ana wondered at the border between reality and fantasy. All caution was about to fly right out the window, she knew it, but she wasn't strong enough to resist the temptation of the man in front of her.

Without any warning, Andree scooped her up in his arms. When he let her down, between kisses and whispers, she noticed the bedroom around them.

Before she had a chance to see any details besides the oversized bed, Andree took off his shirt and wrapped his arms around her. Everything else disappeared in a vortex of the unimportant. Ana wanted to touch him, badly, but she hesitated.

Andree took her hands in his and kissed them slowly, one at a time, gazing deep into her eyes.

"No more holding back. You want to touch me. I am yours as much as you are mine," he whispered, placing Ana's hands on his chest.

His sharp breath filled her hands and her heart. She couldn't tell who enjoyed it more. Her pulse spiraled out of control.

"Here, do not forget your elixir." Andree handed her the bright-blue vial.

Where did he keep it? I completely forgot about it. She opened the container, still hesitant. "You really think I need it?"

"Yes, you do." Andree gently lifted her hand holding the vial to her lips.

"Tastes good, wild berries." Ana gave him back the bottle after she sipped from it. Andree threw it on a nearby chair and redirected his attention to her.

"Let me see."

His lips claimed hers. The reality, her surroundings started to twirl around. She heard his laughter when he found the delicate garter. His teeth gently grazed her skin pulling it off.

Every inch of his body branded on the surface of her heart, deep inside her mind. When she reconnected to reality, Ana noticed the ripped pillow, right beside her, proof that Andree had lost his control for a second.

"Now you are finally mine, my wife, my Princess."

Andree held her tight against his body. His words rumbled from deep within him. The feeling of finally belonging overwhelmed Ana and tears pooled in her eyes. She had been searching for it her whole life, only to find it in his arms, the arms of a vampire Prince. Could she trust him now?

~ ~ ~

Collin handed Ivan his phone. "Read it."

"When did you get this?"

"Moments ago." Collin adjusted the dark gray jacket he wore.

Ivan finished reading the email sent by Collin's contact. "Seems your outburst didn't demolish the plan after all."

Four days he'd lost sight of where the Prince had taken the human. Now, Ivan knew her whereabouts and the pieces of the puzzle would fall into place.

"I told you that arrogant bastard must have a plan. I knew it. But a child? This world doesn't need another one of his blasted family members." Ivan paced nervously, with his fists tight. "And she's a Veres? This is unbelievable. It could mess up my plans big time, and I just got an audience with the brothers in two weeks." Ivan's lamentation would have been funny in different circumstances.

"It is not common knowledge. You can pretend you don't know," Collin suggested after a few seconds of silence. "I am pretty sure they don't know either."

Ivan stopped in his tracks and stared at his friend.

"Now, more than ever we have to get her. She is too valuable not to. A Veres . . . Did you ever hear about that book they are going to look for?"

Collin shook his head, and Ivan resumed his pacing.

"The address she sent us is on *sacred grounds*. Are you sure you want to attack them there? The sentinels are not going to take a breach lightly."

Ivan's brows furrowed. Collin had a knack for stating the obvious. It was bad enough they would have to fight the elite of the Third Coven. The added sentinels were the last thing they needed.

"We are going to be quick about it. Go in, get the human, and get out. One, two hours maximum." Ivan planned out loud. "By the time they figure it out, we should be long gone. We'll need to rent a private plane." He glanced at Collin, who nodded in response.

"She will give us the heads-up one day ahead. Apparently, we have to wait for some stormy weather to cover our approach." Collin volunteered the details.

"That's an excellent idea. After all this is over, I want to meet this woman. I hope you are serious about her. She seems smart and effective."

Collin smiled.

It wasn't in Ivan's character to offer compliments to anyone, but this was a special occasion. The inside spy proved to be valuable, and Ivan was more than willing to use her to get what he wanted.

"Maybe, we'll see. For now, we need to plan this right."

"Yes, we can't afford another failure." Ivan hoped he could, after all, get his hands on the human that meant so much to his enemy.

The two friends set to planning in front of the wall map in Ivan's office. He needed to make sure this time they snatched

Ana. Her bloodline was too precious to pass up, and a child would have ended their plans.

~ ~ ~

Ana and Andree rested on one of the lounge chairs on the terrace. It was the last day of their week in Azores. Watching the sun set had become their ritual every late afternoon. Ana wished she would have painted the breathtaking view, and she took multiple pictures for later.

The ball of fire, slowly descending into the water sent golden orange rays of light shimmering on the surface of the waves. Their hypnotic movement relaxed her.

Andree's arms closed around her body. Ana cuddled closer to him, familiar now with his body. She needed to be close to him as much as she needed air to breathe.

His heart beat louder than the waves splashing against the sand. Ana closed her eyes for a few moments, indulging in the rhythmic sound.

"Can I ask you something?"

"Anything." He ran his fingers through her hair.

She gazed into his eyes, trying hard not to lose the train of her thoughts. He distracted her every time.

"Jonas said at some point that vampires couldn't be killed by humans. Is that true? What about garlic, crosses, holy water, the silver rod through the heart?"

Andree kissed her hand gently, without taking his eyes off her.

"Jonas is right. Humans cannot kill us. Many, including you, hate garlic. Our heightened senses cause us to smell everything more intense. Garlic itself is harmless. It just stinks."

Ana's giggle interrupted him, and Andree kissed the tip of her nose.

She continued to stare at him, wondering if she could start trusting him. Maybe she could grant him a little access to her heart. One fraction of a second later she tossed the thought at the back of her mind.

"The crosses, we cannot care less about them. It is more about what they are made of. As you know already, we have an intolerance to silver. It burns our skin. We tend to stay away from it. The holy water is just another myth. As for the rod through the heart, well, that would kill anyone. Vampire or not."

Ana tightened her hold on him. She didn't want to think about that possibility.

"In theory, we could die that way. In reality, I want to see the human who is going to catch one of us first. Our speed makes it practically impossible unless we are lured into a trap." She withdrew a few inches away from him. The idea itself caused her to tremble. "Only another vampire can kill a vampire. And it has to be a lethal blow straight through the heart, or decapitation."

Andree shrouded her shiver with an embrace. He hugged her closer to him. Ana didn't like the subject, but she needed to know.

"Even with silver-coated weapons, we can overcome an injury. Scarred, but if it is not a fatal blow, it can be survived. You should not worry about me going to search for the book. I will have Jonas and Ella with me. Mike, Daniel, Karl, Mara, and Veronica will stay with you."

"Wait, is everyone coming?" She inched away from him again, so she could stare into his eyes.

Andree smiled again, causing her bones to melt.

"Yes. I want that book found and us out of there as soon as possible." He eased her back onto his chest.

Chapter 17

"Damn, these people should invest in a serious renovation. This place is stuck in medieval times." Ana's remark made Andree laugh.

The local Transylvanian traditional restaurant where they had dinner kept the historic flair as much as the rest of the small town nestled in between the mountains. Ana liked some of the aspects, but strongly disagreed with others.

"They are preserving history. I thought it was charming. Those cabbage rolls were divine." Andree tried to defend the restaurant and won himself a disapproving glare from his wife.

"I am all for it, but do it in a museum, not in a restaurant. I expected those damn old bricks to fall in my plate any second."

The restaurant in discussion indeed kept the nearly archaic décor. Low, curved ceilings and walls completely covered in exposed, raw brick didn't seem hygienic to Ana.

From the first step inside, she crinkled her nose. An old, musty, and moldy smell mingled with the stench of garlic, filling the poorly ventilated rooms.

Traditional decorations on the walls, white pieces of fabric handsewn and stitched with red and black thread in the area-specific style, were gathered with long garlands of dried garlic.

The wooden tables, worn and polished by excessive use, looked right out of a museum. Ana imagined knights sitting around them, drinking and eating, most probably with their hands. *I bet they didn't wash them either.*

The local music hurt her ears. She had never liked it back then and even less now. Ana was relieved when the band left. At least the food didn't let her down, just as delicious as she had remembered it from long ago. She ate the last bite of *papanasi*, a Romanian cheese dumpling.

"That was so good." She licked a dusting of sugar from one of her fingers. "It's nice out. We should walk back and send Karl ahead with the car."

Andree seemed to think about it for a short second then approved. "Okay. Let's go," He extended his hand waiting for her to stand.

Hand-in-hand with him, Ana walked out of the restaurant, on their way to the house they had rented. The aroma of lime trees mixed with a whiff of fresh-cut grass filled her lungs. A more than welcome change from the stale and suffocating smells from the restaurant.

A dog barked somewhere far away, and more responded in a chorus. The sounds of simple life in a small town in Transylvania relaxed her.

Ana walked beside Andree, her head leaning on his arm, her hand nestled into his. She loved the narrow, side streets, with centuries-old cobblestone pavement. The dark stones smoothed by time and use shone in the moonlight. They were one step up from dirt roads, still in use in some parts of the country. She didn't mind that historic aspect.

Out of nowhere, a memory crept into her mind. She didn't want to remember her ex-husband, or when she fell off his motorcycle. The particular pavement had one downside: in humidity it became slippery.

When the motorcycle wiggled over the slick stones, she had found herself sliding head first, like a penguin over the icy banks of Antarctica. Her clothes ripped and stained, but she didn't get one scratch.

She could still hear her ex yelling at her, accusing her of

wanting to get him in trouble. He didn't even bother asking if she was hurt.

A cold chill coursed Ana's body, triggering a shiver. Her grandmother always used to say that when she had chills like that, it meant Death itself flew by and touched her with a black feathery wing. She should feel lucky it missed her and didn't tear her soul out with its scythe.

Ana believed in luck, especially now, since she was months away from becoming a vampire. A crease in the paved sidewalk caused her heel to slip, and Andree's arms closed around her.

"Are you all right?"

"Yeah, I'm okay. I didn't see the crack."

His reaction confirmed for the millionth time the differences between him and her ex. They were like night and day. *The funny part is that anyone would consider Andree as the night.* She smiled in the darkness surrounding them. The truth was different.

"You are trembling. Are you cold?"

Without waiting for a response, Andree took off his jacket wrapping it around her.

"I'm not cold, I . . ." Ana didn't finish her sentence, lost in the sensations caused by his proximity.

Andree held her close to him. His warm jacket kept his scent. The image of his cologne bottle flashed in her mind, *Chrome.* It suited Andree. Just like him, it was strong and sharp.

Mixed with his natural musk and the smell of the leather jacket, it stirred her senses in a cyclone of desire. Warmth infused her, all the way to the marrow of her bones. His thumb brushed lightly over her lower lip, and Ana trembled under his razor-sharp gaze.

All day, he had been teasing her, staring only to look away when she caught him. He had touched her, lingering for an extra second, enough to heat her senses. Every time he backed away, leaving her wanting more, wanting him.

"What is going on?"

Ana placed her hand over his, leaning her head into his palm.

"What are you talking about?" Andree continued to play, testing her limits.

"You've been acting weird today."

"Does it bother you?"

A worried undertone in his voice and a doubtful look in his eyes attracted Ana's attention. *He is definitely up to something.* She shook her head. Words were hard to find in that moment.

"Do you remember what day it is today?" Andree's arm encircled her shoulders as they continued their walk.

Ana smiled at him. "Our ten-day anniversary?"

"You are correct, and I have a surprise for you." Andree's confirmation made her laugh.

"You are crazy. You've been spoiling me with gifts every day."

Andree stopped and kissed her in the middle of the quiet road. "Only crazy for you." The sound of distant traffic faded away. The whole world around them disappeared for a few seconds.

"Wasn't that our street?" Ana pointed to an intersection they passed.

"We are not going home. I figured we could stay out longer."

Ana didn't insist. She knew he must have something planned since that night he wasn't going to search for the book.

"I wish you would've told me. These shoes are not made for long strolls in the night." She extended her right leg in front of her, showing off her turquoise high heels.

Without a word, Andree scooped her in his arms with the same ease he always did. Ana wrapped her arms around his neck, and a tiny giggle escaped her. She sensed his smile. After a few steps, his voice rumbled from his chest straight into her ears.

"You might want to hold tight. I am going to run. I can't wait any longer."

She kissed his cheek and shut her eyes. Another dog barked nearby, from behind one of the fences, and Ana tightened her hold on him.

It seemed like only seconds passed when Andree placed her down in front of a gate. Karl, who must have been waiting, opened it for them.

Ana lifted her eyes to the construction she recognized. The Black Castle towered before them in the night, sending shivers down her spine.

"What are we doing here? Isn't it closed?"

"It is ours for the night," Andree answered with a devilish grin, and she slipped her hand into his.

The courtyard welcomed them, quiet and dark. The Black Castle lived up to its reputation. Somewhere in the distance, a few owls called in the night, and traffic melted in a background noise.

Ana stayed as close as she could to Andree. She could swear the temperature had dropped at least ten degrees, and she shrugged in his jacket. Her high heels barely touched the uneven stones covering the ground.

"You are safe. I am right here. Karl and Mara are close by. Jonas and Daniel are patrolling around the castle. It is just us." Andree lightly squeezed her hand.

"I know, but this place is creepy."

They walked by an uncanny wooden fountain. Ana avoided looking at it, afraid something would crawl out from the depths.

Under a dark archway, Andree lifted her in his arms again. Not one light broke the pitch black ahead of them.

"Can you see anything?" She noticed his smile before the darkness swallowed them. *Stupid question. He told me he can see in the dark.*

Ana gave up trying to distinguish any forms. She leaned her head against his shoulder, holding him tight. Every step he took up the steep stairs, every muscle tensing and relaxing, echoed in her body.

When Andree stopped, the squeak of a door opening made her lift her head.

A dim lit bedroom welcomed them, and Ana's eyes roamed with surprise and avidity. Candles filled the room, and the lights danced with shadows on the rough, uneven walls. An impressive canopy bed flanked with heavy velvet dominated the far wall.

"This was Vlad's room." Andree whispered close, his lips touching her ear as if sharing the biggest secret of the century.

"Are you sure?"

Skeptical as always, Ana took a second peek at the massive, heavy-looking bed. *Is that where he died the day his daughter was born?*

"Jonas confirmed it. This is the room." He kissed her temple. "The bed is a replica."

Andree finally let her stand on her own feet. The huge fireplace occupying most of the opposite wall attracted Ana. A happy, crackling fire spread more of the ever-moving light into the room. The warmth of the flames welcomed her. In front of the age worn stone structure, on the floor, a soft, white bearskin, covered in multicolored pillows and blankets, invited them.

At the side, a champagne bottle and two glasses waited surrounded by more candles. She knew he must've planned the night long before they arrived in the city.

"This is amazing. I didn't know you were this romantic." Ana turned to Andree with teary eyes.

"I am not." He shook his head. "But I know you are, and tonight it is all about you."

His words washed over her with a wave of uncontrollable lust. Ana let his jacket slip off her shoulders, and Andree took off his shirt. The intermittent light from the fire and candles caressed his body, over and around every single one of his defined, hard muscles.

Desire shimmered silver in his eyes. Her blood hummed with mischief and thrill. All of the tension he built in the past few hours caught up with her. Under Andree's touches, whispers, and kisses Ana finally stopped fighting. She let go and abandoned herself in his arms.

A couple of hours later, she snuggled next to him, in front of the fire, between ripped pillows. Tiny pieces of fluff stuck in her hair, sparkling in the light of the flames. Some still floated in the air around them, like snow. Andree picked a few out.

"I have to stop asking for down-stuffed pillows."

~ ~ ~

Andree sat on the terrace that morning, after yet another failure. Every single night, after Ana fell asleep, he went out with Jonas and Ella in search of the book. Everyone else stayed with Ana, making sure she was safe. They weren't the only vampires in the area. He didn't want any surprises, even if they were on sacred grounds and according to the law, any fighting was forbidden.

Daniel joined his friend in silence. For a while they watched the sunrise. The dark sky breaking into lighter shades of blue revealed the breathtaking valley beyond the backyard.

Rolling green hills, decorated with homes and farms, were visible for miles. Summer neared its end, making early mornings and nights cooler. The crisp air filled his lungs, refreshing and clean. A few early birds started their morning songs.

Daniel turned to face Andree. "Congratulations."

"We did not find it yet." Frustration set in. "I do not understand what have we missed? What is it we . . .?" Andree stopped and stared at Daniel, taking in the grin on his face. "What are you congratulating me for?"

"You, my friend, are going to be a father."

Andree jumped from his seat. All his emotions bent out of shape. His pulse drummed in his ears. For centuries he had lost hope that one day he would hear the words he just did. "Are you sure?" It sounded to good to be true.

"I'm positive. I had my suspicions after the first night here, in the Black Castle. I wanted to make sure first, so I waited a few days."

"Ana is going to be ecstatic."

"Which reminds me." Daniel took out of his pocket a small vial containing a bright pink liquid. "I have reformulated her elixir. This should help her, especially now."

"Thank you."

The vision Ella had the night before their wedding flashed in front of Andree's eyes. Every single detail matched reality, down to the candles and the color of the pillows spread in front of the centuries-old fireplace. She had foreseen the night Ana got pregnant, which he had asked her to keep between them.

"Now you have to pick a date for her turning." Daniel's reminder brought Andree back to reality.

"And I have not found that blasted book yet." He ran an opened hand over his face. "I have to, and quick. We are running short on time."

Andree joined Ana, still asleep in the comfortable bed. The sheets, crisp and fragrant, welcomed him. In that part of the world, people still dried the laundry outside, on a line, a through back from the past that brought forth nostalgia.

Ana woke up minutes later bathed in his smile.

"You found it?" she asked excitedly, sitting up in the middle of the bed. "I can tell from the glow in your eyes."

He had explained to her how the lights in his eyes brightened when his emotions ran high.

"No. But I do have great news." Andree drew her back into his arms.

He let the warmth of her body distract him for a moment. Her image, in his arms, wasn't something he could get used to. It always made his heart beat faster, his breath shallow, and his blood boil hotter than the sun. He loved her essence.

"Do you remember our first night here, at the castle?"

Ana's cheeks and the tips of her ears colored pink before she answered. "How could I ever forget it?"

"That night, you, my love, got pregnant."

A whole range of emotions, from happiness all the way to doubt, crossed over her face. Her eyes sparkled, dimmed down, only to shimmer again.

"Are you sure?"

"Daniel is."

Ana burst into tears before he had the chance to say anything else and hid her face in his chest.

Andree held her tight against his body. He knew she found comfort in his arms. She had admitted that much to him. Her warmth and softness played havoc with his senses. His fangs started to descend, and Andree did his best to control his reaction. Instinct kicked in, provoked by the sweet scent of her blood. He closed his eyes, relaxing. His calm always found its way to her.

"Andree." He could barely understand her whisper between the sobs and the tears burning his skin like liquid fire.

"Shhh. I am right here, my love. We are going to have a baby. It is real," he added to reassure her she wasn't dreaming.

He held her until reality set in Ana's mind and her tears stopped.

"You have made me the happiest man ever." Andree wiped away the last of her tears.

"All those years I thought I couldn't have children. Then you come along, and . . . It doesn't seem possible." Ana tried to smile, but more tears pooled in her eyes. "Do you have any idea how happy I am right now?"

~ ~ ~

"I'm leaving in a couple of hours. The audience is scheduled for tomorrow night, and I would like to have some extra time. Perhaps go over everything one more time." Ivan straightened his clothes with a hint of nervousness.

"You're going to be fine." Collin glanced at his friend. "How's the recruiting going?"

"Over two hundred people already." The sense of pride in Ivan's words made Collin nod.

"Amazing. If the brothers buy it, we have excellent—"

A beep, letting him know an incoming message waited, interrupted Collin, and he reached for his phone.

One quick glance at the screen made his brows furrow. Message read: *Set for tomorrow.*

"Damn it." Collin clenched his teeth and tightened his fists. Without another word, he handed the phone to his friend.

Shaking his head, Ivan read the message.

"No. We can't do it tomorrow. I just told you." He threw the phone delivering bad news on the couch.

His hands raked through his dark hair, pushing it back from his face.

Collin picked up the phone and shoved it in his pocket.

Taking a couple of steps, he stopped and turned around to face Ivan.

"There's only one way to do it. We need to split up."

Ivan stared at him and continued to shake his head. "No. I'm not letting you go alone."

"I'm not. I'll have the group with me."

"No." Ivan's hand cut through the air in front of him. "I have to be there. I want to be there. That bastard is dangerous and—"

Collin lifted his hands in front of Ivan and tried to calm him. "I know he is, but the point of this plan is to avoid facing him. It's why we are going to attack when he's out of there, looking for that stupid book."

Ivan continued to oppose Collin's suggestion. They had planned everything carefully, had a small plane on standby. Everything perfected down to the last detail. Only the day was all wrong.

"Why did it have to be the same time as my meeting? Maybe I can cancel it."

"No." It was Collin's turn to shake his head. "That meeting is important for our plan to work. You don't just blow off a meeting with the Veres brothers."

"I can't be in two places at the same damn time." Ivan raised his tone with frustration.

"It's why we have to split up." Collin enforced his idea. "You go to your meeting and get those two on our side. I'll take the group and go get the human."

"I don't like it." A shadow of pessimism in Ivan's voice caused Collin to shrug.

"Well, I'm not crazy about it either, but it is what it is. Besides, my contact will help us there. She's coming back with me, by the way." Collin sounded more convinced and optimistic. "My friend, you must weigh out our chances."

"Fine," scoffed Ivan.

Where Collin stood, it appeared to be the only logical way to proceed, if not for the awful feeling tightening around his throat. The worst possible scenarios played in his mind.

"The hard part is on you," Collin said. "Without the brothers' help we can't do anything. All I have to do is get past four people protecting the human, grab her, and jump back on the plane. We should be in and out of there in minutes."

Ivan had doubt, Collin could see it. Many things could go wrong.

"What if he comes back while you are still in the house?" Ivan named just one of the possibilities.

"He's on a tight schedule. They leave after eleven and come back around five in the morning, before the sunrise." Collin paused and walked back to the sofa. "We should get there around two." He sat and stared at his friend "Even if he does, we still outnumber him."

A deep sigh left Ivan's chest. "Call me before you go in and as soon as you have her."

"I will," Collin said. "Now go. We'll see each other in two days, in Toronto. Oh, make sure that safe house is at least clean."

Ivan's brows furrowed, and after a quick nod he rushed out of his friend's house.

~ ~ ~

"You look happy, future mommy." Ella sat beside Ana in the tall grass, smiling.

"I've never been this happy in my life," she admitted and smiled.

Ana lay in the grass, watching the white and fluffy clouds blow overhead with Ella. She allowed herself to dream about the future for almost an hour. Visions of herself and a baby flooded her mind. She was already planning birthday parties and picking a school. A light giggle escaped her lips, and both Ana's and Ella's laughter filled the warm afternoon air.

"Ella, Jonas needs you." Andree's voice boomed behind her.

"Back to work," Ella joked and ran inside the house leaving Ana with Andree.

He helped her to her feet. "We will have to pick a date for your turning."

In his arms, her mind melted from the perfection surrounding her. For a few moments, she couldn't think of anything but her bright future.

"Hey, lovebirds." Mike interrupted. "Hate to break it up, but Andree is needed."

"Did you guys figure out something new?" Andree quickly turned toward his friend.

"Not exactly, but they want to try a new approach."

"I'll be right back." Andree kissed Ana's lips.

"Andree." She stopped him before going inside the house. "Don't go out tonight, please."

"I need to find the book. Time is not our friend right now. We only have a couple of months left." He touched her abdomen.

"Apparently there'll be a storm tonight." Ana lowered her gaze. "I have a terrible feeling. Please, stay with me." She lifted her eyes to his, pleading.

Andree cupped her face in the palms of his hands and gazed deep into her eyes.

"You will be safe." He lightly kissed the tip of her nose, a habit he picked up in the last few days. "Please understand it is something I have to do."

She let out a deep sigh. "Just come back as soon as you can."

"I promise." Andree sealed his oath with a kiss, and they both entered the house before joining everyone in the basement.

Chapter 18

The crack of thunder shook the whole house. Ana sat straight up in the middle of the bed, with her eyes wide open, her breathing short and fast.

A blinding light flashed, flooding the room. Her hands went straight over her ears, and her eyes shut tight. She knew another one would come. The rolling thunder made her insides vibrate, even with the muffled sound. She hated thunder. It terrified her since she was a little girl.

The alarm clock on the nightstand displayed the time, almost two o'clock. *No way I'm going back to sleep.* She ran to the window, hoping to see Andree rushing home.

White lighting ripped across the darkness in thin lines, like drunken spiders that played in the sky. Ana's jaw dropped, and her eyes opened wider at the spectacle.

"Whoa."

She squeezed her head between her hands again, knowing that after such a show of lights, a serious boom of thunder would shake the ground. Round, heavy rain drops came first, running along the window in tiny lines merging and separating out in a game of chase. In only seconds, a steady stream washed down the cold glass. As expected, the thunder followed.

Ana backed away from the vibrating window. The bottom of her feet recognized different patterns in the thickness of the carpet. With no sign of Andree, a sigh escaped her lips. She wrapped a robe around her body and yawned with a lazy move.

Unable to sleep, she joined everyone else downstairs for

a drink of water and maybe even one of those crunchy almond cookies that were in the kitchen at all times. She loved them. *Oh, never mind the water, I'll have a glass of milk.*

Mara and Daniel sat talking in hushed voices in the living room. Another rumble of thunder covered their words.

"Your Majesty." Daniel was the first to stand.

"The storm woke me, and there's no way I'm going back to sleep now."

"I can help you," Mara offered, jumping to her feet.

"No, please don't. I think I am going to have a couple of cookies and some water or milk."

"If Mike left any," Daniel joked and followed her to the kitchen with Mara at his side.

Mike sat at the island in the kitchen, enjoying some cookies with a glass of milk in front of him.

"Any of those left?" Ana asked, amused. "Where's Karl?"

"Right here, Your Majesty." Karl entered the room from behind her. "I had to check all the windows, make sure we weren't getting any of that rain inside."

Ana twirled toward the direction of his voice. The cold kitchen floor under her bare feet made her toes curl.

"Good call." Ana approved his initiative and darted across the frigid tiles, sliding onto a bar stool. "Anyone going to join us? We have cookies." She dangled the half-full bag over her head.

Everyone gathered around the large island Ana liked to refer to as "big enough to have its own government."

She poured herself a glass of milk and took a bite of one of the almond cookies, passing the bag around. Her elbows rested on the white marble top with black veins and speckles throughout.

"Mmm . . ." Her eyes closed with delight.

~ ~ ~

The small plane shook, fighting its way through the storm. Collin hated flying in weather like this just as much as—if not more than—the rough landing to come. Once on the ground, his group of ten ran quickly out of the aircraft and over the open field, into the forest nearby.

The storm intensified and rain came down in a heavy curtain. Their wet coats shone, soaked in the cold water, every time lightning flashed. *I hope we can take off in this weather once we have the human. We might have to leave in a hurry.* Collin led his people, but he kept glancing behind, making sure everyone followed.

He let nothing slow them down. "We have to keep going." He had to yell over the hammering of the rain. Collin and his group continued running with constant speed through the compact forest. After going up and over a couple of slippery hills, Collin stopped and scoured the surrounding area. In front of them, up the next hill, he located their objective.

"There." He pointed in the right direction, just to make sure there was no misunderstanding. They resumed their trot through the heavy rain. The well-maintained yard, covered now in water, made each inch they covered a test of agility.

With careful steps, Collin's group approached the house and divided into three predesignated groups. Two stood near the double windows, and the third in front of the back door.

For a couple of seconds, they didn't move a muscle, true dark statues under the downpour. Collin glanced at each of them and touched his right temple with his index and middle finger together. It was the signal they were all waiting for.

~ ~ ~

"Your Majesty, you should go back to sleep. Andree is going to kill us if . . ." Mike jumped to his feet drawing his sword.

Mara followed, and the crossed swords swished in her

hands, ready to slash through enemies. She sniffed the air. They all did.

"What is it?" Ana asked in a whisper.

Daniel and Karl flanked her, making their weapons ready as well. They couldn't all be wrong. A chill traveled her back.

"Uninvited guests," Karl whispered.

The next second, both double windows shattered. Hundreds of pieces of glass fell on the immaculate kitchen floor, only steps away from Ana. She jumped to her feet, knocking over the glass in front of her. Milk spilled on the marble countertop, over the half-eaten cookie, and then splashed to the floor. *What a mess.*

Her nostrils flared, her pupils dilated, and her heart fluttered like a hummingbird in distress. A small yelp escaped her lips at the sight of the group attacking them.

They flooded the kitchen through the broken windows and kicked in the back door. Hisses filled the air and fangs glimmered. There were ten of them, and Ana knew she and the others were in trouble, seriously outnumbered.

She took a couple of steps back and glanced at the kitchen knives in the slick, stainless steel support. She grabbed a chef's knife, one of the big ones, with a wide blade. Her tiny hand closed around the thick handle.

"Give us the human," one of the attackers demanded.

"Collin." Ana's eyes opened wide, and the blade shook in her hand.

"You are one sore loser." Daniel's sword slashed the air in front of him, forcing Collin back.

"Over my dead body." Hissing again, Mara stood her ground.

They formed a wall between Ana and the intruders quickly, protecting her from three sides. With the fridge behind her, Ana found herself surrounded.

"You heard her." Collin gave the signal and launched at Mara.

Karl killed the nearest attacker in one swift move. Mike did the same, and they were down to two enemies each.

Ana wanted to scream. Terror tightened around her throat. Out of instinct, she held the knife in front of her, ready to defend herself and her baby if any should pass the others.

Mara landed one clean stab right through the heart of one of the two she fought. Ana saw it happen, only steps away from her.

His body started to glow brighter and brighter. It seemed made of hot, burning lava. It exploded soundlessly, in tiny pieces of fire, only to turn into ashes the same instant. The black flakes of ash feathered on the white floor, and his weapons clinked on the cold ceramic tiles.

Almost a month ago, on the beach, darkness and distance stopped her from seeing any details. Now she did, and Ana shivered, terrified.

A scream attracted her attention just in time to see another one of the attackers turned into ashes. A painful growl caused Ana to turn her head back. A long cut along Mara's left arm glowed for a second. The glimmer dimmed down quickly and started to bleed. It wasn't a fatal wound, but Collin managed to hurt her. Ana opened her mouth to scream, but no sound came.

From the living room, Veronica ran into the kitchen. For the first time Ana saw her wearing something other than her dark gray uniform with long skirts. Suited up in leather armor, the maid rushed to her, with a dagger in her right hand.

Too terrified to smile, gratefulness filled Ana's eyes, and she lowered her knife, still holding it tight in her hand. They could use any help at this point.

Mike got hurt next. He growled, and Ana's head turned

in his direction. Her mind flew to Ella, and guilt suffocated her. *What if everyone dies because of me?*

People she cared about were getting hurt because of her. Everything happened too fast for her to follow. Tears started to stream down her face.

A cold blade pressed against her throat and stopped her from breathing. Veronica's arm held her across the chest, immobilizing her arms.

"I got her," Veronica dragged Ana toward the opened back door.

"What are you doing?" Ana trembled.

"I never doubted you, beautiful." Collin's answer rose over the sounds of swords and daggers.

Beautiful? What? They've been planning this together, all this time? Ana's mind slowly processed Collin's words.

"Veronica," Ana whispered, shocked. Her stomach tied into a knot, the taste of betrayal bitter in her mouth.

"Mike!" Ella jumped out of nowhere to her husband's side, taking on one of the two men he fought. "Are you okay?" she asked him, quickly glancing at his opened wound.

They are back. Andree is here. Hope sparked in Ana's mind.

"I'll be fine. Good timing," Mike added, focusing on the one attacker.

The torrential rain continued to downpour right behind her. They were a step away from the back door. Ana remembered the knife. With her hand still tight around the handle, she thrust it behind her with all the strength and desperation she could gather.

She figured at that point, she had nothing to lose. Ana knew she couldn't kill any of them, but she hoped for a break, anything to work in her advantage.

"You little bitch," Veronica murmured.

The resistance in the blade assured Ana she managed, at least, to hurt the woman betraying them, one tiny victory.

"Traitor."

The low growl came from behind them, and Ana recognized Andree's voice. For one split second, Veronica loosened her hold.

Jonas rushed in from the living room and yanked Ana into his arms, away from the cold blade. Waterdrops shimmered in his beard.

She turned around in time to see Andree severing Veronica's head. It fell on the floor with a thud, rolling a couple of times. Long, deep-brown hair partially covered the lifeless eyes before it turned into the same glowing amber as the rest of the slumped body.

"No!" Collin's scream rose above all other sounds.

He glanced at Veronica's ashes. Mara's sword cut a deep gash along the side his face, neck, and split his jacket open.

Veronica's blood dripped from the blade. Ana let go of the bloody knife and covered her mouth with her hands. Her domestic weapon of choice hit the white tiles and bounced back a couple of times with a cold clang. *I stabbed a vampire. I can't believe it.*

Ana stared at Andree between tears and strands of hair. He barely resembled the man she knew.

Soaked from the rain, water glistened on Andree's body. A small pool formed at his feet. His eyes, cold and empty, scanned his surroundings, evaluating the situation. Steel would've had more life in it.

Every muscle in his body tensed. He resembled a beast, ready to attack, and hissed. His fangs seemed longer than before, deadly weapons on their own. The sword in his right hand appeared huge, old and terrifying, an extension of the demon within.

Shiver after shiver coursed through Ana's body. She tried to be brave but found herself powerless. Her courage fell fast in front of enraged vampires. For the first time, she glimpsed inside and understood the world she wanted to be a part of. It wasn't a peaceful one.

Two more attackers screamed and vanished in flames. With only three left, Andree cut the air in front of him with his left hand.

"Enough of this." His voice boomed over the sounds of the combat, over the metal blades hitting and sliding against each other. "Yield or die. Choose."

The three remaining attackers knelt. From the focus and determination on Andree's face, it was clear he controlled their minds, and everyone exhaled with relief for the first time since the fight started.

"Who sent you?" His question, short and to the point, demanded an answer. Andree advanced to the middle of the kitchen, approaching the kneeling men. His heavy boots swooshed over the water mixed with ashes leaving an inky mess.

"Go to hell!" one of the three yelled.

Andree's sword made one fluid pass and separated the man's head from his body.

Ana's muffled yelp got ignored by everyone except Jonas. He held her close to him, safe. She searched for an emotion of any kind on Andree's face. She couldn't find any. He was colder than an ice sculpture. The man who held her, touched her, fathered her child had turned into a monster before her eyes.

"Wrong answer. Who sent you?" Andree stopped in the front of the next attacker in line.

"I will never tell you." The man spit at Andree.

"Your choice." Andree hissed, and the second man shared the same fate as the others.

His ashes joined the black mixture staining what used to be an immaculate floor.

Ana turned quickly and hid her face in Jonas's soaked

coat. She definitely didn't have the stomach for everything happening in front of her eyes.

"Time to switch strategies." She turned around in time to see him placing his sword in the special scabbard on his back.

With all his attention focused on Collin, Andree didn't even pay any attention to anyone else. The sole survivor of the group that attacked them started to moan in pain holding his head.

"Collin, we meet again, which is unfortunate for you." Andree kept an unnatural calm, more terrifying than if he had raised his voice. "Who sent you?"

"What are you doing to me?" Collin's voice revealed unbearable pain. A thin line of blood trickled from his left nostril.

"I will rip your mind to shreds and get the answers I want." Andree pointed to the other man's head. "Talk, or it will only get worse."

Collin clenched his teeth in agony and hunched forward refusing to talk. A phone buzzed in his pocket.

Andree retrieved the ringing device, and a single name flashed across the screen.

"Ivan . . ." The name flew off Andree's lips with a hiss.

A freezing void filled the large kitchen. Andree's hand closed into a fist, then relaxed. Ana's eyes followed the hypnotic dance of the muscles along his strong arms, under the wet skin. Serpents crawling came to her mind.

When the phone went silent, Andree hit the redial button and set it to video chat. A couple of rings broke the silence.

"Collin, my friend, tell me you . . ." Ivan's voice trailed off.

Andree turned the phone around, from Collin, to the scattered ashes and weapons, only to return to the kneeled man. In front of Ivan's eyes, Andree's sword plunged into Collin's chest. Ana covered her ears again and closed her eyes. She reopened them quickly, not wanting to miss anything.

A bright lava glow spread from Andree's blade, taking over Collin's convulsing body. The half of cookie she had before all hell broke loose did backflips in her stomach, threatening to come up. She fought to keep it down.

"Your men are dead. It is time for us to settle this." Andree's voice was unrecognizable. "Just you and me."

"You smug, arrogant bastard. I'm going to kill you!" Ivan yelled with frustration and anger.

"Pick a place and time. I will be there." Andree threw the phone on the floor and smashed it with the heel of his boot, on top of Collin's ashes.

Ana's robe was stained, her hands and face smeared with Veronica's blood.

Andree rushed to her. "Are you hurt?" He checked quickly, making sure it wasn't her blood.

She shook her head. The beast within him receded, letting the man she knew surface again.

"Are you all right?" Andree insisted, hugging her tight against him.

Ana shook her head again and held on to him. Her body shivered against his.

Daniel rushed to check everyone's injuries. They were superficial, mostly scratches, and he started to work quickly.

Andree took a few steps with Ana toward the living room.

"What is going on here?" A solemn voice came from the opened back door.

The rain had stopped. The smell of wet, saturated dirt filled the air, fresh and rich, and Ana liked it. A group of about twelve people stood in the doorway. Vampires.

"Who are you?" Andree asked, not letting go of Ana.

They seemed neither hostile, nor friendly. Hisses rose,

fangs glimmered, and a few weapons swished out of their scabbards.

"We are the Sentinels of the Sacred Grounds," answered one of the newcomers.

He seemed to be in charge. His auburn hair glistened in the cold, white light of the kitchen.

"That's a pretentious title," Jonas said, turning to the door with a smirk on his face.

"Jonas? You're alive?"

"George, my old friend." Jonas smiled and embraced the man, which brought a sigh of relief around the room.

George took a step back. His head tilted to the side.

"What am I sensing?" he asked and stared straight at Jonas.

"I thought your awareness dulled." Jonas stood tall. "Let me introduce you to two of the most important people you will ever meet. Prince Andree De Croix, of the Third Coven, and Princess Ana." He waved his hand in formal greeting as if introducing the King and Queen of England. "This is my friend, George Myers. He's as old as me. We were turned at the same time, by the same people."

"It is an honor, Your Majesties." George bowed. His eyes intently studied Ana. "You are human, but there is something about you."

Ana glanced at Andree, hardly controlling herself. *Here we go again.* She wanted to roll her eyes, but their guest seemed to be someone important, or at least his title implied so. She didn't want to be impolite.

"You are correct, my friend. Princess Ana is Vlad's blood descendant."

George took a step back and examined her for another few seconds. He dropped onto one knee, followed shortly by the men and the three women in his group.

"My Lady." His right hand covered the left side of his chest.

"If you do not mind, let us go into the living room. My wife is still shaken after everything that just happened." Andree waved at the weapons and ashes littering the floor.

Ana's legs barely supported her body. Coming back from the shock exhausted her. She sat next to Andree with Jonas on the other side. A few of the sentinels, silent and alert, entered the room with George. Most of them remained in the kitchen, with Daniel and the rest of the group. Ana allowed the tension in her neck to relax. They weren't enemies, at least, not at the moment.

"How is this possible?" George's confusion saturated the air.

"It will be morning soon." Jonas intervened before anyone could say another word. "Come, my friend, I will explain everything." He opened the door that hid a set of stairs. "Our Princess needs to rest." Jonas invited George to follow him into the basement.

"I appreciate it." Ana thanked Jonas and smiled with gratitude.

Andree rose and took a step. Ana grabbed his arm.

"Where are you going?" She swallowed hard.

"To the kitchen." He gently released her hold. "I will be right back. You are safe."

Andree stood in the kitchen's doorframe. With his head turned away from her, and his voice low, she couldn't hear him and wished she had his enhanced senses.

When he turned around, Andree voiced over his shoulder. "When the storm clears, we'll leave." He approached Ana.

"We're leaving?" Ana's eyes sparkled with curiosity and excitement. "Did you find the book?"

Andree lifted her in his arms.

"We did. It is why we came home early."

Chapter 19

Ana stared at the Mediterranean-style mansion in awe. The impressive manor surpassed any expectations. Bright-red clay tiles on the roof contrasted with the white walls and the lush, landscaped vegetation.

After the remainder of their honeymoon spent in Hawaii, they arrived home. Andree carried her in his arms inside, through the wide opened double doors.

A five-foot tall floral arrangement sat on a table in the middle of the round foyer, under the domed glass ceiling. The sweet and fresh scent of the multicolored flowers perfumed the air.

Immaculate white marble floors welcomed them, echoing under their steps.

She recognized the black marble crest and made a mental note to ask Andree what it symbolized. Ana had wanted to ask him or his mother since she first noticed it, but every time something else came up.

"Ready for the tour?" Andree took her by the hand and showed her their home.

She couldn't remember much from one room to the next, except her brand-new studio. He had surprised her by changing one of the multiple guest rooms into her painting heaven.

The room contained all her paintings from storage. Her old brushes along with some new ones, and enough paints to last her for a good while, lined one side of the room. Bright light coming through the glass wall caressed her paintings, breathing life into them. The sand sparkled under the rays of light, creating the illusion of movement on the canvas.

"Does this place come with a map?" Ana had to ask when they finally sat on the terrace with cold, refreshing drinks.

Andree's laughter warmed her heart. The lush backyard competed for her attention.

A large patio, partially shaded by a pergola, continued in a regular pattern to the swimming pool. Flat, white slabs of stone each lay separated from the next by a couple of inches of well-maintained grass.

On the right side, a swimming pool dominated, creating a true oasis—the absolute image of relaxation. White lounge chairs with deep-blue pillows neatly lined one side of the yard. At the opposite end, covered with white, light fabric wafting in the breeze, a cabana overlooked the crystal-clear water.

"You will get used to it in no time." Andree kissed her temple.

Ana smiled and turned to the rest of their backyard, the beach. Beyond the patio stones, a grassy area delighted her eyes, with groomed bushes strategically placed around majestic palm trees.

A path led to the beach. Ana couldn't wait to sink her feet into the fine grains. Turquoise waves stroked the white sand with every pass.

"Are you sure this is our home?" Ana asked, completely dazed. "Are we going to live here?"

"No. We broke into someone else's, and we are taking it over," Andree joked, and for a split second, she stared at him, stunned. "Of course, we are going to live here. Unless you do not like it and want to move."

His words made her laugh, cuddling closer to him. The light breeze carried the welcoming song of the waves mixed with the whispers of the lush palm tree leaves.

"What does the crest represent?" Ana toyed with the black medallion around Andree's neck.

"It is a shield, which means we are protectors." He indicated on the round coin like pendant. "The heart and the tree symbolize love and life. The sun and the moon stand for day and night." Andree touched each icon. "We are eternal protectors of life and love."

Guardians of life and love, and I married him to become a vampire.

~ ~ ~

"A grandmother." The Queen's eyes darted back and forth, from Andree to Ana. "Are you sure?"

"Daniel confirmed." Andree leaned back on the couch in his mother's suite.

"When did you find out?" Queen Emelia clasped her hands together with sparkling eyes.

"A few days ago, but we wanted to tell you in person." Ana smiled and laced her fingers with Andree's.

"Wait, there's more. Jonas managed to translate the part in the book about the alternative way of turning." Joy filled his heart. "There is another way, and it will be possible for Ana to retain most of her humanity." Aware of the increased danger, Andree planned to start training for the new method. He knew he would need all the restraint he could muster to pass the self-control test.

"How difficult is going to be?" Concern creased the Queen's forehead.

Andree kissed Ana's hand and refocused his attention on his mother. "The way we all know involves a five to ten seconds bite. Simple and efficient, it stood the test of time."

"And the new one?" Queen Emelia leaned forward.

"The new method, more complicated, involves an initial bite for five seconds, then a release for three." Andree wrapped his arm around Ana's shoulders. "The second one must last exactly three seconds with a five seconds release, followed by a last bite for another three seconds." He sensed Ana's excitement and had to smile—a bitter-sweet smile. Andree was concerned about the release times when he had to let go. A one-second delay could cost him Ana's life. He had two months to practice.

~ ~ ~

Ana hardly contained the excitement about her turning ceremony and the preparations already started. Her dream, her fantasy, finally in her reach, was about to become reality.

During the next few days, she noticed Andree's wariness. "What troubles you?"

"It is this new turning method. I have been working on it every night, but I still have trouble with the release times."

His concern caused Ana to ask for details. "What do you mean, trouble with the release?"

After a deep, heavy sigh, he explained everything. He didn't hide that one second off the timing could kill her.

"Can I help in any way?" Ana leaned back, on the soft cushion.

Andree smiled and touched the side of her face, caressing her jaw. Ana tilted her chin, resting her head in the palm of his hand. It relaxed her every time and brought her the feeling of safety.

"This is all on me. I have to get those times right. You just take care of our baby." His other hand covered her still-flat stomach.

Ana smiled back, her eyebrows shot up, and she leaped from the couch.

"Ana." Andree reached for her, but she slipped through his fingers and ran to the bathroom, emptying the contents of her stomach. It had become a daily occurrence.

"I am calling Daniel." Andree took his phone out and

swiped his finger on the screen. "There must be something he can do."

"I don't think there is. This is normal, at least as far as I know." She plopped on the couch to rest.

About a half hour later, Daniel dropped by. "How are my two favorite people doing?"

"Why, I didn't know you cared." Andree smirked and drew Ana into his arms, cocooning her to his chest.

"I wasn't talking about you." Daniel approached and sat across from them.

"As my mother would say, *touché.*" Andree smiled and kissed the top of Ana's head.

"How are you feeling?" Daniel's attention shifted to her.

"Okay, a little sick earlier, but I don't think we should have bothered you. It wasn't the first time." She glared at Andree, then reached for a handful of nuts.

Daniel shook his head slowly and turned his attention to his friend. "How's the bite training going?"

"I'm concerned about the timing." Andree sat and released Ana from his embrace.

"I already know you will get it. It's a matter of practice." Daniel hesitated for a couple of seconds.

"What are you not saying?" Andree noticed Ana's stretched hand, trying to reach a plate with snacks, and passed it to her.

She smiled and bit a cookie. Since her earlier incident, she was famished.

"At your wedding ceremony, when you tasted her blood, one drop was enough to bring your fangs out. You controlled yourself admirably that time, but will you be able to do it through this turning process?" Daniel stared at his friend with inquiring eyes.

"I have to," Andree answered without the slightest hesitation.

"Can he train on me?" Still confused, Ana figured it wouldn't hurt to ask.

"Sort of . . ." Daniel stopped again for a brief second. "I can draw a little of your blood every couple of days so he can get used to the taste."

"No." Andree jumped off the couch, clearly against the idea.

"You won't be able to control yourself when you need it most. Look at you. Just the memory of her blood makes you react." Daniel pointed to Andree's fangs.

Ana glanced at him and noticed the reaction, even if he turned his head away in an effort to hide it.

"Do it," Ana said. "I'll be fine." She opened the wrapper of a chocolate bar.

"No, she needs her blood. She needs all the strength for the baby."

"I'll only draw a couple of vials every other day, right before you go to sleep, that way you won't have any discomfort." Daniel watched her chewing the chocolate with crunchy nuts and dried fruits. "Your body will regenerate quickly such a small amount. It's safe."

"I am not comfortable with it." Andree insisted to make his opinion known.

"Would you be more comfortable gambling with her life?"

Andree lowered his head.

"Starting today, I'll be here every night and help you train. Trust me, Andree, you need to do this right or don't even think about it."

~ ~ ~

"For crying out loud, brother, the woman said *no* to you three times. Don't you have any pride at all? We need to reach a decision."

"What does my pride have to do with any of this?"

Gabriel argued back and forth with Mihai for almost two months, since Ivan's first visit. His subsequent appointments only fueled the disagreement.

"She doesn't want you. Get over it and let's end them." Mihai clasped his brother's shoulder.

"This is not about Queen Emelia." Gabriel shook his head. "I do not believe starting a war will make things better for any of us." He took a couple of steps away from Mihai. "Yes, I have tried to form an alliance with the Third Coven, and I am not giving up." His chin jotted forward. "They would be powerful allies." Gabriel stood his ground, staring at his brother. He was determined.

"It's obvious to me they don't want an alliance. For the past two hundred years they only confirmed their arrogance." A glimmer of anger sparkled in his eyes. "I'm done with their superiority complex." Mihai cut the air in front of him with his right hand.

"It is not a complex. I have spent more time with them, I know them better." As a younger brother, he always felt he had to prove himself more. "The Third Coven is superior." Gabriel won himself a growl from his brother.

"That woman has you under her spell." Mihai pointed an index finger toward his brother. "You have feelings for her, and they are clouding your judgment right now."

"I do not. It is purely business."

"Then why not sign a treaty? Why do you want to marry her?"

Under Mihai's scrutiny, Gabriel took a few steps in silence. "Everything we have ever done, all that we are, makes us just as good, if not even better than royalty." The younger brother turned and faced his older one. "I want the damn recognition. Happy now?" He growled.

"I had no idea." Mihai tilted his head to the side. "Recognition would be nice, yes, and a royal in our family would do nicely, but you have to admit, it is not happening."

"And declaring war would help us how?" Gabriel insisted, stubborn. He always fought for what he believed in. This time was no different.

"They have been a pain in our . . . side, for long enough. It is time to eliminate them." Mihai pointed somewhere toward the door, frustration evident in his tone.

"Why? Because a complete nobody came to us crying they stole a human from him?" Gabriel clasped his hands behind him. "His dinner? I do not trust this Ivan guy." He shook his head.

"I don't trust him either. It's why I had him followed and investigated. Nothing notable in his past, you are correct, he's a nobody." Mihai volunteered the information gathered. "Aside from a girlfriend he's visiting a couple of times every week, the rest of his time is spent recruiting. He genuinely hates the Third Coven."

"And you share his feelings? Are you prepared to go to war against your own kind? It is wrong, Mihai." Gabriel tried to reason with him. *Why does he have to be this stubborn? Oh, because we are brothers, that's why. Damned genes.*

After a few seconds of silence, Mihai sat in one of the two impressive, throne-like chairs. The old, dark-colored wood creaked under the weight of his body. A deep crease marked his forehead, and he ran his right hand through his long, blond hair. The black onyx stone in his ring shone under the discreet lights attracting Gabriel's attention.

"Ivan will be here any second now. We have been keeping him waiting long enough. I'm ready to do what must be done with or without you."

Standing in front of his brother, Gabriel tilted his head curtly. "Then without me it is." He spoke with a calm tone and sat in his chair.

Gabriel glanced at his own ring, identical to his brother's. They were gifts from their father. Vlad's ring and sword sat in one of their vaults, waiting for another in their bloodline.

Silence covered him, uncomfortable, suffocating. Gabriel was grateful for Ivan's punctuality, and Mihai seemed relieved by the interruption.

~ ~ ~

"Everything is under control now. I have to admit, I could not have done it without your help these past couple of months. Thank you."

Ana smiled and tried to control the sweet tingles Andree's kiss sent through her body. He laughed and closed his arms around her.

"What's so funny?"

"You are still trying to fight the way I make you feel, refusing to let go." A light sadness appeared in Andree's eyes, and she saw it.

"Is there something wrong?"

"I will miss you, so much. I am not sure how this new method will work." Andree sighed. "I wish I knew more."

Ana rested her hand in the middle of his chest. His sharp breath reminded her of how her touches affected him. Not much different from the way she reacted to his, she imagined.

"Since tonight is your last night as a human, what do you want to do?" He covered her hand with his. "Anything you want. Name it."

Ana stared into his deep blue eyes, as mesmerizing as ever. The three months she had spent with him flashed in her mind. He had not made one mistake, hadn't let her down in any way. Each day she had to put more and more effort in keeping her heart safe.

"I want to be with you." The words left her lips without her consent.

She didn't need enhanced senses or special powers to see the tenderness in his eyes. His chest rose then froze, motionless, under her hand. A few seconds later, slowly, he resumed breathing.

"Anything you want, my Princess. Anything." His whisper carried tension, promise, and an overcharge of lust.

Ana took the vial from his hand with a shy smile. All her senses stirred and were on heightened alert.

"I won't need this anymore," she whispered and sipped the last few drops left.

"True. It is the last time." He threw the bottle carelessly on one of the nearby chairs.

Ana shivered with desire under his deep gaze.

Andree slowly walked a close circle around her, the tension sparking between them. His index finger traced a thin line from her neck, across her shoulder, and back over her collarbone.

His hot touch planted tiny droplets of lava all along, searing through her skin. Ana surrendered to his enchantment. She didn't stand a chance. Not that she wanted to.

For hours they held onto each other, and she relished the feel of his body against hers. Before the elixir wore out, Ana rested her head on his shoulder.

"I hope you will forgive me." His whisper caused Ana to stare at him.

She sat and gathered the white sheet around her form. "Forgive you? Andree, it's what I want. I came to your mother and asked to become one of you." Her fists closed on the soft silk. "Of course, I never knew I was going to find you. All I wanted was to become a vampire." Ana lowered her eyes. "There's nothing to forgive. All I can think of is to thank you, for everything you've given me." She knew she hadn't been entirely fair to him. She had kept her guard up all this time. Sometimes it was so hard to do, she had been tempted to move on.

Andree lounged on his back, with one arm bent under his head. His other hand reached to touch her jawline with the back of his fingers. A tiny smile tugged at the corner of his lips.

"You will change. You will not feel the way you do now. Everything will be different for you, even the way you see the world around us." A tiny devilish light glimmered in his eyes, and Andree hugged her to him. "You will be more passionate. You will not hold back anymore. I am looking forward to that part."

"I'm sure you are."

Andree laughed, and that sound feed her soul. Nothing could touch her while he held her. His body was her fortress.

~ ~ ~

Ivan sat heavily on the comfortable couch in Karina's living room. She remained the only one he fully trusted. That morning, exhaustion caught up with him.

"How did it go?"

He glanced in the direction of her voice. Karina's new hair color suited her. The bright orange flame screamed unusual, but it made her eyes seem deeper, her freckles almost disappeared.

"Not bad. It could've been better, but it could've been a lot worse."

"Are you going to make me guess?" Her playful tone brought a smile to Ivan's lips.

He hadn't smiled since Collin's death before his eyes, courtesy of Prince Andree. Ivan had to hold back a hiss at the memory.

"Mihai and the First Coven are behind me. I have his full support. His brother chose to stay neutral. However, he granted us free passage through his territory."

"That is good news, no?"

"Yes. I would've preferred both of them join me, but I guess I have to take what I can get. I'll have to recruit more." He stretched, the first signs of tiredness settling in.

"The sun will rise soon." Karina checked on the draperies, making sure to light-proof the room. With a seductive sway of her hip and a sparkle in her eyes, she turned to Ivan.

"What if you send some of the people you trust further? They could recruit from Europe, from all over the world."

Ivan weighed her idea. He needed as many people as he could gather. He had promised himself he would avenge his friend's death.

"Not a bad idea at all. I don't expect miracles, though. The further out we go, the lower our chances drop. Those people are not affected by the Third Coven. They have no reason to join us." Ivan thought out loud and Karina tilted her head.

"Maybe, maybe not." Her words came out in a partial purr.

"What are you not saying?" Ivan gazed at her with increased attention.

"The turning ceremony for their Princess is tomorrow. There will be guests coming from all over the world." She toyed with a lock of her bright hair. "And in case you haven't heard, there's quite a stir about that book of theirs."

Her whispered comment made Ivan's lips curl into another smile. She had a point. The Third Coven was known over the whole world. Not everyone liked them, either.

"That's good news. I'll send some people out in the next few days. I'll have to pick up the pace as well." Ivan hugged her to him and she smiled.

"In that case, we should celebrate."

"We should," he agreed. "What do you have in mind?"

Rising, Karina released the tie of her dress, allowing the fabric to slide down her curvy frame. Stepping out of the gown, she offered her hand, and lead him into the bedroom.

Plans swirled around in his head, but in the darkness of the room, one thought, one desire, tugged harder. Ivan drew his lovely cohort into the middle of the bed.

Chapter 20

Andree hated himself. As much as he tried, he couldn't share Ana's excitement. The day her fantasy would become reality found him unprepared. To him, it was the singular moment he would literally suck humanity out of her.

He couldn't tear his eyes from her, not even for a few seconds. Andree knew he had to turn her, but he couldn't ignore the part of him that wanted her to stay human, fragile, and innocent.

Ana's humanity attracted him in the first place. He loved how she blushed, the way she slept, peaceful in his arms. Even her tears were beautiful, tiny drops of sadness or happiness with a dash of salt and shimmer.

Her fragility empowered him. Yes, in his selfishness, he had hoped to keep Ana in need of him. He would have been more than happy to continue providing protection the same way he offered his heart. If the predictions were right, she would become the most powerful vampire since Vlad. She would not need his protection anymore.

In his opinion, humans were innocent, the beasts inside them dormant. With the first drink of blood, Ana would have to face the demon inside her.

Andree remembered the night in Transylvania, when they had to fight. She saw his inner beast for the first time. That night he had let him surface, he needed him. He sensed her fear of his beast.

"What's going on with you?" Mike's question interrupted his thoughts.

"I do not want her to change." Andree leaned against the doorframe to the terrace and crossed his ankles.

"With the new turning method, she'll preserve most of her human side, no? Wasn't that why you needed the book?"

"Yes, but what exactly does it mean? How much?" He fidgeted with his phone. "What will she lose?" Andree let out the torturing questions.

"You know you have to turn her. It's the only way you can keep her alive."

"I know. There is no question about it. I cannot imagine life without her. I wish I knew how much of her I'll lose in the process."

"Think of how much you will gain." His friend leaned in briefly, as if he had just shared the biggest secret of the century.

Andree stared at Mike, awakened from what seemed like a nightmare. The truth hit him like a hammer. He would gain an eternity with her.

Daniel came next to visit, a few minutes later, and found Andree and Ana in each other's arms, laughing.

"That's always a good sign." He tilted his head.

"Daniel, come in. What brings you by?" Andree loosened his hold on Ana and she stepped aside, snacking on some fresh mixed fruits and bits of various cheeses. To his satisfaction, lately, she was hungry all the time.

"This." Daniel handed him a vial of blood.

"I went out last night and fed, just like every night for the past two weeks."

Daniel nodded. "This is the last of Ana's blood. I saved it for today. You should drink it before the ceremony."

"No need. I am fine." Andree rejected the vial.

"This must be safe for her, so drink it." Daniel poked Andree's chest with a finger. "Don't forget that I'll be right there with you, counting the seconds."

"About that . . ." Andree finally pocketed the tiny container, "if you see I have a hard time releasing, please pull her away from me." Andree waited for his friend's promise.

"I'm not sure I can do it. Andree, you're stronger than anyone I know. I don't think anyone could."

"My mother, Mara, and Karl will be there, too. I already asked them the same thing. I need to know that if I am losing it, someone will be there for Ana." Andree pleaded, worried the worst would happen.

"All right, I'll do everything I can." Daniel left after his promise, leaving them alone.

Ana gazed into his eyes. His smile sent hundreds of butterflies migrating through her body, and he sensed every single one of them.

~ ~ ~

With only a few minutes to spare, Ana entered the living room. Andree waited for her. He wore his black leather pants and boots but replaced his usual vest with a white shirt.

A simple white silk dress, elegant and classy, fit her perfectly. The cuffed sleeves made her appear more fragile. For the millionth time, Andree wondered what it was about her that gave her all the power she had over him. *Is it her humanity or Vlad's blood?*

Ana's long, black hair all gathered on the right side of her neck, left the other side exposed.

His eyes found the tiny spot where her pulse throbbed under delicate skin. The thought that in a few minutes he would taste her blood caused him to react. His tongue sampled the air and licked his lips with anticipation.

Andree took out the vial Daniel gave him and drank her blood, hoping it would help with the sudden craving. The edge of the vial touched his fangs. The clinkering sound made him close his eyes for a second and take another deep breath. *I can do this.*

Deep inside, he knew her fresh blood would be his ultimate test.

"Are you all right?" Ana's concern brought him back to reality faster.

"I am now. Everything will be fine." His fangs receded.

Andree seized her hands into his and stared into her eyes again. The same sadness as before surfaced.

"Please forgive me for what I am about to do. It is the only way to keep you with me forever."

"No, thank you for what you are about to do. All I want is to be like you," Ana answered and wrapped her arms around his neck.

Andree buried his nose in her hair, closed his eyes and inhaled her essence. Her scent, which he savored more than life, would change, too.

~ ~ ~

As soon as Ana entered the full amphitheater, everyone rose to their feet in silence. Eyes, unblinking like those in a doll maker's shop, stared with empty gazes. The guests waited for her and Andree to take their places, by the Queen. After a silent, collective bow, the guests sat. There were more than she had expected—far more in attendance than both prior ceremonies.

The news about the book Jonas worked tirelessly to translate stirred all the vampires in the world. Some accepted the proof of their origin. Others, undecided, needed more information. A good portion rejected the idea they had alien blood coursing through their veins. They were more split than ever, and imminent conflict loomed over their society.

Ana noticed Jonas, Mike, and Ella sitting together in the first row of seats. Her friend sent her an encouraging smile. Right beside them, George with a few of his sentinels nodded toward her. At least for the time being, for safety reasons, her true origin remained a secret. Mara and Karl both stood behind Ana and Andree. Daniel joined them next.

Her last moments as a human found her more eager than ever.

"Princess Ana, we all know you want to become one of us, but I have to ask you one more time." The Queen started the ceremony with a slight smile on her lips. "Are you here of your own free will, asking to be turned into one of us?"

"Yes." Ana's answer echoed in the crammed amphitheater.

"Very well, your wish will be granted. Prince Andree, when you are ready." Queen Emelia nodded to her son.

Andree turned to Ana and held her shoulders in his hands. His eyes plunged deep into her soul.

~ ~ ~

"I love you." Andree, seeking to spare her the pain, used his magnetism on her for the last time. He bit into Ana's soft skin and tasted her blood. Warm, sweet, thick, the life-giving fluid sent all his senses in a frenzy. Time slowed around him.

With his left arm, Andree held her against his body. His right hand supported her head under the soft, luscious hair.

One. Two. I do not remember having such a hard time counting, not even as a kid. Ana's warm breath brushed on his skin and made the short hairs on the back of his neck stand.

Three. Andree swallowed the first mouthful of blood and closed his eyes in pleasure. It tasted better than the one in the vials, fresh, straight from her veins.

Four. More blood filled his mouth. He heard Ana's heart beating slow. His raced.

Five. He released and swallowed again. Her blood spread into his body just as his venom dispersed into hers causing her heart to pick up the pace. The irreversible reaction had started.

Three seconds of release ended fast, and he bit again.

One. These must be the longest seconds in my life. Two. I have to release, I have to. His inner demon surfaced. The blood beckoned him, and Andree had to fight. He had to win and not kill the woman he loved.

Three. He released her again.

Even with all his attention focused on Ana, Andree heard the guests moving in their seats, impatient. Their clothes rustled against the pillows they sat on.

His inner beast demanded more blood. Another three seconds stood between Ana's immortality and her death.

One. Two more seconds. I can do this. I have to. Two.

The last second seemed the longest. His venom sped Ana's heart even more. Her blood mixed already. It still tasted sweet. *Three.*

Andree released her quickly. Blood stained the silky skin on her neck. A few drops ran in a thin line from the corner of his lips. *Now you are what you wanted. I can have you forever.*

He executed the bite to perfection. Andree scooped her up in his arms and turned around showing off to the crowd the fresh, still bleeding bite marks on her neck. All the guests rose to their feet cheering, welcoming her into their world. Daniel quickly cleaned the wounds and covered them with a bandage.

Andree didn't allow himself to enjoy the moment. Her inert body, in his arms, reminded him she wouldn't wake up the same.

He rushed Ana inside their suite. Mara and Maggie, her new maid, changed her out of the bloodstained dress into comfortable clothes.

Andree sat beside her on the edge of the bed and held her hand in his. The taste of her blood still coated his mouth, lingered on his lips.

Ana opened her eyes. "Andree."

"Everything is all right, my love." He brushed away from her face a few imaginary hairs. In reality, he only wanted to touch her. "You are going to be fine. Save your strength."

"How did it go?" Ana cradled her abdomen. "Our baby?"

"It went well. You both did great. Now rest."

Ana fought to stay awake. Her eyes closed in spite of her effort. "Thank you," she managed to whisper and tried to lift her hand to touch him. She fell unconscious again. Her hand collapsed on the bed.

Andree smiled and lifted her hand, kissed it and placed it on his cheek. He knew it was what she wanted to do.

To his surprise, in only minutes, Ana started to burn with fever. It was supposed to take hours, maybe a day, before the first symptoms.

"Mara, I need some iced water and a wash cloth." Andree didn't take his eyes off Ana. "Everything will be all right," he whispered.

Mara quickly brought the cold water. A few ice cubes floated, hitting the walls of the glass bowl with a refreshing song.

Andree soaked the washcloth in it for a few seconds before squeezing all water out and started to wipe Ana's face. He needed to lower her temperature.

Powerless, Andree watched her fighting the pain, the convulsions. When she arched her back and let out her first hiss, Andree saw her bleeding gums. The fangs broke through, and a cold sweat covered her whole body. *After only two hours?* Andree asked for more ice and continued to wipe her body in an effort to make her comfortable.

Daniel came to check on her first. "How is she?"

"I am not sure." Andree hesitated. "She is progressing way too fast."

"What do you mean?" Daniel rushed to her side.

"She already has her fangs." Andree lifted her upper lip a little, revealing the bleeding gums.

"Usually the fangs break out in the second or third day. You're right." Daniel nodded, a crease marked his forehead. "This is fast."

A new convulsion interrupted them. Ana rolled on one side and gathered her knees to her chest. The very next second, she arched her back with another hiss.

"Could you check if the baby is all right?" Andree's pleading eyes turned to his friend.

"Sure, if you can manage to keep her still."

As soon as Daniel touched her, her eyes opened wide and empty.

"Hmm . . . Hold her," Daniel leaned over the bed.

"Hmm? What is going on? What's wrong?" Andree panicked, trying to keep her still.

He was used to her being a human. Now she grew strong, and fast. Out of habit, he touched her as gently as he could. He didn't want to hurt her.

Only hours before, he could have immobilized her without any effort. Now, she fought back. She became fast, nimble, and her wet, slippery skin made it harder. In spite of the frustration, and worry, Andree found it amusing.

"Nothing is wrong. It's just . . . Damn it, if she would stop moving for a few seconds." Daniel's frustration produced tension.

"What is going on?" Andree asked Mara for help with one quick glance.

"Calm yourself." Daniel took Andree's right hand and placed it on Ana's abdomen.

"What is it?" Andree asked, panic still present in his voice.

"Something incredible. Just relax and free your senses," Daniel instructed.

Under his touch, Ana calmed. The convulsions stopped. Her whole body relaxed, covered in a sheer layer of sweat.

"I can sense him. Or her. This is amazing." Andree lifted his smiling face to his friend.

"Tell me what you sense." Daniel continued to hold his hand in place.

"His heart. This is . . . Wait, Ana's too?" Confusion replace the worry in Andree's tone. "No, it is not hers. It is like there are two hearts."

"There are." Daniel nodded with a happy smile spreading over his face. "You are having twins."

The word *twins* exploded in his mind. Andree remembered it was Ana's dream since her teenage years. She even had their names picked out.

"Are you sure?" Andree insisted, afraid it would be a mistake.

"Yes, I can see them. I have no idea how I didn't see them until now, but she is always moving and it's not easy. Besides, you can sense both of them now that they are just over ten weeks."

"She is going to be so happy." Andree brushed away a strand of wet hair from Ana's face. "My love, we are going to have twins," he whispered and kissed her icy forehead.

A new wave of convulsions caused her to moan and wiped Andree's smile right off his face.

"Can you do anything about this pain? Can you help her in any way?" Andree hurt as much as she did.

Daniel shook his head. "No. You know as well as I do, there's nothing anyone can do." He clasped Andree's shoulder. "She has to go through it on her own. Nothing would work now."

Queen Emelia and Jonas found Ana running a high fever again, almost an hour later.

"How is she doing?" The Queen asked from the doorway.

Jonas rushed to the bed and touched Ana's head. "She's burning up." He removed the cloth on her forehead, dunked it, and replaced it.

"Mother, come over here," Andree waved his mother in.

"What is it?" She quickly approached.

Andree took his mother's hand and placed it over Ana's abdomen, just like Daniel had done earlier.

Ana's agitation intensified. She turned her head away and hissed loudly, forcing Andree to hold her hands again.

"Open your senses," he whispered to his mother.

"The baby is already so strong. I can feel . . . Wait." The Queen hesitated, an inquiring stare in her eyes. "What is this? I can feel two. You are having twins?" The realization came to her, bringing a smile on her lips.

Andree nodded, and showed her Ana's fangs.

"Already?" A crease marked his mother's forehead, and she glanced at Jonas. "This is not normal."

"It's supposed to be a faster than normal transition," Jonas murmured. "I thought it might be a day or two shorter, but at this pace, she will be done in a couple of days or less."

"Please, go back to that book and see what else you can find out." The plea in Andree's voice put Jonas in motion.

"I am going right now." After a quick bow, the oldest vampire alive left the room in a hurry.

The Queen touched Andree's shoulder and smiled.

"She is already so much stronger. Everything will be fine. You are doing a great job keeping her comfortable."

"I have never been this powerless before. If I could take on this pain myself, I would." Andree's whisper filled the quiet room.

"Think of how she would feel if you were not here with her." His mother's warm, encouraging smile gave him back his confidence.

Usually, transitioning young vampires were isolated. Most would be violent, a threat to everyone around them. Even if Ana had tried to attack him or anyone else, Andree knew he could overpower her. Her possible outbursts didn't concern him, only her safety and the twins mattered, nothing else.

During the transition process, fledgling vampires wake. He didn't want her to be alone, isolated, scared of the changes she would notice. He wanted to be there for her, for their babies.

Unable to aid the process, the Queen and Mara left the room.

"I will leave you two alone. Everyone is nearby if you need us." Daniel let Andree know before he exited and closed the door behind him.

Ana looked peaceful for a change, at least for the moment. Andree glanced over at the clock: almost four hours into transition.

Her temperature dropped again. She had been going from hot to cold and back to hot within seconds. He caressed the side of her face gently, with the back of his hand.

Andree wanted to let her know he was there and carefully probed in her mind. Even if unconscious, she could hear him.

"You are doing great, my love. Try to stay calm, relaxed, and accept the change. Do not fight it. You are going to be one tough little vampire. And we are going to have twins."

Chapter 21

"Andree." Ana opened her eyes. She had whispered his name all during her transition, and every time his heart rushed.

"Ana, you are doing great, my love."

He kissed her hand and caressed her forehead. Her temperature had been normal for a while now.

Ana rewarded him with a smile and touched his arm. "Can I have some water?"

"Of course. Are you sure you want water?" Andree hesitated for a second, and she nodded. He poured some into a glass and held it in front of her.

Thirsty, Ana drank almost all of it.

"How are you feeling?"

"Tired and sore, like the biggest possible truck hit me. I had a weird dream, too. You were telling me that we were having twins." She returned the glass, and Andree placed it back on the nightstand.

"That was not a dream, it is true."

Ana sat, all her tiredness and soreness seemed to vanish with the news. "What? Are you sure?"

He nodded and hugged her close to him. "Yes, even now, I sense them inside you. My mother did too, and Daniel confirmed it. Oh, and you almost bit them." Andree remembered her earlier reactions.

"Really?" Her brows furrowed. "I'm so sorry."

"It is fine. You didn't. You just hissed at everyone touching you, except me." He winked. "I feel special."

Ana gazed in his eyes. "You are."

Andree pulled back and examined her carefully, holding her chin up.

"What is it?"

"Welcome to the family." Andree rushed and grabbed a mirror, holding it in front of her.

Ana stared at her reflection. "I have the lights in my eyes just like yours and your mother's."

"Yes, but yours are gold."

"That looks so cool." Her contagious excitement and giggles widened Andree's grin. "What about fangs? Do I have them, too?" She checked her mouth quickly, pressing a finger to her gums. "Oow." A moan of pain escaped her lips.

"Yes, you do. They are tiny and very, very sharp."

Andree set the mirror down and moved closer, wrapping his arms around her.

"How long has it been?" Her question tickled his neck, her lips touched his skin, and his senses stirred wild.

"Four hours. You are progressing way faster than any of us thought." Andree tried to remain in control of his own body. "Jonas went to see if he can find any more information in the book."

"That's it? I thought I read in one of the books your mother gave me that fangs show up on the second or third day." Her heart raced. "Is it bad I got them already?"

"No. It is unusual, and with the different bite, we are not sure what to expect."

The gold lights in her eyes intensified.

"You are so beautiful." His whisper left his lips without consent. Not that he would've opposed it.

Ana jumped on his lap with her legs on either side of his hips. Mischief settled clear in her now almost golden eyes.

"Ana, we cannot do this now." Andree tried to find reason and gently pushed her away. "You are still in transition." He loved the changes in her so far.

"I want to see how it is." One of her hands slipped under his shirt. Her whisper awakened desire deep in his core. Andree's breath caught in his chest. He found it impossible to resist her.

"Ana . . ."

"Is this my blood on your shirt?"

"Mmm . . ." Andree knew her senses would be wild, and she would have no idea how to control them. He bet she wasn't fully aware of what she was doing.

"Then we need to take it off." With one quick move, Ana ripped his shirt off.

She let go of the soft fabric and covered her mouth with both her hands. "I'm so sorry. I've never done this before."

"I forgot to tell you that you are a lot stronger now. I needed help earlier to hold you," he managed to say before the cold air and her touch ignited his skin. She seemed to be aware now, but he was losing the battle with self-control.

Gently, he took her hands into his, and kissed them one at a time. He fought the lust hitting him in waves.

Her top came off next. It was the end of Andree's control. His hiss met one of her own, filling the room. He rolled her under him in the oversized bed.

~ ~ ~

"So, this is how it's supposed to be," Ana whispered after she recovered, completely lost in his cobalt eyes.

"Being a vampire is good for you." Andree caressed her back. "And for me." He placed a kiss on her shoulder.

"I'm not the fragile human anymore." She snuggled against him, holding him tight. "You don't have to worry about breaking my bones."

"True." A chuckle passed his lips.

Her giggle soothed his soul and claimed his racing mind. He'd been worried about her transition. To see her now, like this, lightened the weight on his heart.

"I'm going to take a shower. Interested?" Ana's sultry voice and the provocative sway of her hips filled his heart and delighted all of his senses.

"If I ever say no to that, please just stake me and put me out of my misery. It means I have lost my mind."

He scooped her into his arms between laughs and tight hugs. She clung to him, like her life depended on it.

With the shower done, Andree wrapped a towel around his waist and turned to Ana.

"I'm a little dizzy." Her body swayed and she collapsed.

Andree caught her before she hit the warm floor tiles and took her quickly back to the bed. Through his link with Daniel he called to him, and asked Maggie to get her some clothes.

Ana returned to transition and Andree couldn't wipe the smirk off his face.

Daniel rushed into the room. "Is she okay?"

Andree reached for a shirt. *At least I managed to put my pants on.*

"What's going on?" Daniel's question brought a little guilt in Andree's eyes.

He was half-dressed, and Ana had different clothes on. The air around saturated with the scent of her soap—a dead give-away of what had happened.

"Did you two . . .?" His friend narrowed his eyes with suspicion.

"She woke up and seduced me," Andree admitted with an impish grin on his face.

"Have you lost your mind? Don't you know you can't do that while she's transitioning?"

Andree noted his friend's effort to remain serious.

"I couldn't resist her." Andree finally managed to get a shirt on after two tries. He couldn't find the sleeves. "Trust me, I tried."

"This could influence her transition. I have no idea what else to tell you." Daniel glanced at his friend. "Try and keep your distance this time." A half-furious and half-amused smile tugged at his lips.

"Yeah. Not so sure that will work." Andree still fought with the buttons of the crisp white shirt.

"I might have found . . . something." Jonas walked in the bedroom with Queen Emelia.

They both stopped. The tension between Andree and Daniel thickened. The fragrant soap smell lingered in the room mixed with the aftermath of their union.

"Ana is wearing different clothes." Anger flickered in the Queen's eyes. "Her hair is wet and no longer up."

"Yes, we can all see . . ." Andree still fidgeted with one of the last buttons of his new, clean shirt.

"Please tell me you didn't . . ." Jonas spoke the words before the Queen could.

"Yes, we did. All right? Why is everyone so surprised? She woke up, she was fine and—" Andree wasn't going to try and hide how he felt about his wife.

"And now you're going to transition as well." Jonas finished the sentence, and everyone stared at him.

"What?" Andree took several steps back. "That is the most absurd thing I ever heard."

"Call your assistants." He turned to the Queen. "We are probably going to need everyone." Approaching Andree, he motioned to the edge of the bed. "Your Majesty, you are going into transition, so please, take a seat." At Jonas's insistence, Andree sat on the edge of the bed. "I found, in the book, one of the side-notes explaining how making love with a transitioning new vampire would force both into it, together."

"You must have misread something in the translation." He caressed Ana's arm. "I was born this way, I don't transition."

"Yes." Jonas stopped for a second then continued. "But this is a different process."

Andree ran his hand through his still-wet hair and glanced at Ana. Finally, his smirk was gone.

"You will share the same powers." Jonas ventured into the details. "You have created a common pool, and both of you shall now share everything, including abilities. I would not be surprised if the children do as well."

"Are you sure?" Andree doubted him.

"Yes. I found this before in my readings."

"And you didn't think to say anything?"

"In my defense, your Majesty, I shouldn't have to tell you not to make love with your wife while she is transitioning." A grin stretched across his face. "Everyone knows that much. Or so I thought."

~ ~ ~

"Well, now I know." Andree collapsed over Ana.

"This is just great." Daniel tossed his arms in the air. Of all the crazy situations he went through the years with Andree, this one took the number one spot.

"The assistants have arrived." The Queen waved them in, and their giggles filled the room. "You will say nothing of this," she hissed.

Jonas and Daniel pulled Andree off and moved him onto the other side of the bed, while the Queen and Mara hid their smirks. Once Andree seemed comfortable on his side of the bed, Daniel started to laugh.

"I'm sorry, but this is funny. Andree told me right before you all came in that Ana had seduced him. I bet that wasn't hard at all," he said between contagious laughs.

Ana's moans interrupted him, and Daniel and the others in the room turned their attention to her. Only seconds later, Andree went into convulsions.

After about an hour, they both seemed to calm down, and Daniel figured it would be a good time to take some blood samples for testing. He took Ana's first, and after securing it in his well-known black leather bag, he walked around the bed to Andree.

The needle barely touched his arm when Ana rose to a sitting position. Her eyes, wide open, didn't seem to see anyone, her irises two golden globes. She hissed and showed fangs.

"Don't touch him." Her words held a serious threat.

Daniel's feet left the floor, and he rose in the air. "What the hell?" Looking around, the Queen, Jonas, and the others in the room shared his predicament along with various objects drifting by.

"This is incredible. What kind of power is this?" Mara asked first after she tried unsuccessfully to free herself.

"I saw Vlad lifting objects like this, a long time ago, but he couldn't control people like she is." Jonas shared his memory with the rest of the group.

"This is actually pretty amazing. She sensed danger and acted from an unconscious state. I'm impressed. But I need the blood sample now even more." Daniel's admiration filled the room.

He stared at Ana. She didn't blink, and it appeared she wasn't awake. Her hands, extended in front of her with her palms up, trembled. Her brows furrowed. She seemed determined.

The power radiating from her charged the air.

"Your Majesty, Princess, it's me, Daniel. I won't hurt Andree. You know none of us would ever harm you or him. I need a blood sample, so I can help you both. Please, let us down." His plea hung in silence for a few seconds.

Her head tilted to one side. The deep crease between her brows smoothed.

"If you hurt him, I'm going to kill you." Ana fell unconscious again.

Her threat sounded funny, but her tone was dead serious. The sudden release, far from smooth, caused Daniel and everyone else to drop back to the floor between the other objects. He approached Andree again, and reached for his arm. After a short hesitation, he drew his friend's blood. Once the blood samples were secured, he figured he should probably check the puncture wounds on her neck, too.

"I'm going to change your bandage, not hurt you," Daniel whispered before touching her and removing it. He didn't want to get suspended in the air again. His eyes opened wide with shock. "Her bite marks, they're completely healed, barely visible."

Queen Emelia reacted first. "This is impossible."

Jonas shook his head. "Vlad learned and trained in the art of healing. He never did it this fast. She's amazing." He didn't even try to hide his admiration. "When he said she would be the most powerful vampire ever, he knew. All of her powers are now combined with Prince Andree's, shared. They both are most powerful."

All eyes turned from Jonas to Ana and Andree, both unconscious in the oversized bed.

Daniel moved first. "I must get these samples to the vault." When he reached for his bag, he touched one of the draperies. The rising sun peeked between the heavy curtains.

Queen Emelia and Jonas turned away.

"It is morning. Your Majesty, you should go to your suite. You, too, Jonas. Karl and I can do this." Mara glanced at the two then wiped Ana's forehead.

"*Très bien.* Let me know if you need us." The Queen nodded to Mara before she left the room with Jonas, followed by Daniel.

~ ~ ~

About an hour later, Mike and Ella came to see Ana, only to find Andree transitioning as well. After Mara and Karl told them what had happened, they both started to laugh. Ella came close to her friend.

"I see you've started your vampire adventure with one of your own," Ella whispered next to Ana's ear. She brushed hair out of her friend's face. Trying to peer into Ana's future, nothing came to her. The wall was still there.

Ana opened her eyes a few minutes later.

"Look who's up, my new favorite vampire." Ella's smile spread to her eyes.

"Where's Andree?" Ana's first thought went to him, surprise evident in her eyes when she didn't see him.

"You don't know?" Ella giggled. "You have him transitioning, too." She pointed to the other side of the bed.

"What? How?" Ana rushed to him and knelt on the bed. Her hands trembled when she touched his arm.

"You two made love. That threw him into transition."

~ ~ ~

Ella's explanation fell on Ana's conscience like a bomb.

She wished she could take it back. But not all of it, just the part with the transition.

"How is he?" Ana's eyes lifted to Karl.

"He is fine now. It seems the worst is over." Andree's assistant slightly bowed his head.

As soon as Karl answered, Andree's body tensed. Convulsions started again and sweat covered his body.

Ana took the cloth from the faithful assistant and started to wipe Andree's heated skin with care and icy water.

"I'm so sorry. It's my fault." Ana murmured. "Please forgive me. I have no idea what to do."

Andree shifted on the bed, his arm encircled her waist.

Guilt suffocated her. Ana wanted to cry. To her surprise,

tears wouldn't form. She remembered Andree had told her that vampires don't cry.

"Your Majesty. What are you doing here?" Mara stumbled over her words. "The light."

Queen Emelia and Jonas had witnessed the scene from the doorway.

Sunlight flooded the room, filtered through the heavy drapes.

"I am fine, we both are. We took a serum." Jonas explained their presence.

"*Chérie*. How are you feeling?" Queen Emelia approached.

"A little dizzy, but okay, I guess." Ana didn't even look at anyone else but Andree. "How am I supposed to be feeling?"

"I am not sure anymore. Your transition is different, fast, nothing from what we have known or seen before applies to you. You have already become powerful." The Queen smiled with a mixture of pride and admiration on her lips.

In the next few minutes, they told Ana about what she had done earlier. She listened to every word in disbelief.

To test everything, Ana glanced at Mara. She could see her thoughts. If not for Andree's unexpected transition, she would've jumped around with joy. She turned her attention back to him. His moans hurt her.

The whole room started to spin. "I don't feel so good."

Faces distorted, as if sucked into a funnel, and swirled around her. Voices became distant and incoherent. Before she had a chance to say anything, her vision dimmed, and she collapsed right by Andree.

~ ~ ~

The Queen and Jonas rushed to the bed and tried to pull Ana away.

Andree's arm tightened around her. His threatening hiss filled the room, and he bared his fangs.

"Step back, everyone," Queen Emelia suggested, and the others nodded in approval. "Maybe we should leave her where she is. It looks like Andree will not let go."

"Are you sure? Won't they hurt each other?" Ella's words revealed how much she cared for both of them. "They are unconscious."

"Even so, they protect each other." The Queen motioned for Ella to retreat. "I doubt either of them would hurt the other. But I can't say the same for us."

Andree's moan echoed louder than before and interrupted his mother. His whole body tensed, and his back arched. In a second, his veins turned black, covering him in dark webbing.

Ana placed her hand in the middle of his chest. She shivered. His pain diminished under her touch, and the black webbing disappeared as quickly as it had appeared.

"Can she heal others as well?" Queen Emelia glanced at Jonas, seeking answers.

"I don't know. Vlad couldn't. He tried once to heal me, but he couldn't. She might. She's unbelievable." Jonas's admiration flooded the room. "Regardless, I'm proud to be her guardian."

~ ~ ~

Around four o'clock in the afternoon, Andree opened his eyes. *Why is everyone here? Did I fall asleep? Ana . . .*

"Andree." The Queen reacted first, relieved. "You are awake."

"How is Ana?"

He turned quickly to her and touched the side of her face with the back of his hand. Her temperature was normal. Andree kissed her forehead first, then her hand.

"She is doing great. How are you feeling?" his mother finally had the chance to ask.

"I'm all right. I'm not sure what happened." Andree sat

and massaged his temples. "I remember Jonas telling me that I would go into transition, then nothing."

"You did. You have been out for about twelve hours." Daniel approached the bed. Andree didn't believe his friend at first and looked into Karl's memory.

An unexpected wave of pride filled his heart when he saw what Ana had done.

"I actually felt her healing, warm and light." His eyes focused on her. "I don't know how to explain it. Thank you, everyone, for being here for us." Andree finally glanced around the room. "I am fine now. You can take a break."

Daniel looked at him with suspicion.

"I'm fine." A sheen of sweat covered his body. "But in serious need of another shower."

After a bathing, he asked Karl to bring him some food and coffee. The shower had energized him. Even if still unconscious, Ana didn't seem to be in pain anymore, which he was grateful for.

As soon as his food arrived, Andree started eating. He was starved. Between bites, he glanced at the clock. Almost twenty-four hours since he had turned her.

"Do I smell coffee?" Ana's question made him laugh.

Andree hurried to her side. "That little nose of yours is impossible to fool." He touched the tip of her nose with his lips. "Yes, I am having coffee. Would you like some?"

She nodded, smiling at him after receiving his kiss. "How are you feeling?" The memory of what she had done earlier filled his mind and hers, through their telepathic connection.

Andree sensed her guilt rising.

"Great. I heard what you did for me. I am impressed." He tried to make her feel better.

"I'm so sorry, Andree. I had no idea."

"Please, do not apologize. I should thank you." He handed her the coffee. "If I understand this right, you made us both incredibly powerful."

Chapter 22

A thin layer of sweat glimmered on her body. Ana shivered and wrapped her arms around her waist. She had been conscious for about an hour, and she hoped she had finished transitioning.

"Are you all right?"

"I'm not sure, a little dizzy, and thirsty." Ana reached for another glass of water.

Andree's left eyebrow arched and he turned her face toward him. He offered her the mirror he used earlier. "Here, you need to see this."

Ana stared at her own image. Her eyes lacked the usual clarity, the golden lights brightened, and tiny red lines covered the white.

He lifted her upper lip, and she jerked back with an involuntary hiss. His touch hurt her gums.

"You are having your first thirst." He took back the mirror and set it aside.

"It's terrible. Is this how it's going to be?"

Everything around her blurred. Ana's vision narrowed to a tunnel leading to the exact spot on Andree's neck, where his pulse throbbed under well-tanned skin. His familiar scent invaded her senses, and she licked her lips.

"Relax, I asked Mara to bring you some blood. It is only the first time. You will learn to control it, anticipate it." His smile had no effect on her. She was too focused on the rhythm of his heart. "And stop staring at my neck. You are not feeding on me," he joked, and Ana shook her head embarrassed, murmuring apologies.

She would have never even considered doing such a thing. Her instincts were wild, and she had no idea how to control them.

"Keep in mind, the first time you might get sick. Most vampires do. Mara should be here any moment."

"You're going to have to teach me how to contact her myself."

"I will." Andree's promise coincided with Mara's arrival.

Ana took the mug from Mara's hands and stared at the deep red liquid inside. Their wedding day flashed in her mind, when she barely touched a drop of his blood with her lips. Andree's blood tasted metallic, like she had licked an old penny.

Her breath accelerated, and her heart was about to explode in her chest. One more glance around her, and she took her first sip of blood. It was sweet, a little salty, and just a bit thicker than red wine. She wanted more, and more. She couldn't stop until she had finished it all.

With the back of her hand she wiped her lips, but there wasn't any wasted drop. The pounding in her head slowed and gradually quieted down.

"I thought it would be gross, but it's actually not bad." Her gaze lifted to Andree.

He laughed and shook his head. "You might have thought it before turning. You are not human anymore, Ana. You are now a vampire."

His words finally registered in her mind. Her years-long fantasy was now reality. She examined her hands. They didn't look any different. Did she expect them to? What exactly did she hope for?

"I need a shower." Ana excused herself.

"You are still you." Andree wrapped his arms around her the moment she returned in the bedroom. "I have not lost you."

"What do you mean?" Ana stared at him, confused.

"I am not sure your transition is over. You might go back in it any second, but for now, you have not lost much from the way you were as a human." Andree kissed the tip of her nose. "You still have this look in your eyes. You are still you."

"Does that mean you still like me?" She provoked him. It was fun to incite him.

"I love you." His low, rumbling voice resonated all the way inside her soul. "This is for you. Your own signature look." He waved at the box waiting on the bed, right beside him.

"Thank you. I probably should go try it on." Ana picked up the box and took a step toward her dressing room.

"What happened to that amazing girl who seduced me a few hours ago?" Andree's grip tightened.

"She's still here." Ana smiled and turned her gaze away. He cupped her head and stared in her eyes.

"You are not blushing anymore."

"Good. I hated it anyways. And I can't cry anymore either. I wanted to when you were unconscious, but I couldn't."

~ ~ ~

Ana examined herself in the full-sized mirror. *Since when do vampires wear white? I love it. I love the new me.* Her leather outfit, identical to the ones Andree wore, was unlike his, white, and half the size. No detail was forgotten, she even had the thin straps tied around her upper arms, with tiny buckles. She touched the hanging ends and giggled. A few more twists and turns in front of the mirror, and Ana left the room, excited to start her new life.

Andree waited for her in the living room, with his mother.

"There you are. How are you feeling, *chérie*?"

"Your Ma . . ."

"Please, it is just us," the Queen interrupted Ana's bow.

"You look amazing." Andree coiled his arm around her waist.

The spark in his eyes made Ana wish they were alone. Desire flared between them like a fire doused with gas.

"Great. Not much different than before, but stronger." Ana refocused her attention on the Queen. "I have more energy. I'm not sure I know how to explain it."

"Andree told me you had been up for over two hours. I think you are done. You had the fastest transition ever, under twenty-four hours."

"Is that bad?" Ana's concern present in her voice.

"No. It is unusual, but again, everything about your turning and transitioning has been that way." She devoured every one of Andree's words.

It didn't matter what he said. His voice echoed in the marrow of her bones. Her blood heated.

"Here. This is for you." The Queen handed her a small jewelry box.

"Thank you."

Ana opened it and covered her mouth, stopping the happy squeal. A pendant identical to the one the Queen wore lay in the black, velvety case. The same one she saw the night they met on the beach, the family's crest.

She remembered thinking it looked like a coin, with some design she couldn't make out at the time. Now she could, and she knew how much it meant to them.

"Now you truly are one of us." A welcoming smile on her lips, the Queen helped her with the delicate clasp. "You are now family and have the right to wear our crest."

"I'm honored. I hope I'll never disappoint." Ana touched the round medallion and the smooth choker around her neck.

"You won't." Andree's assuring words coincided with the doors opening.

"Your Majesties. There is someone here who wants to talk to you." Mara bowed quickly before the three of them.

"Do you know who it is?" The Queen was the first to speak.

"Her name is Rina. I helped her and her husband years ago. She only told me she is paying her debt to me, a matter of life and death."

"Then bring her in." The Queen waved her hand.

"Here?" Mara glanced at Andree for approval.

"No." Andree shook his head. "We should meet in the ballroom."

~ ~ ~

"What is so important?" Andree stood tall and intimidating, causing the woman in front of him to clasp her hands in a nervous gesture.

"Your Majesty." She bowed respectfully. "I'm independent, just like my husband, and yesterday we had a visit . . ." She hesitated for a short second. ". . . from Ivan."

What? Ivan? That guy again? Ana expected bad news. Anything associated with that name made her twitch.

"What does the coward want? I am still waiting for his call." Andree tensed at the sound of the name. "It has been two months since I challenged him."

"He asked us to join his army. He's planning an attack on your coven." Rina lowered her head.

"What? I should have killed him that night on the beach. I am sorry I did not rip his head off." The Queen intervened with silver lights beaming from her azure eyes.

Ana stared at her. Queen Emelia's famous composure and grace completely fled for the moment. Her inner demon surfaced glowing silver, as beautiful as her.

"We told him we would need to think about it. My husband and I owe our lives to Miss Mara, and we knew she had returned here." She glanced toward Mara. "He also said the First Coven is supporting him, and the Second is thinking about it."

"This is insane. What the hell did he tell Mihai to convince him? How is this possible?" Andree sounded dangerously close to the border of losing his cool.

His grinding teeth attracted Ana's attention, and she glanced at him. Even if she tried, she couldn't have missed his struggle to keep his inner beast at bay. She couldn't help but wonder what her own beast looked like.

"We thank you, Rina. You will be rewarded." The Queen returned to her usual calm and grace.

"I don't need any reward. I'm paying my debt." Rina and Mara nodded to each other.

"Do you know how many people have joined him so far?" Andree asked.

"He said he counts on close to one thousand independents, but if the First Coven is supporting him, then . . ."

Confused, Ana pursed her lips. *Then what? How many exactly? I hate it when people don't finish what they have to say.* She knew the Third Coven was the smallest, with less than four hundred members. It sounded like the odds were in Ivan's favor.

"Do you know when?" Andree continued his interrogation.

"In about two months, there wasn't a set date yet. If it's any consolation, we won't join him." Rina bowed, and Mara escorted her out. Their steps echoed in the empty ballroom.

"How bad is all this?" Ana broke the silence.

It seemed to her, the welcoming hours as a vampire didn't appear to be the best. *I guess I have Ivan to thank for this. I was expecting something less threatening and oriented more toward my training. Oh. Maybe, Andree will teach me how to kick Ivan's sorry ass. Yeah! That would make up for this.*

"If it is true, it can get ugly." Andree glanced at his mother.

"One way to find out for sure." The Queen took out her phone and tapped the screen.

"Who are you calling?" Andree translated into words Ana's curiosity.

"I might not be on the best of terms with Mihai Veres, but I am pretty good with Gabriel." She walked away from Andree and Ana in an obvious attempt to get some privacy.

"Is there a way to avoid all this?" Ana turned her attention to her husband.

"Avoid? It is not how we take care of problems." He shook his head. "We do not *avoid*."

"Can't you mind control them or something?" Ana tried to find another way to get some answers. She felt lost in a world she didn't understand yet.

"If it is true and the First Coven joined Ivan, there will be close to two thousand people. I cannot mind control them all at the same time." Andree pinched the bridge of his nose. "I could do maybe four, five hundred, but not all of them. Besides, I would not do it." He turned his attention to her. "They want a fight, and they will have one."

Ana noted his determination. It seemed he had made up his mind already. Two thousand against four hundred didn't sound good.

Queen Emelia returned and pocketed her phone. "Gabriel will be here by midnight."

Steps echoed from the left side of the room, and Ana turned her head. Jonas was approaching them. "Did I hear that right? Is Gabriel coming here?"

"Yes, I asked him to." Andree's mother gazed toward the newcomer. "Apparently we are gong to be under serious siege."

In the next couple of minutes, Ana barely heard the Queen bringing Jonas up to speed with the recent events.

Her mind was busy trying to understand why Andree wanted to fight against such bad odds.

"Will you ask him to join us?" Jonas's curiosity didn't escape Ana.

"No." The Queen moved her head slowly from right to left a couple of times. "I only need to know if it is true and maybe some details. Gabriel will not fight against his brother." Her hand touched her medallion, as if she needed a reminder of her own. "It is the law."

"I know. To be completely accurate, they don't fight against *family*." Jonas's eyes focused on Ana as he accentuated the key word.

"No. I will not use Ana's bloodline to get out of it." Andree's tone rose, and she sensed the anger building up inside him.

"What do you mean?" Curiosity got the best of Ana.

"Mihai and Gabriel Veres are your uncles. If they know who you are, they would not fight against you." Jonas's explanation sounded good to her. It was the needed solution.

"No. Like Andree said, we are not going to hide behind Ana. They will get what they are asking for." Queen Emelia's words held the same determination as her son's. She turned around sharply and left, with Jonas following her closely.

"Why not use what we have? If they won't fight against me, why not avoid people getting hurt?" Ana still tried to understand his logic.

"Simply because it is not our way." Andree cut the air in front of him with his right hand. "We fight. We are proud of who we are, and we stand against anyone challenging us." His hand rolled into a fist. "We always have."

Ana noticed the same superiority she'd seen before. Now she knew it was pride and confidence. She also thought at least this time, it was stupid. They should use the advantage her bloodline brought.

"We should go and get your training weapons," Andree's change of subject got Ana's attention, and her excitement went from zero to one hundred in one second.

The moment they entered the armory, Ana couldn't contain her surprise and admiration. She felt her jaw dropping, and quickly closed her mouth. There must've been thousands of weapons hanging on the uneven walls, laid out on the long wooden table on the left side, or standing against the metal supports spread across the vast room.

"Whoa. Do you have an army somewhere around here?"

"When your combat training is complete, you will master every one of them." He waved to the weapons displayed. "You will know how to use them for either attack or defense." With his hand resting on the small of her back, he directed her toward the display area.

"You mean, I'll know how to use all of them?" Her voice sounded high-pitched from the excitement. "As in everything in here?"

Andree laughed and picked out several daggers, swords, and guns, asking her to hold the weapons. It took them almost an hour, but she was armed to the teeth.

"What do you think?" Andree seemed satisfied with the choices they made. He tilted his head, expectant.

"They're a lot heavier than I thought."

Ana never had any contact with weapons before. Now she had one in every pocket. She expected the soft leather to give up under the weight. Or her knees. She wasn't sure which would go first.

"It is why you will have to get used to them before anything else. You will learn how to use them in no time."

"Okay. What's the first lesson?" Ana took a fighting stance, the way she saw actors doing in the movies. "When do I start?"

"Oh. You will not start combat training for a while. Not

until after you give birth to our babies." Andree killed her buzz the same instant.

"What?" Her arms dropped to her sides.

"Ana, I won't take any chance. You will not do any combat training until—"

"I'm pregnant, not handicapped." She quickly objected. "I can start training." Ana felt revolt and indignation rising her temperature. Her fangs started to descend, hurting her gums. She tasted her own blood.

"No. If you want, we can start training on your powers. You can learn the basics. Combat is out of the question." Andree reached to her.

Ana backed away from him, trying to control her frustration. After only a couple of steps, Andree rushed toward her. The same instant her hands extended in front of her, and she lifted him in the air, immobilized, before he could touch her. *At least I have a decent reaction time. This telekinesis business is sweet.*

"Let me down." Andree's frustration amused her a little.

"Only if you promise to train me." Her stubbornness surfaced.

"I will, just not combat."

Ana frowned and kept holding him. Once the first shock of her action washed over her, she admitted to herself she enjoyed her new abilities.

Every drop of blood flowing through her veins carried an enthralling energy. It filled her body. The incredible power coursed through her, saturating every cell of her being. She had no idea how it worked, but it did. And she loved it.

"Please, try and understand," Andree said. "I could not live with myself if you got hurt, or if anything happened to our children. We cannot have more. It is our last and only chance."

He had turned her, but Ana discovered it wasn't enough to make her a vampire. She wanted to feel, act, and fight like one. Tempted to hold him longer, even if only because she enjoyed it, Ana let him down on the stone floor. He was right, it was their last chance.

~ ~ ~

Andree rushed and hugged her to him the moment she let him down and his feet touched the cold floor. The thought that anything could hurt her, or their unborn children, scared him. For the first time in centuries, he was afraid, and he closed his eyes. Fear touched him with an icy feather, and his whole body shivered.

He was used to sensing other's terror, drinking it, feeding his demon with it, not his own.

"How do I move fast like you?" Her question pushed away his anxiety.

"You really want to start this now?" he smiled with his face buried in her hair. "We are not even sure you are done transitioning."

"I've been up and feeling just fine all this time. Do you think I'd go back?"

"I am not sure what to think anymore." He released her from the shelter of his arms and took a couple of steps away from her. "All right, let's see."

Andree couldn't say no to her. Step by step, he taught her how to move, how to think. Ana was a natural, and eager to learn. She followed his instructions, and shortly, she could run as fast as him.

Her accelerated adaptation to her new abilities surprised Andree. For most vampires it took days just to figure out how to run. It took her only minutes. He figured that when their powers pooled together, she picked up his abilities already developed.

"Your small frame is working to your advantage. You are already faster than me." Andree closed his arms around her.

"That's more like it." She smiled and gazed into his eyes. "I'm starting to feel like a vampire."

Through their link, the Queen requested his and Ana's presence in the ballroom. Andree noticed the time, already midnight.

Hand-in-hand with his wife, he ran through the underground corridors and entered the vast room only seconds later.

"He is Gabriel Veres, your uncle." Andree communicated to his wife, nodding toward the man his mother was talking to. He felt her tiny hand squeezing his.

~ ~ ~

Ivan avoided the pile of paperwork on his desk. All the legal documents arrived shortly after Collin's death, and he figured he could store everything in his office.

In the two months that passed, Ivan fought the temptation to accept Prince Andree's challenge daily. He craved confronting him, avenging his friend's death. Just as many times, he stopped himself from doing so.

It would have been too easy. Killing the man he hated wasn't enough for him. He wanted him to suffer first. Ivan wanted to kill every member of the Third Coven, watch Andree hurt for every one of them.

Next would be the arrogant Queen, and he could see with his mind's eye, her perfect blond hair stained with red blood. Involuntarily, Ivan licked his lips and a loud hiss filled the room. He savored the image for a few more seconds.

Collin had died because of the human, now turned, and part of their blasted family. She would die next. Ivan's breath rushed, he suffocated with anticipation and excitement. His judgment clouded with fury and thirst for revenge.

Last, the Prince would fall to his knees, beg for death. Ivan threw a chair against the nearest wall, turning it to scraps. It was the moment he couldn't wait for.

His sword would take away the life that mattered most, the one that would pay for his friend's.

Ivan needed a few moments to recover from his fantasies. Reality welcomed him cold, silent and dark. Collin's letter caused him to reflect on his own life. Yes, he was a vampire, an immortal, but he could still be killed.

For the first time, he considered he might not come back from the fight. He glanced again at the papers on his desk. The time for him to tie up all loose ends in his life before entering the much-anticipated fight had arrived.

Chapter 23

Gabriel Veres stopped in the middle of his sentence and turned around in the middle of the ballroom.

"Your Majesties." He tilted his head graciously toward the approaching couple.

"Gabriel," Andree responded.

"Nobody told me how beautiful you are, Princess." Ana tilted her head gracefully, just as she had learned. "Wait a minute. Didn't you just turn her yesterday? Should she not be in transition?" Gabriel shifted his attention to Andree.

"She is done transitioning," the Queen attracted their guest's attention to her for one short second.

"In twenty-four hours?" Gabriel asked, with an arched brow and an octave higher than normal tone.

"Twenty-three, to be more exact." Andree placed himself between Gabriel and Ana in a protective stance.

Her heart melted. Aww . . . *He still thinks I need his protection.*

She peeked at her uncle with curiosity. He didn't look a day over thirty-five, but from what she knew, he should've been about sixteen hundred years old. He stood almost as tall as Andree, but slender. His movements were slick, and made Ana think of a panther.

I have a cool uncle. This looks promising.

"Prince Andree, I won't . . ." He stopped, staring at Ana. The hazel speckles throughout his green irises fascinated her, they resembled tiny flakes of gold. "Who are you?"

Ana noticed his aristocratic features. High cheekbones, the long, straight nose, and thin lips reminded her of one of the nobles willing to marry her a little while back. The beginning of a beard, the same dark chestnut as his ponytail, gave him a scruffy look, which somehow matched the brown leather suit he wore.

A blurry form rushed toward them around the marble columns. Ana recognized Jonas' presence and his talent of showing up when you least expect him. "You haven't forgotten."

Gabriel spun around fast. "Jonas."

"Gabriel," Jonas responded. A cold respect blew like a blizzard between the two of them.

"What are you doing here?"

"Jonas is a member of our coven," the Queen explained, short and to the point.

"I see." He turned again to Ana. "Seriously, who are you? I have not sensed this presence in . . . many years." Gabriel sniffed the air.

She didn't miss that twitch in his nose that almost made her laugh. Ana didn't need to sniff around. His sharp cologne mixed with something that took her a couple of seconds to identify: horses. *He didn't come here on a horse, did he?*

Ana noted how Andree bit his lower lip in an effort to contain his laugh. She remembered how soft and demanding his lips were, and her heart did a back flip in her chest.

"He did not. He likes horses and has a few on the ranch where he lives." Ana heard Andree's explanation and laced her fingers with his.

"Princess Ana is your niece. She is your father's blood descendant," Jonas declared with a proud undertone in his voice.

"How is it even possible? My father only had Mihai and me." Disbelief and confusion mixed in Gabriel's words.

"Wrong. Before he died, Vlad also had a daughter." Jonas voice sounded condescending in Ana's mind. She was now sure the two men weren't best friends. "Your sister came into this world the day before your father left it."

The confusion on Gabriel's face looked funny to Ana. Wanting to make a good impression, she focused and stayed serious. Laughing at her uncle didn't seem to be a good start.

Jonas explained to Gabriel how everything had happened, how he was her guardian and sworn to secrecy.

"This is incredible. My father's presence is so strong." He gazed toward Ana again. "Why did he insist on keeping it a secret?"

"At the time, if you remember, you and your brother were power hungry. Both of you wanted to step out of your father's shadow and make a name for yourselves. His daughter would have been vulnerable, a human. He feared you would kill her."

Gabriel faced Ana again and knelt in front of her. Surprised by his action, she moved closer to Andree.

"My lady, please forgive me, for I have not known. This is..." He stopped in the middle of his phrase and studied her. "You are one of us, I can feel your power, even if so young. This can't be right. Are you... with child?" he finally asked.

Ana nodded. Deeply touched by her uncle's reaction, she couldn't speak.

"Yes, she is." Andree's pride surfaced in his answer.

"The first Veres–De Croix generation," Gabriel whispered, still awed, rising back to his feet.

"I prefer De Croix-Veres." Andree squeezed Ana's hand, their fingers still interlaced.

"Of course you do. But the mother is a Veres." Gabriel waved toward Ana. "You should know that always, the mother comes first."

"What is this Veres-De Croix talk?" Ana's genuine curiosity brought smiles all around.

"Our families are the most prestigious in the world, in

our world to be more exact," Gabriel started to explain. His voice sounded soft, soothing, like silk.

I feel so stupid when everyone knows something I never heard of. That has to change. I have to learn more about all this. Mara's going to be busy.

"Veres is the most reputable name, and De Croix is royalty. An alliance between us would have been beneficial to all of us. I have tried unsuccessfully for years to convince Queen Emelia to marry me." Gabriel glanced at Andree's mother.

Ana's attention shifted to Jonas. For one short second his fists tightened, his knuckles whitened, and his jaw clenched. *No way. Jonas is jealous.*

"The alliance has been made already." The Queen smiled in Ana's direction.

"You are right. Ana is family. Mihai will not fight against you." He turned to his newfound niece.

"So, it is true. He joined Ivan against us." Anger bubbled in Andree's voice. "How did that loser convince him?" Andree's question caused Gabriel to sigh.

"Mihai and I have different views when it comes to the Third Coven. I see you as a potential ally. He considers you as a powerful enemy. I tried to sway him, and there was progress, until Ivan appeared out of nowhere." Gabriel ran a hand over the scruffy lower half of his face. "He hates you and found an ally in Mihai. Jonas's book, which apparently confirms our alien origins, did not help. A lot of vampires out there are outraged, and they joined them."

"Apparently?" Jonas jumped in the conversation. "You can see it for yourself if you like. You didn't want to believe me the first time, both you and Mihai made me an outcast." His trembling finger pointed toward an exit, to the rest of the world. "Now I have the proof." His eyes darkened, and for the first time, Ana sensed the power within her guardian.

She felt like a black sun sparked to life, spreading dark

energy. The darkness seemed to crawl on the immaculate floors and coil around her feet. It didn't scare her, it empowered her.

"If it is true, and one of them turned our father, why keep it secret?" Gabriel's voice yanked her back to reality. "He had all the time in the world to tell us."

"Your father believed in not interfering with destiny. He insisted that people were not ready to face the truth." Jonas hurried to answer. "He knew that one day, it would all come out and change our world. It seems that time is now."

The black marble floor carried the sounds of Gabriel's soft-looking boots when he walked away from the group.

"Regardless, when I tell Mihai—"

"You will not," the Queen interrupted, and Gabriel whirled in her direction.

"What do you mean? I have to. If he knows about Princess Ana," he waved to his niece, "he won't fight against your coven. He will want to meet, but he won't fight against you," Gabriel insisted, glancing to every person in the room and finally turning his focus on Ana.

"That is exactly why you are not going to tell him." Andree enforced his mother's words. The determination in his eyes added more weight.

"You people are crazy." Gabriel's hands flopped at his sides. "You don't understand. It is going to be a bloodbath, a massacre." He turned to Andree. "They are close to two thousand." His arms lifted again, as if the high number had to be shown. "You have what, a little over three hundred? That is five to one." His opened hands moved through the air in front in him, imitating an instable balance, enforcing the bad ratio.

"We are going to need a good plan to balance the numbers." Ana sensed in Andree the pride, the confidence she admired so much in him.

Even if at the time she thought it foolish, she stood proud

by his side. Her eyes never left his profile. She couldn't imagine her life with anyone else.

"No plan is going to get you out of this alive." Gabriel seemed defeated by Andree's and the Queen's decision.

"It will be what our destiny is." Queen Amelia closed the subject.

Andree glanced at Ana. Her insistent gaze must have drilled holes on the side of his head. A smile bloomed at the same time on both their lips.

"Could I at least get to know my niece?" Her uncle's hope resonated in the vast room.

"That it is entirely up to her." Andree lifted his right hand, and Gabriel turned to Ana with pleading eyes.

"I would like that," she whispered and smiled at her uncle.

~ ~ ~

"At least now we know that they will attack in two months, from the North." Queen Amelia glanced toward her son and Ana, then to Jonas, all of them still in the ballroom. "And Gabriel will stay neutral." She concluded that night's meeting after their guest left.

Andree released Ana's hand and paced, his mind already planning ahead.

"We might have only three hundred and fifty people, but every single one of them is a lot more powerful than those independents and Mihai's coveners," Andree said out loud. "We need a plan to make up for the numbers and—No," he yelled, turning towards Jonas the same second.

"What is it?" Queen Emelia hurried to ask.

"Your Majesty, it will be—" Jonas started.

"No. It is out of the question." Andree took one threatening step toward Jonas. "Ana will not fight. She is pregnant, and she does not have any training." Andree's fists closed, his brows furrowed. The most terrible scenarios came to his mind. Even a scratch upon her flesh would've been a tragedy to him.

"Wait a minute. Don't I get to say anything?" Ana's question won her a disapproving look from Andree.

"Everybody, calm down," Queen Emelia intervened. "Jonas, what were you thinking?"

"I thought of a plan to make up for the unfavorable numbers." Jonas hesitated in front of Andree's fury. Another of his hisses filled the room and caused Jonas to take a step back. "Against this many, direct combat is suicide. The best way would be to use our combined powers." He glanced toward Ana.

The Queen followed his gaze and nodded.

"What exactly do you mean by that?" Ana asked with confusion in her tone.

"You could probably control them . . ." Jonas let his sentence go unfinished under Andree's threatening glare.

"I said no." Andree finally spoke again, calmer but just as unmovable in his decision. He wasn't going to allow any danger near her. Ana and his unborn twins were everything to him.

"She would be safe, Your Majesty," Jonas insisted. "I have not shown you yet what my ability is. It has been a few hundred years since I last fought, so I might be a little rusty."

Ana's guardian took a few steps away from them and lifted his arms in the air, in front of him, with palms facing up. A light-blue translucent shield appeared like a dome around him, covering a substantial area, about ten feet in diameter.

"What is this?" Queen Emelia advanced to him.

"My protective shield. Anyone under it is completely safe. It is impenetrable by any weapons, and no one from outside can use any powers on the ones inside."

"I cannot get in his mind," Andree admitted. *Hmm. This is new, and it could come in handy. Something to think about.*

The Queen and Ana both touched the shield. Andree attempted to put his fist through the dome that appeared to be made of an impenetrable matter that looked like crystal-clear water.

"Nobody else can get in, either," Jonas said. "I would have to drop it and let you in."

"I see." Andree walked away a few steps.

He turned, and one of his daggers flew toward Jonas. The sound of the metal hitting the marble floor echoed in the ballroom with emptiness and futility.

Jonas relaxed, and the surrounding dome melted away.

~ ~ ~

"How long can you keep it active?" Andree's question brought hope in Jonas' eyes.

"Right now, a few minutes, but with training, maybe thirty to forty minutes."

"It's a great plan." Ana couldn't hold back her excitement. "I'll be safe and I can—"

"No. You will be safe and far away from the battle," Andree interrupted, turning toward her.

"Why? Jonas can keep us safe." She waved toward where the dome was until only seconds ago.

"Because you are my wife, you are carrying our children, and I will not put you in harm's way." Andree's cold and calm explanation sent shivers up her spine.

"Andree, please be reasonable. Think about it. Nobody will have to fight. I can train and—"

"No."

Ana stared at him. She glanced to the Queen, pleading her cause without words. She understood none of them would go against Andree's decision. She could hear their thoughts, and for a moment they drove her dizzy. A reminder that after turning, her husband was responsible for her and her actions. She turned to Andree. He remained her last hope, and the optimism left the room long ago.

Her blood boiled with a mix of anger and frustration. Not even when she caught her ex-husband cheating on her, had Ana been so furious. If she had known how to fight, she would've, right here—right now. Her hands itched.

"You would dismiss a perfectly good plan and put everyone else in danger?" She made an effort to speak with calm.

"The plan is viable, and we will work the details, but I will execute it." Andree stood unmovable in his decision. "I am supposed to have the same powers as you, right?"

"So, it's all right to risk your life, but not mine? Do you think I would want to raise our children without you?" Ana asked.

The chill of a possible future crawled up her spine.

"You will. And you will make sure our children—"

"The hell I will!" Ana yelled.

The Queen didn't even try to hide her smile.

Jonas covered his beard with his hand.

"Ana . . ." Andree reached for her.

Ana backed away from him. She couldn't fight her instincts any longer. The tiny beast inside her screamed to be freed. With her jaw clenched and her lips pursed into a thin line, Ana stared into his blue, mesmerizing pieces of cobalt. Her body tensed.

"I'm not a weak human anymore. I'm part of this coven just like everyone else, whether you like it or not." Ana took a deep breath in an effort to maintain some composure. "I understand and appreciate your concern, but don't you dare treat me like I don't belong here."

Ana whirled on her heels and took advantage of his earlier lessons. With the speed of miniature lightning, she left the room.

~ ~ ~

"She is a quick learner. And she is fast." Queen Emelia's admiration filled her son's ears with pride. His heart wasn't doing so great.

Andree let out a deep sigh. He managed to make Ana mad at him for the second time that night. *This must be some new record... The worst kind.*

Andree found himself in an impossible position, forced to choose between giving Ana what she wanted and her safety. The two were mutually exclusive.

"Andree, I know it is not my business." The Queen started with a warm undertone in her voice. "Ana is your wife, and it is your decision, but we should talk things through for a minute."

He glanced at his mother and nodded in an invitation for her to continue.

"Jonas' shield seems to be the solution we need here. You and Ana share the same powers, so if you both train, you could probably control every single one of the attackers." The Queen tried to support Jonas' plan. "I know you want to do it alone, and keep Ana safe, but under the shield, by your side, she would be safer than anywhere else."

"If I train hard enough, I might be able to do it alone." Andree tried to stick to his strategy.

"Could you mind control them all?" his mother insisted.

"No. There are too many." He shook his head remembering Ana asked him the same question.

"You have been able to control others' minds for a few hundred years." Queen Emelia touched her stubborn son's shoulder. "This new power you just got from Ana, you still have to train."

Andree already knew where she was headed. He didn't like it, not one bit. He needed Ana.

"If you cannot mind control them all, what makes you think that you will be able to control them physically?"

Andree didn't bother to respond, he had no answer. The reality stared him in the face. He needed her combined power to avoid a massacre.

"Mother, please call a general emergency meeting." Andree's voice sounded like ice pellets. "The sooner, the better, we do not have time to waste. We all need to start training."

He turned to Jonas next, and advanced toward him. His steps heavy, his heart slowed down, barely beating in his chest.

"I need you to train harder than ever before. Your shield needs to be the strongest it can be. You are Ana's guardian." Andree jabbed his right index finger at Jonas' chest.

"Yes, Your Majesty."

"I will put our lives and our children's lives in your hands. If you fail"—Andree growled to make sure there was no misunderstanding— "I will kill you myself."

"I didn't know until now. When Vlad asked me to be ready for *the one*, when he entrusted me to be her guardian, he referred to this moment." Jonas' hand pointed to the floor, between them. "I am her guardian." Pride resonated in his tone. "I will die before anything happens to Princess Ana." Jonas' vow assured Andree he would.

He didn't miss the empowered resolution glimmering in Jonas' eyes. Andree didn't doubt Ana's guardian's commitment to do everything in his power to keep her alive. He only feared it wasn't going to be enough.

Andree took a few steps in the general direction of the exit.

"Andree." Queen Emelia called out to her son.

"I need to find Ana. We need to talk."

Chapter 24

Ana ran as fast as she could. She had never lost control like that. The changes within found her unprepared. All the sounds, smells, all the voices in her mind drove her dizzy, and made her angry.

She didn't know how to control the new powers, the strong instincts that took over her judgment. The ocean always helped find her inner balance, and Ana headed that way.

The farther she went from The Castle, the more silence engulfed her. She could hear the sounds in the kitchen: dishes getting prepared, the clinking of silverware and plates.

Somewhere water ran, and a squeaky faucet hurt her ears. Clothes rustling, probably laundry getting folded or people simply walking, pounded in her head.

Moonlight guided her steps. *I knew I was supposed to see in the dark, but never thought I would see almost as well as in daylight.* All her frustration bottled up inside.

She set herself free on the small, isolated beach and hissed loudly. Her fangs descended without any of the pain from the last few hours.

Ana kicked the sand with her brand new white boots, but it wasn't nearly enough. It was like kicking air, unsatisfying. She went straight to one of the massive boulders, and in an uncontrollable excess of fury, she punched it. No pain at all.

Expecting to hear every bone shatter in her right hand, to her surprise the boulder cracked in multiple pieces. They fell in the sand with a heavy thud and clouds of dust rose around them. The ground vibrated under her feet.

"Damn, I'm strong." Ana glanced at her hand. The skin on her knuckles broke and started to bleed. Out of instinct, she shook it.

A second later, she lifted it to her lips. The bleeding had stopped, and after another couple of seconds there wasn't even a scratch. *Is this for real? What the hell?*

Ana dropped into the sand, knees gathered to her chest. Her heart returned to a normal rhythm. She massaged her temples and contemplated the ocean. *Now I can paint at night, too. I have to do it some time.*

Low waves murmured into the night, caressing the coarse sand. The moon reflected off the ever-moving water, and Ana let out a sigh. She wanted to cry, but she couldn't. *One small downside of being a vampire.*

~ ~ ~

Andree stopped for a few seconds to use the link with Ana. Almost immediately, he could see what she saw: the ocean and her fight with the losing boulder. *At least I know where she is. I had hoped she would never have to fight. Damn you, Ivan. You are a dead man.*

Already mad at him, Andree didn't want to make things worse. He still hoped somewhere deep inside he could keep her safe. The circumstances worked against him. An invisible claw grabbed his heart and squeezed it. The place where Ana and his unborn children resided was threatened by the lack of air. Fear gripped him like never before.

Andree found her hidden behind a huge rock, the same spot they had sat the day before their wedding. Only steps away, the rocky rubble from her earlier confrontation attracted Andree's attention, and he smiled.

~ ~ ~

"What did that boulder ever do to you?" Andree sat in the sand, right by her side.

"It looked funny at me. Did you come to control my mind?"

The heat radiating from his body surrounded her. Still mad at him, Ana fought against the soothing effect his proximity had on her.

"No. I already told you I would never do it. I like your mind as is." His words rumbled from deep within his chest, and Ana's body vibrated with the sound of them. "And your mind is not the only thing I like about you." Andree hugged her close to him, and she stopped fighting the calmness.

The sky started to lighten up on the horizon. Different shades of blue danced together breaking the black reigning over the sky until only minutes ago. The morning approached. Ana turned her head and gazed at Andree.

"I'm sorry for earlier. All these changes got to me. I've never reacted like that before."

"I know, and I am sorry, too. I am not used to anyone standing against me, confronting me the way you did." He gently kissed her hand. "Your instincts are a lot stronger now. The reactions are faster than your ability to control them. In time, you will learn to deal with everything."

The beginning of a smile tugged at the corner of his lips.

"I smashed that boulder, and it didn't even hurt." She used her thumb to point over her shoulder, in the direction of the unfortunate rock. "My knuckles bled for a couple of seconds, and then I just healed myself. Is it normal? I don't know what to expect."

"It will take time and training to discover, or rediscover yourself." He set her on his lap. His arms closed around her like a cocoon. "Together, we will learn the full extent of your abilities."

Ana rested her head on his chest, this time accepting the comfort he offered her. She let him soothe her body.

"I love you so much, Ana," he whispered "All I want is for you to be safe, happy, and—"

"I understand why you don't want me in the fight. I know I'm not trained." She quickly interrupted him. "I don't have a clue as to what I am, or what I'm doing, but if I can help, I want to."

Andree let out a deep sigh, and Ana glanced at him. Sadness and worry mixed in his eyes. She regretted her earlier outburst. All this time, she feared he would somehow hurt her. Instead, she was the one hurting him. *I never thought I would be capable of doing anything like this.*

"Do you promise you will do as I say? If things do not go according to plan, I need to know you will go to safety, and—"

"You mean I can fight with you?" She turned to face him.

"I hate to admit it, but I need your help. I cannot do it alone—"

Ana's kiss stopped him for the third time in only seconds. He didn't seem to be able to finish any of his sentences. Desire and desperation made a volatile mix, and Andree hugged her tight against him.

When they needed to breathe, he held her face between the palms of his hands. His eyes bore straight into her soul. "Promise me."

Ana smiled and let her fingers intertwine in his hair. "I promise."

~ ~ ~

Ana sat with Andree on the terrace, in the soft light of the sunset. Long shadows darkened the perfectly maintained lawn, like the creepy fingers of an invisible monster.

"You have become more powerful than I ever thought you would." His whisper brought a smile on her face.

Their last training session marked her success. She held

two thousand logs for almost a half hour without any of his help.

"You made me what I am. Without you, none of this would've been possible." Ana wrapped her arms around his neck as soon as he drew her on his lap. Her pregnancy, now visible, wasn't a secret anymore.

"Ana, when we started all this, you promised you would do what I tell you."

Her gaze drifted to his. "I'm not going to run away and let you die, if that's what you are talking about."

A sigh escaped from his chest. "You promised me." Shadows settled in his eyes.

"It is a woman's prerogative to change her mind. I'm not going anywhere without you." Ana shook her head. "Our children need you just as much, so don't you—"

Andree pressed his lips against hers. She didn't want to think of a life without him when she was just getting used to the one with him. And she liked this new life.

"When I say so, Mara will take you to our jet. You will be going to the Sacred Grounds. George already made arrangements for protection and a safe place for you to stay for a while." He tucked away a lock of hair behind her ear. "There will be an envelope with your new documents. I have already opened an account under your new name, so money will not be a problem." Andree stopped for a few seconds, as if he had lost his words.

Ana's mind shifted into nightmare mode. She imagined herself pregnant, heartbroken, fighting through snow and rain. A barren land lay before her eyes, as empty as her heart.

~ ~ ~

"When things are settled, Gabriel will come for you. He will make sure you and the kids have everything you need." He had to swallow the obstruction in his throat. "I am sure Mihai will accept you, too. You will use your bloodline and make sure those little guys . . ." Andree's voice trailed off and his hand covered the little bump where his unborn children grew.

His touch was met with kicks from the twins, and Ana's hands rested on top of his. Feeling his children alive made it more real, brought even more pain, broke his heart further.

As much as he tried to stay composed, the thought he might not be around even to see them pained him. His heart slowed down, heavy.

"Andree . . ." Ana tried to speak, but he stopped her again. His hungry lips took hers. He didn't want to think, just to feel.

Emotions swirled together, in a vortex, separating him from the world around. The silence only left room for the most terrifying thoughts to surface. He clung to her with the fierceness only desperation could bring. *I can't lose her or the kids.*

"I waited over five hundred years for you to come into my life. I hoped we would have more than just a few months." Andree tried to keep his voice in check, but it fluctuated. "If this is all the time we are going to have together," he could barely link his words together, "I want you to know, it was all worth it." An attempt to a smile failed from the start. "I have never been as happy as I have been with you." His eyes lingered on her lips. "Thank you for every second you have given me, for—"

Ana silenced him with a kiss.

"Our plan, your power, should work in theory." Andree continued, staring into her eyes. They glowed with golden sparks, like two miniature suns. She brightened his life. "The only variable is how the enemy will react. There is a chance they will not fall for it, and I want to be prepared," Andree continued in a low whisper. He couldn't find the strength to speak any louder. "I want to make sure you and our children will make it, even if I do not."

Another embrace meant to keep death away, silenced not only him, but her as well. From his almost six centuries, only the last few months stood out. The day he saw her for the first time, their marriage ceremony, the night she got pregnant, all succeeded with nauseating speed in his mind. He wanted more.

Andree hoped they would survive and raise their children, teach them how to ride a bike, how to drive, how to be vampires, everything he knew. But hopes were just that, not guaranteed.

"We are all going to make it. If I have to, I'll step up there and let everyone know who I am." Ana's rebellion filled his breaking heart. "On our wedding day I vowed to protect you at any cost. I'll be damned if I'm going to do otherwise." She withdrew from his embrace. "Like it or not, you will have to accept it. I am not going to let anyone hurt you or our people. The Third Coven will not be eradicated as long as I have a say."

Determination sparkled in her eyes. He didn't doubt for a second, she would do what she just said. Andree imagined her fighting Mara to stay by his side. He pictured her tiny body avoiding danger, only to yell out, loud and clear, her origin.

"You spoke like a true Princess. The Third Coven is lucky to have you. I am lucky to have you. But your bloodline will remain a secret until after the fight."

Andree knew he cut off her last hope. He had to. If it was his destiny to die, he wanted to go with dignity, doing what he had always done best: protect.

He spent the remaining hours in their bedroom. The dark clouds of a possible outcome cocooned him and his wife within. In the nightmare land, both of them only had each other. And each of them was going to fight for their future.

~ ~ ~

"Do what I couldn't. If I make it out alive, I promise to make up for the lost time." His own words echoed in his mind long after he hung up the phone. He intended to keep that promise.

Ivan's trip to Europe left him drained, emotionally exhausted. After two centuries a lot had changed, but he didn't expect to find the transformation inside himself. He visited places close to his heart and made sure he took care of all loose ends.

His recruiting exceeded his expectations. He had more independents than Mihai had coveners.

Hours before the decisive battle, they all met in the woods at the border between the Second and Third Coven territories. Ivan stared at the people gathered there, under his command. *My army. Collin would be so proud of me right now. That's okay my friend, you will be avenged.* He glared at the stars blinking in the sky. He didn't think that Collin was up there, but he knew for sure he wasn't in the middle of the vampires mingling in the woods. A chuckle escaped Ivan's lips. His friend would've hated being there. His clothes and boots would've gotten dirty.

The army of vampires waited in the night for their signal to move. They had a couple of hours of light running ahead of them and everyone made sure they were ready.

Ivan pushed everything out of his mind. He purged memories of places, people close to his heart, past experiences and emotions. The focus stayed on eradicating his enemy.

The moment when Collin died at the end of Prince Andree's sword flashed before his eyes. It fueled him with the hate and thirst for revenge driving him.

This is for you, my friend.

With one last deep breath, he signaled, and over two thousand vampires started their march.

~ ~ ~

The day of the attack arrived. Shortly after midnight, Ana and all three hundred and fifty members of the Third Coven, plus a little over a hundred independents, gathered by Jonas and George, positioned in the open field behind The Castle. The forest, containing an unusual calm, surrounded them.

If anyone told me a few months ago I'd be here, leading a vampire army, I would've thought them crazy. She glanced around.

The unmovable army waited for their attackers to show up. *This is so surreal. I can't believe I am actually here.*

When the horizon started to change colors and blue hues took over, Daniel lifted a hand over his head, clutching a vial of daylight serum. "To the Third Coven."

Ana recognized the signal and watched the purebloods emptying their ampoules. "To life and love." The chorus of voices rose in the early morning.

The sun's first rays caressed the tops of the trees. The tip of a silver spike, strategically planted, shone like a star of hope for justice. *I wish I could stake him myself. I should be enjoying preparing to be a mother, not waiting to fight. My feet are going to be so swollen. Damn you, Ivan.*

The army emerged from the forest in straight lines, advancing at a steady pace. Mihai Veres and Ivan led the way into the large clearing.

Ana's eyes stopped on their shining wet boots. The morning dew coated them in a glistening layer. *How long have they been walking?*

"So, you knew we were coming." Hostile and spiteful, Ivan broke the silence.

"Did you think we wouldn't? You are in our territory," Queen Emelia reminded him.

"The Queen's famous last words." Ivan mocked her accent, and sadistic laughs came from behind him.

Does this guy always have stupid hyenas cackling behind him? Ana met him only once before, and it already felt like *déjà vu*.

Ana's attention shifted to the left side. Between the two groups facing each other, Gabriel showed up with a group of his people.

"Brother." Ana heard for the first time her other uncle speak. "You have finally decided to join us." Mihai's raspy voice echoed in the fresh morning air.

Ana stared at him. Even with about a hundred yards between them, she noticed the resemblance to his brother. Not so much in appearance, as in the way they both stood, their dominating presence. Ana straightened her frame. If they were related, she might as well look the part. Mihai's blond hair was gathered in a low ponytail, and the rising sun reflected off the golden locks. *Him and Gabriel rock the long hair. I kind of like it on them.*

His features seemed chiseled in granite. The deep dimple in his chin softened the warrior appearance. Ana remembered Gabriel telling her in one of his visits that once Mihai likes and trusts someone, he's nothing more than a teddy bear. *Yeah, I can see that.*

Andree and the Queen glanced at each other, and both turned to Ana. She sensed their uneasiness and smiled with confidence.

"I am not here to join. I am, and will, stay neutral." Gabriel spoke, and Ana sensed the relief in Andree's next breath. "But I will ask you one more time to reconsider this. Brother, it is not your fight. You can still—"

"You are wasting your time," Mihai turned his attention in front of him. His eyes darkened, filled with the essence of his beast. His lips stretched over even teeth, in a grimace of superiority. "I see you gathered every member of your coven. Good. We wouldn't want any loose ends."

"If I were you, I would not rush to claim victory yet." Andree's remark came across as sarcastic and smug, as usual.

Ana giggled inside. *You tell him.*

"You've been a pain in my side for way too long. Your love for humans is revolting. You married one," Ivan provoked, pointing in Ana's direction.

She saw Andree's smile, so cold it could freeze hell itself. He took one step forward, glaring at Ivan with superiority, and confidence. Ana sensed his decision to anger him further.

"I did. She is the same one you sent your people after, all the way to the Sacred Grounds." Andree paused and glanced at her. "I have also turned her, and she is going to wipe that smirk off your face before I kill you."

At the mention of Sacred Grounds, Ana's ears detected the murmurs floating high in the fresh morning air. Mihai and Gabriel glanced at each other as if to ask: *Why didn't we know about it?*

Ivan advanced a couple of steps. Ana hid a shiver under his uncomfortable stare. She recognized the same demons-haunted eyes from the night on the beach. That seemed so long ago. Back then she ran, now, she would fight.

"She looks like the dinner I missed a while ago." His words brought more laughs from his followers.

Ana's blood heated up. She wanted to scratch his eyes out, to give him another scar, to make him suffer.

"You are right, Ivan." Andree's eyes glowed silver. "She is the one you didn't get to kill. What an irony." He lifted his right arm with his hand opened, the signal. "She will be the end of you."

Jonas activated his shield, the luminous dome flowing from about ten feet high, all the way to the lush grass.

"Now," Andree murmured only for her ears.

Ana focused on the energy buzzing between her and Andree, and imagined the attackers floating in a void. Every man and woman in the opposition hung in the air.

Chapter 25

From where he stood, Gabriel noticed the smallest details in both of the confronting groups. He had no idea about the magnitude of Ana and Andree's powers, about their plan, or what had just happened. He was astounded.

Gabriel looked first to his right, where the Third Coven gathered that day. In front of them, Jonas' translucent, magnificent shield, offered safety to the small group underneath it. Celina, Mara, and Karl grouped around him. The Queen stood one step in front of him, in all her splendor. *I really could see myself with her. Oh well, it wasn't to be.*

Andree and Ana, both a couple of steps ahead of the rest of the group, had identical stances. They stood with one leg slightly behind the other, arms extended in front of them. Determination and focus deeply set in their eyes. Andree's black leather suit was well-known, but Ana's white one still raised eyebrows. *She is incredible. I have never been this proud of anyone before.*

She seemed a miniature copy in the opposite color to Andree. Since he met her, Gabriel knew his niece was a force to be reckoned with, but never imagined how powerful she had grown. The light morning breeze blew the white and black capes in a hypnotic movement.

Gabriel turned his head to the left, where his brother and the rest of his followers dangled helplessly about ten feet above the ground. *Now I'm even happier I didn't join him. That doesn't look comfortable at all.* In spite of their efforts, they could neither move nor use any of their powers. They hung in the air completely at Andree's and Ana's mercy.

~ ~ ~

"What is this? What is going on?" Mihai's voice didn't hide the surprise or the panic. Andree smelled his fear across the almost one hundred yards separating them.

"This is our answer to your actions." Queen Emelia took a step forward. "Do you care to rethink yet?"

"What kind of sorcery is this?" Ivan desperately and unsuccessfully tried to free himself.

Andree watched him squirm, fear emanated from him in dark waves. *Good, my inner beast is starving.*

"The kind your *missed dinner* can conjure." Ana's lips pursed, and Andree knew it was a combination of anger and focus.

"You can't hold us like this forever." Mihai struggled to lift his hand and grab his sword.

Andree glanced at Ana and nodded, the signal for her to take control—to hold everyone by herself.

Free for the next part of their plan, Andree let his arms down and took another couple of steps before talking. "As you can see, she can hold all of you all by herself."

"Not forever." Ivan's growled, unable to move.

"No need to hold you forever," Andree announced with confidence. "Long enough for me to kill every single one of you will do. Let's start with you, since you are the leader of this operation. Shall we?" Andree's right arm extended in his direction, and he levitated Ivan away from the group.

The training is paying off. This is not even hard. Never mind enjoyable. Andree displayed a satisfied grin.

"Let me down." Ivan yelled. "Fight me!"

"I challenged you four months ago, the same night your people attacked us on Sacred Grounds." Andree tilted his head and examined him with disgust. "You are a coward. You never accepted my challenge. What would Collin think?" He goaded him further. "Instead you gathered an army."

"Ugh. Let me down!" Ivan managed to squirm a little, only because Andree gave him some leeway. He wanted to give him a sliver of fake hope, so he could crush him harder.

From the corner of his eye, Andree saw the Veres brothers glancing at each other again. Mihai started to display signs of doubt. His eyes turned to Ivan as if he was embarrassed to be associated with the man.

"What are you doing?" Ivan soared across the sky. "Let me down!"

"Are you sure that's what you want?" Ana's lips tugged into an impish grin.

Several feet below him, a razor sharp, silver coated spike protruded from the ground.

"If it was possible, I love you even more." Andree had to send his wife the message. She almost caused him to lose control with her remark.

Andree turned his hand sideways, leaning Ivan on his back only inches away from the sharp, shining spike. Stronger waves of fear emanated from him, and Andree's inner beast feasted.

"It is time for you to pay for all the unnecessary deaths you have caused." His voice boomed in the fresh morning air. "It is because of your kind that humans fear us, hate us, and have tried to hunt us for centuries. It is time to clean up our ranks."

"No! Stop. We can talk about this." Ivan tried to escape Andree's clutches.

"We are done talking." Andree dropped him onto the spike.

Ivan's body plunged and ignited in amber flames. There wasn't enough time for him to yell. Seconds later, his ashes fell to the ground under thousands of terrified eyes.

"Now . . . Who is next?" Andree turned to face the rest of the attackers.

"Ana, are you all right? Can you hold them just a little longer?" he asked through their link, glancing briefly in her direction.

"I'm fine. I can hold them a few more minutes. But hurry just in case."

"Prince Andree, you've shown a great deal of power. Between you and your wife, you are a force beyond any imagination." Mihai rushed to speak. "I underestimated you, and I admit my mistake." His words echoed with victory in Andree's ears. Their plan worked.

"Does it mean you are volunteering to be next?" Andree turned abruptly toward him.

"Prince Andree." Gabriel jumped a few steps from where he stood, attempting to stop him.

"It means I admit my mistake. I recognize your power, and I'm offering a peace treaty." The older of the Veres brothers insisted. Hope underlined his tone.

Andree controlled Mihai, leaning him backward. "Why should I trust you?" He indulged in the fear he smelled. He drank it, filling his senses.

"Your prowess in battle is only matched by your ability to get in anyone's mind. See for yourself. I'm speaking the truth," Mihai said.

A few steps ahead of him, Andree admitted out loud. "You do speak the truth, but ultimately, the decision belongs to our Queen."

Andree lifted Mihai into a standing position, moving him closer to the threatening silver spike just because he enjoyed seeing his adversary squirming.

"From where I sit, I do not need your peace treaty." Queen Emelia's left eyebrow arched in a challenge for Mihai to prove her wrong. "In case you have not noticed, we do have the advantage here."

"My Queen," Gabriel started.

She lifted her left hand, silencing him without a word.

"I admit I was wrong," Mihai continued his plea. "I thought I had an opportunity."

Andree let his mother do the talking. *"I am taking half."* He communicated to Ana. Nobody but him saw her relief.

"Thank you." Tiny beads of sweat glistened at her hairline. He knew all too well what it took for her to hold them the way she did. But he also knew she would not ask for help unless she was in real trouble. He had learned that about her in their training when she almost dropped some logs on herself.

"Of course you did. Now I have my opportunity." The Queen stood her ground. "After all this time, I have the chance to eliminate an enemy."

"Or you could gain an ally," Mihai offered.

Silence covered them all, broken only by solitary birds flying by.

Andree searched Mihai's mind, and held back a satisfied grin. Mihai honestly thought his life hung by a thread. He had no idea he had just offered them the last missing piece of the puzzle. His plan succeeded, finally complete, perfectly executed thanks to his wife. *"We got them. It will be over soon, my love."*

"My brother is truthful. He will be the most loyal ally anyone can wish for. I can vouch for him." For the second time, Queen Emelia gestured toward Gabriel, silencing him.

"Fine. Nobody else will die. Never forget today, and never try to betray us." The Queen stared at Mihai. "We will not be lenient a second time."

Andree recognized the signal word—lenient—and released everyone, at the same time with Ana.

Jonas kept his shield around them, just as he had instructed him. For as long as Ana was in the open, Andree had to make sure she was safe.

Mihai started to walk toward Queen Emelia. He reached about halfway between the two groups, when a woman came running from behind him, with daggers ready. Her orange hair flamed in the morning sun.

He reacted fast, and before she passed him, his sword sliced her in half. One single hit. Clean, swift and deadly. Her body ignited in a bright fire just like Ivan's had only minutes earlier. Her ashes blew in the wind and touched the ground near the silver spike.

"She was Ivan's woman. I figured that sooner or later, she would want revenge," Mihai turned to face his people. "Go home, everybody. There will be no fight today or any other day against our allies. If any of you have a problem with it, come forward now." He rotated his wrist, and his sword whistled in a circle. "You will have to go through me first."

Mihai's proof of loyalty was received with whispers and nods by the Third Coven, and Andree couldn't hold back a victorious smile. *This is more like it. Finally, we have them where we want.*

Since nobody else moved, Mihai placed his sword on his back, in the scabbard, and continued his way toward the Queen, followed by three of his lieutenants.

~ ~ ~

Jonas dropped his shield. After he'd been protecting everyone for close to an hour, he took a well-deserved break.

The closer Mihai walked, the stronger the presence he recognized.

"Queen Emelia." He tilted his head in front of the Third Coven's Queen.

"Mihai," she answered.

"Prince Andree," he continued, and Andree nodded in his direction.

"Princess Ana, I'm impressed." Mihai stared at her with interest.

Ana didn't answer him, just tilted her head.

"Jonas, you're more powerful than I remember." He greeted even the man he had once banished. Judging by the cold glare in the other man's eyes, he didn't forgive him.

Jonas didn't answer him either, just nodded in silence.

Yeah. He still hates me. Oh well, I can't please everyone.

Mihai turned to Ana. He sensed all the power that radiated from her, the presence surrounding her.

"Who are you?" His dark eyes bored through her. He expected an answer.

Gabriel placed a hand on his brother's shoulder.

"She is our niece."

"What? How is that possible?" Mihai's surprise caused his voice to rise.

Jonas explained the ancestral connection, as he did for Gabriel only a couple of months ago. Even without all the details, Mihai recognized her right away as family. His father's presence, as strong as if he stood there. Just like his brother, Mihai knelt in front of Ana.

"My Princess, I'm honored." He bowed his head. "You're incredibly powerful. Even more than my father used to be."

"She is the reason you are alive." Queen Emelia spoke with an explanatory undertone. "We would not kill family."

He finally understood the reason Gabriel didn't join him and Ivan. Everything made sense. Mihai rose back to his feet and turned to his brother. "You knew. You should have told me."

"We asked him not to." Andree walked closer to Ana, resting an arm on her waist. "Gabriel was bound by his word."

"Why? None of this would have happened." Mihai waved at their surroundings.

"That is exactly why." Andree declared with conviction. "Everyone should know that even if we do not have the numbers, we are not powerless. Now it is all settled." Andree's words clicked in Mihai's mind. It made sense. He would have probably done the same. *Hm. I am starting to like this guy. I hated his guts all this time, but I have to admit, he is worthy.*

"We can sign the treaty right now if you like," Mihai offered and turned again toward Ana. "You are with child."

Ana nodded, glancing in Andree's direction.

"Children, we are having twins," Andree puffed his chest.

"This is extraordinary." Mihai clasped Andree's shoulder. "The first Veres–De Croix generation."

Ana giggled.

Andree shook his head.

"We should all get inside before the serums wear off." Queen Emelia gestured toward The Castle.

~ ~ ~

"We won't let you betray us," one of the three lieutenants, the one with a patch covering his left eye, growled and fired a shot from the gun pointed at Mihai.

Unlike before, when most fights happened too fast for her to see, this time Ana's eyes registered every move, as if she watched a movie in slow motion, a terrifying one.

Gabriel swung his sword cutting the rebel's hand and head in one long, fluid motion. But the bullet had already left the barrel, heading to its trajectory. The head and half the man's arm, still holding the gun, fell on the ground in tandem. Mihai avoided the tiny projectile, and Karl's sword deflected it shortly after.

The high-pitched sound of the bullet colliding with the sword coincided with a second bullet fired by another one of the lieutenants, the stocky one, with crazy, beady eyes under bushy brows. Ana wondered if those brows would somehow impair his vision. The third one, the youngest looking one, pulled a sword and a dagger.

The second bullet was destined for Queen Emelia. Celina threw herself in front of the Queen, and the bullet pierced the woman's shoulder. *Damn it, those brows didn't stop him.* Ana hissed.

"No!" the Queen yelled.

One of her daggers whistled through the air, stopping in the lieutenant's heart.

By the time his body ignited in amber flames, the Queen had caught Celina, breaking her fall in the wet grass. Ana saw it wasn't a lethal wound. She allowed herself to hope that The Queen's assistant would make it.

Ana's eyes traveled from Celina to the fight now unfolding.

Mihai fought the last of the lieutenants. The sound and sight of their swords hurt Ana's eyes and ears. Andree turned her around. He held her tight, against his body. She couldn't see her uncle anymore, but heard Gabriel joining in the fight with a roar.

A scream filled her ears with terror. Ana freed herself from Andree's arms and turned around just in time to see the terrible end of the short fight. Reaching around her waist, he yanked her back, holding her close.

Mihai fell to his knees, a dagger sticking out of his chest. She knew it must've been aimed at his heart, but it'd missed. His attacker's body fell to the ground. Gabriel held his sword impaled into the rebel's heart with both his hands, until ashes flew from the disintegrating body.

"Brother." Gabriel kneeled beside Mihai, holding his head and easing his brother onto the lush grass. His sword lay beside him, reflecting the bright light.

The silver coated dagger spread the burn, and the amber glow covered Mihai's chest. Thick blood stained his clothes.

"Pull it out . . ." Mihai's hand closed around the handle.

"You are going to bleed to death." Gabriel stopped him quickly.

Daniel rushed from behind, examining the wound. "There's nothing I can do. If I pull the dagger, he'll be dead within seconds. It missed the heart by an inch but cut his aorta." His explanations seemed to fall on deaf ears. "The dagger is keeping him alive, but not for long. The silver burn will reach his heart eventually." Daniel lowered his eyes, powerless.

Ana glanced around.

The Queen knelt beside Celina, trying to stop her bleeding. The bullet was still in her shoulder.

Gabriel hunched beside his brother.

Blood roared in her ears. She didn't hear her own hiss.

"Let me go." Ana removed herself from Andree's hold, rushing to kneel beside Mihai.

His breath shallowed and the amber glow spread fast, like lava through a chute.

"Hold him." She turned to Gabriel, who nodded. "I'm going to try something."

"No, Ana." Andree's hand clasped on her shoulder. "You have not trained for this. You never healed a wound this serious."

"I have to try. It's the only way to save him," Ana insisted.

"Your energy is depleted." Andre knelt beside her in the dew-coated lush grass.

Ana turned and stared into his eyes. Andree was right. She had no idea what to do. Her power was close to nonexistent. All of the effort from earlier left her barely standing.

"I can't let him die," she whispered.

"My Princess," Daniel intervened. "There is nothing any of us can do. He doesn't have your blood."

Ana's head jolted up. "No, he doesn't." Mihai's hand closed around her arm.

"Listen to him . . ." Crimson-colored life slipped out of his body quickly. "I'm glad I met you, even if only . . ." His eyes closed, and his grip on her arm faded away.

"No!" Ana yelled, and Andree caught her shoulders in his hands, trying to drag her away from her dying uncle.

Her fangs lowered, and Ana bit into her left wrist. Blood rushed into her mouth. With her right hand, she pulled the dagger out of Mihai's chest. His scream flew over the tops of the surrounding forest, piercing her ears. Scared birds flopped their wings, rising into the sky.

She placed her bleeding wrist on top of his wound. Her blood trickled into his body, mixing with his own. Almost instantly, the silver burn receded, and Mihai reopened his eyes seconds later. Her life-giving, self-healing blood worked inside Mihai's body. Life returned to his clouded eyes.

"This is incredible. Her blood is healing him from the inside. His aorta is regenerating," Daniel explained to everyone gathered around.

Ana withdrew her hand. Her bite marks faded.

Within seconds, Mihai's injury became a memory. Not even a scar remained where only seconds ago the silver-coated blade drained his life away.

Ana was more surprised than anyone, acting from desperation. After just meeting her uncle, Ana sensed he would be a big part of her life.

She didn't want to lose him. Not without trying everything. She stood speechless and tired. Everything that happened, between the efforts and the emotions, had left her exhausted. Her body shivered.

"I'll never forget this. You have my gratitude, my loyalty, and my sword for as long as I shall draw breath." Mihai stared at her.

Eyes, the same shade as hers, stared at her like a mirror through centuries.

"It's not why I did it." Her answer caused Mihai to smile.

"I know. I felt it, too," he whispered.

Ana sensed the bond between them, like invisible chains tied them together. Their destinies, she knew, linked her to him in a way none of them understood. At least not yet.

Andree offered her the comfort and strength of his body. She gratefully accepted it. *Is it over?*

"Celina." Ana turned around.

"I got her. Everything is fine." Daniel had already extracted the bullet and worked on a bandage.

Ana closed her eyes for a second. *Everyone made it out alive. Well, except Ivan and the orange-haired woman.*

As soon as Mihai could walk, minutes later, they all left. Andree and Ana stayed behind.

"You did it." Ana placed her hand in the middle of his chest. "You killed Ivan." She let out a relieved breath. Ana would've preferred if she had killed him, but at least she helped. It was almost as good.

Shadows ran over his face. "Yes, but you never kill only one person."

"What do you mean?"

"There is always more behind that one. We are safe for now. Let's go." He turned away from the opened area, guiding Ana toward The Castle.

She pushed all the dark scenarios from thought and peeked one more time behind, to the place of her first fight.

The silver spike sparkled in the sun. It seemed to her, everyone forgot about the ashes scattered in the wind. *Funny how vampires live so long, and when they finally die, there's only ashes left behind. It's like they never existed.*

~ ~ ~

The next day, Ana and Andree returned home. At her insistence, they went for a walk on the beach. After the last two months spent at The Castle, in training, she missed walking barefoot in the fine sand, the breeze messing up her hair, the smell of the ocean filling her senses.

"What am I going to train for next?"

Ana kicked the sand playfully, and gazed at Andree, waiting for his answer.

"How about taking a break? You trained hard for the last couple of months."

"And what do you suggest I do to pass the time? Sit around and look pretty?" Ana pursed her lips, a sure sign she was ready for a confrontation.

"Since we are done fighting for a while, I thought we could concentrate on what is most important."

"And what would that be?" She asked smiling, remembering how he left her wondering just like that, the night she accepted to marry him.

Andree stopped and folded his arms around her body, holding her close to him. "Us, our family. I want those little ones to have everything, including the happiest mom."

"I'm happy. But I could be happier if you would stop treating me like I'm going to break if I move. I want to continue training, please."

"It is not fair." Andree shook his head. "You know I cannot say no to you, and you take advantage of it." He stared in her eyes. "If you insist on training, you will, but not like this past couple of months. Only a few hours, maybe three or four times a week."

"And the rest of the time?" Ana insisted.

"The rest of the time you could go back to what you love, painting. Or, focus your energy on me." He gazed at her with an arched eyebrow and that impish smile she loved.

She knew that same instant, he would not hurt her, he had proven himself over and over again. It was time to trust him, and for the first time since they'd met, she dropped her guard. "Andree," she whispered and wrapped her arms around his neck.

"Yes . . ."

"I love you."

Andree's lips claimed hers, his arms tightened around her body.

A peace fell over her, as if their souls finally met. His kiss caused her toes to curl in the sand.

"It took you long enough to figure it out."

Her gaze quickly rose to him. "Wait a minute. Did you know?"

Andree nodded. "Since the instant it happened." Her confusion caused him to whisper into her ear, "About two seconds after I fell in love with you."

"You are right." She moved closer to his lips. "I loved you all this time. Ever since you entered that room." She kissed him, and Andree lifted her in his arms.

"So," he winked at her, "does this mean that you are going to focus your attention on me for a while?"

Ana's laugh widened his smile.

"I guess I could do that now that I have time."

"You did not have time before?"

Ana stared in his eyes for a few seconds, the same shards of blue heaven that always mesmerized her. It was good to let herself love again, allow him into her heart.

"Before my time was limited. Now, I have all the time in the world to show you how much I love you. I'm a vampire."

Epilogue

In the comfort and privacy of their own home, Ana took Andree's hand. They both entered their living room, each carrying one of the twins. Both babies had to be in their carriers, with minimum to no contact. It was the first twenty-four hours since birth when they had to be tested.

Feeding them bottles and changing diapers had to be done with gloves, and Ana couldn't wait for the process to be over and done, so she could hug her twins. The last four hours, since she brought them into the world, had been a challenge for her to keep her distance.

"It will be over soon." Andree placed one of the carriers—their son's—on the table.

"I am looking forward to it," Ana whispered and placed Theodora by her brother, in her carrier.

Ana looked into the eyes of her daughter, just as blue as her brother's, and smiled. Both children inherited Andree's deep blue eyes and her jet-black hair.

Jonas entered the spacious living room followed by George and Syrena, the two responsible for testing and prophecies.

Mihai and Gabriel eyed the black boxes George and Syrena carried. They resembled the book. Made from the same black metal, they had identical glowing glyphs in the middle of the covers.

Ana glanced at her twins. Both had just fallen asleep. *They are so beautiful. I can't wait to hold them.*

"We have all gathered here today to witness these tests." George was the first to speak and motioned for Ana and

Andree to step back from the babies. "They will determine whether or not these children will be the leaders of Europe, Asia, and Africa. If our suspicions are right, they are our future." He glanced to Syrena, right beside him.

"If they are, and the prophecies are about to be fulfilled, it means the New World is upon us." Ana stared at her. "First, the tests. We'll talk about the rest after."

New World? What's that? What about the old one? What is she talking about?

Without wasting any time, George approached Theodor first. Slowly, he opened his box and took out a black velvet pouch.

Ana squeezed Andree's hand and cuddled closer to him.

"Let's see if you are the one destined to rule Europe in the future, little one."

George opened the satchel and revealed the black stone inside.

Ana glanced with doubt at the ordinary rock. *It isn't even pretty. What's a damn stone going to prove?*

George loosened up the soft blanket and placed the flat pebble on the baby's bare chest. He bowed his head and took a few steps back, joining the rest of the group.

The stone came to life, glowing in a blinding blue light. Theodor opened his eyes, filled with the same glow.

Ana covered her mouth, and her gaze lifted to her husband. Andree wrapped his arms around her and kissed her temple.

"The stone chose him," he whispered in her ear.

I hope that's a good thing. If not, that stone is going to skip straight into the ocean. For one short second, Ana glanced out the opened back door, to the beach.

"He is the one," George confirmed.

Ana struggled breathlessly to control her emotions: pride, happiness, and joy. The stone had chosen her son, and from what she could see, he accepted it. *Wait, that means he will go to Europe? When? What about us?*

George placed the stone back into the pouch and tightened the blanket around Theodor's tiny body. With the stone back in the box, he placed it at the baby's feet.

"The stone is yours to keep. Use it well." With a bow, George rejoined the group, and Syrena stepped forward.

She wore silks and tulle wrapped around her body, instead of leather outfits like most vampires. Syrena brought an exotic air with her every time she was around. Ana smelled the desert in her proximity, a sea of sand dunes, moved by mysterious, whispering winds.

Syrena approached Theodora and loosened the blanket around her. The tiny girl opened her eyes, looking at the woman beside her. Just like George earlier, she took out a black satchel from the second box and loosened the shiny silk tassel.

"Your test is harder, little one, but your reward will be greater," she whispered and lifted the satchel up, turning it upside down.

Black sand started to fall, in a thin but steady stream. Ana stared at the grains on their trip down. Instead of falling on Theodora's body, they stopped about an inch before touching her skin. A glowing blue hue mixed in. With the pouch empty, Syrena took a few steps back, waiting for the reaction.

Theodora closed her tiny hands in miniature fists, and the sand moved around, taking the shape of a young woman.

Whispers filled the room, and the baby girl turned her head to where everyone stood. When Theodora moved her arms up and down, the woman jumped and laughed.

The black sand radiating a blue glow attracted Theodora's eyes. The beginning of a smile tugged at her tiny pink lips. It was her, in the future, and they smiled at each other. For a few seconds, illuminating lights danced in both their eyes.

She looks so happy. Those blue glowing eyes suit her and Theo. So far so good, but what does all this mean? How will it affect their lives? Is she going to have to live all the way across the world? Nope. That's not happening. I am not letting either of them leave.

With a twirl, the woman disintegrated, and the sand fell in a small mound above Theodora's chest. Syrena scooped it back into the satchel and smiled satisfied.

"Needless to say, this baby girl is our future Princess." She placed the bag in the black box at Theodora's feet. "And the sand is yours to keep. Make good use of it."

A general sound of relief filled Ana's ears. Family and friends gathered to share the special day. Both babies fell back asleep.

Now that she could hug and kiss them, Ana rushed to her children with Andree on her heels. They each took one of the twins and finally welcomed them into the world with a loving embrace.

Proud of them both, Ana let everyone hold them. She couldn't hear enough praise of her babies.

"There you are. I missed you," Ana whispered to her daughter. She kissed her forehead as soon as she made it back into her arms.

With the wave of emotions washing off, Ana sat. She and Andree switched the twins and gazed at each other. Their hearts smiled.

"Now that it is official, would you like to know about the prophecies?" George asked and waited for Ana's approval.

She lifted her eyes to him and nodded in agreement.

This better be good.

Andree's right arm encircled Ana's shoulders, and she cuddled closer to him, each holding one of the babies.

"I will start with Theodor, and Syrena will continue with his sister, Theodora."

Silence broken only by the sound of waves washing over the sand and the whispering palm trees surrounded everyone, a thick blanket of anticipation.

"Prince Theodor De Croix, or Theo, as you decided to call him, will be the most powerful of us ever in existence. He will unite vampires from Europe and parts of Asia in the New World. Unfortunately, his quest won't be easy. He is going to fight for everything. Every single one of his accomplishments will be a struggle. The New World will be a test for all of us, but he will adapt to it and lead with justice. The first five hundred years of his life will be the hardest."

Ana's eyes moved from her son to Andree and back. It seemed even the breeze stopped and the waves ceased to stroke the shore. She wasn't sure what to do or say. *I could use my tears right about now.* Why did he have to fight and struggle? At least he would be powerful enough to do so.

Theodora's tiny cry broke the silence. Ana turned her gaze to the tiny girl the same instant.

"I guess she wants to hear her future," Andree gently rocked his daughter.

Syrena smiled and nodded at the baby girl.

"Princess Theodora De Croix, Thora, as she will be known, will be just as powerful as her brother. The people of Africa and the remaining part of Asia will welcome and recognize her as their leader. She will discover in the desert the one destined to her, a mysterious, ancient creature. A powerful, untamed alien, this man will be a challenge. Thora will have to make hard choices. The future of our world will be in her hands. The New World will present her with this challenge after her five-hundredth birthday."

Andree patted Ana's arm. She stared at their babies and wanted to cry. Both their futures seemed good and bad at the same time.

"What's this New World you both mentioned?" Ana had to ask, before she forgot.

George spoke first. "We are not sure. Our visions are vague. They show very little of the world." He paused and stroked his chin. "I saw Prince Theodor in cities with tall, dark buildings, flying sort of cars without wheels, like a science-fiction movie."

"Princess Theodora came into my visions living in a palace, in the desert, surrounded by luxury and advanced technology unknown to us." Syrena shared her revelations. "She also appeared at times in cities that don't yet exist."

Silence crept up around them again.

That sounds all right. What about their struggles? Can that be avoided? Can I do anything to help? She leaned her head on Andree's shoulder. He would have helped too, she was sure of it.

"I could try and look into their future as well." Ella stepped forward and clasped her hands before her. "Maybe I can see more details?"

"Yes, please." Ana rushed to answer, grateful for her friend's offer.

"That would be great." Andree made room for Ella to sit.

With both twins on her lap, Ella closed her eyes and held them, concentrating. There was movement behind her eyelids. Ana tried to see into her friend's mind, but she was too emotional to stay focused. She pursed her lips and waited like everyone else.

A few times Ella's eyebrows furrowed, and she seemed out of breath, but recovered and continued. After about a half hour she opened her eyes. She looked like something terrible threw her out from her trance.

Ana took back her son, and Andree reached for his daughter. Ella stood massaging her temples. "First, the kids will be fine."

Ana smiled, relieved, and after she kissed her son, turned her attention back to Ella. She took a few more steps and then turned to face everyone.

"I have focused more on the world around them, but your prophecies are true. Theo will fight for everything he will obtain, and Thora will be forced to make hard choices."

Andree touched Thora's cheek with the back of his fingers. A tiny smile tugged at her daughter's lips, the exact same reaction she always had, and Ana smiled. *She's my girl all right.* She moved Theodor closer to his father for the same treatment. Unlike his sister, he didn't smile. *So he's the serious one. Well, I guess I can't have them both be like me.*

"The world as we know it today will be literally washed away." Ana turned her attention to Ella. "A sudden, terrifying flood will devastate Earth. More than half the population will be gone. I didn't see what will cause it, just the aftermath." Ella stopped for a few seconds. She seemed to be sorting her thoughts. "Entire species will go extinct, countries will disappear. I saw humans drinking blood. The destruction will be beyond any imagination." She clasped and unclasped her hands. "But the survivors will rebuild. New cities, new technology, everything will be different." Ella stopped again, visibly troubled by what she'd seen.

"When will all this happen?" Ana asked, afraid to hear the answer.

Ella shook her head lightly and glanced at her friend.

"On their birthday. I saw you eating cake," she added and turned to Mihai.

"Me? I don't eat cake. I'm pureblood," Mihai rushed to clarify, hoping for a mistake.

"You did in my vision." Ella insisted, and she shrugged her left shoulder.

"Which birthday?" Ana insisted, now terrified of her children's future.

"Their one-hundredth."

Mike hugged his wife to him, and Ella accepted the comfort, leaning her head on his shoulder.

"Oh, and at your five-hundredth anniversary, you will wear red," Ella added and smiled in Ana's direction.

"We have one hundred years to prepare for what is to come." Andree thought out loud, and Ana noticed all eyes turning to her husband.

He looked at her, and they both gazed at the twins.

"Everything is going to be all right. Mommy and Daddy are right here." Ana kissed the foreheads of her twins.

CPSIA information can be obtained
at www.ICGtesting.com
Printed in the USA
FFOW03n0424190518
46696984-48797FF